Praise for
A Sound Among the Trees

"In *A Sound Among the Trees,* author Meissner transports readers to an-other time and place to weave her lyrical tale of love, loss, forgiveness, and letting go. Her beautifully drawn characters are flawed yet likable, their courage and resilience echoing in the halls of Holly Oak for generations. A surprising conclusion and startling redemption make this book a page-turner, but the setting—the beautiful old Holly Oak and all of its ghosts—is what will seep into the reader's bones, making *A Sound Among the Trees* a book you don't want to put down.'
—KAREN WHITE, *New York Times* best-selling author
of *The Beach Trees*

"My eyes welled up more than once! And I thought it especially fitting that, having already shown us the shape of mercy in a previous novel, Susan Meissner is now showing us the many shapes of love. *A Sound Among the Trees* is a hauntingly lyrical book that will make you believe a house can indeed have a memory...and maybe a heart. A beautiful story of love, loss, and sacrifice, and of the bonds that connect us through time."
—SUSANNA KEARSLEY, *New York Times* best-selling author
of *The Winter Sea*

"I have a dozen things to do (like sleep!), but here I huddle through the night, turning pages, mesmerized by yet another Susan Meissner novel. How does Susan create characters that stay with me long after I close the book? How does she transport a reader so easily to a mansion in the South, in this century, bringing one family's challenge of the Civil War to speak to contemporary times? How does she address the emotions and memories that hold us hostage with such grace? How do her turns of phrase bring tears unbidden to my eyes? I keep reading, knowing I'll discover a fascinating story and hoping I'll infuse some of the skill and craft that Susan weaves to make it. *A Sound Among the Trees* is one more exceptional novel from a world-class storyteller. Jodi Picoult, make room at the top."

—JANE KIRKPATRICK, award-winning author
of *The Daughter's Walk*

"*A Sound Among the Trees* is another Meissner masterpiece filled with well-shaped characters, a compelling plot, and haunting questions: are our memories reliable enough to grow us, or do we cling to them as an excuse not to live? Meissner stunned me as she skillfully grappled with those mysteries. I left the book resolved to live joyfully in the sacredness of today."

—MARY DEMUTH, author of *The Muir House*

A SOUND AMONG *the* TREES

A NOVEL

SUSAN MEISSNER

author of *The Shape of Mercy* and *Lady in Waiting*

WATERBROOK
PRESS

A Sound Among the Trees

Trade Paperback ISBN 978-0-307-45885-8
eBook ISBN 978-0-307-45886-5

Cover design by Kelly L. Howard

Published in the United States by WaterBrook, an imprint of the Crown Publishing Group, a division of Penguin Random House LLC, New York.

WATERBROOK® and its deer colophon are registered trademarks of Penguin Random House LLC.

Library of Congress Cataloging-in-Publication Data
Meissner, Susan, 1961–
    A sound among the trees : a novel / by Susan Meissner. — 1st ed.
        p. cm.
    ISBN 978-0-307-45885-8 — ISBN 978-0-307-45886-5 (ebk.)
    1. Haunted houses—Virginia—Fredericksburg—Fiction. 2. Fredericksburg
(Va.)—History—Civil War, 1861–1865—Fiction. 3. Psychological fiction. I. Title.
    PS3613.E435S68 2011
    813'.6—dc22

                                                2011013220

There's a sound among the forest trees, away, boys,
Away to the battlefield, hurrah!
Hear its thunders from the mountain, no delay, boys.
We'll gird on the sword and shield.
Shall we falter on the threshold of our fame, boys?

FANNY CROSBY, 1861

Part One

THE GARDEN

he bride stood in a circle of Virginia sunlight, her narrow heels clicking on Holly Oak's patio stones as she greeted strangers in the receiving line. Her wedding dress was a simple A-line, strapless, with a gauzy skirt of white that breezed about her ankles like lacy curtains at an open window. She had pulled her unveiled brunette curls into a loose arrangement dotted with tiny flowers that she'd kept alive on her flight from Phoenix. Her only jewelry was a white topaz pendant at her throat and the band of platinum on her left ring finger. Tall, slender, and tanned from the famed and relentless Arizona sun, hers was a girl-next-door look: pretty but not quite beautiful. Adelaide thought it odd that Marielle held no bouquet.

From the parlor window Adelaide watched as her grandson-in-law, resplendent in a black tuxedo next to his bride, bent toward the guests and greeted them by name, saying, "This is Marielle." An explanation seemed ready to spring from his lips each time he shook the hand of someone who had known Sara, her deceased granddaughter. His first wife. Carson stood inches from Marielle, touching her elbow every so often, perhaps to assure himself that after four years a widower he had indeed patently and finally moved on from grief.

Smatterings of conversations wafted about on the May breeze and into the parlor as received guests strolled toward trays of sweet tea and champagne. Adelaide heard snippets from her place at the window. Hudson and Brette, her great-grandchildren, had moved away from the snaking line of gray suits and pastel dresses within minutes of the first guests' arrival and were now studying the flower-festooned gift table under the window ledge, touching the bows, fingering the silvery white wrappings. Above the children, an old oak's youngest branches shimmied to the tunes a string quartet produced from the gazebo beyond the receiving line.

Adelaide raised a teacup to her lips and sipped the last of its contents, allowing the lemony warmth to linger at the back of her throat. She had spent the better part of the morning readying the garden for Carson and Marielle's wedding reception, plucking spent geranium blossoms, ordering the catering staff about, and straightening the rented linen tablecloths. She needed to join the party now that it had begun. The Blue-Haired Old Ladies would be wondering where she was.

Her friends had been the first to arrive, coming through the garden gate on the south side of the house at five minutes before the hour. She'd watched as Carson introduced them to Marielle, witnessed how they cocked their necks in blue-headed unison to sweetly scrutinize her grandson-in-law's new wife, and heard their welcoming remarks through the open window.

Deloris gushed about how lovely Marielle's wedding dress was and what, pray tell, was the name of that divine purple flower she had in her hair?

Pearl invited Marielle to her bridge club next Tuesday afternoon and asked her if she believed in ghosts.

Maxine asked her how Carson and she had met—though Adelaide had told her weeks ago that Carson met Marielle on the Internet—and why on earth Arizona didn't like daylight-saving time.

Marielle had smiled, sweet and knowing—like the kindergarten teacher who finds the bluntness of five-year-olds endearing—and answered the many questions.

Mojave asters. She didn't know how to play bridge. She'd never en-

countered a ghost so she couldn't really say but most likely not. She and
Carson met online. There's no need to save what one has an abundance of.

Carson had cupped her elbow in his hand, and his thumb caressed
the inside of her arm while she spoke.

Adelaide swiftly set the cup down on the table by the window, whisk-
ing away the remembered tenderness of that same caress on Sara's arm.

Carson had every right to remarry.

Sara had been dead for four years.

She turned from the bridal tableau outside and inhaled deeply the
gardenia-scented air in the parlor. Unbidden thoughts of her granddaughter sitting with her in that very room gently nudged her. Sara at six
cutting out paper dolls. Memorizing multiplication tables at age eight.
Sewing brass buttons onto gray wool coats at eleven. Sara reciting a poem
for English Lit at sixteen, comparing college acceptance letters at eighteen,
sharing a chance letter from her estranged mother at nineteen, showing
Adelaide her engagement ring at twenty-four. Coming back home to
Holly Oak with Carson when Hudson was born. Nursing Brette in that
armchair by the fireplace. Leaning against the door frame and telling Adelaide that she was expecting her third child.

Right there Sara had done those things while Adelaide sat at the
long table in the center of the room, empty now but usually awash in
yards of stiff Confederate gray, glistening gold braid, and tiny piles of
brass buttons—the shining elements of officer reenactment uniforms before they see war.

Adelaide ran her fingers along the table's polished surface, the warm
wood as old as the house itself. Carson had come to her just a few months
ago while she sat at that table piecing together a sharpshooter's forest green
jacket. He had taken a chair across from her as Adelaide pinned a collar,
and he'd said he needed to tell her something.

He'd met someone.

When she'd said nothing, he added, "It's been four years, Adelaide."

"I know how long it's been." The pins made a tiny plucking sound as their pointed ends pricked the fabric.

"She lives in Phoenix."

"You've never been to Phoenix."

"Mimi." He said the name Sara had given her gently, as a father might. A tender reprimand. He waited until she looked up at him. "I don't think Sara would want me to live the rest of my life alone. I really don't. And I don't think she would want Hudson and Brette not to have a mother."

"Those children have a mother."

"You know what I mean. They need to be mothered. I'm gone all day at work. I only have the weekends with them. And you won't always be here. You're a wonderful great-grandmother, but they need someone to mother them, Mimi."

She pulled the pin cushion closer to her and swallowed. "I know they do."

He leaned forward in his chair. "And I...I miss having someone to share my life with. I miss the companionship. I miss being in love. I miss having someone love me."

Adelaide smoothed the pieces of the collar. "So. You are in love?"

He had taken a moment to answer. "Yes. I think I am."

Carson hadn't brought anyone home to the house, and he hadn't been on any dates. But he had lately spent many nights after the children were in bed in his study—the former library—with the door closed. When she'd pass by, Adelaide would hear the low bass notes of his voice as he spoke softly into his phone. She knew that gentle sound. She had heard it before, years ago when Sara and Carson would sit in the study and talk about their day. His voice, deep and resonant. Hers, soft and melodic.

"Are you going to marry her?"

Carson had laughed. "Don't you even want to know her name?"

She had not cared at that moment about a name. The specter of being alone in Holly Oak shoved itself forward in her mind. If he remarried, he'd likely move out and take the children with him. "Are you taking the children? Are you leaving Holly Oak?"

"Adelaide—"

"Will you be leaving?"

Several seconds of silence had hung suspended between them. Carson and Sara had moved into Holly Oak ten years earlier to care for Adelaide after heart surgery and had simply stayed. Ownership of Holly Oak had been Sara's birthright and was now Hudson and Brette's future inheritance. Carson stayed on after Sara died because, in her grief, Adelaide asked him to, and in his grief, Carson said yes.

"Will you be leaving?" she asked again.

"Would you want me to leave?" He sounded unsure.

"You would stay?"

Carson had sat back in his chair. "I don't know if it's a good idea to take Hudson and Brette out of the only home they've known. They've already had to deal with more than any kid should."

"So you would marry this woman and bring her here. To this house."

Carson had hesitated only a moment. "Yes."

She knew without asking that they were not talking solely about the effects moving would have on a ten-year-old boy and a six-year-old girl. They were talking about the strange biology of their grief. Sara had been taken from them both, and Holly Oak nurtured their common sorrow in the most kind and savage of ways. Happy memories were one way of keeping someone attached to a house and its people. Grief was the other. Surely Carson knew this. An inner nudging prompted her to consider asking him what his new bride would want.

"What is her name?" she asked instead.

And he answered, "Marielle..."

The present rushed back in around her as the parlor door opened and a boy stood in the doorway, eyes wide. Adelaide took a step back from the table. She had seen this child arrive earlier that day with his parents when she was still puttering about in the garden. Members of Marielle's family. She had not met them yet.

The boy wore a black button-down vest and a scarlet bow tie that pointed to eight o'clock. Most of his hair had been slicked into obedience. Most of it.

"Wait. This isn't a bathroom," he announced.

Adelaide composed herself. "No. It is not. The bathroom is the second door on the left. Not the first."

The boy looked over his shoulder. "I think someone's in there. The door's closed."

"Then I suppose you will have to wait."

The boy cast a glance about the parlor and then looked back at Adelaide. "So are you the old lady who lives in this house?"

She stiffened. "This is indeed my house. Who are you?"

"I'm Kirby. I live in Santa Fe. That's in New Mexico."

"Kirby. Your parents named you Kirby."

"Not curb-y like the street. Kirby. With a K."

Adelaide moved toward the boy and the parlor door. She put her hand on the handle as if to close it behind her. But he stood unmoving in the doorway, oblivious.

"So this house was here before the Civil War? It's that old?" he asked.

"Yes."

The boy took a step inside the room. "There's an old lady outside who says it's haunted."

"You shouldn't believe everything you hear."

"I don't. I don't believe in that stuff."

She made another attempt to close the door. The boy seemed not to notice.

"So you make Civil War uniforms in here? My aunt says you do. But I don't see any."

"And who might your aunt be?"

"Marielle. You know, the bride. 'Course she's not a real bride now. They were married last weekend in Arizona. I went to the wedding." He cocked his head. "You weren't there."

"No."

"Didn't they invite you?"

"Of course they invited me. Perhaps we should join everyone in the garden. Have you met my great-grandson, Hudson? He's probably your age."

The boy didn't move. "I met him in Arizona. But he's not my age. He's ten. And I'm nearly twelve. My mom said old people are sometimes afraid of airplanes. Are you afraid of airplanes?"

"Shall we?" Adelaide motioned them away from the room.

Kirby took a hesitant step back into the hallway. "So do you make Civil War uniforms in that room?"

"I do."

"I'm just wondering why you do that. That war has been over for a long time. The North won."

"Yes. Here we go." She closed the door and they now stood in the hall. The air in the hall seemed stiff. Unmoving.

"Do you make them for museums or something? Because that seems dumb to me. Museums are supposed to have the real thing. Not copies of the real thing. Don't museums here have real Civil War uniforms?"

"Yes...they do. Perhaps you would like to use the bathroom at the top of the stairs?" Adelaide felt as if the walls were pressing in now, listening. It was a familiar feeling.

"I can wait," Kirby answered. "So if you don't make them for museums, why do you make them?"

People were moving about the lower level of the house, in and out of the large patio doors off the main dining room. Caterers were bustling between the kitchen and the garden, and attendants at the front door were helping people with their gifts and cards for the newlyweds. No one appeared to be looking for the boy.

"I make them for reenactments."

"For what?"

"Reenactments. It's like pretend. People wear them for pretend. They pretend they are in the Civil War, and they wear them. Surely you know what pretend is." Adelaide headed for the patio doors and the clean air outside the house.

The boy followed her. "But why do they do that?"

"Because...I suppose because you learn things by experience that you can't learn just by reading about it in a history book."

"Huh?"

Adelaide stepped aside as a caterer swept past them with a tray of sliced ham.

"They do it for fun," she continued a second later. The outside air was just steps away.

"Yeah, but everybody knows how it ends. You can't pretend that part. The North won. Everybody knows that. What's the fun in pretending if you can't pretend what you want?"

"Who says you can't pretend what you want?" Adelaide stepped across the threshold, caressing the door frame as she walked past it, her eyes scanning the garden for her Blue-Haired Old Ladies.

arielle sank into a white padded folding chair and kicked off one open-toed pump. She plunged her bare foot into the succulent grass and let the coolness soothe the skin on the balls of her feet. Behind her the quartet was playing a racing tune that made her think of birds in flight. Guests were seated in chairs all around, on the grass and the stone patio, eating off glass plates and sipping drinks. The lilt of their subtle Southern accents lifted above the music as her brother, Chad, spoke to her from across the table.

"Wow. Quite the party," he said.

Marielle settled back in the chair. "This is how it's done in the South. Or so I've been told."

Chad smiled. "How what is done?"

"A proper garden party." Marielle waved toward the buffet tables and gloved catering staff. "Carson thinks all this finery is Adelaide's way of making up for not being at the wedding last week. I would've been fine with tapas on paper plates. But she wanted elegance."

Chad's smile widened. "Do they even know what tapas are here?"

Marielle kicked off her other shoe. "I told Adelaide that Carson and I had the rehearsal dinner in Phoenix at a tapas bar, and she thought I said topless bar."

Her brother tossed his head back and laughed. Marielle joined him.

"Funny, right?" Marielle said. "Oh, and this morning I asked her if the local grocery store here has cilantro, and she told me she's never seen any label from a place called Salon Trowe."

"You sure you're ready for this?" Chad said, laughing harder.

"It's a little late to have *that* conversation again, don't you think? Have you noticed what I'm wearing?" She grabbed a fold of wedding dress above her knee and fluffed it upward. The gentle fabric fell away like water when she let go.

"I suppose you're right about that." His smile, half its weight now, graced just one side of his mouth.

Marielle cast a glance about her. Carson was several yards away, talking to a man from his office in DC. Hudson and Brette were far off in the lower part of the garden with her and Chad's parents. Adelaide was eating a piece of cake at a table on the edge of the garden, surrounded by her elderly friends, all wearing Easter-colored polyester. "You're still happy for me, though, right?"

Chad raised his champagne flute. "Of course I'm happy for you."

She watched him take a sip and place his glass back on the table.

"I really do know what I'm doing," she said.

"I thought you didn't want to have this conversation again."

"I don't."

"Fine, then let's not have it."

"Just because we're not having it doesn't mean I don't know what you're thinking. I have a right to be happy with someone. I'm thirty-four, in case you've forgotten. You still had zits when you married Lisa."

He grinned. "I did not still have zits."

"You were twenty-three. You still had zits."

"Hey, I totally agree. Not about the zits; about you having the right to be happy with someone. If you've met your soul mate in Carson, then I'm genuinely happy for you. Really."

Marielle crossed her arms across the tabletop. "But there you go. You said 'if.' You don't think I have."

Chad cocked his head. He opened his mouth, then shut it.

They were quiet for a moment. One of the tiny asters in Marielle's hair fluttered to the table. She gently slid it back into her hair.

Chad stroked the stem of his glass. When he spoke again, his voice was tender. "Look. I really like Carson. And his kids. And if you're totally fine living in the same house where he lived with his first wife, then more power to you. Just please tell me you're not sleeping in the bedroom she slept in."

"Not that it's any of your business, but no, we're not. We're sleeping in a room Sara never spent any time in."

Chad crinkled an eyebrow. "Okay, well, that just doesn't seem possible. She grew up in this house, right? You told me her mother practically abandoned her and Adelaide raised her here. This house is big, but it's not that big."

Marielle's gaze rose involuntarily to the gabled windows of Holly Oak's second floor. All the bedroom windows looked the same from that part of the garden. A long exhale escaped her lungs. "It's big enough."

Chad paused a moment before continuing. "You know, Carson seems like a nice guy, Elle. He seems like the kind of guy who would understand if you wanted to have your own place."

Marielle lowered her eyes to meet her brother's gaze, "Carson would have moved us into our own place if I had insisted. I didn't insist. This has been the kids' only home. I didn't want to do that to them."

Chad's forehead wrinkled in puzzlement. "Do what to them? You and I moved four times when we were kids. It's not the end of the world."

"This is their home."

Her brother leaned back in his chair. "Yeah, but any house can be a home if you're with the people you love and who love you. I'm sure I read that on a poster somewhere."

Marielle shook her head, and another aster fell from her curls. "Well, I don't live my life on poster philosophy. I'm sure you don't either."

Chad nodded, but his thoughts were unreadable. She couldn't tell what he was agreeing to.

"I didn't insist," she continued in a gentler tone. "I could've, but I didn't. This is a lovely house. A beautiful house."

"Adelaide's house."

"And she's going to be ninety on her next birthday. In the not so distant future it will be Hudson and Brette's house."

"I suppose."

Marielle huffed a breath past a quick smile. "What's to suppose? She's old. She's frail…"

"She doesn't look frail to me. I'm surprised she didn't come to the wedding—"

"She likes staying close to the house. And she's going to be *ninety,* Chad!"

Her brother raised his glass and drained the last of his champagne. He nodded as he swallowed. "You're right. It's a beautiful house." He set the glass down.

Marielle narrowed her eyes. "What?"

"What do you mean, what?"

"What else are you not saying?"

"I'm out of champagne."

"Coward."

He smiled. An easy, relaxed smile. Different than the ones from the last few minutes. She waited.

"Funny that you would call me a coward, Elle. Because I think you are very brave."

"Ha ha. So very funny."

He lifted his glass toward a passing waiter who held a tray of champagne flutes. "It's true. You are brave. You fell in love with a guy you met online and dated for just four months, and now you're living in his dead wife's house, with the grandmother who raised her, and you're mothering her children, and you've moved far away from the desert and everything that's familiar. And you're okay with all of it." The waiter handed Chad a new glass, and he saluted her with it.

The gesture felt like an unexpected jab from a trusted ally. She flinched from surprise and the tender sting of her brother's candor. "That was low," she murmured. "You'd say that to a girl in her wedding dress?"

Chad set the glass down and reached across the table for her hands. "Hey, I wasn't being sarcastic. I meant every word. You are brave. Braver than me. I'm in awe, actually. It's a compliment, Elle. I promise you."

"Yeah, well, that's not what it felt like—"

"I'm totally serious. I'm the coward. And you're the brave one." He released her hands.

"Tell that to Mom and Dad. That's not what they think. Or my friends back in Phoenix. They think I married Carson because I was desperate."

"No, they don't."

"They do. They just won't say it. But they do. I see Mom looking at me and looking at Carson and these two stepgrandchildren I've thrown into her lap, and I know she worries I'd grown desperate and that's why I married Carson. And I'm pretty sure Adelaide thinks it too, and she barely knows me."

"Marielle."

He waited until she looked up at him.

"You know what I think?" he asked. "I think you need to stop wondering what everyone else thinks. You love him. He loves you. That's all that matters, right? Love is enough. I *know* I saw that on a poster somewhere. Love and cilantro. I will make sure to send you some seeds so you can grow your own."

Marielle smiled as the tense moment evaporated. "And serrano peppers, too."

"Want to change the subject?" Chad asked.

"Absolutely."

"Kirby tells me there's a cannonball buried in the stonework on the north side of the house. Compliments of the Yankees."

"Oh right. The cannonball. I'll get Carson, and he can show it to you. I suppose Kirby told you the house is haunted, too?"

"By a ghost named Susannah. A spy, I hear. A spy for the Union." Chad rose from his chair.

"A spy? Who'd you hear that from?" Marielle slipped her shoes back on her feet and stood.

Chad motioned with his head toward Adelaide's table. "One of Adelaide's cronies over there."

Marielle turned toward the table at the edge of the sun-drenched garden. Adelaide lifted her head at that moment and met her gaze. The two women regarded each other from across the patio. Marielle tipped her head in a silent greeting, and Adelaide slowly returned the nod.

As she and Chad moved away from the table, an aster fluttered from her hair and landed on the grass by her feet.

From her table at the edge of the patio Adelaide watched Marielle and her brother approach Carson as he talked with a colleague. She saw Carson brighten at her approach and lift his arm as almost an afterthought to encircle her waist. Marielle said something to him; the colleague leaned forward in interest.

"Cannonball!" the man exclaimed.

Carson said something, and then the four of them moved away, toward the back of the house.

"She's a nice girl, Adelaide. And my goodness, she's tall," Pearl said.

Adelaide swiveled her head to face her three table companions, women she had known since their children were in diapers. On her right, Pearl sat in a coral-hued dress and hat. Deloris and Maxine, one in creamy yellow and the other in lavender, sat across from her. A fourth woman, Frances, whose jet black hair warred with the deeply set wrinkles in her eighty-five-year-old face, slowly ate her piece of cake. She was new to Fredericksburg and her circle of friends at First Presbyterian—definitely not one of the Blue-Haired Old Ladies. Maxine had brought her.

"I never said Marielle was nasty and short," Adelaide said.

Maxine laughed.

"So what does she do?" Frances asked.

Adelaide rearranged the napkin on her lap. "She writes grants for environmental groups."

Several blank faces stared back at her.

"What exactly does that mean? What's an environmental group? Is she one of those the-sky-is-falling liberals?" Deloris's brow crinkled in disdain. "Does she think we're all melting the North Pole?"

"I seriously doubt she thinks the sky is falling, Deloris," Adelaide replied. "And I don't think she spends much time thinking about the North Pole. She's lived in Arizona all of her life. Her specialty is desert conservation. Or something like that."

"The desert. Her specialty is the desert?" Deloris's tone was dubious. "What on earth is she going to do here in Fredericksburg?"

"She's not going to try to find a job right away, is she?" Maxine asked. "I mean, those children haven't had a mother in four years. The least she could do is be here at the house for them when they get home from school."

Three blue-haired heads and one raven-haired one turned to Adelaide, the unspoken observation obvious on their faces. If Marielle wasn't going to be working, then what would she do all day while the kids were in school? in Adelaide's house?

"I don't know what Marielle's plans are. They've only been here for a few days, and I've tried to give them as much privacy as I can." Adelaide brought her teacup to her lips. The liquid inside had cooled. She looked about for one of the waitstaff she'd hired to freshen her cup. No sign of one.

"So how exactly is that working out?" Deloris leaned forward in her chair. "I mean, the privacy thing and all. With your bedrooms on the same floor."

"Deloris!" Pearl blushed crimson.

"What? They are!"

Adelaide turned back to face her friends. "Holly Oak is plenty big enough for the five of us, Deloris. I am sure we'll manage to stay out of each other's bedrooms."

"I haven't seen Marielle spend much time with the children today." Frances cocked her head toward Hudson and Brette, who were on the lower level of the garden near the entrance to their mother's former art studio—and the last remaining echo of slave quarters at Holly Oak. Marielle's parents and Carson's mother were with them, talking quietly together while the children played with a lop-eared rabbit, Hudson's new pet.

"Oh, Frances. It's a wedding reception. Look at all the guests Marielle has had to greet," Pearl said. "Isn't that right, Adelaide?"

Adelaide's gaze traced the sloping lawn to the vine-covered walls of Sara's studio and her great-grandchildren playing in front of it. She looked first to Hudson and then Brette.

"Hudson and Brette are adapting very well to Marielle's being here," Adelaide said absently.

"Did you know Carson and Marielle are taking the children with them on their honeymoon?" Deloris said, turning to Frances. "They're spending a week in Orlando. At Disney World. Can you imagine? Children on your honeymoon?"

"I think it's very sweet of them," Pearl said. "Those children are as much a part of this marriage as the two of them are. I think it's a lovely thing to do. There will be plenty of time for Carson and Marielle to have trips of their own."

"Well, it just seems odd to me. Especially taking them out of school for four days when there's only a month left." Maxine said, but Adelaide had slowly disengaged from the conversation. Her gaze lingered on Brette, off in the distance playing on the front step to the studio, bending down to touch the rabbit, and squealing as it hopped away from her.

Frances pushed her plate away. "I suppose they need this time alone together to bond as a family. That's what I heard on the TV. When two people marry and there are kids already, it's like a new family is being forged out of untried steel."

Adelaide watched Brette run to Marielle's mother, Ellen. The woman reached down and adjusted the bow in Brette's hair. Brette said something and Ellen laughed. Ellen knelt down and hugged the girl, and Brette's slender arms easily went around Ellen's neck. Adelaide marveled at the intimacy, and it took her several seconds to remember Brette didn't meet Ellen for the first time last night as Adelaide had. Brette met Ellen at the wedding. Brette stayed in Ellen's house. Ellen had bought her a bracelet made by Hopi Indians.

A name on the periphery of her consciousness tugged at Adelaide as she watched Brette disengage from Ellen's tender embrace.

Caroline.

"So you haven't heard from Caroline, then," someone at the table was saying.

"Frances," another voice said, in quiet reproof.

Adelaide turned back to the table. "What was that?"

"I just asked if you'd heard from Caroline." Frances replied as the other women stared at her.

Adelaide lifted her teacup and nearly raised it to her mouth before remembering it had grown tepid. She set the cup back down. "No. I haven't."

Pearl patted Adelaide's hand.

"What?" Frances looked about the table, from old woman to old woman. "Isn't that her daughter's name?" Frances faced Adelaide. "Isn't that your daughter's name? I was told that was her name."

Adelaide licked her lips. "That is her name."

Maxine leaned across the table. "And I also told you not to bring it up!" she growled in a half whisper.

"You told me she probably wouldn't be at the reception. That's what you told me. You didn't say I couldn't say her name!"

"I most certainly did say that," Maxine muttered.

Pearl clucked her tongue.

"What? Why can't I ask where she is? Is she in prison somewhere? Is she living in a commune in San Francisco?" Frances directed these questions to Pearl.

An uncomfortable silence stretched across the table. Again, Adelaide's gaze sought her great-granddaughter's form, now in the dappled shade of a crab apple in bloom at the garden's westernmost edge. "She could be in either of those places, I suppose," Adelaide replied.

"What?" Frances blinked.

"Adelaide, we don't have to talk about Caroline," Deloris said.

"What did she say?" Frances turned to Pearl. "Did she say she's in both of those places? They have communes in the prisons in San Francisco?"

"Honestly, Frances!" Pearl exclaimed.

"What?" Frances's voice rose in multiple decibels.

"I don't know where Caroline is," Adelaide turned to address Frances and her glistening black hair. "I don't see her very often, Frances. It's been four years since I've seen or heard from her. And I haven't known where Caroline is in decades."

"You haven't seen her in four years?" Frances echoed, eyes wide.

"The last time I saw her was at Sara's funeral. I don't know how she heard Sara had died, but she did. She came to the funeral and then she left, and I haven't heard from her since."

Frances's mouth was an open O. For a second she said nothing. Then she spoke, and this time no one shushed her.

"Why? Why don't you know where she is?"

Adelaide shrugged. "That's how she wants it. That's how she has wanted it since she placed her infant daughter in my arms and disappeared. Before then actually."

"My word! How long ago was that?"

"Sara would've turned thirty-eight on Tuesday." Adelaide rubbed an age spot on her arm. "And Caroline is sixty-four."

No one said anything for a long stretch of seconds.

"Did you quarrel?" Frances's tone was incredulous. "Could the two of you not make it right between you all these years?"

Again, no one shushed her.

"I have no quarrel with my daughter, Frances. She is unwell and she misuses drugs. She always has. It's as simple as that."

Frances puffed out her cheeks in indignation. "There is nothing simple in that at all. You are her mother. How could you just let her throw her life away like that?"

Pearl gasped, and Maxine, reaching to clap her hand over her mouth, knocked over her coffee cup. Deloris whispered the name of Jesus. A prayer perhaps.

"How, indeed." Adelaide's voice was soft and unhurried.

"Frances, you really don't know what you are talking about!" Maxine began to mop up the spilled coffee with her napkin. "Caroline made her own choices. Adelaide did the best she could. It wasn't easy raising a teenage girl without her father. I was here. I saw it all. When Adelaide's husband had his heart attack, Caroline's emotional problems just got worse. And she turned to drugs that her doctor didn't prescribe. It wasn't Adelaide's fault."

"Please, let's talk about something else!" Pearl pleaded, reaching for her water glass.

Frances waved toward the hulking frame of Holly Oak. "You've been alone in this house with no husband since your daughter was a teenager? Nigh on fifty years?"

Adelaide slowly turned her head to face Frances. "I have not been alone."

"Not alone?" Frances paused, puzzlement crossing her wrinkled face for several seconds. "Oh. You mean the ghost."

Pearl spewed the water out of her mouth, then proceeded to gasp and sputter. Deloris reached over and patted her back.

"Frances! For heaven's sake, I told you not to mention that either!" Maxine turned to Adelaide. "I am sorry, Adelaide."

Adelaide blinked slowly. "What have you got to be sorry about, Maxine?"

Maxine lowered her voice. "I brought her."

"I told you not to mention the ghost," Pearl wheezed at Frances, her silvery eyes glistening with moisture.

"Pearl, I know you tell everyone who comes to Holly Oak about the ghost you think I have living here," Adelaide said calmly. "I know you told the boy with the vacuum cleaner name, and I know you've probably told Marielle and her parents and her brother and his wife, so why would I assume you did not also tell Frances?"

Pearl coughed. "I'm sorry, Adelaide. I can't help it."

"So there is no ghost?" Frances looked from one woman to the other.

Adelaide removed her napkin from her lap and stood. She reached for her teacup. "You are welcome to peek inside every nook and cranny at Holly Oak to look for my ghost, Frances. If you find one, let me know. And I haven't been alone because I raised Sara here. And she brought Carson here and blessed me with two great-grandchildren here. Poke about as you please—but mind the cellar. Apparently, the ghost has a nasty grudge against the cellar. I need more tea."

Adelaide turned from the table and, with teacup in hand, headed for the kitchen and a hot kettle.

⌁

Six decades later she could still remember the ache of hoping against fate for a boy. After all those second-trimester miscarriages, Adelaide had reasoned that the only child she had finally been able to carry to term would certainly be male; the lost ones were all female.

The moment the delivering doctor pronounced the squalling thing in his hands was a girl, the slow waltz of destiny that fell on all women born to Holly Oak began, and Adelaide, spent and sweating, had no choice but to fall in step. What else could she do? She and her infant daughter would surely be pulled along anyway, as had her mother and her grandmother in those years after the war. It was an unspoken understanding among Holly Oak women—for who on the outside would believe it?—that the house had never grasped the notion that it was no longer a battleground, a hospital, a hiding place, a graveyard...no longer a refuge stripped of its meaning by the women who had lived inside it. It was still a house of penance, the cannonball on the north wall a tangible reminder of the indictments against it, and its women the apparent objects of its remorse.

Her great-grandmother Susannah had intimated that Holly Oak seemed to bear a grudge, a notion reinforced when Adelaide was young by neighbors who pointed to the house and murmured that a female Union spy had lived there and that the house was haunted by Yankee soldiers buried in its cellar.

Adelaide had said nothing of this to the delivery room doctor or nurses, nor to her husband, Charles, who was brought into the room after the child had been washed of the evidences of human nativity and placed in her arms. No one but a Holly Oak woman could possibly understand the strange psychosis of a house that could not reinvent itself. No one else but a Holly Oak woman would need to.

Charles McClane, whom Adelaide had married in 1945, was a decorated Air Corps pilot and the son of an affluent Richmond family. His money had financed Holly Oak's first major updating since the Civil War, and he would've found Adelaide's perception that the house was stuck in a strange limbo of regret—eighty years after the war's end—to be utter nonsense. Everything was new inside. And besides, houses aren't sentient beings. The suggestion that Holly Oak would likely exact another toll, this time on Caroline, simply by virtue of her sex, would've sounded preposterous. So Adelaide did not suggest it. Once, in a moment of weakness, she proposed to Charles that they sell Holly Oak and build a new house, and when he said, "Whatever for?" she had no answer for him.

Adelaide's mother, Margaret, was still alive when Caroline was born in 1947, and when she held her granddaughter for the first time, she had whispered to Adelaide that with every new generation, past grievances lose some of their weight. Margaret had a debilitating stroke the year Caroline turned eight, however, and dissolved into a world where she recognized neither magnificence nor malevolence. Margaret wasn't aware when Caroline began to exhibit mood swings that doctors attributed to inconsistent parenting and an indulged lifestyle. Adelaide's mother passed through the fog of her last years unable to recall that she had imagined Caroline's life might be different.

Adelaide raised her daughter at a cautious distance, as if the house watched her every parenting move, reminding Adelaide when she might've lavished intimacy on Caroline that a Holly Oak daughter was destined for misfortune. Charles raised Caroline with the rules and structure he'd learned in the military. Caroline's response to caution was to mistrust it and to authority, to test it. So when Charles died of a heart attack the year Caroline turned seventeen, she seemed to lose her method for measuring authority's ability to make life safe. The depression she succumbed to was treated with cognitive therapies that should've worked and didn't, and antidepressants that awoke in her a hunger for altered states which was never satisfied.

Caroline left Holly Oak in 1965, on the one-year anniversary of her father's death, with a hundred dollars in one back pocket and five foil-wrapped LSD-laced sugar cubes in the other.

Adelaide heard from her daughter three times over the next eight years. Twice by phone to borrow money, and once she came back to Holly Oak in person.

With a baby girl in her arms.

The cannonball, firmly wedged between timber and stone, was an arm's stretch on tiptoe. Its domed face beckoned from the flatness of the north wall of Holly Oak like a button to be pressed, an invitation to revisit the cold December day it hurtled into the house. On either side of it, clematis vines climbed skyward, bypassing the sunken orb as though it were a slumbering threat.

Marielle watched as Chad extended his arm to touch the ball's flinty surface. He turned to Carson and the co-worker who had followed them to the other side of the house.

"Is this the only one?" Chad asked.

"It's the only one still imbedded in the house." Carson slipped his hands into his pockets. "There were probably others. All the houses in this part of old downtown were shelled during the First Battle of Fredericksburg, especially along the river here. You can see from the upstairs bedroom windows one of the places where the Yankees built a pontoon bridge to cross the river. A lot of the houses on this street were destroyed. Holly Oak lucked out. The town was pretty much leveled."

Chad stepped back, and Carson's co-worker Len moved forward to scrape his fingertips across the ball's exposed arc.

"But you're not from around here, right? DC?" Chad asked. "You had to learn all this from someone else, I take it?"

Carson smiled. "I guess you could say I've lived here long enough to know the history. This house is on the National Register; a number on this street are. Sometimes Adelaide will share a tale or two about what happened here during the war."

Chad laughed. "Adelaide? She that old?"

Carson laughed as well and then seemed to notice anew that Marielle was beside him. He pulled a hand out of his pocket and reached for her. She took a step to shorten the distance between them. "Her great-grandmother lived in this house during the war. Adelaide remembers her. Sara knew all the stories too."

Marielle flinched slightly at Sara's name, and Carson's arm around her momentarily stiffened in response.

Chad quickly filled the strained seconds of silence.

"This great-grandmother wasn't named Susannah, was she?" he asked.

Carson stroked Marielle's back with his thumb. "I suppose you heard that name from Pearl."

"Sweet old lady in a flowered hat who likes to tell people you've got a ghost named Susannah living in the house?"

"That would be her."

Len stepped back from the wall. "A ghost?"

"So the legend goes. I've never seen any ghost, and I've lived here for ten years."

"So why does Pearl think there's a ghost?" Marielle asked. "It was the first thing she wanted me to know when she got me alone today. It's not like you've ever mentioned it."

Carson smiled. "It's her story, not mine. Pearl's got a cousin who claims she's clairvoyant or a medium or something. That cousin came here once and felt the presence of a ghost—or so she says."

"How did this cousin know it was Susannah's ghost?" Chad asked.

"My guess is she's heard the stories. A lot of people around here know Susannah Page hid some Union soldiers in the house and helped them escape. Apparently she was also suspected of spying for the Union by marrying a Confederate officer named Nathaniel Page, who apparently got shot during the escape. Nearly killed him."

"So she was bad news, huh?" Chad said.

"Oh, I don't know. I think she probably had a terribly troubled life for such a young woman. Divided loyalties, unable to choose sides but living in a place where you simply had to. After all, she and her mother had only been living in the South for a year when the war broke. Pearl said her cousin heard Susannah's ghost weeping over how her heart had literally been torn in two."

The image of a grieving faceless apparition, gray from age and death, glided into Marielle's mind and then morphed into the young version of Susannah she'd seen in the portrait on the stairs inside Holly Oak. That Susannah looked about Marielle's age. Sara's age, too, when she died. Marielle pushed the image away. "Pearl doesn't talk about a ghost when the kids are around, does she?" Marielle asked.

"No, but I think it's gotten back to Hudson. He knows Pearl thinks there's a ghost. Of course, he thinks that's cool."

"Pearl should be more careful. Brette's too young to be hearing ghost stories," Marielle murmured.

Her brother turned to again study the north side of the house, starting with its rooftop spires, and Marielle watched as his gaze finally settled on the convex aberration of the cannonball. "A house this old probably has a boatload of memories inside it. I could almost believe there's a ghost in there."

Marielle had no desire to continue contemplating the memories lodged inside Holly Oak. Or the dead people who had made them. "Can we talk about something else?"

Chad turned back around to face her. "Sorry, Elle. No more talk of ghosts. I'm going to go find Lisa. She'll want to see this."

Her brother began to walk back to the other side of the garden, and Len fell in step with him. Carson kissed Marielle at her temple as they turned away from the side of the house.

"Having a good time?" he murmured.

She laughed lightly. "Until we started talking about ghosts."

He squeezed her shoulders as they began to stroll slowly back to the other side of the house and the reception. "Don't pay any attention to Pearl and her stories. She's just a funny old lady with an overactive imagination. There are no ghosts inside that house, I assure you."

"Does Adelaide believe there's a ghost?"

Carson took several steps in silence. "No," he finally said.

"You hesitated."

Carson shrugged. "She has kind of an eerie respect for this house. It's kind of quirky sometimes."

Marielle had only spent scattered moments in Adelaide's presence in the week since she and Carson and the children had returned from Phoenix. Not enough to know what Carson was alluding to.

"What do you mean by quirky?" she asked.

"Oh, nothing, I guess. Anyway, she's pretty quick to brush off Pearl's stories. Pearl's kind of, well, she's a bit dramatic and silly sometimes. It surprises me that she and Mimi are such good friends. Mimi's not that way at all. I guess sometimes opposites do attract..." He broke off and cracked a lopsided grin. "Hey. Weren't you the one who wanted to talk about something else? You were having a lovely time until the subject of ghosts came up, right? Mimi did okay with the planning?"

Marielle let her question fall away. "It's been a lovely reception. She did a wonderful job."

"Didn't she, though? I originally thought she'd rather we had the reception at one of the hotel ballrooms or the country club or even the church because—" He stopped abruptly, seeming to nearly choke on his words. He shot a look toward her.

"Because you had your reception with Sara here," Marielle finished for him.

"Marielle, I'm sorry. I can't believe I said that."

"We agreed not to eggshell this, right? You had your reception with Sara here. I'm sure it was lovely too."

He inhaled and exhaled audibly. "Yes. It was. And it was a long time ago."

"But a lot of these same people came to it, I suppose."

"Some. Yes."

The back of Holly Oak loomed over them as they turned at the northwest corner of the house. Marielle felt its shadow fall over them.

Her thoughts carried her to the conversation she and Carson had after he proposed and she accepted. They had met up in DC—their second in-person meeting—and then driven to Fredericksburg the next day so that she could meet Hudson and Brette. Marielle had been awed by the house's age and size, and she'd remarked to him what a beautiful house it was. As they stood at the window on the second floor landing overlooking the south-side garden and patio, he asked if she would be okay with living at Holly Oak after their wedding. He'd said the house would be jointly owned in trust by his children at Adelaide's passing and that since they had never lived anywhere else, he was reluctant to move them. Her first thought was one of caution.

"You don't want us to have our own place?"

"We kind of will have our own place. It's a big house, Marielle. And Mimi's almost ninety. We can keep the maid service I hired if you want, or I'll let them go. Whatever you want. The kitchen can be all yours. Mimi makes all her own meals anyway."

She had stared at the bedroom doors that flanked her on all sides.

"Which room did you and Sara share?" she had asked.

Carson had turned his head toward a door at the southwest corner. "It's just a guest room now."

And then he'd told her she would never even have to go into that room if she didn't want to. There were plenty of bedrooms on the second floor and even one on the third floor where the kids slept.

"Do you ever go in that room?" she asked.

He had paused for just a second. "I used to. But I don't anymore."

The resolve in his voice moved her. She said yes, that she was okay with it. Now as they walked in Holly Oak's shadow, a trickle of doubt ribboned through her for the third time that day.

"So, this is still what you think we should do, right? Live here? In this house?" she asked.

Carson glanced up at the house's massive backside before turning to face the lawn that stretched ahead of them. Hudson and Brette, twenty-some feet away, were sitting on the steps to the old slaves' quarters, the rabbit sandwiched in between them. He tightened his arm around Marielle's waist as if he'd started to fall and was catching himself. "I don't want to be afraid to live here. I don't want to think that I can't be with you. Here."

"I know what you *don't* want; I'm just a little… I mean, I know it's only been a week, but…I wonder if maybe we're asking too much of ourselves."

"It's going to be fine. We're going to be fine. You and I…"

But his voice fell away, and he did not finish his thought.

This time, Marielle did not attempt to finish it for him. She had no idea what it was he had started to say.

Brette raised her head from where she sat with her skirted knees up against her chest. Rising from the steps, she ran toward them. Marielle couldn't tell if the little girl was running toward her, toward Carson, or toward the in-between place that separated them.

～～～～～

Marielle hadn't planned to correspond with anyone on her online dating account who didn't already live in the southwest. It was the fourth time in five years Marielle was giving online dating a try, and she had formulated several deal-breaker rules that she'd promised herself she would not renege on. No one younger than she by more than five years. No one recently divorced. No one who didn't call back when they said they would. No one who called her Mary Ellen. No one who wanted to meet up at a cocktail lounge in a hotel lobby. No one who didn't live within a couple of hours' drive. Experience had taught her that a few ground rules were a good thing.

When a glitch deposited a Virginia man's profile into her inbox, Marielle had been a mere keystroke away from deleting it when she saw that Carson Bishop didn't like chocolate. At all.

Having never met a person who also did not like chocolate, she perused the rest of his profile and discovered he also didn't like roller coasters or tight spaces or shellfish. Marielle's first correspondence to Carson was a simple e-mail quipping that she had begun to believe she was the only person on the planet who didn't like Hershey's on the half shell. She had no intention of continuing to e-mail him. She told him plainly in her e-mail that it was too bad he did not live closer as she might've pursued a friendship with him.

When he e-mailed back commenting that he too wished she lived closer, a tiny fissure formed in her tightly constructed parameters. She e-mailed him back.

And the electronic conversation continued.

She learned Carson was forty and the widowed father of a son and daughter. His wife, Sara, had died four years earlier from complications of an ectopic pregnancy. He was a systems engineer for a defense contractor in DC and lived with his kids and their great-grandmother in a one-hundred-sixty-year-old mansion in Fredericksburg's oldest neighborhood.

A graduate of William and Mary as well as Virginia Tech, he liked live stage over film, Tim Hortons coffee when he could get it, playing tennis, and the color green. Raised Methodist. Wore his sandy brown hair cut short and rimless glasses. Loved to watch old movies and hang out with his kids. Unskilled at instigating a relationship with a woman, his friends at work had spent the last year coercing him to try online dating. He hadn't yet corresponded with anyone he'd been matched with. Marielle was the first person to respond to his profile that he had replied back to.

He'd confided in her because she was safe. She was too far away to worry about having to meet in person right away or take out on a date. It had been a long time since he'd been on a date. She had found his vulnerability strangely endearing.

After eight weeks of e-mails and then dozens of phone calls, Marielle began to feel like their random meeting online hadn't been random at all.

"I know I haven't even met him yet, but I think I'm falling in love with him," she told her mother. "He's not like the other guys I've dated. He's always more interested in finding out how my day was than he is telling me about his. He calls me when he says he's going to call, he laughs at my jokes, he asks about you and Dad. He…he just makes me feel like I'm important."

"But…what if you meet him and there are just…no sparks?" her mother had cautioned.

In the last decade Marielle had learned to mistrust relationships that started out with fireworks like the Fourth of July and then fizzled on any ordinary gray day in November. She could already tell there was something different about her attraction for Carson. He made her feel relaxed and peaceful. There was no pounding *kaboom*. No eye-popping dazzle. It felt very natural. And she liked it.

"I'm not worried about that," she'd answered.

Her mother had paused for a moment before adding, "You do know there aren't any deserts in Virginia."

Marielle had nodded. She loved the desert.

But the desert was not a lover.

The last of the wedding presents—a tall, lead crystal water pitcher that stood atop a crush of white tissue paper—lay open on Marielle's lap. The cut glass caught sunlight at odd angles and splashed prisms in all directions onto the garden's patio stones. Adelaide poked at a miraged rainbow drop with her foot, and Hudson, sitting next to her, laughed and stomped on the one nearest him.

"It's beautiful, thank you." Marielle beamed toward Pearl, who sat one table away in the shade with the rest of the Blue-Haired Old Ladies. Most of the guests hadn't stayed for the opening of the presents, just family and close friends. But the Ladies had.

"I know Adelaide's got dozens of water pitchers, but you need one of your own!" Pearl seemed quite pleased with herself.

Hudson leaned toward his great-grandmother. "Does she, Mimi?" he whispered. "Does she need one of her own?"

Adelaide peered at him. "Let Pearl have her little delusions," she whispered back.

"What?"

"I'm not sharing my water pitchers."

Hudson's mouth broke into a slow grin. "You're teasing me."

"It's been a long day."

"It's been a *boring* day. I'm bored." Hudson looked to the table of opened presents, the remains of the cake, the empty champagne bottles. "We're done now, right?"

Adelaide rubbed a callous on her finger, formed by sewing brass buttons and golden braid for years on end. "Depends on what you mean by
'done.'"

"I mean, I can go now, right? That's what I mean."

Adelaide regarded her great-grandson, studied his face. People said he
favored Adelaide's side, that he had Sara's eyes, Caroline's chin, and her
nose. She saw the resemblance—who couldn't?—and it pleased her. She
resisted the urge to lay a wrinkled hand on his head—he hated that—to
feel the comfort in his boyness. There hadn't been a boy born at Holly
Oak until Hudson since 1863. Adelaide's gaze rose instinctively to Brette,
who sat across from her, practically on Marielle's mother's lap, toying with
the woman's charm bracelet. The child was drunk on grandmotherly attention from a woman whose only grandchild to that point was a chatty
boy with a vacuum cleaner name.

Adelaide wasn't sure what the future held for Brette. Hudson's arrival
hadn't kept Sara alive, hadn't brought Caroline crawling back. Hudson
would surely, if not eventually, usher in something new, but that wouldn't
change what had happened before. Nothing could do that.

"I know what you mean, Hudson," she murmured. "But we have
guests. And it would not be fair to Kirby for you to disappear into the
house and leave him here in the garden."

Adelaide motioned with her head to where Kirby sat next to his parents on the opposite side of the tables of spectators. He was thumbing
through a large, colorful cookbook—one of the gifts. The bow tie he had
on earlier was now peeking out of his front pants pocket.

"He won't care, Mimi. He thinks I'm a kid."

"You are."

"He thinks he's older than me."

"He is older than you."

"He won't care."

"If you are going into the house to play a game or to watch the television you will need to ask that boy who thinks he is older than you if he would like to join you."

Hudson stood. "He won't care." Her great-grandson tossed the three words over his shoulder.

"Well, I care. You are a gentleman."

"You said I'm a kid."

"Who is learning to be a gentleman."

Hudson shuffled away. Adelaide watched him approach Kirby, watched the vacuum-cleaner boy shrug, stand, and then place the cookbook on his chair. They began to walk toward the open dining room doors. Brette dashed away without a word from the lap on which she was leaning to follow them, leaving Marielle's mother to look thoughtfully after her.

Carson stood to address the thirty or so people who had remained. "Marielle and I just want to thank you all again for coming today. I'm especially glad Marielle's family could be here from Arizona and New Mexico and that all of you could meet them. It's been so wonderful to share this day with you all."

"You deserve to be happy again, Carson," Maxine interjected.

Adelaide sighed. Leave it to Maxine to painfully state the obvious at the most unnecessary time.

"Yes, well, uh, thanks again, everyone." Carson reached for Marielle, putting his arm across her shoulders. "It really means a lot to us that you came."

Chairs made little scraping sounds on the patio stones as people stood and stretched and began short conversations that would inevitably end with a soon-to-be-spoken good-bye. Except for the Blue-Haired Old Ladies. They signaled the waitstaff to bring them more coffee. Marielle's mother, Ellen, walked over to Adelaide and sat down in the chair Hudson had occupied.

"Thanks so much for having the reception here, Mrs. McClane," Ellen said. "It was so lovely. You have such a beautiful home."

"It was my pleasure. Anything worth celebrating has always been celebrated here in the garden. So, where else could we have it but here?"

Ellen nodded. "Well, it was just wonderful. Carson has told me so much about this house."

"Has he." Adelaide didn't frame it like a question. It wasn't a question.

"Mmm, yes. He said this house has been in your family since before the Civil War. And survived a horrible battle. That's amazing to me."

Adelaide swallowed. "Indeed."

"Marielle tells me you sew uniforms for Civil War reenactments. That's a very interesting hobby. How long have you been doing that?"

Adelaide repositioned herself in her chair. "It's actually more than a hobby. Hobbies tend to cost you money. This actually pays for my brandy and cigars."

Ellen laughed nervously.

"I am kidding, dear," Adelaide continued, and the woman visibly relaxed. "I prefer port over brandy—and without the cigar. And never while I am sewing."

"Well. That's…that's fascinating."

"I use the original patterns, you see, and sew everything but the interior seams by hand. I won't sell an officer's decorated greatcoat for less than $350—that's quite a bit more than most of my competitors. But I don't care. People buy them. I always have a waiting list. And I've been doing it since I retired from teaching. Twenty-five years, if you're into the math."

"So interesting." Ellen seemed genuinely intrigued. "And how did you get involved in reenactments, if you don't mind my asking?"

Adelaide shrugged. "I don't mind. My great-grandmother and her mother and grandmother sewed uniforms in the same parlor I sew mine in. But theirs were real, if you know what I mean. Many women were called upon to sew uniforms in their parlors during the War Between the States. I have picked up where they left off, you might say."

"Wow." Ellen breathed in deeply, taking in the sweep of the patio, the lawns, and the west end of the garden at their backs. "There's just so much history here." Then she pointed toward the back of the yard. "Carson said those two buildings at the edge of the garden there used to be slaves' quarters."

Adelaide followed Ellen's line of vision to the stone buildings festooned with ivy.

"Yes. Those are the last two. Hudson keeps his rabbit in one of them."

"And the other one?"

Adelaide was about to speak when an oozy realization crept over her. Marielle's mother surely knew the other one had been Sara's art studio. Ellen had been at its steps with the children for the better part of the reception. She had no doubt looked in the windows and asked the children about it. She'd surely seen the pitched tabletops where Sara experimented with paint, fabric, clay, and metal. Had seen the remnants of Sara's unconventional creativity. Artist friends had long ago taken away the usable elements Sara had left behind, like leftover tubes of paint and fabric. What remained was what Sara had barely started, a few haphazard, gestational pieces whose imagined final appearance no one could guess. They still sat in the studio, covered in dust, visible from the windows.

"Sara had a studio in the other." Adelaide turned to face Ellen.

Marielle's mother murmured a "hmm" that dissipated into the afternoon air.

"No one is using it at the moment," Adelaide continued.

"Right." But Ellen's eyes were on the studio, as if its door were wide open, declaring its current usefulness. Or perhaps its shrinelike aura. Adelaide recognized the look of a mother whose concern for her child gnawed at her.

"You needn't worry about the studio, Ellen," Adelaide said. "Most of Sara's things have been cleared away. What's left is rather unremarkable. Things she had barely begun to work on."

Ellen slowly turned away from the old buildings at the edge of the garden, her face pained. "I'm sorry, Mrs. McClane. I didn't mean to bring up anything painful. Has...has this been a hard day for you?"

The woman's question surprised Adelaide a little. Of all the people who might've asked how she was feeling about the day, Marielle's mother was the last person she had expected would ask. She barely knew the woman. Adelaide thought of the moments in the parlor, much earlier that day, before the vacuum boy had intruded on her privacy and the lingering memories of her granddaughter.

"A little," Adelaide replied. "I raised Sara, you know. She lived here. Her children began their lives here. Yes, today's been a little difficult."

"And Carson? Do you think it's been a hard day for him? Maybe just a little?"

Carson stood several yards away, his hand on the small of Marielle's back, talking to the man who had twice been his best man. "I don't know," Adelaide said. "But I would imagine he would not be the gentle soul that he is if it didn't still hurt just a little." She brought her gaze back to the woman who sat next to her.

Ellen smiled, the kind of slow, measured grin that an honest answer evokes. "I suppose you have a point." She turned her head to look at Marielle and Carson, who were now walking with a few guests to the garden gate. "I worry that they took this all a little too fast," she continued, almost as if to no one.

"Maybe they did," Adelaide replied, and Ellen swiveled her head back to look at her.

"You think maybe they should've known each other a little longer, don't you?" Ellen's quiet voice was laced with subtle urgency and sad camaraderie. She seemed to think she had an ally in Adelaide.

Adelaide patted the woman's hand and then withdrew her arm. "It doesn't really matter what you and I think. It's done. They are married. And if there's one thing I have learned in almost ninety years on this planet, it's that you cannot undo the past by wishing it undone."

late afternoon breeze sent a pair of crumpled mauve napkins dodging about the caterers' feet as they pushed their black rolling totes across the patio stones. Marielle watched the last evidences of her wedding celebration disappear from the garden—in the form of the waitstaff dressed in bridal white, whose hushed service had sent the guests away content. They closed the gate behind them, waving to her as they left. The guests and string quartet were gone as well, and the garden was noiseless now except for a choir of songbirds in the birches and the sound of a neighbor's lawn mower.

Marielle's parents and brother and his family were touring the national cemetery and Marye's Heights with Carson before the sun went down. She had been to the sites with Brette and Hudson on her first visit to Fredericksburg, and since the children had not wanted to go again, Marielle opted to stay at Holly Oak with them. Adelaide had gone up to her bedroom to rest, and the silence that now enveloped her was welcoming.

She turned away from the gate and the empty patio. Sunlight through the trees freckled the stones with a messy ballet of light, and the leaves responded to the breeze with an obedient rustle; applauding the day, perhaps.

It had been a good day for the most part. Meeting friends and family who had known Sara, loved Sara, hadn't been as awkward as she had imagined. Everyone seemed to genuinely accept her, some nearly congratulating her for steering Carson out of his pitiable aloneness. The smiles had been kind and sincere. But there had been scattered sideways glances she was most likely not meant to see, accompanied by a cocked head or pressed lip or crinkled forehead.

Some were wondering.

Marielle could read, even peripherally, their unspoken concern. Was she really content with living in the same house where the first wife had lived? with the first wife's grandmother? Those few perplexed glances hadn't truly surprised her. Her parents—and Chad—had practically the same looks on their faces when she told them where she and Carson would be living after they married.

She'd returned from the East Coast with Carson's engagement ring on her finger, and her parents had hastily arranged a dinner party to celebrate. Chad, a regional sales director, had used some frequent flyer miles and flown in from Santa Fe. When the guests left, and as her parents, Chad, and she finished up the last of the coffee and dessert, her father asked if she and Carson would be moving closer to DC after the wedding.

"That's quite a commute he's got," her father had said.

Marielle had set her coffee cup down carefully and answered no, they would not. They would live at Holly Oak.

No one had to ask what Holly Oak was. She had shown them the pictures of the mansion, both inside and out. Her parents and brother knew it was on the National Register. That it survived the shelling of downtown Fredericksburg during the Civil War. They knew how impressive it was. And who had lived there.

"At Holly Oak," her father had echoed. And as Marielle looked up from her coffee cup, she saw the surprised look people have when they ask a question they think they already know the answer to. They all wore that look. The three of them had assumed she and Carson would make their home somewhere other than Holly Oak. It wasn't even Carson's house, after all. It belonged to his dead first wife's grandmother. And she still lived in it.

"It's a beautiful house," Marielle had said. "A beautiful, *big* house that has everything. You guys can stop worrying. I'm okay with this. I'm not afraid to live there."

For a long moment no one said anything. Then Chad spoke into the strained seconds of silence. "So what are you going to do with all the toasters and Crock-Pots you're going to get?"

Gentle laughter filled the room.

"I'm keeping the ones I like best, of course. And using them."

"But Carson has such a long drive," her mother said, her brows furrowed with unease that seemed meant for a different concern altogether.

"Everyone who works in DC has a long commute, Mom. It's not a place to live; it's a place to work. Everyone in Carson's department lives outside the Beltway. Most of them live in Virginia, actually."

"He must be on the road for more than an hour each way," her father said.

Marielle shrugged. "That's the East Coast, Dad."

Again, there was silence.

"It's a beautiful house," Marielle said again. "Just wait till you see it."

"Looking forward to it." Her father's tone suggested he knew it was not his place to decide where his married daughter should live. Her mother smiled, stood to clear away the dessert plates, and asked Marielle which department store she'd like to register with…

At her far right, the door to the dining room now swung open and Brette popped her head out.

"Marielle, Hudson won't let me play the Wii. It's my turn. And he won't let me."

An empty space where the rented tables had been placed stretched between her and Brette. Marielle wasn't quite ready to go in. She wasn't ready to step out of her wedding dress or referee her first squabble between her stepchildren.

"I'll be there in a little bit, Brette."

The girl frowned.

Marielle turned toward the edge of the garden and the long sloping lawn. "I promise. I won't be long."

Brette mumbled, "Okay," and the french door closed.

Marielle walked to the edge of the patio stones, slipped off her shoes, and set them by steps that led to the garden's stretch of grass and trees in the ample backyard. The cool flagstones massaged her bare feet as she walked down the steps onto the sloping lawn. The back of her dress trailed on the tops of the blades of grass, and she liked the way it looked and felt. Behind her, Holly Oak was bathed in an amber glow of sunlight as the sun hovered low on the western horizon. Ahead of her were the old slaves' quarters and Sara's studio, their entrances shadowed now since the sun had fallen behind them. She stepped to the edge of the quarters and winced as the grass gave way to dirt and little stones. Marielle put out a hand on a stone wall to steady herself and flick a pebble from between her toes when a voice startled her.

"Looking for me?"

Marielle pushed herself away from the ancient wall and gasped. Adelaide sat on a wood-and-iron bench that overlooked a line of trees and the rooftops of houses on the next street.

"Oh my goodness, Mimi!" Marielle exclaimed. "You scared me! I thought you were inside resting."

Adelaide turned her head toward the woods. "I tried to. But I can't make myself tired just because people think I should be. Everyone thought I should lie down. So I did. And then when everyone left me alone, I came out here."

"Oh."

A tiny span of silence followed.

The old woman looked up at her. "I would ask you to sit down, but you will ruin your dress. This bench is unkind to organza."

"That's all right. I don't need to sit down. I...can leave if you want."

Adelaide seemed not to have heard her. "Was it a nice party for you, Marielle?"

"It was a lovely party. Wonderful. Thank you so much for hosting it."

Adelaide swiveled her head back to face the trees. For a second she said nothing. Then she spoke. "You know, slaves used to sit on this bench at the end of the day and smoke their pipes and tell stories and rock their children to sleep. Right here. On this bench."

Marielle stared at the woman. "Um. No, I didn't know that."

"My great-great-great-grandfather Eldon Pembroke owned a woolen mill. And sheep. And a good many slaves. And my great-great-great-grandmother had a haberdashery a few blocks away from here on Caroline Street."

"A haberdashery. That's like a fabric shop, right?"

"No. Not a fabric shop. Hers was a men's haberdashery. It was an accessory store for men back when men wore accessories. Gloves, hats, walking sticks, ascots. Things like that. They tailored men's suits too."

Movement far above her on the patio caught her eye. Marielle saw Brette emerge from the dining room onto the patio, looking for her. "Sounds like those were nice times, when men wore accessories," Marielle said absently, worried that she had already botched her first opportunity to mother the children on her own. Marielle waved. The girl went back into the house, apparently not having seen her.

Marielle turned back to Adelaide and saw that the woman was staring at her.

"My great-great-aunt Eliza worked at the haberdashery until it closed during the war," Adelaide continued. "And so did my great-grandmother. Susannah Page."

"Susannah. She's been quite popular today."

Adelaide nodded. "Pearl told you, I assume. Whenever there's an event at Holly Oak, Pearl has to bring up Susannah. And now that you've heard Pearl's theory, I just wanted you to know that I've lived in this house all my life and I've never seen a ghost here."

Marielle laughed lightly. "I'm glad to hear that."

"And I think I should also let you know that the room you and Carson have chosen was Susannah's room. I am only telling you because Pearl will make a fuss over it when she hears you're in that bedroom. I'd rather she didn't have the thrill of seeing your surprised face when she asks which bedroom you're in and you tell her and she announces to you you're sleeping in Susannah's room."

"Susannah's room?" Marielle sensed a flicker of uneasiness zip through her.

"That is the very look that would fuel her stories for the next decade, assuming she lives that long. It's better that you know now."

The subtle disquiet spread despite Adelaide's downplaying.

"But you don't believe in ghosts. Do you?" Marielle asked.

Adelaide seemed to regard her thoughtfully before she answered. "Ghosts are not what I believe in," the old woman finally said. Then she stretched out her hand.

Marielle blinked at it.

"I am afraid I need a little help off this bench, Marielle. I've been sitting here too long. And it's too low."

"Oh! Of course!" Marielle took a step toward her and placed her hand under the older woman's elbow as she rose to her feet.

"Do...do you want me to keep my hand here?"

Adelaide smiled at her. "No, dear. I will be fine. You can let go, and I'll race you to the top."

Marielle dropped her hand and took a stutter step.

"I am kidding," Adelaide said.

They began to walk up the lawn, and Marielle cast a glance at the studio as they passed it.

"I do hope you will be happy here, Marielle," Adelaide said, looking up at Holly Oak.

"Thank you. I'm sure I will be." Marielle chanced a peek at the older woman and decided to ask the question that had been niggling at the back of her mind since Carson first introduced her to Adelaide. "Have you been happy here?"

Adelaide slowly nodded, as if to confirm the unspoken observation that accompanied Marielle's question, that Adelaide had known much sadness at Holly Oak. Her husband had died young. Her only child, a drug-abuser, had run away from home at seventeen, and the grand-daughter she had raised had died at the age of thirty-four.

"I don't know that my life would have been any different had I lived it in some other house. Maybe it would've been worse. Who can say?" Adelaide said. "Holly Oak isn't to blame, not really."

"To blame?"

"Some people have said this house is cursed."

Adelaide's serenely spoken but odd words prickled Marielle. "Who says the house is cursed?"

"Ignorant people. It's not a curse."

"What…what's not a curse?"

Adelaide paused a moment before answering. "You are probably too young to remember record players. But sometimes when you'd play a record, way back when, there'd be a nasty scratch and the needle would just get stuck. And when that happened, the record just kept playing the same bit of music over and over. The needle couldn't move past it. It didn't know how, you see. It wasn't designed to know how. But it wasn't the needle's fault."

Adelaide stopped and turned to look at Marielle. "Do you hear what I am saying? It wasn't the needle's fault. It was the scratch."

Marielle stared at her. It was the first time Adelaide had done or said something that suggested to Marielle that the woman's age was perhaps messing with her mind. Carson had said from the beginning that mentally Adelaide was still as sharp as a tack. But Marielle had no idea what to make of what Adelaide was saying to her now. Movement above them on the patio eased her gaze away for a moment. Carson and the others had returned.

"It wasn't the needle's fault," Adelaide said again.

"No, of course not." Marielle forced her gaze back on Adelaide.

"You gouge a record deep enough and the needle can't get past it. It tries but it can't, so it keeps playing the last thing it *could* play, over and over and over. And that, Marielle, is not a curse. That is the evidence of the needle's limitations, despite its wish to do what it was created to do. Do you see the difference?"

Carson didn't see her on the lawn below the stairs. His back was to her.

"Do you want to go back up to the house now?" Marielle faked a light tone. She had no idea what Adelaide was saying. None.

Adelaide frowned. "Did you hear anything I just said?"

"I…I heard you."

"Well?"

Adelaide was staring at her, displeasure washing across her weathered face. It surprised Marielle how much Adelaide's disappointment bothered her. But the woman was talking in riddles. "I don't know what you want me to say, Mimi."

The older woman pinched her brows in apparent disgust. "Did you not *understand* any of it?"

Carson, please, please, turn around.

"You said it's not the needle's fault. It's the scratch."

"Yes, but what is the needle?" Adelaide asked.

Turn around, turn around.

"I…I don't… The needle plays the music?"

Adelaide sighed and shook her head as if Marielle were a naive adolescent. "No, dear. The needle is this *house*. Do you see? The needle is Holly Oak."

At last Carson turned. He saw her. He waved.

"Do you understand what I am telling you, Marielle?"

Carson began to take the steps quickly down to the lawn. Marielle felt the tension inside begin to shift from not understanding a word Adelaide was saying to wanting Carson to hear it for himself. "Not really," she said.

Adelaide turned, noticed that Carson was approaching them. She sighed audibly.

"Never mind," Adelaide muttered. "You are a different kind of girl. You arrived here later. The rest of us were born here. Maybe you won't have to understand it."

Carson was now at her side.

"What are you ladies doing way down here? I figured you'd be inside with your feet up." He smiled wide, looking from Adelaide to Marielle. Pleased, it seemed, that they had been walking in the garden together.

"We were just talking," Adelaide murmured, resuming her stroll up the sloping lawn.

Carson's smile widened. "What about?" Again, that pleased tone.

Marielle shrugged her shoulders, a suitable reply impossible to conjure.

"Girl talk," Adelaide answered.

Part Two

THE PARLOR

*T*he yards of gray wool stretched across the cutting board like a sheet of dull tin. Adelaide ran her hand along the folded edge, pressing it down, her fingers whispering across the coarse fabric as if reading Braille. The parlor was bathed in silence except for murmurs of cloth falling across wood. The children had already left the house for their last day of school, and Carson was out of the house before dawn for a 7:00 a.m. conference call. Adelaide heard the kitchen door open and close. Marielle had gone out into the garden to sip her third cup of coffee.

Adelaide reached for the muslin pattern pieces on the chair behind her and began to lay them on the wool, fastening them to the material with T-shaped quilting pins. On a second chair lay folded pieces of cotton twill for the pockets, cotton duck for the cuffs, green silk for the lining, fourteen brass buttons for the double-breasted coat, a looping twirl of gold braid for a colonel's insignia, yellow wool piping that would turn wheat-colored in the play of cannon smoke and gunpowder.

She reached for her shears, shiny Ginghers that could slice off a fingernail if you're weren't careful, and opened them to make the first cut. As she moved the blades, the wool gave way without protest and remnants began to slide away, some of the fragments dropping to the floor. Adelaide had four uniform sets to cut after finally receiving measurements via the e-mail account Carson monitored for her. The order for an upcoming August reenactment in Pennsylvania had come while Carson, Marielle, and the children were in Orlando. Adelaide normally didn't accept more than one order at a time, but the timing for this one had been providential; she needed something substantial to occupy herself in the summer months with the children home and Marielle wandering about the house. Making four complete uniforms—frock coats, trousers, and undergarments— would fill the long summer days with details.

The first few days after Marielle and Carson returned from their honeymoon, well-wishers came by the house every day and the distractions had been welcome ones. Adelaide invited Marielle to use the formal living room to receive her guests, and Marielle, a bit overwhelmed, it seemed, with ceaseless Southern hospitality, agreed with a smile and a shrug. Neighbors and church women came by for ten days straight to greet Carson's new wife, bringing as tokens of their welcome plates of pralines and peanut clusters, densely sweet pound cake and little jars of gingham-topped strawberry-rhubarb preserves. The Blue-Haired Old Ladies also stopped by—one or two at a time—to pump the bride for additional insights on how a woman can fall in love with a man she's never met because a robotic machine— the vast and unknowable Internet—had seemingly drawn their names out of a hat.

The visits had dwindled though, and Adelaide was relieved to have a mountain of sewing to do to occupy her time. It surprised her how highly aware she was of Marielle's presence in the house, and it equally surprised her how much she sometimes wanted to shoo her away. Not away from Carson or the kids, just away from her. Carson seemed quietly happy to be married again and the children eager to please their new stepmother. But Marielle wasn't a replacement granddaughter. Adelaide hadn't contemplated how that wouldn't change one iota when she pictured Marielle living at Holly Oak. Carson had a new wife and the kids had a new mother, but she did not have a new granddaughter. She didn't know what she had, but it was not a new granddaughter.

A four-uniform order also gave her sufficient reason to hide away in the parlor if she wanted privacy to sort all this out mentally. The parlor was the one room she told Carson she wished to keep just as it was, despite there being a new "woman of the house." Marielle could do, within reason, whatever she wanted to with the other rooms, but the parlor—the one room where time seemed to be a hushed afterthought—was hers.

Adelaide had always felt that way about the parlor, since that long-ago day her great-grandmother Susannah described how she had sewn Confederate uniforms at the long oak table and once had hidden two of the uniforms inside her feather bed. Her great-grandmother had told her of other events that had happened in the parlor, the echoes of which, Susannah had said, still rippled through Holly Oak. Susannah told her she'd read her marriage proposal from Nathaniel Page by letter in the parlor. She was accused of being a spy for the Union in the parlor. She served tea to the man she loved in that parlor and held a dying baby in the parlor. And—with an emancipated slave—planned the escape of two hidden Union scouts in that parlor. Susannah had taught her wounded husband how to walk again and gave permission for her daughter, Annabel, to marry in that parlor. And the most significant thing? The parlor had been a makeshift field hospital during the Battle of Fredericksburg. Yankees, shot to bits on the frozen flatland below Marye's Heights had been dragged back to town to the houses they hadn't obliterated by shelling the day before, to die or be bandaged or be sewn. In Holly Oak's parlor, a dozen or more wounded Union soldiers had bled and died on the floor, slumped in corners, and even on top of the table where Susannah had sewn together Confederate uniforms—the strangest kind of irony. Two soldiers had been buried in the cellar, and later, so her great-grandmother said, were exhumed and laid to rest at the national cemetery, a hill of green that overlooked the very spot where they had fallen.

Adelaide remembered asking her great-grandmother how she knew there were echoes rippling in the house—she had been eight—because she had listened for the echoes and had heard only silence inside and woodpeckers outside. Susannah had said a house is meant to be a place of safety and refuge, not a place for spilled blood and lies and broken promises. Adelaide could still recall, even eighty-some years later, the images that filled her head as she tried to hear those echoes of violence and lies and broken promises. She had bad dreams for several nights afterward, and she might have had worse nightmares had Susannah expounded, but her grandmother Annabel had stepped into the parlor at that moment and told Susannah not to tell Adelaide any more stories like that, that it was Susannah's fault the notion that the house was cursed perpetuated year after year and for pity's sake to stop it. Before she was hushed a second time, her great-grandmother had told Adelaide to listen carefully and she would hear them, the echoes, and that only the women of Holly Oak could hear them. And when Adelaide asked her in a whisper if it was true that she had been a spy—gossip at school and on the streets was that she had been—Susannah told Adelaide to let the house tell her if she had been a spy or not.

The parlor became the center of the house's mystery after that day, since Adelaide's great-grandmother passed away a few months later, having never mentioned the echoes again, and her grandmother and mother would not discuss it. But Adelaide began to sense the rippling effect of time crumpled in on itself—echoes perhaps—the year her father died, and again much later when her husband Charles died, and again when dementia swallowed up her mother, all amid the whispered consensus of local gossipers and rumormongers that Holly Oak's women were cursed because of what happened in the war. Because of what Susannah Page did.

And didn't do.

In her adult years Adelaide found a stack of her great-grandmother's letters to her cousin Eleanor Towsley of Maine shoved to the back of Annabel's escritoire, written in the early years of the Civil War and returned to Susannah by a family member upon Eleanor's death in 1920. But Susannah's letters portrayed her as merely a young woman in love with a man who happened to be a Union Army scout. Eliza Pembroke, Susannah's aunt, was the one accused of Union loyalties. Adelaide didn't know where the letters were now. She'd given them to Caroline when her daughter was sixteen. Likely as not, Caroline had carelessly tossed them in the trash or sold them for drug money. Caroline hadn't believed that the house still echoed with reverberations from the past. Caroline hadn't believed in much of anything.

Adelaide shared her great-grandmother's stories of crippling echoes and Holly Oak's strange fascination with its women with her good friend Pearl decades later, to her utter regret. It wasn't long after that that Pearl, as a self-proclaimed favor to Adelaide, asked her so-called clairvoyant cousin Eldora Meeks to verify the existence of ghostly activity.

That had been a mistake. The woman knew nothing about houses. Eldora Meeks may or may not have the ability to talk to spirits, but she surely had no gift for talking to houses. Yet Pearl passed the story of her cousin's unsubstantiated discovery of the ghost of Susannah Page to anyone with the slightest interest, despite Adelaide's persistent requests that she shut up about it. Susannah Page didn't haunt the halls.

Undeterred, Pearl had told Adelaide that sooner or later someone was going to have to make peace with Susannah's ghost.

And Adelaide had said that was proof enough that Eldora hadn't the slightest idea what she was talking about.

There was no peace to be made with Susannah. Susannah wasn't the one at war.

Adelaide now set the cut pieces of the frock coat on a third chair and folded the wool. She spread out the green silk lining and reached for her pin cushion. She heard the kitchen door open and close again. Marielle had come back inside.

The doorbell rang, and Adelaide stood motionless for a moment. It was early, only a little after nine. Too early for even the Blue-Haired Old Ladies to make a social call. She listened as Marielle opened the door, heard a man's voice say he had a package for a Mr. Carson Bishop, heard Marielle say that she could sign for it; she was his wife.

Adelaide went back to pinning the weightless length of silk, glad that Pearl or Maxine or Deloris hadn't decided to stop in. The Blue-Haired Old Ladies were making stops at Holly Oak even after the other neighborly welcomes had ceased. Pearl had been by just the day before to visit for a spell in the kitchen and invite Marielle to lunch the following week.

And just as Adelaide had predicted, Pearl's reaction to finding out Carson and Marielle were sleeping in Susannah Page's bedroom had been swift and animated.

"Oh dearie, are you sure that's wise?" Pearl had said to Marielle. "I mean, of all the bedrooms, *that* one?"

To which Marielle had replied, "But nothing happened in that room. Right?"

Adelaide had patted Marielle's hand. "Nothing happened in that room."

Pearl had leaned forward in her chair, vigorous concern multiplying the wrinkles around her eyes. "She *slept* in there, Marielle."

"What difference does that make?" Adelaide had said.

"Well, where do you think her ghost would feel most comfortable? Where do you think her ghost would want to be?" Pearl replied. "Wouldn't she want to be in her own bedroom?"

Adelaide reached for her teacup. "To do what? Sleep? I wasn't aware that ghosts needed sleep."

Pearl loudly clucked her tongue. "That is my point exactly! Carson and Marielle are sleeping in a room occupied by a ghost who doesn't sleep!" Pearl turned to Marielle. "You really should consider moving into a different bedroom."

"That's enough, Pearl." Adelaide had taken a sip of her tea and replaced the cup. Pearl clamped her mouth shut. And Marielle offered to refresh all their teacups.

After Pearl left, Marielle hadn't asked Adelaide for any more information about Susannah or the room she was sleeping in except to say that

Pearl was nothing if not insistent. And Adelaide had reassured her that Pearl's imagination had always been hanging on one hinge and to pay her no mind. But Marielle's mood seemed thoughtful the rest of the day, brooding almost. Pearl's persistence that Susannah was an unhappy ghost traipsing about Holly Oak had obviously unnerved her. Adelaide had wondered if Marielle told Carson about Pearl's visit and warnings. But since Carson hadn't said anything, not even a gentle request that Adelaide tell Pearl to mind her own business, she assumed she had not.

Adelaide felt a kink in her back from bending over the table, and she stood and stretched carefully. Another cup of tea would be nice. She opened the door of the parlor and took a step toward the kitchen but stopped when she saw Marielle standing statue-still, looking at the family photographs that lined the lower half of the staircase. She stood on the third step, her arms crossed loosely in front of her, unaware that Adelaide had opened the parlor door and now watched her. Adelaide took a step back, wanting to silently close the door and pretend she never had the thought to get another cup of tea. But she couldn't take her eyes off Marielle as the young woman's gaze traveled the wall, resting first on the sepia-toned portrait of Susannah Page seated with her young daughter, Annabel, standing next to her, then Annabel's wedding portrait, and then Adelaide in her mother's arms with her christening dress flowing over her mother's skirt, then her father wearing his army uniform. Then Adelaide's engagement photo, Caroline as a child on a tricycle, Caroline's senior portrait, Sara in a prom dress, and then Sara in front of her studio with baby Brette in her arms and Hudson embracing her from behind.

Marielle studied the wall from the bend in the stairs at the landing where the first portrait hung to the bottom stair where the gallery ended with Sara and the children. Then she lifted her head to start at the top again, her neck slowly guiding her gaze down the wall of photographs.

Adelaide pushed the door closed without a sound, the hankering for another cup of tea dismissed.

arielle sat on the floor of Brette's room, an eruption of Barbie dresses blooming in her lap. Brette sat next to her, tugging at a tiny pink warmup suit on a flaxen-haired doll. The roar of the air conditioner pushing cooled air into the room muted the other sounds in the house; Marielle would not hear Carson come home from work unless she opened the bedroom door or the A/C switched off, which was highly improbable.

She had been warned about Virginia heat in June. Two college friends back in Phoenix—East Coast transplants, both of them—had warned her at her bridal shower with knowing looks and clublike solidarity that she hadn't felt heat until she lived through a humid Southeast summer.

Marielle had reminded them that it's usually 115 degrees in Phoenix on any day in the summer, and the two friends had just laughed.

"You don't know what you're in for, hon," one of them had said. And the other had nodded empathetically.

Marielle now gently moved the dresses off her lap and stood.

"Where are you going?" Brette said, her face at once morphing into worry.

"Just opening the door so we can hear when Daddy comes home."

"I don't want Hudson coming in."

Marielle walked over to the door and opened it. "I don't think he will." She could hear the sounds of the TV two floors down in the family room. SpongeBob turned up too loud.

She came back to the rug and retook her spot, pulling her cell phone out of her pocket as she sat down and setting it where she could see its windowed face. If Carson called to say he would be late, which she was learning happened a lot, she didn't want to fumble in her pocket for the phone and miss talking to him.

She missed their phone conversations. For the first three months of their relationship, the phone had been their sole tether to each other. They spent an hour or more every night talking across a span of miles that didn't separate them anymore. He hardly ever called her now. Of course, he wouldn't. Why would he? They weren't dating. They were married. They lived in the same house. They talked face to face every day, but somehow it was different.

It had been three weeks since she and Carson and the children had returned from the family honeymoon at Disney World, and it needled her that she was instantly aware of how long it had been. Marielle had expected some transitional stress with the move, the marriage, and instant mother-hood. She wasn't naive. Her mother had warned her she would probably have it; so had her matron of honor, Jill, and just about everybody back in Arizona—as if she didn't know there might be some tough days, especially since she was moving into a house which didn't require a towel, a fork, or even so much as a light bulb from her apartment in Phoenix.

Chad had been right about toasters and Crock-Pots. Holly Oak al-ready had those. Holly Oak already had everything.

All it really needed was a wife and mother—roles it was used to hav-ing but which she barely understood. She got that. There would be some transitional stress.

But no one could have prepared her for the oddities of living in a house with so profound a past. Photographs of Holly Oak's former and current residents lined the halls. Downstairs, sepia-toned portraits of Mona Lisa–faced women in full skirts, uniformed men with handlebar mustaches, a child in a christening gown, black-and-white wedding photos, and high school senior pictures and babies and prom photos—they covered the walls like curious spectators. Carson had taken down a few of Sara's photos, but he asked to leave up a couple for the sake of the children. How could she say no to that? She didn't. He removed his old engagement and wedding photos, but he'd left the eight by ten of Sara sitting on the step in front of her studio with Brette in her arms, fat-cheeked and diapered, and Hudson hanging over her back, his arms necklaced around her. It hung next to the third stair, between baby pictures of Hudson and Brette. And Marielle walked past it all the time.

No one had any prenuptial advice about how to walk past a photo gallery like that every day.

And no one had advice on how to put away dishes that Adelaide had been using in the kitchen for decades or how to buy a different kind of detergent than what was on the laundry room shelf or how to handle the rumor that the house was haunted by a ghost, that dead Yankees had been buried in its cellar, and that there may or may not be a curse, depending on who you talked to.

Driving the children to and from school, attending their end-of-year art shows and soccer games, and familiarizing herself with what they liked and didn't like had filled her days when they first returned from Florida. And so had the neighborly visits. But now school was out. It was the middle of June and the visits had stopped. The summer months stretched ahead of her like a thorny chore she was unprepared to touch. And the oppressive heat outside seemed to confirm that she was no match for the weeks that lay ahead.

She had been stupid to think she wouldn't need a job right away; some outside task to give her life meaning beyond dishes, ghosts, and making peanut-butter-and-jelly sandwiches for two kids she barely knew and yet felt constrained to love.

She did love them.

She loved them.

But loving them didn't mean she couldn't love other things. Like a job. Like having a purpose outside of the house. Carson had told her he would help her find a new job if she wanted, and she'd said she was fine for now just spending time getting to know the children. Besides, there weren't desert conservation groups in Fredericksburg needing grant writers. She was going to have to reinvent herself careerwise, and there was enough reinventing going on in her life already...

"Marielle! I said I can't snap this."

Brette was kneeling in front of her, an arm outstretched with a half-clothed doll in her hand.

"Sorry." Marielle took the doll and snapped the tight bodice. "There you go."

"She's going on her honeymoon. Like we did." Brette jammed the doll, alone, into a blue plastic sports car.

"Where's her groom?" Marielle asked.

Brette looked about the room, littered with Barbie clothes, plastic furniture, and four or five additional blond-headed female dolls. "I don't know where he is." She turned back to the doll in the car. "She doesn't need him. She can go on her honeymoon by herself."

Marielle watched as Brette zoomed the car around the oval rug in her room, running over little shoes and purses and plastic dishes. A few popped into the air and fell back down like jacks. As Brette pushed the car around the room, Marielle began to wonder how hard it would be to freelance out of the house. Set up a grant-writing business and work out of the room off the kitchen, perhaps? Maybe it wouldn't be so hard to diversify after all. There had to be plenty of nonprofits on the East Coast that needed contracted grant writers; she didn't have to solely work on environmental projects. Maybe she could do a little copyediting or proposal writing...

"Now she's at Disney World!" Brette lifted the doll out of the car, held her high for a moment, and then lowered her to the floor. She turned to Marielle. "Want to see my mom's Barbie clothes? I have them. Mimi gave them to me."

The word *mom* pulled Marielle's attention back to Brette. "Sure," she replied, mentally massaging away the poking reminder that she wasn't the girl's first mother. Her only.

Brette hopped up to her feet and opened her closet. She withdrew a vintage cosmetic case, upholstered in pink vinyl with a black handle, and sat back down with it. "They kind of smell. They're old."

The girl opened the case and began to pull out tiny outfits, purses, and hats, releasing an odor of aged fabric. Marielle recognized a few pieces from her own childhood Barbie collection. The chef's apron with its tiny black-checked potholders, the pink ballerina tutu with the white diamond-shaped sparkles, the black lamé sheath.

"And look!" Brette said. "Her bride dress."

Brette pulled out a white lacy concoction that frothed tulle and acetate. She handed it to Marielle.

"Wow. These are all lovely."

"They were my mom's," Brette said again, and Marielle nodded.

"Did you know my mom?" the girl asked, her head cocked in doubt.

"No. I didn't."

"I don't remember her. But we have movies. Sometimes I like to watch them."

Marielle smoothed out the wrinkles in the tiny wedding dress. "That sounds like a great way to remember her."

Brette stared at her. "Do you want to watch them sometime?"

Marielle blinked. A dozen indescribable responses, minuscule and lacking definition, pinged in her head. "Um. Maybe. Sometime."

"My mommy had blond hair."

"Like you," Marielle said stiffly.

"Yours is brown."

"Yes."

"But I like it."

Marielle instinctively reached for her, and Brette climbed in her lap. "I'm glad."

Brette lay her head against Marielle's chest, and for several seconds neither one said anything.

For a moment, the room felt right. The moments-ago urgency to set up a business, to fit in, to not count the weeks, drifted a bit, gave up some of its weight. With the little girl in her lap, warm against her skin, Marielle sensed a tender weakening inside. Not just inside her. But inside every-thing—inside the air around them, the wood floors, the plaster walls that had been painted over and over and over. As if a tumbler had moved into place, just one of many inside a very old lock.

She leaned her chin on Brette's head, silently reassuring herself that soon she would not be counting the weeks. Soon she would use her own dishes in the kitchen. Soon her portraits would be done and her own wed-ding picture would hang on the wall. And then a day would come, maybe next year, when she would forget she had been counting weeks, and per-haps they would be a family of five then, and Adelaide's secrets about curses and record players and ghosts would not matter anymore, and she would not have to convince herself that she loved Carson enough to have married him and his past.

She could see the tip of that future day as she sat with Brette snug in her embrace.

Brette sighed against her. Marielle kissed the top of her head.

"Sometimes I want to call you Mommy," Brette said.

Marielle nodded.

"But sometimes I don't."

The front door opened downstairs. Carson was home.

Brette jumped off her lap and dashed to the door and then the stairs. Marielle stood slowly, and the little wedding dress floated to the floor.

fingernail moon sliced the twilight sky as Adelaide looked out one of the utility room's windows. On either side of her, shelves filled with canned beans, jars of pickles, and unopened bottles of salad dressing shone in a mix of twilight and incandescence from the single bulb above her. Boxes of juice drinks and spray bottles of sunscreen lay in easy reach on other shelves, along with plastic crates of balls, croquet mallets, and squirt guns. Rolls of paper towels, boxes of cereal, cans of bug spray, and an assortment of flashlights, old phone books, and Christmas lawn ornaments crowded other shelves. A mishmash of empty boxes and bags of foam peanuts and stacks of shopping bags with cord handles swarmed in the corner by a door to the outside that no one ever used. It had been called a utility room since Adelaide was little, but it was more a place to put things until you needed them. A waiting room, really.

Before the Civil War, the room off the kitchen was known simply as Cook's room. Susannah's grandfather Eldon Pembroke, who built Holly Oak the summer of 1850, had been a slave owner like most Virginia landowners and kept a contingent of slaves at the house in town while the rest lived at his sheep farm and shearing barns outside of town. The houseworkers slept in the slaves' quarters at the edge of the garden, with the exception of Cook, whose name no one remembered because no one had called her by her name.

By the time Adelaide was born in 1921, her father—a science teacher at the local high school and a World War I veteran—had renamed it the utility room after having recently spent eighteen months in trenches, longing for a place to store things you might need later.

Three decades after that, when Adelaide's husband, Charles, financed the house's first major renovation, the utility room was shortened by several feet to enlarge the kitchen. A long row of windows was set into the south-facing wall so that Adelaide's mother could tend her collection of needy, fur-leafed African violets. New shelves and cabinets replaced sagging boards and cubbies. Tile was laid over a new cement floor. A couple of decades after that, when Adelaide's mother was finally placed in a home for people who can no longer remember that fire can burn down a house or that the river can drown you, the violets died and the room became solely a depository of things waiting for their shot at usefulness.

Now Adelaide stood in the center of it with Carson at her side. Marielle was upstairs getting the children ready for bed. "It's been a long time since this room has been gone through," Adelaide said.

"I know. I've been meaning to take care of it since...well, since before...a long time," Carson replied.

She turned to him. "I thought you were finished with stumbling over that," she said.

He smiled halfheartedly. "Sometimes I forget I'm finished with it."

She watched Carson look about the room, assessing the work ahead of him to clear it of clutter so that Marielle could have it as an office space. Assessing other things too, perhaps.

After four years they had both reached a point where Sara's absence seemed normal instead of a cruel deviation. Carson's marrying Marielle had reminded them both what normal used to be and was no longer.

"Sometimes I forget I am finished with it too, Carson," she said.

He moved his shoulders as if to shake off the momentary weakness. "It shouldn't take me long to clear this junk out of here. Half of this stuff can go out in the garage. And if Marielle rearranges the pantry, we can move the extra food in there and maybe stop stockpiling so much of it. This will be a nice room for her to work in, actually, once we get that stuff cleared away from the windows and open it up a bit. She can bring her laptop in here and some of her books and her photographs of the desert. It will be nice." Carson nodded his head as if in agreement with someone.

Adelaide pursed her lips together, picturing Marielle clacking away at her laptop while Brette and Hudson hung about the parlor doors, bored.

"What about the children? What are they supposed to do when she's in here?" she asked.

"This really isn't any different than when Sara set up the art studio in the old slaves' quarters, Mimi. Same thing, really. And Hudson was younger than Brette is now when she started working in there."

Carson had a point. But something about Marielle having an office in Holly Oak for a purpose that had nothing to do with Holly Oak needled her. She didn't know why. "They will come to me if they get restless."

Carson shook his head. "You won't have to do anything. Marielle will be right here in the house. The kids don't need her every waking minute. Besides, when they go to my parents' house for those three weeks, Marielle is going to need something to do. Something that she's familiar with and knows. It's…it's not been easy for her. She's…" His voice fell away.

"I know it's not been easy."

He swiveled his head to face her. "Has she said anything to you? Did she say something?"

"No, she hasn't. But I'm not blind, Carson. She relinquished a lot to marry you. I know that. I'm sure you do too."

Carson said nothing. A flicker of pain moved across his face. "Marielle loves me. And I love her."

"I didn't say she doesn't love you; I said she relinquished a lot to marry you. She gave up her home, her job, her friends, her independence. And you made her an instant mother; don't forget that. And then you plunked her down into the house you shared with Sara. This house of ghosts."

"Don't start on the whole ghost thing, please." Carson picked up an empty box and began to toss random items inside it: rain boots, a jump rope, citronella candles, and a faded box of rose food. "The last thing Marielle needs to hear now is that you *do* think there are ghosts in this house."

"But what is a ghost exactly, if not a startling shimmer of the past that you still see from time to time? I've been thinking about this. A ghost doesn't have to be a person. Pearl doesn't know what she's talking about."

Carson threw a bottle of car-wash detergent into the box. "I don't want to talk about this. Marielle will be back down here any minute to tell me the kids are ready for bed. All this ghost talk of Pearl's is only making it harder for Marielle to feel at home here. I wish she'd stop. It's unsettling for Marielle."

Adelaide sighed. "Yes, I am sure it is. All of it."

Carson dropped a whiffle ball into the box and looked at her. "What's that supposed to mean?"

Adelaide grabbed a couple of boxes of cereal to take to the pantry in the kitchen. "I think we all have our ghosts, in some shape or form. How can we not?"

"Ghosts and memories are not the same thing," Carson said quietly as he taped the box shut. "Memories are things we get to keep. I'm not going to forget I loved Sara. Marielle and I talked about this, before I ever proposed to her. She doesn't expect me to forget I loved her. I don't feel about Sara the way you feel about this house or the way Pearl feels about your great-grandmother. Sara isn't a ghost. Give me those." He reached for the cereal boxes.

"I can help empty this room," Adelaide said.

"You don't have to. Marielle and I can do this. I think it will be good for her and me to finish this together. Besides, you're missing *Jeopardy*."

She handed him the boxes, and he took them, turning swiftly away from her.

"I'm sorry I said that," she said.

"Said what?"

"Well, whatever I said that made you say what you just said."

He put the cereal boxes into an empty Rubbermaid tote. "That you're missing *Jeopardy*?"

She smiled.

Carson peeked over his shoulder at her and grinned easily.

"I mean, about all of us hanging on to our ghosts," Adelaide said. "I shouldn't have said that. I miss Sara too."

Carson reached for two boxes of graham crackers and said nothing as he placed them in the tote on top of the cereal.

"I speak my mind too freely. I know that. I am sorry."

"Look. I don't care so much what you say around me. But I do care what gets said around Marielle. I don't want her having to handle more than what she's already having to deal with. She doesn't need to know what you believe about this house, Mimi."

Adelaide at once remembered what she had said to Marielle the day of the reception about the record player and the needle. She'd already said too much.

At her silence, Carson looked at her. He frowned. "What did you tell her?"

Adelaide shrugged. "Hardly anything."

"What did you tell her?"

"I only said that the people who say Holly Oak is cursed don't know what they're talking about. It's not the house's fault."

Carson tossed a carton of granola bars into the tote and stood erect. "Was that really necessary?"

Adelaide sniffed. "Few things are necessary, Carson. And I'll have you know she asked me if I've been happy here. And she asked me because, if you will recall, *you* brought her here to live and now you expect *her* to be happy here. So I told her that all the things that have happened to me are not the house's fault."

"For crying out loud—"

Adelaide's breath and voice tightened in her throat. Carson didn't often raise his voice. He was mad at her. She felt behind her for the shelving unit and grasped a metal rung for moral support. "What? It's not the house's fault my father had cancer or my mother had dementia or that Charles died of a heart attack in his fifties or that Caroline became an addict or that Sara was taken from the both of us when she was only thirty-four!"

"Adelaide!"

"It doesn't know how to get past the scratch! I've told you that before!" She tottered slightly for a moment and grasped the rung tighter. Carson did not notice.

He lifted the tote of food off the floor. "This is exactly what I don't want you telling Marielle," he said quietly. "It's nonsense. And you can think it if you want, but I told you a long time ago that I didn't want you talking this way around the kids—"

"I haven't!" Adelaide exclaimed.

"And I would appreciate it if you also didn't talk this way around Marielle."

"She asked me."

"She asked if you had been happy here."

They stood there for a strained moment, staring at each other.

"You called me Adelaide," she finally said.

Carson's facial features took on a conciliatory look. "I'm sorry, Mimi. How about if we just move past this. Please?"

Another long moment of silence passed between them.

"She's having lunch with Pearl next week," Adelaide finally said.

Carson began to walk past her with the box in his arms. "All the more reason to drop this. I don't think Marielle believes Pearl. But I'm afraid she could believe you."

And he stepped past her with the tote in his arms, leaving her alone in the mix of light and shadow.

The drumming whir of a sewing machine greeted Marielle as she stepped off the last stair and made her way to the slightly ajar parlor door. The house was silent except for the mechanical piercing of the needle into fabric. She had already taken Brette and Hudson to swimming lessons, and a family friend had offered to pick them up so that Marielle could have lunch with Pearl and not worry about the time. She was glad. It surprised her a little that she was looking forward to lunch with Pearl. She tapped lightly and the whirring ceased.

"Yes?" Adelaide said from within.

Marielle gently pushed the door open. Adelaide was seated at her sewing table with folds of gray frothing at her hands. A gooseneck lamp perched over her sewing machine looked as though it were inspecting her work. She looked up as Marielle poked her head inside the room.

"Just wanted to let you know I was leaving," Marielle said.

Adelaide cocked her head as she studied the gauzy, violet-hued cotton dress Marielle had chosen to wear. "You look nice. Lavender looks good on you. And it's Pearl's favorite color. She'll think you wore it for her."

Marielle smiled. "Should I just let her think it?"

Adelaide reached for her scissors and clipped a dangling thread on the seam she had just sewn shut. "Pearl will think what she wants, dear, no matter what you do. Keep that in mind."

There was unspoken weight under Adelaide's words. A warning. "Um.

Thanks. I will. The kids are all set to go home with Lynn Jarrel. I'll pick them up from there on my way home from Pearl's."

Adelaide snipped another thread. "You don't need directions to Pearl's?"

"I'll be fine. I'll just use my phone."

"Your phone."

"I have GPS on my phone. I'll be fine."

Adelaide pulled the half-sewn jacket out from under the raised needle. "I know I should know what that is, but today I am just not interested in knowing. Call me if you get lost. I know you can do that on your phone."

Marielle laughed lightly. "I will."

She turned to go, but Adelaide called out her name. Marielle turned around.

"Look, maybe I shouldn't be saying this, Marielle, but Carson doesn't want you having to deal with any more ghost talk. And I know Pearl. She'll bring it up."

Marielle took a step into the room. "Carson said that? When was this?"

Adelaide turned back to her sewing machine. "When we were cleaning out the utility room for you, I said something about this being a house of ghosts. I shouldn't have. That's when he said he didn't want you to have to hear any more of Pearl's stories."

Marielle sensed hesitancy. Back-pedaling. "Mimi, Pearl's stories don't scare me. The first day I heard about them it was a little weird, but it's not like I'm having nightmares. Is that what Carson thinks? That I'm afraid?"

Adelaide stuffed the jacket back underneath the needle. "I think it's more that you shouldn't have to deal with Pearl's ghost on top of having to get used to me and this house and the humidity outside. And he knows I told you about the scratch, and he doesn't like that either."

Carson was miffed that Adelaide had told her her theory about the scratch? A theory that made absolutely no sense?

"It's not what you think," Adelaide quickly added. "We only talked about it for a minute. A minute. All I am saying is when you go to Pearl's today and she starts talking about ghosts, you can tell her to shut up. That's all."

"But maybe I don't want her to shut up about it," Marielle said, now very glad she had called Pearl the day before with a suggestion.

Adelaide turned her head to look at her. "I beg your pardon?"

"Pearl's stories don't scare me. Just like they don't scare you. Maybe I want to hear her stories."

"Whatever for?"

Marielle shrugged. She had been giving the matter some thought. It shouldn't be a big surprise that she was daily becoming more interested in what remained in a house after someone died. She was curious. That was all. "Maybe it will help me understand what you were telling me about the scratch."

Adelaide raised an eyebrow. "Pearl doesn't believe in the scratch. Only the ghost."

"I'll keep that in mind."

Marielle stood for a moment longer, but Adelaide said nothing else. The woman turned back to the sewing machine, pressed her foot to the pedal, and the needle began to flash with purpose. "I'll see you later, then, Mimi."

Adelaide nodded. "Yes. Have a nice time, dear."

Marielle stepped back into the entry hall. Her face was warm. Adelaide probably hadn't been completely honest with her, but neither had she.

She had asked Pearl to invite a third person to join them for lunch.

Eldora Meeks.

⁓

Fragments of cucumber sandwiches, chicken salad, and melon balls dotted the creamy blue china plates as the three women sat in Pearl's sunroom.

They had eaten as soon as Marielle arrived, forgoing a stroll through the garden, owing to the heat and Eldora's needing to be in Yorktown by five.

Over lunch, Pearl had described in ebullient detail how Marielle and Carson had met and fell in love, as if Marielle were not sitting right there at the table with them. Marielle didn't mind, even though Pearl kept embellishing the story. The chatter gave her a chance to study Eldora Meeks without attracting attention.

Marielle had never met someone who claimed to have special sight or a connection to the spirit world or the ability to talk to the dead. She had never met anyone with any kind of psychic ability at all.

Eldora looked to be in her late sixties, plump, with silvery red hair and eyes that narrowed into slits when she smiled. She wore a pale pink warmup suit trimmed in white and flicked her tongue to the corner of her mouth every time she said something. Her accent was more fluid than Pearl's or Adelaide's and reminded Marielle of taffy being pulled by slowly moving blades. She looked like a kind grandma who watches the shopping channel, makes quilts, and collects porcelain dolls.

Marielle reached for her glass of sweet tea and took a sip just as Eldora turned to her and smiled, her eyes disappearing into lash-fringed seams.

"That sure sounds like a right sweet love story," Eldora said. "But you probably have many questions, don't you, Marielle? That's why you asked Pearl to invite me to come today. What can I do for you?"

"She wants to know about the ghost," Pearl interjected, and Eldora raised a hand.

"Now, Pearl, why don't we let Marielle ask her own questions, shall we?"

Pearl sat back in her chair, her lips puckered as if she'd swallowed a lime. "I'll try to be quiet," she murmured.

"Are you sensing a troubled spirit inside the house, dear?" Eldora asked Marielle.

Marielle shook her head slowly. "Well, no, not really. I just... I actually just want to know what you saw or heard at Holly Oak when you were there."

"And why is that?" Eldora's voice was still kind and accommodating.

"Because…because Adelaide said something to me about the *house* being troubled. That doesn't make any sense. I don't understand what she means by that."

Pearl leaned forward. "Adelaide doesn't believe in the ghost, Eldora."

"Yes, I know, Pearl. I'm aware of that. But we're lettin' Marielle ask the questions, remember?"

Pearl sank back in her chair. "Sorry," she mumbled.

Eldora turned back to Marielle. "Did you ask Adelaide what she means?"

"What?"

"Did you ask her what she means when she says it's the house that is troubled?"

Adelaide's strange words on the lawn floated back to Marielle. "She said it's like a record player that keeps playing the same part of a song over and over because it can't get past a scratch."

Eldora nodded. "I see. And did you ask her what she meant by that?"

"She tried to explain it, but we were interrupted. I never really had the chance to bring it up again because it seemed to be something she wanted to keep just between us. But Carson knows now she told me. And he's not exactly happy about it."

"I wonder why he feels that way." Eldora laced her fingers together and sat comfortably back in her chair.

"He doesn't believe in ghosts either!" Pearl said, and then clamped her hand over her mouth.

Eldora smiled at Pearl and then turned back to Marielle. "And how about you, dear? What do you believe about ghosts?"

Marielle shrugged a shoulder. "I've never had any reason to believe they exist."

"But now you are wonderin' if you do?"

"I'm just trying to understand this. I'm living in that house now. It's my home."

Eldora reached for Marielle's hands. She flinched at the woman's touch and then slowly relaxed. Eldora's manicured fingers gently stroked Marielle's hands.

"Here's the thing, Marielle. I can tell you what I felt inside that house. Ten years later I can still feel it. And I am happy to tell you. But I can't make y'all understand anything. I think in the end it's you who is goin' to have to decide where you land on all of this."

Marielle swallowed. "All right."

Eldora let go of her hands and smiled. "First, you need to know that I didn't ask for this gift I have. It just came to me. My grandmother had it and so did her aunt. I didn't know I had it until I was fifteen. And at first I didn't know what to do with it. And I can't see the future or make objects move or hear y'all's thoughts. I see and hear things in the spiritual realm, things that ordinary people can't see and hear. Lots of people don't like to think there is a spiritual realm, and those that do don't like to imagine that some of us can see it and hear it when they can't. Are you with me so far?"

Marielle nodded her head slowly. "So you can see...people who are dead? You can hear them?"

Eldora's tongue flicked the left corner of her mouth. "I believe I can."

"She can!" Pearl whispered.

"Did you see a ghost at Holly Oak?" Marielle asked.

Eldora tipped her chin and hesitated for only a second. "I sensed a heavy spirit of sorrow and betrayal in Holly Oak, the most intense I have ever felt. Deep and pervasive. And yes, I felt the presence of someone who believed themselves responsible for it."

"Susannah...," Pearl murmured, practically under her breath.

Marielle felt a prickling on her skin and shook it off. "Was it? Was it Susannah?" she asked, matter-of-factly.

Eldora breathed in and out deeply, reconnecting, perhaps, with the sensation she felt when she was inside Holly Oak. "I believe so, yes. Who else could it be? She was a woman who surely had many regrets. It's widely held that Susannah Page hid Yankees inside Holly Oak, that she married a Confederate officer to hide her alliances with the North. That same officer, Lt. Page, was later betrayed by those same Yankees. They shot him in the head, nearly killed him. Yes, I think it could be her."

Again Marielle felt a tingling on her arms and again she willed it away. "But you didn't actually *see* her. You didn't talk to her."

"No."

For a moment the three women were silent.

"Do the history books say what you just told me?" Marielle finally asked. "About Susannah?"

Eldora only paused for a second. "No. They do not. Susannah was questioned only once about her Union loyalties. It was a well-known fact she had family in the North and a cousin who served in the Twentieth Maine. She was accused of hiding Yankees, but she was never charged. And her husband, Lt. Page, was indeed wounded terribly at Gettysburg. He was a supply officer. He wasn't even on the front lines. Y'all hear what I'm sayin'? He wasn't even on the front lines. That's what the history books say."

"So, assuming you're right about…about her ghost, what do you think Susannah wants?"

Eldora again laced her fingers on the tabletop. "Well, I would imagine she wants what all ghosts want, Marielle. She wants peace."

"That's right," Pearl breathed. "She wants peace, poor thing."

In her mind Marielle pictured the record, spinning madly on its turntable, the needle unable to move past the crooked gouge but refusing to give up trying.

"And how is she supposed to get it?" Marielle asked.

"That's just it. She can't. That's why she's still here. She can't undo what she did."

"That's why Adelaide sews the uniforms, dear," Pearl said, peeking at Eldora for approval for her comment.

"What do you mean?" Marielle asked.

"You know," Pearl continued. "The uniforms. Susannah sewed uniforms too. Real ones. In the parlor. Adelaide is trying to go back to the beginning. Make things right for Susannah. Like a do-over."

"But Adelaide doesn't believe Susannah is a ghost," Marielle said.

"Yes, but she thinks the house is."

"Is what?" Marielle asked.

"A ghost. Adelaide thinks the house is a ghost. It's the same thing." Pearl crossed her legs and lifted her tea glass, looking satisfied with her contributions to the conversation.

Marielle turned to Eldora.

"Adelaide thinks the house is stuck, unable to move forward in time with the people who live in it," Eldora said. "Horrible things happened inside Holly Oak. Horrible things happened in this town. And Susannah made it worse somehow, so the house keeps exacting a toll on its women. It needs restitution to get past its past."

"What do you mean, a toll? Are you saying the house has it in for me?" Marielle laughed nervously.

"No. Not like that. Adelaide would say the house withholds protection over its women to make atonement for Susannah's many wrongs. That's why some people think there is a curse on the house."

It's not the house's fault. It's not the house's fault. The echo of Adelaide's quiet declaration at her reception played back in her mind. *It's not the house's fault.* As if the house had a sense of justice—and the means to dole it out.

"You actually think the house *feels* like it's been wronged? That's impossible."

"I didn't say I thought that," Eldora replied. "I said that's what Adelaide thinks. I think the grieving presence is Susannah. Adelaide thinks it's the house."

Pearl patted Marielle's arm. "It's really the same thing when you think about it."

Ridiculous images of the house swallowing her whole, of the doors and windows becoming solid wall and trapping her inside, pressed in on her. She shooed the cartoonlike notion away.

"Houses don't feel things," Marielle said.

"No, but people do." Eldora took her napkin off her lap, folded it neatly, and placed it on the table. "Susannah did and Adelaide does. And so do you. Isn't that why you asked me to come here?"

"I asked you to come because I need to know how I'm supposed to live in a house that everyone seems to think is haunted."

Eldora shook her head. "Actually, dear, you might want to keep Adelaide's word for it in mind. Be easier for you. Not haunted. Stuck. Adelaide thinks the house is stuck. I think it's Susannah who's stuck."

"Stuck," Pearl echoed.

Marielle pulled her own napkin off her lap and tossed it onto the table. "Look. I need to make this work somehow. I need to know how to live in that house. What am I supposed to do?"

Pearl tapped the table with a ringed pointer finger. "First thing you need to do is move out of that bedroom!"

"Pearl, please." Eldora held up a hand to silence her.

"Well, Eldora! They are sleeping in her bedroom!"

Eldora turned to Marielle. "I don't suggest you move out of Susannah's bedroom unless you sense tension and disquiet there. Do you?"

"It's just a room," Marielle replied.

"I'll take that as a no. I didn't either when I was there. The rooms where I sensed the most unrest were the parlor, the cellar, and the slaves' quarters. Oh, and the garden. But that's not a room."

"Are you telling me to stay out of those rooms?"

Eldora reached out and squeezed her hand. "Actually, I suggest you try being very intentional about going into those rooms. I suggest you speak absolution to those rooms whenever you can, whenever you are alone in them. I think Susannah has forgotten that God is forgiving. It is more in His nature to forgive than to punish."

"You want me to say that to the rooms." The words sounded silly in her ears as she said them.

Eldora nodded. "It won't be as hard as you think, Marielle." She squeezed her hand again and then pulled her hand away.

"Why didn't you say those things when you were in the house?" Marielle asked.

"I am no one to Susannah Page. I have no right to say anything to her. You live in her house. You are raising her descendants. I think she will listen to you."

"And should I say anything to Adelaide about this?"

Eldora was thoughtful for a moment. "Do you think you should?"

Marielle didn't know what to think.

"Adelaide doesn't like it when we talk about Susannah's ghost," Pearl offered.

"I'm not even sure I can do what you're suggesting," Marielle looked away, toward the tall windows that looked out onto Pearl's backyard and a long row of bushy peonies bursting with color. "I don't even know if I believe any of it."

Eldora smiled at her graciously. Kindly. "Yes, dear, but your life is playing out as if you do."

The sweet, almost tangy odor of pressed fabric under a hot iron wafted about the silent parlor as Adelaide set the appliance down and guided the still-warm jacket—minus its braid and buttons—onto a padded hanger.

She stepped back to examine her work, making sure there wasn't a hint of asymmetry in the coat's proportions. A few threads dangled from the side seams, and she bent to snip them. She liked constructing coats the best. They exuded an air of elegance despite their intended purpose.

A *Richmond Times-Dispatch* features reporter had once done a story on her uniform making, years ago, when Sara was home for a summer break from college. Adelaide had been making a coat just like this one the day the reporter had come, and it was at the same stage of completion. Without their buttons, the coats always looked sightless and meek. The man had taken pictures of her sewing a button. He had taken pictures of the parlor too. And the cannonball on the side of the house.

And the portraits in the hallway. He had asked to borrow a few photographs of Susannah Page, and Adelaide had kindly declined his request. "I don't feel comfortable with any of my photographs leaving the house," she said. He said he would take very good care of them and return them promptly. She said no. The reporter turned to Sara then, wordlessly, it seemed, asking her to come to his aid. Sara suggested he take a picture of the photos on the stairway instead, and that's what he did.

The interview began in the parlor, though she hadn't wanted it to.

Sara, bless her, commented that it was such a lovely day in the garden, perhaps the reporter would like to interview her grandmother out there, and that she would bring them sweet tea and homemade macaroons.

Adelaide had been wise to wait to grant the interview until Sara was home on summer break. The man kept dragging the questions back to Susannah's suspected espionage, and Sara valiantly attempted to redirect the conversation back to uniform making.

Adelaide finally asked the man if what he really wanted to talk about was Susannah Page.

"It will make the story more interesting, Mrs. McClane," he said.

"What is it you want to know?"

"Was she a loyalist? Actually, was she a spy for the Union? Did she hide Yankee soldiers in this house? Was she one of Pinkerton's agents?"

Adelaide played with a crumb of toasted coconut on her plate. Sara whispered to her that she didn't have to talk about anything she didn't want to.

There had been a gentle breeze that afternoon and little humidity. Whatever she said would be carried on the breeze to who knew where— out past the shuttered slaves' quarters and into the woods or straight into the open windows of Holly Oak.

"My great-grandmother was a teenager when the war began, and she was loyal to her family, not a cause. She hid a cousin and his best friend, a young man she was very fond of, in this house, and yes, they were Union soldiers. But I know of only the one time she did it. It was before Gettysburg. She told me her husband was not even at Holly Oak at the time, so obviously he was not wounded during their escape. Susannah's aunt Eliza Pembroke was charged with passing secrets on to the Union Army, not Susannah, and it was Eliza who was imprisoned in Castle Thunder, not Susannah. And I seriously doubt Susannah was one of Pinkerton's agents."

The reporter, who was taping their conversation with a tiny tape recorder, still took notes on a slim, spiral-bound notebook. She read later, in

the article, that he had been noting her tone of voice, the confident countenance on her face, and even the accompanying breeze that set her wind
chimes to a tinkling applause.

"I understand you remember your great-grandmother. You were eight,
I believe, when she died?"

"That is correct."

"So she told you all of this?"

"No."

The man looked up from this notepad. "So your grandmother or
mother did?"

"No."

The man waited.

"Susannah wrote letters to her cousin Eleanor Towsley. The Towsleys
were her father's family in Maine, and John Towsley was the cousin Susan-
nah hid in the spring of 1863. Eleanor and John were brother and sister.
Susannah was very close to her cousins. Not geographically, of course.
Susannah and her parents had been living in Washington DC, where
Susannah was born. They spent several weeks in Maine every summer.
When her father died of influenza in 1860, Susannah and her mother came
back to Holly Oak."

The man sat forward in his chair. "Do you still have those letters? Are
they in a museum somewhere?"

"I don't know where they are, I'm afraid." Adelaide glanced at Sara.
And Sara looked down at her hands.

"But you actually saw these letters? You read them?" the man asked.

"Oh yes. I read them many times."

"But you don't know what happened to them? Were they stolen?"

Adelaide had shook her head. "I...I gave them to a family member.
And that person lost track of them."

The man looked from Sara to Adelaide. "Well, that's a downright
shame. They'd be worth a lot of money, I'd wager."

Adelaide had told him they probably would.

"So. These letters. Susannah Page wrote them during the war? And somehow they made it through the mail to Maine? How did you come to have them in your possession?"

"As I said, she and Eleanor were close. When Eleanor died in 1920, her family sent the letters back to Susannah. And no, she didn't write them during the entirety of the war. She stopped writing them in the summer of 1862, before the First Battle of Fredericksburg, before she married Lt. Page. Before a lot of things."

The man scribbled something in his notebook. "And she gave them to you?"

"I found them in an escritoire after my grandmother died. Stuffed to the back."

The man looked up. "And you didn't notify anyone, like a museum curator or a historian or something?"

That had never occurred to Adelaide. Not then. Not ever. "No. They were personal letters."

"But of historical significance."

"There is nothing significant in the letters that you could not read in any of the mountains of literature written on the Civil War."

"Well, except for any parts that would exonerate your great-grandmother."

Adelaide stiffened. "My great-grandmother never required exoneration. She was never charged with any wrongdoing."

The man smiled. "Yes, but the perception is that she—"

Adelaide cut him off. "Young man, you are a journalist. You deal with facts, not perceptions. You of all people should know this. People will think what they want. They will always think what they want."

The newspaper's design staff had lifted that quote and set it off by itself in a shaded box with large type.

The reporter then said he'd like to close by asking her if she had any comments for those with perceptions about her great-grandmother that were untrue.

"I shouldn't have to tell the world that things aren't always what they seem," Adelaide had said. "Just because you hear a rustle in the trees, that doesn't mean that the bogeyman is preparing to pounce on you the minute you turn your back. Sometimes the rustling is just God sending a breeze to cool your skin after a hard day in the blazing sun. But I suppose the notion of the bogeyman makes the story more interesting."

The man laughed. He told her he enjoyed their interview immensely and that Sara's macaroons had been exquisite. He promised to send copies of the story after it was published, and then Sara showed him to the door. When she returned to the patio, Adelaide still sat at the table, wondering if she had said too much.

Sara reached for one of the empty glasses on the patio table and picked it up. "When you said you gave the letters to a family member, you meant my mom, didn't you?"

Adelaide snapped her head up, infant hope blooming inside her that Sara knew where the letters might be. "Has she told you about them? Have you seen them?"

Sara shook her head. "She told me about them, but she never offered to show them to me. She did tell me that none of us has the remotest idea what happened here, that she was the only one who did. She said Holly Oak should be...should be leveled."

Adelaide still felt the sting of those words at the mere remembrance of that short conversation with Sara after the reporter left. Picturing Holly Oak in ruins, in the state of devastation it was spared over a century earlier, pained her.

"When did she tell you this?" she had asked Sara.

"Couple of years ago. The last time she was here."

Sara had been sixteen. Caroline had come home out of nowhere to get a copy of her birth certificate to get a new passport. And she'd asked for some money. She only stayed for two days and left in the middle of the night without saying good-bye to either one of them.

"Your mother hasn't… She hasn't always had a firm grip on reality," Adelaide had responded.

Sara picked up another empty glass. "I know," she said. And she reached for the third glass and headed back into the house.

The story had been published two weeks later, and for a short while Adelaide was a bit of a celebrity among her friends and neighbors in Fredericksburg. But then the novelty wore off, people went back to believing whatever they wanted about Susannah Page, and Adelaide went back to sewing uniforms in obscurity.

Adelaide hadn't looked at the article in nearly a decade. As the aroma of hot fabric now dissipated, Adelaide turned to a bookcase and withdrew an album from a middle shelf. She leafed through the pages until she found the article folded inside a page protector. She withdrew it and spread it out flat on the table: "Fade to Gray: Descendent of Suspected Union Spy Sews Confederate Reenactment Uniforms in Her Historic Fredericksburg Home."

Adelaide shook her head. "Suspected union spy," she mumbled to no one. She studied the photos. Sara had said the photographs of her were wonderful, that Adelaide hadn't looked a day over sixty. There was one of her sitting at the patio table with Holly Oak in the background, one of her sewing on a button, and one of a finished uniform on a headless mannequin, straight and true, as if the camera had been able to peek into time and catch a glimpse inside Stonewall Jackson's closet.

And then there was the long photo of the portraits on the stairs. The one of Susannah, in particular, seemed to stare back at her, peeved at the interruption that had whisked her onto the pages of a Richmond newspaper.

Adelaide began to read the story, which opened with a nod to the uniform-making business but seemed to rather quickly morph into a commentary on who the real Susannah Page might have been.

Adelaide suddenly became aware that she was not alone.

Marielle had stepped inside the room.

"My word! I didn't even hear you come in." Adelaide looked past Marielle for the children. She saw no one. "Where are Brette and Hudson?"

"They wanted to stay at Lynn's and play for a while longer. She said she'd bring them home by supper time." Marielle came to the table and stood by her.

"Did you have a good time at Pearl's?" Adelaide asked.

Marielle nodded. "Very nice."

"I suppose she peppered you with questions about your personal life?" Adelaide said as she started to fold the article to put it away.

"Not too many. What is that?" Marielle peered at the article, moving in closer to read its headline.

Adelaide suddenly wished she had put the album away sooner. Or perhaps not taken it out at all. "Oh. Just an old article someone wrote about me and the sewing." She had forgotten how transparent she had been with that reporter.

"May I read it?"

Adelaide couldn't think of a good reason why Marielle shouldn't read the article. Carson wouldn't get after her for it, would he? There was no mention at all of a ghost in the story. Eldora Meeks hadn't been to the house yet.

"All right." Adelaide pushed the album toward Marielle, who pulled out a chair, smoothed out the newsprint and began to read. Adelaide returned to her own chair and threaded a needle to stitch the hem of the coat.

A few minutes later, Marielle raised her head. "That's a very interesting story. I liked what you said about the rustle in the trees."

Adelaide felt a warm rush across her cheeks. She hadn't blushed in years. "Thank you."

Marielle folded the article and placed it back inside its protective covering. "Can I ask you who you gave those letters to?"

Adelaide poked the needle through the fabric. "I gave them to Caroline."

"Oh."

There was a momentary lull.

"You're probably wondering why I gave them to someone as irresponsible as Caroline."

Marielle started to shake her head, but Adelaide continued.

"It was before she ran away. Right after Charles died. She took her father's death so very hard. And she wasn't emotionally healthy to begin with. I gave her the letters because I thought it would comfort her to know that Susannah lost her father when she was a teenager too. I thought she would find a connection to Susannah that would help her. But I don't think that's what happened."

"What do you think happened?"

Adelaide shrugged. "I don't know what Caroline did with those letters. Maybe she burned them; maybe she sold them to buy drugs. I don't know. But I don't think they did for her what I hoped they would. She hates this house and everything about it."

Adelaide heard Marielle's voice catch in her throat.

"She hates this house?" Marielle echoed.

"She's one of those people who thinks..." Adelaide didn't finish. If Carson were here he wouldn't approve. She needed to shut up.

"Who thinks what?" Marielle asked.

"Nothing."

"Who thinks what, Mimi?"

"That it *is* the house's fault. That it is cursed. What I told you the day of the party—we shouldn't be talking about this."

But Marielle closed the album and took a step toward her. "Did she tell you that?"

Caroline didn't have to.

"I've seen it in her eyes. Every time she comes here, which I know is not often. She hates this house. And she's not well, you know. She has mental issues. I am sure Carson has told you."

"But surely she didn't hate Sara. And she doesn't hate her grand-children?"

Adelaide set the coat down and ran her finger across the tiny new stitches. "No. I think she loved Sara as best she could. That's why she left Sara with me, even though Caroline hated this house. She told Sara once she was safer with me at this horrible house than with her anywhere. She was probably right about that. And I think in her own strange way she loves Hudson and Brette too."

The two women were silent for a moment.

"Do you miss her?" Marielle asked.

Adelaide reached for her scissors to cut the thread. "I miss everything that could've been."

Marielle said nothing. She stood and reached out to touch Adelaide on the shoulder. Then she turned to leave. "I'll make us some tea."

Adelaide turned her head as Marielle walked away and hesitated for a second at the doorway. Marielle then touched the door frame with both hands on both sides, a lingering caress, it seemed, with her fingertips, and stepped out into the hallway.

arielle lay next to Carson, her head tucked into the hollow of his underarm. He was quiet, as he often was after they'd made love. In the first couple of weeks of their marriage she had wondered where his thoughts traveled after they'd been intimate, but the usual caress of his fingers on her shoulders suggested he was not far. She wanted to believe he was not far. He hadn't loved anyone since Sara, in any kind of way. And he hadn't loved anyone before her. She liked to imagine that in his contemplative silence following sex, Carson was merely lost in wonder at having found love again.

Marielle turned her head in the shadowy darkness to look at him. A second passed before he seemed aware of her gaze. He bent his neck to kiss the top of her head.

"What is it?" he murmured.

She had no suitable answer for him. She smiled though he probably could not see it. "Nothing."

Just wondering what you're thinking.

He shifted his body and drew her closer. "I'm glad you had a nice time at Pearl's today," he said. "You were sweet to accept her invite. I'm sure you probably would've liked to have spent that time getting your office up and running."

"I didn't mind." She lowered her head to his chest.

"Must've been a bit awkward, though, trying to find things to talk about. Or did she do enough talking for the two of you?"

A moment passed before she spoke. "Actually, there was a third person there."

"Maxine?"

"No." Marielle inhaled deeply, quietly. "Eldora Meeks."

Carson's head lifted off his pillow. "You're kidding."

"No."

"She just showed up?"

Marielle tipped her head upward, but she could barely make out Carson's face in the darkness. "I asked Pearl to invite her. I wasn't going to bring it up that I had. But it felt like lying to let you assume it was just the two of us when it wasn't."

"Why did you want her there?" He sounded dumbfounded.

"I wanted to talk to her. It's not that I believe any of that stuff about Susannah's ghost or anything," Marielle replied. "And I know Adelaide doesn't believe it either. But she believes *something*, Carson. There is something about this house that compels her. Something I think I need to understand if I'm going to live here. In this house. With her."

Carson said nothing and Marielle continued. "On the day of our reception here, you told me Adelaide has a deep respect for this house, remember? But it's more than that. It's like...it's like she thinks the house has a memory, a soul. And it's in some kind of turmoil."

Carson hesitated before he spoke. "Adelaide is an old woman who has known a lot of sadness."

"Yes, but you know about this, right? How she feels about the house?"

"Yes."

"So, were you not going to tell me?"

Carson's arm around her loosened somewhat. "I just didn't want you thinking she's crazy. I wanted you to get to know her first. She's not crazy. She's just... I guess she's what people would call eccentric. I'm sorry I didn't tell you before now."

He sounded genuinely disappointed in himself.

"It's okay," Marielle said.

He began to stroke her arm again, slow and measured.

"What did Eldora tell you?" he said.

"She thinks Susannah is stuck here, unable to get past her horrible crimes against the house."

"Crimes against the house? Is that what she said?"

Marielle leaned away from Carson and propped her head on an up-turned elbow. "No. But I think that's what she means. Eldora thinks Susannah's loyalties to the Union were the cause of too much sorrow and so she has regrets. Or maybe it's that Susannah is still torn between her loyalties, like you said on the day of the reception. Adelaide, on the other hand, thinks the house has some sort of awareness that what Susannah did was an act of treason against the house. And that's why the house takes out all its frustrations on its women. It wants penance. Or absolution."

"That's...that's absurd," Carson muttered, but Marielle sensed a hint of guardedness in his tone. "I really don't think it's wise to head down this road with Pearl. Or Eldora. You take either one of them too seriously and they'll start up again with it. And I just don't see what's the good in that."

"Start up with what again?"

Carson turned on his side, drawing up an arm under his head. "The whole wanting-to-set-Susannah's-ghost-free thing. Pearl and Eldora were all over it when Eldora came here. It was ridiculous."

"Were you and Sara here then?"

"Eldora came just a few weeks before we moved here. Before Adelaide had her heart attack and we came to care for her after her surgery."

Marielle thought for a moment. "Wait. You're saying Adelaide had a heart attack right after Eldora toured the house?"

Carson paused for a second. "Come on, Marielle. Don't even start with that."

Marielle folded her arm and positioned her head on her pillow. "I was just kidding. So have you ever met Eldora?"

"No."

"Did Sara meet her?"

Again, Carson paused before answering. "Yes."

"She did? Did...did Sara think Eldora was the real deal?"

Carson sighed. "I don't know. We'd heard that Eldora had helped the cops find a missing person a couple of times. But there were also times when she couldn't. Personally I think she just got lucky the few times she was able to help them."

"What did Sara think about her?"

Carson didn't speak for several long moments. "Honestly, Marielle. Does it really matter?" His voice sounded sad.

Marielle knew she should drop the subject, but she had to know one more thing. The topic might not come up again for some time. And it was such a trivial thing. Tiny compared to the other unasked questions she had.

"Did Sara know about letters Susannah wrote to her cousin in Maine during the war? Adelaide gave them to Caroline before Sara was even born. But now no one knows where they are."

"Where'd you hear about those?"

"I read a newspaper article about Adelaide and asked what became of them. I was thinking if Caroline had given them to Sara, maybe they're still here somewhere."

"What difference would it make if they were?"

"Well, the article says they prove Susannah was just a girl in love, not a spy. I just think it's interesting that the one thing that could clear all this up is missing. Maybe if Sara had known—"

"Is this really that important to you?"

She heard in his voice a heaviness, a weight she had not felt before and which startled her. A bubble of heated fear rose within her. Small but distinct.

"I just want to know if Sara ever mentioned the letters. And if Caroline still had them."

Carson exhaled heavily. "I don't know. I don't think so."

"You don't think she knew if Caroline still had them?"

"It's not like it was a topic that came up when Caroline would drop in out of the blue. Sara never mentioned she knew where the letters were, if that's what you mean." He paused for a moment before adding, "Where are you going with this?"

Wasn't it obvious? "If the letters exonerate Susannah, then she had no horrible crimes against this house," Marielle replied. "And if there are no crimes against the house, then there is no ghost."

"Well, of course there is no ghost," Carson said gently. "You don't need letters to prove that." He kissed her temple and then turned over to face the wall. He pulled the covers over his bare shoulders. "I've actually got an early day tomorrow."

Marielle frowned. "So we're done talking about this, I guess."

Carson lifted his head from his pillow but didn't turn around. His voice was kind but tired. "Aren't we? I mean, what's there to talk about? I don't know where the letters are. Nobody does." He paused, waiting for her to acknowledge him. "Okay?" he asked gently.

"I just don't see why people think the way they do about this house when no one really seems to know what happened in it."

He turned, reached for her cheek, and touched it. "Don't worry about it so much." Then he turned again to the wall.

Marielle lay on her pillow, feeling decidedly not sleepy. Her thoughts began to somersault inside her brain. Maybe Caroline hadn't destroyed the letters—what would have been the purpose in that? Caroline only had the letters for a year when she ran away from home, most likely without taking the letters with her, which means she left them here. And it seemed un-likely to Marielle that Caroline had sold them for drug money. The collec-tor who bought them wouldn't have kept them a secret. So if Caroline hadn't disposed of them, then didn't it stand to reason the letters were still inside Holly Oak somewhere? Hidden. What if it were the letters Eldora sensed when she had been inside the house? Not Susannah herself, but her letters.

If the letters were found, perhaps the elusive sense of peace that the house or Susannah needed would be granted. If, of course, Marielle decided to even believe the house or dead Susannah were capable of needing anything…

Finding those letters would at least lay to rest the cursed house rumors, even if only for her.

But where could the letters be? And what kind of shape would they be in?

The minutes ticked away as Marielle lay sleepless on her bed, a few too many thoughts tumbling in her head. Next to her Carson's breathing had become low and rhythmic.

The rest of the house she knew also lay in quiet slumber.

Adelaide. Hudson. Brette.

She was alone in the house, but not alone.

Marielle sat up in bed, highly aware of the deep silence in the house. She suddenly had the uncanny and impossible sensation that she was being watched. Evaluated.

She swung her legs to the side of the bed. The notion was ridiculous. She needed air. Outside air. She needed to fill her lungs with air from the world outside this house.

Marielle stood, slipped into a pair of flip-flops and grabbed a cotton bathrobe from the chair beside the bed. She began putting it on as she walked toward the door.

The second-floor landing and stairs were tinged with tiny bursts of amber radiance from night-lights that glimmered from several electrical sockets. But the air seemed deathly still, the very antithesis of luster.

Marielle took to the stairs and was in her office off the kitchen in seconds. She flipped on a light and headed for the door to the outside that Carson had just repainted a robust red. She opened it and felt a press of moist night air, still warm from the hours-gone day. The curtain of sticky air surprised her. The desert in Arizona left few vestiges of the sun's relentlessness when night fell. But here in the South, there was never a night off from the contest of wills. She breathed in deeply anyway, closing her eyes and pretending for a moment that she was back on her balcony with a view of the Sedona mountains embracing her. She imagined the sand still warm but purple now in the night's palette of midnight colors. She pictured saguaro cactus, tall as giraffes, saluting the sky. And she imagined she could hear the far-off call of a coyote and the sound the wind makes when there are no trees to slam against. Marielle opened her eyes and looked skyward, but the massive oak in front of her marred her view, the only one of its size and age in the yard. She stepped out onto the brick walkway and walked briskly to the patio for an unobstructed view of the stars. A few stray fireflies sparked in the distance.

She passed the locked doors of the cellar, angled to greet her and pale white in the moon's glow, and made her way to the open patio. Below her, the old slaves' quarters shone in the moonlight. Sara's old art studio.

Caroline might have handed the letters over to Sara at some point, and Adelaide just didn't know that she had. Perhaps Sara had stashed them in the studio...

Marielle wondered if there would be any resistance to getting a key to look inside. Carson had said he needed to clean it out but still had done nothing toward that end. If she asked for the key to look for the letters, it might hasten that little project, which was actually not a bad idea.

She sat down on one of the patio chairs and stared at the black faces of the studio's two windows. Would he ask her to let him do it by himself? She certainly hoped he wouldn't insist on doing it alone. But what if he did?

Marielle shook her head to dispel thoughts she had no cause to ponder.

She sat back in the chair and again tried to picture the expanse of the open desert spread out all around her. She tipped her head back to gaze at the night sky.

Nothing looked familiar.

It was as if all the stars were in the wrong places.

udson sat cross-legged on the parlor rug, his back against a table leg and a gaming device in his hands. Blips of melodic tones pinged from the tiny console as he worked the controls, a frown creasing his lips. Adelaide sat in a chair next to him, hemming a pair of uniform pants.

"I hate this game!" the boy moaned.

"Then why do you play it?" Adelaide guided the needle into the fabric.

"Because I want to win."

Hudson bent forward, punching the buttons with fervor.

"I thought you were supposed to be upstairs packing for New York," Adelaide said.

"I'm done."

"Did Marielle help you?"

Hudson sat back against the table leg again and drew his knees up against his chest. "I didn't need help."

"Did she offer to help you?"

"I don't need help, Mimi. I'm ten. I know what to pack. Besides, Brette wanted her."

The needle slipped into the fabric and out again, silent and purposeful. "She might have liked to help you, Hudson. She's never packed a boy off to spend three weeks with his grandparents before."

"But I didn't need help."

Adelaide let it go. "So who is watching your rabbit while you're gone?"

"Marielle said she would. I showed her everything."

"That's very nice of her."

The boy shrugged. "I guess."

She set the pants down on her lap. "Well, isn't it? Isn't it nice?"

Hudson poked at the buttons and cocked his head. "But isn't that what moms are supposed to do? If my real mom was here, she'd take care of Ziggy and nobody would say, 'Oh, that's nice!' You wouldn't."

"Hudson."

He looked up at her. "What?"

"Might I suggest you use the words 'first mom' not 'real mom' around Marielle?"

He blinked. "Why?"

Adelaide picked up the pair of pants and the needle. "Because no one likes to feel like they aren't real."

Hudson went back to his game. "I guess."

A moment later Carson stepped into the parlor with keys in his hands. "You all set?" he asked Hudson.

"I've been ready for a long time." Hudson stood.

"Give Mimi a hug good-bye, then." Carson spun out of the room and headed for the stairs, calling for Brette.

Her great-grandson turned to her and put his arms around her neck. She inhaled his clumsy boyness. "Be careful, Hudson. Remember what we've told you about strangers. Be nice to Brette. Don't fight with her. Watch out for her. Come home safe."

"I know all that, Mimi."

"Yes, but I need to say it."

A moment later Brette was in the parlor with her arms around Adelaide. "Bye, Mimi!"

"Good-bye, sweetheart. Mind your grandma and grandpa."

"Okay."

The girl dashed away, grabbing the handle of her suitcase and chasing after Hudson to be the first in the car. Adelaide stood and walked to the foyer to say good-bye to Carson. He had Marielle in a tight hug, and Adelaide looked away until they parted.

"If the traffic's not too bad I might try and make it back by late tonight, but I'll call you." He kissed her lightly on the cheek, mindful, it seemed, of Adelaide's presence.

"Don't drive it if you're tired," Marielle said. "I know your parents want you to stay tonight with them. Mimi and I will be fine."

Carson looked past Marielle to Adelaide standing at the doorway to the parlor. "I'll play it by ear. You ladies have a nice day today."

Adelaide tipped her chin. "Say hello to your parents for me."

"Will do."

Marielle looped her arms through his. "I'll walk out with you."

Adelaide watched as the couple walked away. She went back into the parlor and resettled into her chair to hem the other pant leg.

Several minutes later she heard the door to the outside open and shut. And then Marielle was at the parlor entrance, her arms crossed easily across her chest. She leaned against the door frame.

"Can I get you anything, Mimi?"

"No, dear. I am fine. Thank you, though. You going to work in your office today?"

Marielle nodded. "I have some proposals to write and my Web site to work on. It will keep me busy, I think."

"That sounds like a good plan."

Marielle lingered at the door.

"Something on your mind, Marielle?" Adelaide asked.

"Actually, yes. I'd like… Would it be all right if I got the key to Sara's studio?"

The needle slipped a bit, and Adelaide grazed the tip of her finger.

"And I suppose you kindly waited until Carson and the kids were all gone for the day before asking for it."

"Yes. I didn't want them to… I didn't want it to be awkward for them. I just want to see inside it. I want to see what Sara was working on. You know, what she found interesting."

Adelaide hadn't been to the studio since the month after Sara died, when she and Carson opened it and realized Sara hadn't completed much of anything. There had been a dozen different projects, all in various stages of creation, but none of them finished.

"What Sara found beautiful was actually the act of hatching an idea, not executing it. She wasn't in the habit of finishing anything, you know."

Marielle smiled. "No. I didn't know. I wondered why there was nothing in the house that she had done."

"The butterfly painting that hangs in Brette's room was nearly finished when she died. A friend of hers finished it for her so that Brette could have it." Adelaide looked up and met Marielle's gaze. "Brette doesn't know anyone else touched it."

"Oh. I won't say anything. Ever."

She looked back to her hemming. "Thank you. There were a few other pieces that needed just a bit of attention. Carson put up one of her wall hangings in the library. It's not signed or anything, so you wouldn't know it's hers. It's that strange one with all the fabric and colors and slivers of mirror going every which way."

Marielle nodded. "Yes. I know the one you mean. It's very beautiful. Reminds me of the desert at sunrise, actually."

"Well. That's nice to know. And I have one of her sculptures in my bedroom. It's a blossom coming out of a human hand. Rather odd. But she made it, so it is precious to me."

"Sure."

Adelaide set the pants down on her lap and cut the thread from the needle. "What's left in the studio are all the bits and pieces of stuff none of her other artist friends could use. What I'm saying is, it's a bit of a mess in there. And no doubt full of spider webs and dust."

Marielle shrugged. "I'd like to see it anyway."

"You'd like to have it cleaned out, perhaps?" Adelaide tied off the hem.

"Maybe. Yes, probably. Can you think of a reason why it shouldn't be cleaned out?"

"Well, the kids know it belonged to their mother..."

Marielle tightened her crossed arms. "But you just said it's full of spider webs and dust. Do you think *that* image is good for the kids? What if we turned it into something they could actually use? Like a playroom or something?"

Adelaide snipped the tied threads. Marielle was right. "I hadn't thought of that before. You've got a point. I don't suppose you are thinking of making any changes today..."

"Of course not. I wouldn't take anything out of there until I could talk to Carson about it. But I would like to see it."

"The key is in there." Adelaide nodded toward the library across the foyer, where Carson had his desk and computer. "Bottom drawer of Carson's desk. In the Altoids tin."

"Thanks, Mimi." Marielle uncrossed her arms. "Are you sure there's nothing I can get for you before I go outside?"

"No, dear. I'll be fine."

Marielle turned to leave, and Adelaide called out her name.

"Yes?"

"Be careful, dear," Adelaide said. "Some of Virginia's spiders have a nasty bite."

Marielle smiled, nodded, and was gone.

The next hour and half passed quickly as Adelaide finished the pants, then set to work on piecing the next jacket. By eleven thirty she still hadn't heard Marielle return from the studio. The woman had been down there for nearly two hours—longer than it should take to peruse Sara's odd, artistic remains.

Adelaide set down the pieces of the collar she was working on and went to the window. The garden's foliage, in full midsummer bloom, blocked her view of the old slaves' quarters. She couldn't see the door unless she went upstairs and looked out her bedroom window. Adelaide headed for the stairs and ascended them carefully. At the top of the stairs she walked down the long hallway to her bedroom and stepped inside, then moved to the window that overlooked the garden. She could see that the door to the studio was ajar. But the paned windows were too clouded with dirt and too far away for her to see inside. And since it was daytime and no need for Marielle to have a flashlight, there was no bouncing luminescence to indicate that Marielle was still there. What on earth was Marielle doing in there for two hours? She said she wouldn't start cleaning out the studio until she talked to Carson first. Had she changed her mind? Had she lied?

Adelaide turned from the window. She'd have to go see for herself. She walked back to the stairs and took the first half. At the bend she switched hands and reached for the railing on her left. Her eyes suddenly met Susannah's in the portrait as she grasped for the railing. The visual connection startled her. Susannah's gaze was tight on her, her mouth an even line, impossible to describe. Adelaide stepped back involuntarily and wavered on the step. She again reached for the railing, unable to take her eyes off Susannah.

Her hand felt only air.

Adelaide tumbled forward. Her outstretched arm met the step below her, and she heard the miserable sound of cracking bone and felt a fiery pain in her wrist. The remaining photographs on the wall were a chaotic mosaic of rectangles zooming past her as the rest of her body pitched forward. She smacked her head hard, and as she tumbled down the rest of the stairs, an inky blackness swallowed her.

Then she heard a far-off voice in the darkness, speaking her name.

A cold fog embraced her, and she heard her name a second time.

And the swishing of a skirt.

Part Three

THE STUDIO

hen Holly Oak was newly built, Carson had told Marielle, its row of slaves' quarters numbered half a dozen stone-and-timber cottages that featured real glass windows—a luxury not afforded the laborers on the Pembroke sheep farm outside of town. The Holly Oak quarters were as cozy as a slave could expect to have.

Each one had a stone fireplace for cooking, evening chats, and to keep the winter chill from seeping into weary bones. Two of the larger cottages—gone now—had separate sleeping rooms. The two that remained were single-roomed units that shared a common wall and a common history. But as Marielle made her way across the grass, the only commonality she saw now was the weathered exterior. Inside one were a hutch and a rabbit. Inside the other, echoes of her new husband's first wife.

She'd decided not to tell Adelaide she was poking about the studio for Susannah's letters. If she found them, she wanted the discovery to be a surprise for Adelaide. If she didn't, she didn't want the embarrassment of having naively supposed they were in there.

Marielle climbed the three stone steps that led to Sara's studio. The key slipped into the lock, definitely a newer mechanism, and the handle turned at her touch. The hinges squawked a weak protest as she opened the door and stepped inside the half-shadowed room.

The air was tinged with the odor of dust and age and mouse droppings. Sunlight cutting through the haze of stale air revealed messy mosaics of disintegrating cobwebs. She could make out shelves on one wall and a collection of empty fruit crates and closed boxes along another, two tables with pitched tops for drawing, and another table with a flat surface sporting tall and squat shapes. An easel stood at attention, covered in a canvas tarp. She reached along the wall to see if the place had ever been wired for electricity but found no light switch.

Marielle took another step and waited for her eyes to adjust to the dim light in the room. Sara couldn't have worked in here in such darkness. She must have had battery lamps or a generator. Even with the sun reaching higher into the midmorning sky, Marielle couldn't see how Sara could've found inspiration in such a dull, lifeless room. She pushed the door fully open behind her to let in more light and then stepped farther inside. Marielle lifted the canvas tarp on the easel and peered at what lay underneath—a rectangular stretch of nubby fabric and the beginnings of a woman's face outlined in thick black paint: only brows, a dot for the mouth and a brush stroke for the nose were visible on the face's oval outline. She replaced the tarp.

Marielle moved to the drafting tables, empty except for cups of pencil nubs, rusty X-Acto knives, and dull metal rulers. On the flat table she saw a cookie tin containing shards of colored glass, a basket of long strips of curling leather, and a nearly empty bolt of netting, gray with filth. A tall unfinished sculpture—a tree, perhaps—rested near one edge of the table, a half-completed basket made of torn and lacquered cookbook pages rested on the other.

On the shelves, various-sized containers of metal buttons, door pulls, and keys rested next to each other. She looked behind each tray and those just like them on the lower and upper shelves, looking for a cigar box or hat box or some other compartment someone might use to stow old letters inside. Nothing.

She pulled the tarp off the easel and spread it on the floor by the boxes, checking for spiders as she sat down and gingerly opened the first one. Inside, old crafting magazines, art show fliers, and paint-spattered smocks lay in disarray. She checked the next box, and the next, finding more magazines, half skeins of yarn and twine, spools of wire, and opened bags of glass beads—some holding only a solitary example of what the bag originally contained.

Sara had been a bit of a pack rat. That surprised her. In the half-dozen conversations they'd had about his deceased wife, Carson had made it seem like Sara was a textbook only child, organized and efficient. Marielle stood and reached for the last box on the top shelf, tearing away a weave of webs that seemed to hold it fast like Gulliver on the Lilliputian beach, tiny bands stretched with stoic but flawed intentions.

The box, made of wood and stained ebony, had been decoupaged with emptied flower seed packets. Sara had painted her name in one corner. It was the size of the felt-lined box her mother kept the good silverware in; bigger than the greater Phoenix phone book, smaller than a suitcase.

Marielle brushed her hand across the top, dislodging the airy remains of webs and dust, and sat back down on the tarp. She waited before opening the box, sensing that she had uncovered something that probably didn't contain old brochures and paint smocks.

It seemed the kind of box Marielle might've hidden letters in if she'd had some she wanted to keep secret. Made of permanent material with a tightly fitting lid, it had been tucked away from eyes and hands that might've come across it in the house.

She lifted the lid.

Guidebooks to the Smithsonian, the Metropolitan Museum of Art, and other art galleries lay in a subdued, glossy pile.

Marielle frowned. No wonder no one had bothered with this box when the usable art supplies had been removed after Sara died. She picked up the guidebooks, all at least fifteen years old, revealing a plain-covered book with just a hint of gold embossing on its edges. Definitely not a museum catalog. A journal perhaps? She lifted it and found another. And still another. Intrigued, Marielle pulled the three volumes out of the box to see if a bundle of old letters had been stashed underneath the journals. But her hand met only the wooden surface of the bottom.

No letters.

She opened the first plain-cover book, revealing pages of loopy handwriting, swirling with arcs and sweeps—the kind of script she'd expect an artist to have. She leafed through the second and third one. Each entry was dated, some going as far back as twenty years. Some, only six.

The pages were full of poems and bits of prose, all of them signed with a fat, swirling capital S.

Sara.

A tremor wiggled its way through her as Marielle realized Carson probably didn't know these journals existed. Surely if he did, they wouldn't have been left in the studio among useless remnants of Sara's past, miscellany that no one at Holly Oak treasured and yet which no one had been able to scrape away.

And if Carson didn't know the journals were in the studio, perhaps he didn't know they existed at all.

Was it disrespectful to read them? Obviously Sara had kept them in a place where she expected they would be safe. Secret. And the journals weren't mere high school scribblings kept back for sentimentality. Some of the poems had been written just a few years before she died.

The journals weren't some old thing Sara had kept for memory's sake. They were part of her life as an adult. And she had kept them secret.

Marielle smoothed back the first page. Sara had entitled the first poem "Suitcase." It was dated February 12, 1990.

Suitcase

Your letter came
A fold of pink
Your announcement
Home for a few days
But you don't live here
And this is not Home
For you

You rang the bell
The button guests touch
Your announcement
Home for a few days
But you waited for the door to open
For this is not Home
For you

You said my name softly
The one you gave me
Your warning
Home for a few days
You carry no suitcase
Because this is not Home
For you

You left in darkness
A touch on my cheek
Your apology
Home for a few days
And you disappeared as always

Leaving me in this Home, to ever watch from
    its windows
For you

A tightness gathered in Marielle's chest. The pained words of a teenager mourning the absence of her mother tugged at her. She turned the page and read the next one.

Imagine

I see you in the man at the library…
Who wears a striped vest and combs his hair straight
Who chews his pencil and hates to be late
Who wears a gold ring and canvas shoes
When I see that man
I see you

I see you in the man at the park…
Who jogs with his dog and wears a blue shirt
Who helped the young girl who fell and got hurt
Who told me once the day is new
When I see that man
I see you

I see you in the man at the store…
Who smiles at me and says my name
Who laughs at my jokes and likes to play games
Who has a new baby and a love that's true
When I see that man
I see you

I see you in the man in my dreams...
Who sings me to sleep and kills the fears
Who fixes my car and kisses the tears
Who always knows the right thing to do
When I see that man,
I see you

Marielle sat back against the leg of the table, holding the book up to her chest, awash in Sara's long-ago ache of missing her parents. Carson had told her no one knew who Sara's father was. Not even Caroline. Sara had grieved over this.

She contemplated continuing to read or replacing the journals and showing them to Carson later when he got home. What if he decided they needed to stay private? He might even decide to read them on his own and not share them with her.

But surely Sara had kept them secret because she never intended Carson to read them. Maybe if Sara were here she would tell Marielle under no circumstances was she to show the journals to Carson.

The only way to know for sure was to keep reading.

Marielle pulled the book away from her chest and turned the page.

For the next hour she read the entirety of the first journal. Sara wrote of other things besides her missing parents. She wrote about the house, the cannonball, the river, the trees at the edge of the garden, her friends at school, love, boyfriends, art, God, and dreams.

She also wrote several poems about soft voices she heard when she closed her eyes and how she wished she knew if they were voices she was to trust or fear. She couldn't tell. She wondered if she was hearing the whispers of her own conscience—an angel on one shoulder and a demon on the other—or messengers from heaven, or ghosts from the past trying to communicate with her.

The last poem in the first book made Marielle's skin tingle.

Whispers

The river whispers
A steady voice
Reminding me I have a choice

The trees whisper
A swaying tune
Telling me of former ruin

The garden whispers
A quiet twitter
Life is grand, life is bitter

The house whispers
A rasping melee
I turn away, I run, I flee

Marielle closed the book. Sara had written the poem long before Eldora Meeks visited Holly Oak. Long before Pearl had any reason to tell the
world Holly Oak had a ghost.

Carson hadn't actually told her whether or not Sara believed in Holly
Oak's ghost or if she had bought into Adelaide's strange belief that the
house demanded restitution. But clearly Sara had sensed something...

Marielle's back ached and her eyes hurt from squinting in the poor
light. She decided to go back to the house to get a camping light, something to drink, and a cushion to sit on to read the rest. Bringing the books
into the house seemed a little risky, even with the kids gone for three
weeks. She could perhaps put them in her little office off the kitchen, but

Carson was still in and out of that room, making little improvements for her. It would be too hard to conceal the books in there. No, it was best for now to keep them here in the studio until she had read them.

She set the journals on top of the museum catalogs and got up. She made her way to the open door and paused for a moment before emerging into the late morning sunshine. As she stood there, she remembered the little bench at the back, where she had come across Adelaide on the day of her reception. Perhaps she could come back and read the other two journals on the bench instead of the darkness of the studio.

That was a much better idea than reading by camping light in the musty studio.

Marielle walked up the grassy slope to the patio steps and across the garden to her office door. The house was completely silent when she stepped inside. She didn't even hear the whir of Adelaide's sewing machine. Marielle walked past her desk chair on her way to the kitchen, and her arm brushed a dress-up gown Brette had left over the back of it. Brette had given it to Marielle to mend. She grabbed the dress to hand over to Adelaide on her way back outside. Sewing was not Marielle's forte. She stepped into the kitchen, grabbed a can of Coke to take with her, and then headed for the parlor. A muffled grunt caught her attention, and she turned toward the sound.

Adelaide lay in a quivering heap at the bottom of the stairs, a gash on her forehead bleeding crimson on the floor.

She felt hands touching her, heard the rustle of a skirt, and the sound of her name. Her wrist was on fire. And her head. Her back. Everything was on fire. The house was on fire.

She had been wrong about the house.

Eldora was right. It was Susannah all along. Susannah, the tortured woman who could not forgive herself. It was all Susannah. Not the house. It was Susannah's cursed presence who had spoken dementia into her mother, who somehow took all those baby girls Adelaide had lost, who had caused Charles's heart attack, foisted on Caroline a host of emotional issues and drug addictions, and caused Sara's third child to begin its life in a place destined to kill both child and mother.

It had been Susannah all along, making everyone else pay for her sins.

Not the house valiantly trying to purge itself of the wrongs committed against it.

No. Susannah. Mad Susannah. Holly Oak's ghost.

Holly Oak's curse.

She had been wrong. Eldora was right. Pearl was right.

It was Susannah who pushed her down the stairs.

Susannah who stood now at her mangled body, dousing her with fire.

"Adelaide!" The ghost wailed. "Adelaide!"

Adelaide opened her mouth to beg for mercy, but only a moan escaped her lips.

Susannah leaned over her.

"I've got you."

And Adelaide let the ghost take her.

~~~~~~~~~~~~

And then there were lights.

Blinking lights.

And voices.

"Pupils are responsive."

"Adelaide."

She felt movement. She was in a wagon. Susannah was taking her to the graveyard in a wagon.

"Adelaide."

"Mrs. McClane, can you hear me?"

She opened her mouth. "Susannah...," she whispered.

"Who is Susannah? Is that her daughter?"

"No. That's... No, that's not her daughter."

She didn't recognize the man's voice. But the other one. That was Marielle. Good heavens, Susannah was after Marielle, too...

"Marielle." Her voice was a raspy mutter.

"I'm right here, Mimi. You fell. We're taking you to the hospital. Okay? You're in an ambulance."

She opened her eyes; they were so heavy. She saw Marielle leaning over her.

"The house is on fire! It was Susannah!" she whispered.

Marielle looked up. There was a man on the other side of her. He was wearing a uniform. The man looked at Marielle.

"She hit her head pretty hard," he said.

Marielle looked back down at her, and her eyes were glistening.

"Did you see her?" Adelaide whispered.

Marielle bit her lip. "We're almost there," she said.

And the wagon sped away as darkness again crept in.

~~~~~~~~

When she awoke, she felt something soft and cool on her head. She was surrounded by white. She felt light. Weightless. A curly clear tube poked out of her arm, and a face leaned in.

Marielle.

"Mimi, you're at the hospital. They're going to take some x-rays, okay? But I'm going to be right here. I'll be right here when you're done."

"She isn't here, is she?"

Marielle shook her head slowly. "No. She's not. You're safe here."

"And the house? Did she burn down the house?"

"No. The house is fine. And you're going to be fine."

Adelaide reached for Marielle's hand.

"Don't go back there. It's not safe."

Marielle's eyes widened, but she said nothing.

"Don't go back there." Adelaide said again.

Marielle opened her mouth to say something, but two smiling men in scrubs walked into the white room and announced she was going to have her picture taken.

~~~~~~~~

A doctor stood over her. He held an x-ray in his hands. She did not remember being wheeled into this room. Marielle was nowhere in sight.

"Mrs. McClane, you are very lucky," the doctor was saying. "You've a fracture in your wrist, but that's the only broken bone. The bruising on your back will make it hard for you to go dancing for a while, and you'll have a sizable knot on your head, but I've never seen someone your age survive a fall like that without a broken hip—or worse."

Adelaide studied the negative image of her arm in his hands. A claw. A skeleton.

He held the picture up to a backlight. "So you broke both the ulna and the radius here. Fairly clean breaks, though. But we're going to have to set them in surgery and use a few pins to coax the bones back together. I'm thinking with some therapy you're looking at full range of motion within six months."

"Six months?" Adelaide echoed.

"With therapy."

"I need to sew."

"I'm thinking you'll be able to sew again. If you keep your therapy appointments. Now, your daughter-in-law tells me you're able to sign your own release, is that correct?"

"She's not my daughter-in-law. She's married to my grandson-in-law. Where is she?"

The doctor nodded toward the hallway. "I believe she's out in the waiting area talking on the phone to your..."

"Grandson-in-law. And yes, I can sign my own release."

The doctor flipped off the backlight. "Okay. We'll have the staff get the forms in here and get you set for surgery. Your records say you had heart surgery here before. Correct? Ten years ago?"

"Yes."

"Okay. We'll take a quick look-see at your records and see how you tolerated the anesthesia and all that. Any questions before I see you again in the OR?"

Adelaide shook her head. The movement made her wince.

She awoke again to blessed numbness. Nothing hurt.

Her throat felt thick, as if she had been asleep for a thousand years. She tried to clear her throat, but the effort proved impossible.

Suddenly there was movement beside her.

"Would you like a drink, Mimi?"

Adelaide turned her head. Marielle sat in a chair close to the bed, a magazine folded open in her lap. Adelaide nodded.

Marielle reached for a cup with a bent straw sticking out of it. She poured water from a plastic pitcher.

"Here. I'll raise your bed a little bit."

Marielle touched a switch on a remote, and the bed began to fold into an L. She stopped it and then reached for the cup, setting it just under Adelaide's chin. Marielle guided the straw into her mouth, and she drank. The liquid felt like heaven.

"Thank you," Adelaide murmured when she pulled away from the cup.

Marielle sat back down.

Adelaide tried to remember what day it was. Tuesday? Saturday? The kids left for New York today. So it was Saturday. "What time is it?"

"A little after five."

Adelaide motioned for the water, and Marielle rose to hold it for her. She took another long swallow.

"So I guess I missed lunch?"

Marielle smiled. "Dinner's on the way, though I hear it's chicken cacciatore."

"I suppose Carson is all bent out of shape because I fell while he was gone?"

Marielle set the cup back down on the tray. "He was pretty worried when I called. But I told him your surgery went very well and that you were expected to come home tomorrow."

"He's not trying to dash home tonight, is he?"

Marielle sat back down again. "It's raining hard up there. I told him not to worry. To come home tomorrow like he planned. But if you want, I can call him and tell him you'd rather he came home tonight."

Adelaide shook her head. "No, no. You did the right thing. I can't stand it when people fuss over me."

Adelaide looked down at her arms. One sprouted tubes that were busily transmitting information to a collection of monitors; the other was fat with hard foam and gauze. "So I'm all in one piece again?"

"Yes. The doctor said everything went fine in surgery. They put a couple of stitches in your forehead too, to minimize the scar."

Adelaide raised her good arm to her head and touched the padded bandage. "I must've scared the living daylights out of you."

Marielle smiled. "Actually, you did."

"What happened?"

"You...you don't remember?"

Adelaide closed her eyes. "I was on the stairs. You were...you were outside in the studio. I reached for the railing..."

A sudden recollection of the house turning upside down on her flooded her mind. She saw the pictures on the wall tumbling, eyes turning, watching her spiral. She remembered the rustle of a dress. Susannah's voice calling her name...

She shuddered.

"Mimi? You okay?" Marielle rose to her feet.

Adelaide swallowed hard. "Yes. Yes, I'm all right." She took several deep breaths.

Marielle slowly sat back down.

"Good Lord, it seemed so real," Adelaide said.

"What? What seemed so real?"

"I heard a voice calling my name. It sounded like my great-grandmother. I heard the rustle of her skirt. I felt flames all around me. It was like she was...reaching for me. Like she had pushed me down the stairs and set the house on fire. I heard her voice, Marielle. She said, 'I've got you.'"

Marielle leaned forward and clasped Adelaide's good hand. "That was me. I came in from the studio and found you at the bottom of the stairs. You were bleeding and trying to crawl for help. I said your name. And I had Brette's play dress in my arms. That's the rustling you heard."

"You called my name?"

"I didn't think to call out, 'Mimi.' I said, 'Adelaide.' It's the name that popped out first."

Adelaide eased back onto the pillows, exhaustion creeping over her. "It just seemed so real..."

"You...you hit your head pretty hard, Mimi."

Adelaide turned her head on the pillow to look at Marielle. "I said some crazy things to you, didn't I?"

Marielle squeezed her hand. "It's okay. You're back to being you."

The door to her hospital room opened, and an orderly in purple scrubs walked into the room with a covered plate. "Hello, Mrs. McClane. I've got a nice hot meal for you." The orderly set the meal onto the wheeled tray and pushed it close to Adelaide. "Want me to cut your food for you, or would you like to have your granddaughter do it for you?"

Marielle opened her mouth, but Adelaide spoke before she could say anything.

"We'll manage. Thank you."

The orderly left.

"So would you like me to cut your food for you, Mimi?"

Adelaide nodded.

Marielle stood, removed the plastic cover, and began to cut the chicken and pasta into bite-sized bits. "Would you like me to stay while you eat?"

"You've been here all day with me, haven't you?"

Marielle nodded.

"No, dear. You go on home. I am going to eat and then sleep. I feel like I could sleep for a year. You feel okay about sleeping there alone?"

"Of course."

Marielle finished and then reached for her purse on the floor. "I'll come back in the morning. Carson's planning to leave Long Island at daybreak, if the weather permits."

"That sounds fine, dear."

Marielle squeezed her hand. "See you tomorrow. Call me if you need anything."

"Will do."

Marielle was almost at the door when Adelaide called her name.

"Yes?"

"Thank you. For everything you did today."

"You're welcome." Then she left.

Adelaide ate her meal, one-handed, in silence. She couldn't recall the last time she had slept in a room other than the one at the house. As she chewed, she tried to think back to the last time she had spent a night outside Holly Oak.

Ten years ago. At this same hospital.

Adelaide pushed the tray away. The world outside her window was turning gray as the sun disappeared behind fat clouds.

The sweep of the storm's arc was increasing. It was moving south.

The first raindrops began to spatter on the windshield as Marielle neared Holly Oak. She fed the accelerator a bit more gas, anxious to get home. She had left the door to the studio open that morning, expecting to return to it within minutes. The journals were sitting on top of the wooden box she had found them in. Exposed. Anyone walking past the garden on the street could stand on tiptoe and look over the gate. If the angle was right, they could see that the studio door was open. The house's security system didn't include the garden or the studio. If someone wanted to climb the fence and see inside the studio, there was nothing to stop them.

She thought of Sara's journals, her most private thoughts, laid bare, and her heart began to pound. The sprinkling turned to heavy drops of rain.

Marielle pulled into the driveway and threw the gear into park. Grabbing a canvas shopping bag to cover her head, she dashed from her car to the side gate to the garden. Rain pelted in plump, generous drops, and her sandaled feet were soon soaked. She ran across the flagstone patio and kicked off her shoes at the stone steps that led to the lawn and the studio at the edge of the yard. She sprinted across the wet grass, nearly slipping twice, and darted through the open studio door. Water was already seeping onto the stone floor, puddling on its uneven surface. Marielle pulled up the tarp she had been sitting on and reached for the journals, dry except for a sheen of glistening moisture on the top book. She rubbed it across her chest and placed it in the center of the tarp along with the other two and folded the edges over. Then she placed the wooden top back on the box and replaced it on the top shelf.

A peal of thunder rocked the sky as she grabbed the bundle and headed for the door. She reached for the studio key in her pocket as rain hammered her back. With the door locked and the journals carefully wrapped, Marielle ran up the sloping lawn, her purse slung over her shoulder clapping her on the back. She grabbed her drenched sandals at the top of the patio steps and dashed for her office door, fumbling in her purse for her house keys. When at last she was inside, she closed the door behind her and leaned against it to catch her breath.

Marielle shook her wet hair out of her eyes and walked into the laundry room, just off her office. She set the damp, tarp-covered bundle on the washer and dropped her shoes to the tile floor.

First a shower and dry clothes.

Then a bowl of pasta and parmesan and a glass of wine.

Then the journals.

The house was eerily quiet inside as the storm raged outside. Marielle turned on lights in the kitchen and foyer, closed the parlor doors and was about to head up the stairs when she noticed spots of blood on the floor at the bottom of the stairs from where Adelaide hit her head. She headed back into the kitchen for paper towels and window cleaner.

As she knelt to clean the stain, she noticed the pictures on the wall were crooked, as if Adelaide had bumped them all when she fell. All except Susannah's. She hadn't bumped up against Susannah's...

Marielle finished and left the cleaner by the stairs to put away later. She righted all the portraits as she took the stairs, stopping at Susannah's for just a moment. She pictured the photographer asking Susannah and Annabel to stand like statues as he readied his camera. Susannah's hands were folded in her lap, empty, curled into each other. Her head was turned and tipped, just a bit, to perhaps better catch the light. The sepia tones gave only hints of the color of Susannah's eyes, not dark like brown. Blue, maybe. Or gray. A small upturn in her closed mouth suggested she might've smiled had she been given the freedom to. Her full skirt spilled into the photo like a bell made of foam. Annabel, in white, stood at her side, her countenance like her mother's—obliged into solemnity by an outside force.

Marielle reached out to touch Susannah's face, the size of a half-dollar under the glass...

A low rumble of thunder sounded and she slowly withdrew her hand.

She turned and continued up the stairs, aware she was walking into Susannah's old bedroom to shower and put on dry clothes.

An hour later, Marielle sat in the family room, the former drawing room, with the TV on low for company. A plate with a few tangled coils of linguini sat on the coffee table in front of her. Her cell phone was next to the plate, still warm from talking to Carson. He had apologized again, the third time that day, for not being there when Adelaide fell, for not having been able to spend the day at the hospital with her. He was sorry she had to spend the night alone at the house.

And she'd laughed and reminded him she'd lived alone in her condo in Phoenix for eight years. "So I suppose you didn't get a lot done today," he had said, after a moment's pause.

The journals were sitting next to her on the sofa when he said this. She fingered the spine of one of them. She wanted to tell him about the journals with as much intensity as she didn't want to tell him. It felt awkward not to tell him.

"I didn't have a lot on the agenda to get done today," she answered.

And then she had changed the subject and asked how his parents were and what the kids had done that afternoon after the long drive. They had talked for twenty more minutes about the children, his parents, the lovely mundane. Just like old times.

Marielle stood, took her plate to the kitchen and rinsed it. Outside, rain fell in chaotic cadence against the house as she poured a second glass of Chardonnay. She went back into the family room, turning off lights as she walked, but then she returned to each switch and turned the lights back on. Too much talk of ghosts.

She settled back onto the couch and picked up Sara's second journal. The first entries were dated from what was probably Sara's first year at college. She wrote about the rhythm of the city, the plight of the poor, the beauty of the seasons, the grandeur and anguish of romantic love. The heady exhilaration of stretching her wings. The hell of being rejected by her parents.

Sara had felt a rush of release and vulnerability when she left Holly Oak for college, a loosening, like a scab that suddenly releases its grip on the tender new skin underneath.

She'd written of relationships Marielle was fairly certain Carson knew nothing about, but also about falling in love with Carson, of their engagement, their wedding, the birth of her first child, and of being pulled back to Holly Oak like a magnet that she couldn't resist.

An hour later Marielle closed Sara's third and final journal, running her hand across its stretched leather back. She reached for her wine glass and swallowed the last of it, warm from sitting out, its sweetness flattened by the temperature of the room.

Sara had been a different girl than Carson's descriptions had led her to believe. She was not just the busy, outgoing woman with unconventional artistic flair but also an unsure woman, wounded by rejection, and needing her art to help her stay focused on beauty rather than ugliness.

Or perhaps Carson had just seen what he wanted to see, as men in love can sometimes do.

On their third phone call, when Marielle was first beginning to feel the pull of romance, she had asked Carson to tell her about his first wife. She had wanted to know what the woman who'd first won Carson's heart had been like.

Carson seemed relieved to be able to tell Marielle that Sara had been creative, engaging, devoted to her family, thoughtful, a good mother, and a giving person. She didn't like waste or pretense.

And when Carson told Marielle that Sara had no idea who fathered her and had been abandoned by a substance-abusing mother, she'd asked how a person overcomes hurdles like those. Carson said Sara had been one of those people who managed to flourish despite hardship. The conditions of her upbringing had made her resilient rather than needy and bitter.

But the journals revealed a different kind of girl.

It seemed to Marielle that Sara had been able to relax her apparent resilience when she wrote in her journals. The poems and bits of prose spoke of a woman dealt a heavy hand, a girl grasping for handholds, for meaning, just as Marielle imagined she might have if the same destiny had been handed her.

Sara had wrestled with bouts of depression, with flash-thoughts of suicide during college, and had sought escape in temporary relation-ships—before she met Carson—which Marielle knew she had not told him about.

Marielle now knew that Sara had sensed something amiss about the house, just like Adelaide, just like Eldora, and she had released those misgivings onto the pages of her journals, writing of a sense of liberation when she left for college and of a veiled reticence when she returned seven years later with a husband.

One of her last poems had been about Hudson's presence somehow diluting the aura of regret. Hudson wasn't an extension of Susannah's troubled spirit. He was a boy.

He was different.

Carson couldn't have known Sara had toyed with thoughts like these. She wondered if Adelaide knew.

Sitting there in the quiet, a room Sara had surely been in hundreds of times, it was almost as if Marielle was being invited into the secret. And she didn't know what she was going to do about it.

A peal of thunder rumbled in the distance, sounding like a great stone being rolled from the mouth of a cave. Marielle closed her eyes and pictured standing at the entrance. If she showed the journals to Carson, would it change anything between them? Would he love her more and Sara's memory less? Or would these new discoveries about the wife he thought he knew open the door to grief he'd told Marielle was closed for good? Marielle had been up-front about relationship choices that she now wished she could go back and unmake, but Sara had led Carson to believe she had never been with anyone else.

She pondered what would change if Carson knew Sara's resiliency was actually a thin veneer she excelled at keeping intact, that his first wife contemplated thoughts of suicide the year before she died.

If she put them back in the studio, he would surely come upon them. He'd already told her the studio needed to be emptied of Sara's artistic remnants. That chore was long overdue.

Which meant the journals were destined to be discovered if she put them back. He would find them, and she would have to say something like, "What are those?" And it would feel wrong and deceitful.

Marielle leaned forward and massaged her temples. What to do? She needed an unbiased opinion from someone she trusted. She reached for her cell phone and scrolled down her contacts to Chad's name. She pressed the call button. A few seconds later he answered.

"Married Marielle," he said, and she could hear the smile in his voice.

"Hey, Chad."

"You get the seeds I sent? Did you see I sent poblano peppers too? I figured, what the heck."

"I got them. And thanks. I just... I've come across something, and I'm not sure what I should do. You got a minute?"

"Sure. What's up?"

Marielle spent the next ten minutes updating her brother on her lunch with Pearl and Eldora, Adelaide's fall that day, why she went into the studio, and the discovery of Sara's journals. And what she'd read inside them.

"And now I don't know what to do with them," she said.

"What do you mean?"

"I mean, should I put them back and pretend like I never saw them, or should I hide them away somewhere else? Or should I just show them to Carson?"

"What makes you think you shouldn't just put them back?" he said easily. Too easily. Like there was nothing to think about.

"Because then I'll have to pretend I've never seen them," she answered. "We're going to clean the studio out. It's highly likely we're going to come across those journals while we're together."

"Why pretend anything, Elle? Just put them back, and when he comes home tomorrow tell him you found some of Sara's journals in her studio and you're not sure what he wants done with them."

"But I think Sara kept them hidden from Carson for a reason," she said. "And I think if she were alive she'd want them kept secret."

"But she's not alive. And keeping secrets from your husband usually isn't a great idea, Elle. He's your husband now, not hers."

Marielle felt her cheeks grow warm. "I know that! I just feel like some of the stuff she wrote will hurt him. Will change the way he thinks about her. And maybe it will change the way he thinks about me."

Chad hesitated a moment. "Well, I think you should just put them back. And let what would've happened anyway, happen. Tell him you found them but you put them back. Or tell him nothing and let him find them."

She frowned. "I don't like that idea."

"They aren't yours, Marielle. Have you thought about that?"

"I know they aren't mine. I just... I need to think about what to do."

Chad sighed. "Don't wait too long to decide, Elle. If he finds them in the house, that could be awkward. And I don't mean just for him."

"I won't wait too long. Thanks, Chad."

"No prob."

Marielle clicked off her phone and tossed it onto the couch.

Chad was right about one thing for sure. The journals weren't hers. She needed to put them somewhere safe until she could decide if they should go back to the studio, somewhere inside the house, in a room no one spent time in.

She could only think of one room like that.

Marielle grabbed the journals and headed for the stairs, keeping her eyes on her feet—away from the faces in the photographs.

At the second floor landing, she stepped into her bedroom and grabbed a flashlight from her bedside table. Then she went back into the hall and made her way to the last bedroom at the back of the house.

The room Carson said he didn't go into anymore.

The room he had shared with Sara.

Marielle opened the door and reached for the light switch. She'd peeked into this room before. The master bedroom furniture had been removed and replaced with a brass day bed and wicker end tables, chairs, and a settee. The cabbage-rose upholstery sang pink and cornflower blue. Adelaide had told her the redecorating of the room had taken place the summer before. Prior to that, the room had been empty for a year. Before that, it had housed Carson and Sara's bedroom furniture, and Carson had slept in it alone for two years after Sara's death.

Marielle had been glad Carson had already been out of this room when he met her. It had been more than just his bedroom with Sara; it had been Sara's bedroom since she was a child.

Marielle walked over to the closet and opened it, hoping that inside she would find what she had seen in every other closet on the second floor—a crawl space.

Boxes lined the floor, folded throw rugs and bed pillows lay on top. Marielle knelt and moved the boxes away from the wall and saw the glimmer of a glass knob, the handle of a crawl space. She opened it, flipped on the flashlight, and peered inside. Stuffed animals like the kind from county fairs sat against the wall, looking tall under the low ceiling. Around them, high school yearbooks, swim team trophies, ribbons from debates gathered dust. A neat stack of books lined the opposite wall, covered in plastic. Marielle could read a couple of the spines in the dim light. *Island of the Blue Dolphins. The Pigman. The Secret Garden. Where the Red Fern Grows.*

She moved an ample-sized yellow bear, his paws outstretched as if to say, "Give them to me." The space behind him was dry and clean. She reached for one of the throw rugs behind her, wrapped the journals inside, and set them down on the wood floor. She shoved the bear against them, concealing them completely.

She sat back on her knees, staring at the bear and his cartoonlike eyes.

The things in this space were Sara's. These were things that had been kept.

Adelaide might be the one to find the journals if she left them here.

And getting the journals out of this room once Carson and Adelaide were back home might be difficult to do without attracting attention.

No.

Marielle shoved her hand under the bear and pulled the rug-wrapped bundle out from underneath it. She'd have to find another place.

Maybe there was no other place.

Maybe she'd just have to put them back in the studio tomorrow where she found them. Before Carson got home.

Or maybe she'd just show them to Carson and avoid waiting for him to stumble across them. Let fate play itself out...

She didn't have to decide tonight. She would sleep on it. In the morning maybe the best solution would be clear. Marielle pulled the journals out from the folds of the throw rug.

She was backing out of the crawlspace and the closet on her knees when she sensed movement behind her.

And then a woman's voice, low and accusatory.

"What are you doing?

Marielle fell back against the closet door, childlike dread gripping her as she wheeled her upper body around. All that she knew of reason and reality seemed to hang in the balance as she turned, crazily expecting to see a ghost.

But the figure in the room with her was not Susannah.

 lilting voice, raised and insistent, intruded on her slumber, and Adelaide awoke.

"But I'll only be a minute."

Pearl.

Adelaide opened her eyes and struggled for a moment to make sense of her surroundings. She lay in a bed, but not her bed. And the room was not in Holly Oak. She tried to raise herself, but her body felt like one of Sara's clay sculptures set out in the sun to harden.

"I'm afraid visiting hours are over unless you're family," said another voice.

She was in a hospital.

"I just want to give her these flowers, and I'll scoot right out."

Pearl's voice came from just outside her half-open door.

She remembered then the fall and the curious way the portrait faces— even her mother's—watched her tumble down the stairs.

She remembered the rustle of a skirt.

And the voice of a ghost.

"I don't even know if she's awake," the nurse said.

"I'll just take a look-see. I promise not a peep if she's sleeping." Pearl managed to sound sweetly compliant even when breaking the rules.

"Well, as long as you just set the flowers inside and come right out."

"Oh yes. I promise."

A second later Pearl emerged from behind a suit-striped privacy curtain, a vase of tightly closed tulips in her hands. The vase was wet and so was she. A clear rain bonnet on her blue-hued hair sparkled with moisture.

"Oh, Adelaide! You're awake. Oh my. Just look at you."

"Pearl. Please tell me you didn't drive down here in the pouring rain to tell me to look at myself."

Pearl stepped fully inside. "Oh no. I had my nephew Charlie bring me. He's waiting in the car. He doesn't like hospitals."

Adelaide wanted to sit up, but she didn't know where to begin to accomplish such a task. Her left arm on its bed of pillows felt like it was encased in lead, and her head was swimming in a soupy fog.

"So tell me, dear. What happened?" Pearl set the vase down on the bedside table. "Maxine said you fell down the cellar stairs. What on earth were you doing fooling around the cellar stairs?"

Adelaide fumbled for the remote Marielle had used earlier and pushed a button. The foot of the bed began to curl upward, and she let go of the button to stop it. "I wasn't on the cellar stairs. And how in the world would Maxine know anything about what I have or haven't done today? I only fell this morning. It is still Saturday, isn't it?"

"Dorothy called Maxine. She volunteers in the gift shop here. Remember?"

"Dorothy."

"Yes. Dorothy called Maxine, and Maxine called me."

Adelaide pushed another button, and the head of the bed began to rise. "Well, in that case, what took you so long?"

"Oh, I apologize for that. I was at the church for that memorial for Harriet Conrad's sister. I was in charge of the little ham sandwiches. I didn't get Maxine's message until I got home. I came right over."

Adelaide released the button to stop and let the remote fall by her side. "How nice."

"Well, I didn't come right over. I had to find you some tulips first. I know how much you love tulips. They'll be prettier tomorrow."

Adelaide turned her head slowly to look at the vase of flowers at her bedside. Yellow tulips. Sara's favorite flower. "Thank you, Pearl."

"You're welcome, dear. Now tell me, please, before that nurse kicks me out, what you were thinking traipsing down the cellar stairs! You know how I feel about that cellar. I can't believe Marielle let you do that. You're not a young woman anymore, Adelaide."

Adelaide licked her lips. They felt dry and old. "As I've already said, I was not on the cellar stairs. I was in the house. I misjudged the distance to the railing, and I fell. On the regular stairs. Not the cellar stairs."

"Oh! Oh my goodness. All the way? Did you fall all the way?"

"No. Just halfway." *From where the portraits start.*

"You know, you're a lucky ducky that you didn't break your hip. Or your neck. Oh my goodness. Can you imagine?"

Yes. Yes, she could.

Pearl patted down her bedspread. "But a broken wrist isn't the end of the world, though."

Adelaide looked down at the white mound that was her arm, raised as if she were about to hurl something skyward. "I'll never get those uniforms done on time. That family will be so disappointed. They're for a man and his three teenage sons. I've never been unable to fulfill an order before. They will probably have to go elsewhere and get something not half as nice."

Pearl sat down on the chair by the side table, a look of wonderment on her face. "Oh, but Adelaide! I could help you, couldn't I? And Marielle. She's not doing anything with the children gone for three weeks."

"You haven't sewn anything since your own maternity clothes. Need I remind you how long that's been?"

Pearl opened her mouth to protest and then shut it. "Well, okay, that's true," she said a second later. "But how much can it have changed? Women have been sewing since the Garden of Eden."

Adelaide coughed and reached for her water, taking a sip before answering. "A great deal has changed. I don't mean since the Garden of Eden. I don't use a treadle, you know."

Pearl tossed a wrinkled and jeweled hand in the air. "I know that. You can show us, and Marielle certainly has used a more modern machine. We'll be fine. And Maxine can help. She can sew on buttons."

Adelaide replaced the water cup and sat back on her pillows. "I don't know..."

"It will be fine, you'll see! We can just have Carson bring your machine and all your materials to my house. I've seen your machine. It's portable. And I'll make a caramel cake. This will be like a party!"

"For heaven's sake, why would I have Carson drag everything over to your house?"

Pearl scrunched her weathered face. "Well, we couldn't... I mean I wouldn't want to... You know how I feel about that parlor, Adelaide."

Pearl was afraid of the parlor. She was afraid of a lot of things when it came to Holly Oak. It was the only thing about their decades-long friendship that bothered Adelaide. Pearl's silliness about other things was entertaining, even endearing. But not this. And not today. Adelaide turned her head toward the window in her room. The curtains were still open, and rain glittered on the glass.

"Eldora says—," Pearl began.

"I know what Eldora says."

"Maybe we could move everything into the old drawing room if you don't want to move it all to my house. I could probably handle that. Probably."

Adelaide said nothing, and Pearl mistook her silence for irritation. She patted Adelaide's good arm.

"I can't help it, Adelaide. I know how you feel about that house. I know how devoted you are to it. It's just... There are some rooms I can't go in. Please don't be cross with me. Eldora says—"

Adelaide cut her off. "I am not cross with you." She kept her head toward the window and watched rivulets race each other to the sill and fall away into the dark.

"But you're not saying anything."

Adelaide knew she might regret it later, but she felt compelled to tell Pearl about the strange sensation she had when she fell. Pearl believed Eldora knew what she was talking about. Adelaide hadn't seen Eldora in a decade, and up to that point, had no desire to see her.

But she was having doubts about everything she had ever believed about the house.

And about her great-grandmother.

"Something happened when I fell, Pearl," she murmured.

"What, dear?" Adelaide felt Pearl leaning closer in her chair.

Adelaide turned her head from the window but she did not look at her friend. "Marielle was out in the studio this morning, and she had been out there for a long time."

"The old slaves' quarters?" Pearl breathed.

"And I began to worry that she was messing with what's left in there. She told me she was just going to look inside, but she was gone for so long. I couldn't see if she was still in the studio from the parlor window, so I had gone upstairs to look from my bedroom. I could see that the studio door was still open, so I knew she was still in there. I didn't want her throwing anything out without talking to Carson first. So I was going to go out there and make sure, and I started down the stairs. I got to the landing in the middle, and I turned to start down the second set of stairs. I reached for the railing, and my eyes met Susannah's eyes behind the glass of her portrait, and I...I don't know. I reached for the railing, and it wasn't there. It was like...like someone had moved it."

Pearl gasped and placed a hand over her mouth as she whispered Adelaide's name.

"And I began to fall," Adelaide continued. "I could see all those other faces on the wall watching me as I tumbled. Annabel's. My mother's. Sara's. Even my own. It was like…like I had been pushed, Pearl. Like someone was mad that I had allowed Marielle in the studio and had left her there for so long. I blacked out for a moment at the bottom. And when I came to, I heard a rustling skirt and a voice saying, 'I've got you.'"

"Oh dear. Oh my lands! Oh, sweet Mary and Joseph!" Pearl sputtered. "Was it Susannah? Did you see her?"

Adelaide shook her head gently and turned to look at Pearl. "No. Marielle told me she was the one who said, 'I've got you.' She said she had one of Brette's dress-up gowns in her arms when she found me and that was the rustle I heard."

"Oh." Pearl bit her lip, the look of one unconvinced.

Adelaide's gaze was drawn again to the zooming water paths on her window. "I'm wondering if I've been wrong about the house. I've always thought the house somehow needed some sort of release, forgiveness maybe. I've never thought Eldora was right. I thought the house had a burden it wanted lifted; I never believed it was Susannah haunting us all with her regrets."

"But now…now you think it *is* her?"

Adelaide shook her head. "I don't know."

Pearl inched the chair closer and reached for Adelaide's good arm. She clasped Adelaide's hand. "Let me call Eldora. Let's have her come back to the house. Maybe she can figure out what Susannah wants."

Adelaide shook her head, her brow creased in consternation. "I don't know if that's what I should do."

Pearl clucked her tongue. "Lordamercy, Adelaide. Why on earth have you kept that house? I don't see how you've been able to live there all these years with all that has happened to you there. Why haven't you sold it and moved to a happier house?"

"I've always believed that somehow I could make it stop because I understood and because I had lost so much. When Sara brought Hudson home, I was sure I had done it. I had given the house what it needed. But then Sara died, and I've been wondering if Hudson's birth had been just a temporary reprieve. That nothing has really changed."

Pearl squeezed her hand. "Let me call Eldora. Please. She'll know what to do."

"How do you know she'll know what to do?"

"Well, okay, I don't. But she'll know more than you do."

Adelaide sighed. "Maybe. I'll think about it."

They were quiet for a moment.

Pearl shook her head woefully. "I wish you weren't going back there tomorrow. She'll likely strangle you in your bed tomorrow night."

"Thank you for your empathy, Pearl. If Susannah really wanted me dead, I'd be dead already."

"I just don't like it..." Pearl shook her head and then abruptly stopped and jerked in her chair. "Oh my goodness! Is Marielle home alone? Is she all alone in that house tonight?"

Adelaide nodded and patted Pearl's hand in hers before she let go. "I don't think Marielle is in any danger tonight. She's not like the rest of us Holly Oak women. Not yet."

*M*arielle gaped at the drenched figure standing in front of her. The woman's gray-brown hair hung in wet coils down her shoulders, and her dark skirt clung to her calves like a Grecian drape. She wore a faded denim jacket, frayed in places and which appeared to be a size too big. Her face was Adelaide's in a younger life.

For a moment Marielle almost believed the apparition in front of her was a time-travelled version of Adelaide as a middle-aged woman. This staggering thought tore at her as she grabbed the fallen journals and struggled to her feet.

But then realization flooded her. "Caroline…," she sputtered

The woman's eyes widened. "Who are you? I don't know you." Her tone bristled. "Where's my mother? Where are the children?"

"I'm… I…" Marielle was suddenly unable to recall if Caroline knew Sara was dead. A half-second later she remembered Adelaide had told her Caroline had shown up at the funeral and left the next day without a word to anyone. "My name's Marielle Bishop."

"Bishop? Your last name is Bishop?"

"Yes. I'm married to Carson."

Caroline seemed to need a second to process this information. She stood staring at Marielle for several awkward seconds. "You know who I am," she finally said.

"Yes."

"Well, where is everyone? Where's my mother? Where are my grand-children?"

"Carson and the children are on Long Island at his parents'. He's re-turning home tomorrow morning, but the children will be there for three weeks. And Adelaide fell and broke her wrist today. She's at the hospital, but she's supposed to be released tomorrow."

Caroline's wet brows rose. "She broke her *wrist,* and she's in the hospital?"

Marielle swallowed, pushing back murmurings of inadequacy. "She fell down the stairs, actually. The break required surgery. And she hit her head too. Her doctor wanted her to stay overnight as a precaution."

Caroline stood unmoving and dripping rainwater onto the rug under her sandaled feet.

"Can I get you a towel or some dry clothes?" Marielle asked.

"What are you doing in this room?" Caroline's gaze dropped to the journals in Marielle's arms.

Marielle had no intention of telling Caroline what she carried. "Why don't I help you find some dry clothes?"

"I have clothes, Mary-whatever-your-name-is—"

"Marielle."

"Marielle. I want to know what you're doing in this room."

A shot of anger zoomed forward, replacing the intimidation she felt only seconds earlier. "I know who this room belonged to, and I'm sorry for your loss, really I am. But this is a spare bedroom in the house where I now live. I live here. And you're dripping water on the rug."

Caroline looked down at her feet and the amoeba-shaped puddle that surrounded them. She slowly raised her head. "You live here."

"Yes."

A second of silence.

"Well then, how about that towel," Caroline said.

Marielle moved past her, holding the journals tight to her chest. She made her way to the large bathroom on the north side of the hallway and flipped on the light switch. "The towels are in the cupboard on your left."

Caroline walked past her. "I know where the towels are."

"Come downstairs when you're done. I'll make us some tea."

Caroline nodded and then closed the door.

Marielle spun around and walked quickly to her bedroom. Before she could even begin to make sense of Caroline's being there, she had to find a place to stash Sara's journals. She opened her closet, shoved the journals under a pile of sweaters and then withdrew them again. She knelt on the closet floor, opened the little door to her own crawlspace but then closed it.

She pulled out her laptop case and placed the journals inside, then zipped it closed. She set it back against the wall, behind her dresses. Then she stood and closed the closet doors and made her way downstairs to put water in a kettle.

In the foyer Marielle nearly tripped over something square and dark as she hurried past the front door.

A suitcase.

Caroline had brought a suitcase.

For a moment, Marielle stared at the wet evidence that Caroline might be thinking of staying more than a day. Then she took the suitcase upstairs and set it just outside the bathroom door.

⁓

Caroline stepped into the kitchen wearing a pair of jeans and a flowing top that fell to her hips. She had combed her wet hair and pulled it into a ponytail. In the warm light of the kitchen Marielle could see that Caroline's face was heavily lined with creases and wrinkles, marks of a life spent in the sun—or in worry.

"Thanks for bringing up my suitcase." Caroline pulled out a chair at the table in the kitchen's alcove and sat.

"Sure. No problem." Marielle set a cup of tea before her and a sugar bowl. "Need any milk or cream in that?"

Caroline pulled the cup toward her, studying its painted porcelain face. "No. Thank you."

Marielle sat down across from her with her own cup. A dozen half-formed questions zoomed across her brain as she stared at the woman across from her. Caroline. Caroline the addict. Caroline the runaway. Caroline the horrible mother. Caroline who knew where the letters were. Adelaide's estranged daughter. No one had seen or heard from her in four years, and now here she was—out of nowhere—sitting in the kitchen with Marielle and drinking tea.

"You shouldn't leave the front door unlocked like that. Anybody could've come in here." Caroline took a sip from her cup.

Stunned, Marielle rummaged for a suitable reply, but Caroline spoke again before she could respond.

"I remember these cups. My mother got them the summer before my father died."

Marielle said nothing as she watched Caroline set the teacup carefully down on its saucer.

"So how long have you and Carson been married?" Caroline looked up at Marielle, but her hand was still on the cup. She was stroking its question-mark handle.

"A couple of months."

"And you're living here? You and Carson and the kids are living here?"

Marielle took another sip of her tea. "Yes. We're living here." She set the cup down. It made a tender clinking sound.

"Why?"

"I...I beg your pardon?"

"Why on earth are you living here?"

None of your business, thank you, came quickly to her mind, and Marielle squelched it before it spewed itself out her mouth. She wondered what Carson would say. He had never described Caroline as being overly blunt. Perhaps he didn't know. He had only seen her a couple of times in the ten years he was married to Sara. Perhaps this was a side of her he hadn't had time to see.

"We decided it was the best arrangement for the children right now. And for Adelaide," Marielle replied coolly, amazement giving way to annoyance.

Caroline shrugged and took another sip of tea. "Best," she echoed as she set the cup down. Then she looked up at Marielle, folding her hands under her chin on upturned elbows. "You're not from around here, are you?"

Neither are you, Marielle wanted to say. "I'm from Phoenix."

Caroline opened her mouth, as if ready with a quip about Marielle's very non-Southern hometown, but then she closed it. Softness fell across her facial features. When she opened her mouth again, her voice was gentle.

"Never made it to Phoenix," she murmured. "Been to the Grand Canyon, though. I went there thinking you could jump off the edge of it. Turns out it's not that easy."

Marielle waited in silence. She could think of nothing to say in response.

Caroline unfolded her hands and placed them in her lap. Her gaze fell on the cup in front of her. "I suppose my mother told you all about me."

"A little."

Caroline looked up. "There are reasons why I left. Reasons why I stayed away."

Marielle shrugged. "You don't owe me any explanations."

"But you're raising my grandchildren so I would like you to know."

Caroline's frankness, which had angered her moments earlier, now made Marielle uncomfortable.

"That's okay. You don't even know me," Marielle said.

"And you don't know me either."

Caroline sounded just like Adelaide.

"I made a lot of really bad choices when I was younger," she continued. "And I got myself into situations I couldn't get out of. I wasn't well, and I chose all the wrong ways to remedy that. I know what people think of me, and I can guess what you probably think, but Sara was better off here with my mother than she ever would have been with me."

A sudden boldness came over Marielle. "How do you know she was better off without you? You weren't even here."

Caroline stared at her. "Did you know Sara? Were you a friend of hers?"

Marielle thought of the journals hidden upstairs in her bedroom. "No. I just don't see how you could know she was better off without you."

"Because I was a terrible mother. I was an alcoholic and addicted to painkillers and who-knows-what-else. I heard voices in my head. I slept with whoever kept me warm and fed, and I couldn't keep a job or a roof over our heads. I was a pathetic excuse for a mother. That's how I know. If I had stayed here, she would've ended up hating me, or I would've ended up dead. I…I was a different person back then."

"But what about your grandchildren?" Marielle asked, aware of a sudden swell of maternal concern regarding Hudson and Brette.

"What about my grandchildren?"

"Doesn't it bother you that they don't even know you?"

Caroline sat back in her chair. "Well, until recently, I didn't want them to." She turned to look out the alcove windows. The rain had lessened to a gentle shower, and the glass glittered. "But now I do. I've…I've had an experience. A resurrection—for lack of a better word. I don't expect my mother or Carson or anyone else to understand. But I feel different. And I'm under the care of a doctor and am taking medication the way I'm supposed to—that's a first. I feel…whole. For the first time in my life I don't feel like a fragment of a person."

"Is…is that why you came back?" Marielle asked.

Caroline turned to face her. "I want to see my grandchildren. They're still young. There's still time for me to get to know them and for them to get to know me. It's too late for me to be a mother to Sara but it's not too late for me to be a grandmother to Hudson and Brette."

"So…you're here to stay?" Marielle's thoughts flew to sharing her home with not just a ninety-year-old matriarch but now the matriarch's sixty-something renegade daughter. And maybe a ghost…

"No," Caroline answered. "Not to stay. I have no desire to live in this house." She shook her head. "Not this house."

Marielle waited for Caroline to offer some kind of explanation for her feelings toward Holly Oak. But Caroline said nothing else. And Marielle didn't quite know how to ask if it was because Caroline believed the house was haunted. It seemed a juvenile thing to say, like asking Caroline if she believed in the tooth fairy.

The two women sat quietly for a moment.

"I'm sorry the children aren't here," Marielle finally said.

Caroline inhaled, a cleansing breath perhaps. "Maybe it will be better this way. I can use the time to make some sort of peace with my mother before they come home. That is, if you will allow me to stay here until then. I promise not to stay more than a week after they come home."

"Of course. You have somewhere else to go?"

"I'll be living with a friend in Bethesda for a while. Until I can get my own place. Never had my own place before. But I'd like to visit Holly Oak from time to time. And come for Thanksgiving and Christmas—if that's all right."

"Of course," Marielle said. "This is more your home than mine."

Caroline cocked her head, as if to consider deeply what Marielle had just said. A question or comment seemed to form on her lips, and then it slipped away.

"Would you like to come with Carson and me when we go to the hospital to pick up Adelaide tomorrow?" Marielle asked.

Caroline shook her head. "I think I'll just wait here. You can tell her I'm here. I'd rather she knew and didn't faint dead away at the sight of me and break something else."

Marielle smiled. "Sure. Carson's hoping to be home by eleven o'clock, and then we're going to go get her."

"Carson. Nice guy. I always liked him." Caroline stood. "I'm very tired, Marielle. In a lot of ways. If you don't mind, I think I will go on upstairs and go to bed. It's been a long day."

Marielle stood also. "I don't even know which room was yours."

Caroline laughed weakly. "It looks like you're in it. I peeked on my way down. It has the master bedroom look about it. And your wedding photo on the dresser."

"I'm sorry, Caroline. Adelaide said it had been Sus—" Marielle stopped, Susannah's name frozen on her tongue.

Caroline narrowed her eyes a bit. "Susannah's room. So you've heard about Susannah."

Marielle nodded.

"I don't know what you've been told about this house and about Susannah Page but you should just know, Marielle, that things aren't always what they seem. Thanks for the tea." Caroline turned and started out of the kitchen. "I'll be happy to sleep in Sara's room—your guest room."

*I*n the sterile quiet of her hospital room, Adelaide dreamed of her great-grandmother. It was a dream she'd dreamed before, many times, though it had been years since the last time and more than eight decades since the first. The setting of the dream was always the same, Susannah's eighty-fifth birthday, a real event.

And then the dream would morph into something unreal.

On the day of Susannah's eighty-fifth birthday, Adelaide had been eight.

Her great-grandmother had not wanted to be fussed over or to have a multitude of well-wishers traipsing inside Holly Oak. She agreed to a small gathering in the garden with just close family and friends. Adelaide could still taste the tang of raspberry lemonade on her tongue, even eight decades later. She had never had it before.

Late in the afternoon, her great-grandmother had sent Adelaide into the parlor to fetch a shawl, and when she returned with it, Susannah thanked her and then murmured, "I do believe I am not long for this world, Adelaide Rose."

Adelaide hadn't known what she meant.

Susannah leaned close to her. "I can't say that around your grand-mother and mother. They don't want to hear it. They don't want to hear a lot of things. The thing about you, Adelaide, is you are too young to understand about the echoes in this house and too young to want to. I want you to remember this, child: I did everything I could. I did everything I could. Someday when you want to know the truth, you'll find it beneath you. Under your feet. You walk upon it. We all do."

Adelaide had stood transfixed, pondering her great-grandmother's strange words. She remembered looking down at the paving stones at her feet. Then she opened her mouth to ask her great-grandmother what she meant, but a trio of guests intruded upon them to say their good-byes. Susannah looked at Adelaide and laid a finger to her lips.

That was the last conversation Adelaide had with her great-grandmother.

The next morning, an hour after a brilliant April sunrise, Adelaide found her great-grandmother dead in the wingback chair in her room, having passed from one life to the next in those stray moments between sleep and consciousness. Adelaide did not know Susannah was dead. She thought her great-grandmother had fallen asleep in her chair again. She went downstairs and told her mother Nana wouldn't wake up for breakfast.

After the funeral, and for many months afterward, Adelaide dreamed of finding Susannah alive in her chair and hearing her great-grandmother repeating those odd words from the party.

Sometimes she would dream of finding Susannah in her chair in the parlor or in the garden or in the slave's quarters that Susannah said had been Tessie's room. Her great-grandmother would always be in her nightgown, the one Adelaide found her dead in, but she would always be warm and alive and talking. Not cold and stiff and silent like Adelaide had found her.

And she would always repeat the message.

I did what I could.

The answers are beneath you.

After awhile the dream faded away, and Adelaide would only experience it again if someone mentioned Susannah's name or if she lingered too long on the stairs and caught her great-grandmother's young eye at the portrait near the landing.

But it had been twenty years since Adelaide had had that dream.

Until she had it again at the hospital.

She dreamed Susannah was sitting in her wingback chair in her bedroom as Adelaide remembered it, her white floss hair tumbling down her shoulders like a bridal veil. Susannah's hands were folded in her lap, and her head was bowed as if in prayer. Adelaide couldn't make out her great-grandmother's facial features; it was as though a sheet of water, like the backside of a waterfall, separated them. Adelaide took a step closer and was instantly aware that every part of her body ached, and her left arm felt as though a vice encircled it. She looked down at her misshaped wrist, its unnatural curl. It was broken. Anger soared inside her, and she looked up at her great-grandmother.

"Haven't I suffered enough for you?" she heard herself rasping. "Haven't we all suffered enough?"

The sheet of water fell away, and her great-grandmother raised her head. But instead of seeing the old woman of eighty-five, Adelaide was looking into the eyes of the young Susannah whose portrait hung at the top of the stairs. This Susannah now reached for Adelaide, grabbed her broken wrist and squeezed, clamping down on the vice with all her might. Adelaide crumpled to the floor in anguish, screaming for help, but hearing only a muffled wheeze coming from her mouth.

And then she awoke.

She was aware first that she was not back at Holly Oak; she was in a hospital bed. No one was squeezing her broken wrist; it was pulsating with pain of its own accord. She turned to the window and grimaced as pain rippled through her. The rain had stopped, and washed sunlight was sliding through blinds that no one had closed from the night before.

Her arm felt like it was on fire.

The privacy curtain was suddenly wrenched open, the metal rings scraping across the pole like nails shaken in a tin can. A smiling, black-haired nurse appeared with a breakfast tray.

"And how are we feeling today, Mrs. McClane?" the woman said.

"Like I've been thrown down the stairs by an angry ghost," Adelaide muttered.

And the nurse threw back her head and laughed.

———

The doctor had been by and pronounced her well enough to go home by the time Carson and Marielle arrived at noon. She was sitting in the chair in her room waiting for them, with her tulips in her lap—balanced with her good arm—in the clothes she had arrived in the day before. Her left arm hung in a sling—navy blue with white trim. And her head was a bit mushy from the painkiller the nurse had given her.

"You didn't both have to come," she said when they walked into her room.

"Sorry I wasn't here yesterday, Mimi." Carson bent over her and kissed her forehead, "Really sorry."

"It wouldn't have changed anything if you had been." But Adelaide immediately wondered if she was mistaken. If Carson had been there, Marielle wouldn't have been snooping around in the studio. And if Marielle hadn't been in the studio, Adelaide wouldn't have been on the stairs wondering what Marielle was doing.

"Sleep okay?" Marielle asked.

"Until the drugs wore off." Adelaide put out her arm, and Carson helped her out of the chair.

"They're going to want you to ride down to the car in a wheelchair, Mimi," Carson said.

"Nonsense. I broke a wrist, not a leg."

"But they—"

"All right, all right." Adelaide sat back down in the chair. "Do you have the prescriptions for the pharmacy?"

"Got them right here." Carson patted his shirt pocket. "We can stop by Goolrick's on the way home. And I've got your post-op instructions too. You're all set. Don't worry. We'll take good care of you."

"I'm not worried. Why should I be worried? It's just a broken wrist."

Carson looked at Marielle, and an unspoken comment passed between them. Something was up. Something they weren't telling her.

"It is just a broken wrist, right?" She looked from one to the other.

"Yes. Only a broken wrist," Marielle said quickly.

"What is it? What's wrong?"

"There's something we need to tell you, Mimi," Carson's voice was laced with concern.

"What? Is it one of the children? Did something happen to one of the children?"

"No. Nothing like that." Carson replied quickly. "It's Caroline. She's back."

The air in the room seemed to thicken. "What did you say?" Adelaide whispered.

"Caroline's home."

The police hadn't looked for Caroline the day she ran away. She had been just a few weeks shy of her eighteenth birthday, nearly the age when leaving home was a celebratory event accompanied by mortarboard tassels and shopping for dorm furniture.

Nearly a year had passed before Adelaide got a phone call from her.

"I just wanted you to know I'm okay," Caroline had said, sounding very far away.

"Please come home." Adelaide replied, keeping her emotions in check.

"No." The response had been swift. Rehearsed, perhaps.

"Caroline. Whatever it is that you've done, I don't care. I just want—"

"Whatever *I* have done?" A whooshing sound filled the space behind her daughter's voice, barely masking her indignation. Her daughter was calling from a pay phone on a busy street. Adelaide could still feel the knife blade of her daughter's quick reproof.

"You're saying it's *my* fault you don't want to come home?" Adelaide had asked.

Caroline had paused for just a moment. When she spoke, her voice was hot with anger. "What is with you and that house and someone having to be at fault for everything?" Her daughter swore, and Adelaide closed her eyes against the sound of those ugly words.

"I just... I don't understand, Caroline!" she had blurted, anger now fusing her words together.

"You know what, Mother? Neither do I. I gotta go."

"Caroline! Please. You need help! You need a doctor."

"Good-bye."

"Please! Call me again, will you?"

But Caroline had hung up without promising anything.

She called again, a couple of times. Showed up a few times in her early twenties. Never promising anything.

Except when she was twenty-six and arrived at Holly Oak with a baby named Sara.

She had promised something then.

"I won't ask you to give her back to me," Caroline had said, after she asked Adelaide to take Sara. "I'll sign whatever papers I have to. I promise I won't ask you to give her back."

And she didn't.

It surprised Adelaide how little Caroline had changed physically in the nearly fifty years her daughter had been in and mostly out of her life. The shape of her nose—Charles's—and the plucky swell of her cheekbones—Adelaide's—and the silvery blue hue of her eyes—Caroline's own—were time-stopping icons of the past. Only the lines in Caroline's skin, the steel-gray strands in her hair, and Adelaide's own sense of impending mortality suggested decades had swept past them both.

When Adelaide arrived home from the hospital, her daughter was waiting for her in the garden, sipping a glass of sweet tea and reading from a slim volume, the title of which Adelaide could not see. The book looked old and treasured. Caroline set the book down on the glass-topped table in front of her when Adelaide stepped out onto the patio.

"Hello, Mother." Caroline rose from her chair and came to her, hesitant for only a moment. Then she put her hands on Adelaide's shoulders, as if in benediction, leaned in, and kissed her on the nonbandaged side of her forehead.

"Caroline." Her daughter's name fell off her lips more in wonder than greeting. Caroline seemed not to notice the difference. Caroline touched the strap of the sling over Adelaide's shoulder and followed it down to the hammock of cloth that kept her arm close to her heart.

"Are you in much pain?" Caroline said, her brows knitted in concern.

The irony of those five words caught Adelaide at a strange place, and she nearly laughed out loud. *Come now, Caroline. I live at Holly Oak.* She shook her head. "Not too bad. Doctor says I should recover well. No sewing for a while, though. Pearl is going to help me finish an order I'm working on."

Caroline laughed lightly. "Pearl. So there goes any hope of a quiet homecoming for me."

Several awkward seconds of silence followed. Adelaide had a million questions on her mind but found herself unable to give voice to any of them.

Caroline raised her gaze. "I hope you don't mind that I didn't call first."

"I've never minded before, Caroline. I wouldn't start now." Her response sounded caustic and she immediately regretted saying it. But Caroline smiled, laughed a little.

"It's so good to see you, Mother," she said. "Want to sit a bit?" Caroline pulled out a chair, and Adelaide settled into it. "Want anything from the kitchen?" Caroline asked.

"No, thank you."

Caroline retook her seat and crossed her legs at the ankles. She wore a gauzy tan skirt that fell about her legs and skimmed the surface of the patio stones. Her blue tank top was studded with cloudy rhinestones in a floral pattern, some missing. At her neck was a gold cross, small but sparkling. New. Caroline looked completely comfortable and content. Adelaide couldn't remember the last time Caroline looked that way. She tried, but she couldn't.

"Is it true?" Adelaide said, suddenly overcome with emotion. "Is it over?"

The words came out wrong. Marielle had told her everything Caroline had said, about wanting to know her grandchildren, about having a real address in Bethesda, about finally being under the care of a doctor, about having had some kind of cleansing revelation. Adelaide meant to ask something like, "Are you really home for good?" but Caroline seemed to know what she meant.

"Yes." Caroline's one-word reply, weighted by the years, was whispered across the table, heavy despite its softness. "I'm home."

Adelaide closed her eyes, needing a few seconds of solitude to attempt to embrace the thing she had always wanted. For a moment she felt stripped of sensation, as if the impact of finally having Caroline home had sent her crashing into an abysslike void. The pulsing pain of her broken wrist was the rhythmic meter that ticked like a metronome, reeling her back in.

When she opened her eyes, Caroline was still calmly sitting in her chair, her hands folded in front of her, her skirt the only thing moving as a summer breeze kicked its hem.

"You're different," Adelaide said.

"Yes."

Adelaide's aching head was suddenly filled with the images of Caroline's random past visits home. Strung out, broke, homeless, angry, a child in her arms, needle tracks in her arms, nothing in her arms.

"What happened to you?" Adelaide murmured. "You're not...not the same."

Caroline looked away for just a moment, searching for the right words, perhaps. "I guess you could say I came to the end. The very end of it all. I didn't know there was a door at the end, but there is. And somehow in that dark nothingness I fell against that door, and it opened for me. A nun came to visit me in the hospital. She invited me to spend a few months at a place where people like me, people who fall against the last door on earth, find out how to crawl through it."

"Hospital?" Adelaide echoed, but Caroline raised a hand to whisk the question away. To whisk all of Adelaide's questions away.

"I'm not the person I was when I left here all those years ago. And I'm really sorry for everything I put you through, Mother. Truly sorry. I hope you can forgive me, even just a little."

Adelaide felt tears slipping down her ancient cheeks. She wanted to say yes, but her lips would not obey. Caroline went on.

"I can't get back the years I threw away. I can't...I can't make it up to Sara. I know that. And I've forgiven myself for that, but I want to make it up to my grandchildren. I know you have no reason to trust me, but I am asking you to let me have the opportunity to be a grandmother to them. And a daughter to you. Please."

"I never thought this day would come. I stopped hoping it would," Adelaide said, again closing her eyes to somehow lessen the sensory overload.

"I know. I'm sorry. I'm so very sorry, Mother."

Adelaide opened her eyes and wiped away her tears with her good hand. Caroline's eyes were dry, her face composed, as though she was used to being a different person.

"How long…how long have you been well?" Adelaide asked.

"Two years."

A stab of surprise made Adelaide flinch in her chair. "Two years?"

"I had to be sure. I had to be sure the change was real. I was too used to the counterfeit." Caroline's voice was as calm and gentle as the moment Adelaide had stepped out on the patio. "The last thing on earth I wanted to do was to come home thinking I was finally free, only to find out I had fooled myself into thinking there was hope for someone like me. I had to be sure it was true, that there *was* hope for someone like me. And that I had found it."

Adelaide reached her good hand across the table, and Caroline took hold of it. "Stay here," Adelaide pleaded. "Don't go back to Bethesda."

Caroline shook her head slowly. "No."

"But we have plenty of room—"

"I will stay for a month. Until the children get back from New York and then another week after that, but then I'm going back. I'll be back to visit often; I promise you that. But I can't live here." She let go of Adelaide's hand.

"Why not?" But Adelaide knew why. Holly Oak was a house of ghosts, of regrets.

Caroline didn't answer. Instead she leaned forward in her chair, moved the book out of her way, and crossed her arms on the table, easy and unrushed. "Why did Carson stay here after he remarried?"

"What?"

"I need to know why Carson and Marielle are here. Why aren't they in their own place? Are you not well? Is that why they are here?"

Adelaide again flinched in her chair. For a second she couldn't quite remember why Carson and Marielle lived there. Then clarity fell over her. "They thought it would be best for the children. And they thought I was too elderly to live here alone."

"They?"

"Carson and Marielle."

"And is that what you think? That it's best for the children?"

"This was their mother's *home*," Adelaide let the little verbal barb fly across the table.

Caroline didn't so much as flinch. "Yes, of course, this was Sara's home. But it's not Sara's home any longer."

Adelaide's head and arm began to throb in a dancing ache. "They made the decision to stay here with me in this house. I didn't ask them to."

"I see." Caroline looked away again, past the little grove of trees at the west edge of the garden.

Adelaide wordlessly sought her daughter's gaze. But it was several long moments before Caroline turned from the trees that marked Holly Oak's boundaries.

"She seems like a lovely woman," Caroline said.

Adelaide suddenly was bone-weary. "Yes, she is... Do you suppose we could go in now? I think I need to rest."

Caroline rose to her feet. "Of course." She reached for the book to put under her arm. As Caroline helped Adelaide out of the chair, she caught a glimpse of the title. The book was a psalter.

Caroline had been reading the Psalms.

arielle stood at the door to her makeshift office off the kitchen, her gaze on the half of the studio that she could see from her vantage point. Morning sunlight played on the vines that grew up the sides. For the third time in as many days, she pondered taking Sara's journals out of their hiding place in her closet and returning them to the box where she found them. Knowing they were hidden in her closet was setting her on edge, making her feel like the house was somehow folding itself in around her. She didn't like it.

Perhaps when she went to feed the rabbit she would take them and put them back. After Carson left for work. She would need to get the key out of his study…

Carson had seemed only slightly taken aback when she told him she'd been in the studio when Adelaide fell. She hadn't told him she'd been in there for a couple of hours, and apparently Adelaide hadn't said anything to Carson about how long Marielle had been gone. Surely if Adelaide had mentioned it in passing, Carson would wonder what Marielle found so interesting in the dregs of Sara's creativity. And Carson seemed to care only what prompted Marielle to take a peek inside the studio, not what prompted Adelaide to be on the stairs when she fell.

Marielle had simply told Carson she wanted to see inside it.

A touch on her shoulder made her jump. Carson had come up behind her. He had a cup of coffee in his hand.

"Carson! I didn't hear you!"

"Sorry. Didn't mean to scare you." He said it kindly, but his gaze was on the studio, where hers had been. "Big plans today?"

"Sort of. Pearl is coming over. Caroline and Pearl and I are going to try to help Adelaide finish up those uniforms today."

Carson pulled his gaze from the studio, and he smiled at her. "You didn't tell me you could sew."

"I can't. Pearl thinks it's positively criminal. I barely know how to thread a needle. Caroline said she would show me how to hem and sew on buttons. I guess I can be taught how to do that."

"Caroline? Really?"

She nodded.

"I've never pictured Caroline as having been around a sewing machine much either," he said. "Not that I'm comparing her to you." He took a sip of his coffee.

Marielle smiled. "Apparently that was one of the many jobs she had over the years. She worked for a designer in the garment district in Los Angeles. He taught her."

"He taught her to sew?" Carson sounded incredulous.

"Well, I don't think that's exactly what he hired her for." Marielle turned from the window, away from the view of the old slaves' quarters. "I didn't ask her to elaborate."

Carson studied her for a few moments. "So are you okay with Caroline being here?"

She shrugged. "This is her home."

He moved closer and touched her cheek. "It's your home, too."

"I suppose." It was out of her mouth before she could think it through. The two words surprised them both.

"You're not feeling like this is your home?" Carson's voice was laced with part surprise and part something else. Disappointment?

"It's...it's a little harder than I thought it would be. There are just a lot of reminders of former lives here. Sometimes it's hard to compete with them."

Carson set his coffee cup down on her desk and held his arms out to her. Marielle let herself be folded into them. "It's an old house," he cooed. "Old houses can feel that way, I think. But we're putting our own imprint on this house—you and me and the kids. There will be reminders of us here someday." He kissed the top of her head. "Caroline has made it clear she doesn't want to live here, and Adelaide is getting on in years. In a little while it will be just the four of us."

She lifted her head to look at him and frowned. "Just the four of us?"

He blinked, wide eyed, and then laughed. "Well, sure. Just the four of us. You're not telling me we should be counting the ghost too, do you?"

"I didn't mean ghosts, Carson. I meant children. Our children. Yours and mine."

The smile on his face vanished and then returned a second later. He kissed her again. "Of course. I didn't mean... I wasn't suggesting there would only be the four of us... I only meant. Oh, for Pete's sake, I need to stop. I'm making it worse." He squeezed her affectionately. "Of course someday there will be more than just the four of us."

Marielle turned her head back to the window, to the outline of the studio at the far end of her view. She felt Carson lift his head and follow her gaze. For several moments they stood there in silence, looking at the same structure.

"I guess you want to start cleaning it out?" he murmured.

"Don't you?" she asked.

He leaned his head against hers. "Yes."

"I think we should do it while the children are in New York. I was thinking we could make the studio into a playroom for them. A surprise for when they get home."

"We?"

She turned to face him. "I think we should clean it out together."

He nodded thoughtfully, though not exactly in agreement.

"This weekend, maybe?" she said.

He grabbed his coffee cup. "Sounds like a plan." He kissed her lightly on the mouth. "Gotta go."

Carson turned and left. Marielle stood there a moment longer before heading upstairs to shower and dress. She didn't contemplate long Carson's not being one hundred percent on board with the plan to clean out the studio together because there was something more pressing to think about. Saturday was only three days away. She had three days to decide what to do with Sara's journals.

Leave them hidden or put them back. Leave them hidden or let them be found.

By ten o'clock that morning, Marielle and Caroline had moved the long table into the family room and brought in Adelaide's sewing machine and notions baskets. They had also spread out the uniform pieces, all in varying stages of completion. Adelaide said the old drawing room would give them all more room to move about, but Marielle wondered if there was another reason they weren't going to be sewing in the parlor.

Her ponderings were proven correct the moment Pearl stepped into Holly Oak's foyer at ten thirty, her arms full of cake, a sewing basket, and past issues of *Southern Living*. "We're not in the parlor, are we?" she asked as Marielle welcomed her inside. Marielle told her they'd be working in the old drawing room.

"Oh, thank heaven! Lordamercy, I almost didn't come!" She handed the magazines to Marielle. "These are for Adelaide, sweetie, so she doesn't go plum crazy with boredom watching us sew. Where's the injured little darling?"

Pearl swept past Marielle into the family room, where Adelaide and Caroline sat on a leather sofa. Caroline had her legs tucked up underneath her, and Adelaide had a couple of bed pillows under her arm. Marielle followed her inside. Pearl set the cake and the basket on the long table and then dashed over to Adelaide with barely a nod to Caroline. "Oh, my dear. And how are we doing today?"

"We're doing fine, Pearl."

"Oh, lovely. I brought my *Southern Living*s for you, dear. I cut out the recipes, of course, but you don't like entertaining anyway so you won't miss them." She turned to Caroline. "Hello there. I am Pearl Sibley, Adelaide's oldest and dearest—well, not oldest because I'm only seventy-nine, but—"

Pearl clamped her mouth shut. When she opened it again, one word fell out. "Caroline."

"Hello, Pearl," Caroline said with a gentle nod of her head.

"Lordamercy. It's Caroline." Pearl turned to Marielle, who stood a few feet behind her. "Marielle, it's Caroline."

"Yes. We've met." Marielle said.

Pearl turned to face the couch again. "My stars! Caroline!" She rushed forward and pulled Caroline to her feet to embrace her. Then she stepped back with her hands on Caroline's shoulders. "Look at you! Why, you don't look a day over fifty. Maybe fifty-five. You know, I saw you at poor Sara's funeral, and I thought to myself, that girl is finally looking her age. But not today. Why, today you look near radiant. Doesn't she, Adelaide?"

Adelaide opened her mouth—to agree or disagree, it was impossible for Marielle to tell. Pearl went on before Adelaide could speak.

"Are you here for more than a day? Because if you are here for more than a day, you should come to my jewelry party Friday night. That's in two days. Marielle, you should come too. You should both come. Adelaide, dear, I'd ask you but I know you'll just say no."

"Yes, I'm here for more than a day, but I'm not sure I'm ready for a jewelry party yet. Thank you for the invitation, though. That's very kind." Caroline sat back down on the couch.

"Well, this is just splendid! Will you be sewing with us, Caroline? I think it would be so much fun if you did. I've been brushing up the last few days on my Singer. Like getting back on a bike."

"Yes, I thought I might."

"Goody. I am sure there is something we can find for you to do, isn't there, Adelaide?"

"Caroline has actually done quite a bit of sewing, Pearl. I don't think we will have any trouble finding something for her to do." Adelaide sat forward on the couch, and Marielle moved to help her stand. "Now then. Let me show you girls what needs to be done. We need to move Pearl's caramel cake into the kitchen, though."

Caroline stood as well, and Marielle reached for the cake. As she left for the kitchen, Pearl began to ask Caroline where she had been the last few years and what she had been doing. She was still pumping Caroline for details when Marielle returned a few minutes later.

"So you became a nun?" Pearl was saying. "Because I didn't know you could do that after living like, well, like you have lived. Because, I mean you've slept with so many men and had a child and all."

"Good Lord, Pearl—," Adelaide said.

"No, I didn't become a nun," Caroline replied, lifting a uniform coat off the table. "I spent some time with some. At a convent. Turned out to be just what I needed. But I didn't become a nun."

"Really? Well, isn't that something? Did you hear that, Marielle? She wanted to become a nun but they wouldn't let her." Pearl turned back to the table. "But we're glad you're here instead of kneeling in a church for hours on end! So glad. What a nice surprise!"

"How about if we get started?" Adelaide said.

For the next few minutes, Adelaide showed them the hand sewing that needed to be done and the few seams that were left to do and all the linings that had to be tacked down. Marielle was shown how to attach the buttons, and she settled onto the couch next to Adelaide to begin the task. Adelaide watched her sew the first few and told her she was doing a fine job. Caroline took on the hems and lining, and Pearl sat at the machine and sewed up the remaining open seams. They would work on the gold trim and braid that afternoon.

An hour had passed, with Pearl providing a running commentary on the social scene in Fredericksburg, when the doorbell rang.

"I'll get that," Marielle stood and put the jacket she was working on on the cushion next to her.

"Oh! I think I might know who that is," Pearl said.

"What do you mean?" Adelaide looked up from taking a peek at Marielle's work.

"I invited someone to lunch."

All eyes turned to her.

"Who did you invite, Pearl?" Adelaide asked.

"It's a surprise."

The doorbell rang again, and Marielle walked quickly to the foyer and opened the door. Standing on the welcome mat was a stout, smiling woman in a powder blue sweat suit trimmed in white.

Eldora Meeks.

delaide heard a woman's voice, one that she recognized but couldn't place. She heard the front door close and Marielle saying something. Footsteps sounded on the foyer's tile floor. Caroline took a step toward the drawing room doors.

"Who is here, Pearl?" Caroline sounded anxious. There were few people in Fredericksburg her daughter wanted to see; Adelaide was fairly certain of that.

But before Pearl could answer, Marielle was showing the guest into the drawing room.

It had been more than a decade since Adelaide had seen Eldora Meeks. But the woman hadn't changed much in all those years. Adelaide would've known the woman anywhere.

"Eldora…," Adelaide breathed.

Eldora turned to her. "Hello, Adelaide. It's so nice to see you again."

"Yes!" Pearl was triumphant. "Eldora is here!" She turned to Caroline. "I don't think you've ever met my cousin, Caroline. This is Eldora Meeks. She's clairvoyant."

Eldora, smiling, thrust her hand toward Caroline. "Nice to meet you, Caroline."

Caroline took it tentatively.

"And Marielle you've already met," Pearl was saying, but Adelaide's eyes were on Eldora and Caroline. Their hands were still touching, their handshake frozen for a moment as if time had stopped at their hands.

Then Eldora abruptly pulled her hand away, gulping a breath of air as she did so. She smiled at Caroline, a mixture of awe and surprise on her face. "Very nice to meet you," she said again.

"Likewise," Caroline said, but she stared at Eldora as if she felt differently.

"I'm having sandwiches delivered from Pandora's at noonish," Pearl announced. "So we'll have some time to chat before we eat. Adelaide, I told Eldora what you told me in the hospital and—"

Adelaide cut her off. "Pearl, could I see you in the kitchen for a moment?" Adelaide didn't wait for an answer. She turned to the drawing room doors and was halfway across the foyer tiles when Pearl caught up with her.

"What is it, dear?"

Adelaide waited until they were in the kitchen. Then she drew Pearl close to her. "Why didn't you tell me you had asked Eldora to come today?"

"Adelaide, you seem upset with me. I only did what you asked me to. You told me you wanted to see Eldora again. I invited her over. I thought you'd be grateful."

Adelaide sighed. "Did you really think I'd want to have Eldora come over with Marielle and Caroline here?"

Pearl lifted her chin. "I had no idea Caroline was at Holly Oak. Seems to me you could've told me *that*. And as for Marielle, I don't see what difference that makes. Marielle and Eldora have already met. If you're upset, it's your own fault for not telling me Caroline was here, dear."

"What on earth do you mean, Marielle and Eldora have already met?"

Pearl brought a hand up to her mouth. "Oh. Oh, never mind. Just never mind about that." Pearl started to walk away, but Adelaide used her good arm to stop her.

"Marielle has already met Eldora?" Adelaide asked. "When?"

Pearl patted her arm. "You know what? This really isn't any of my business. I just try to be a good neighbor, that's all. Marielle asked to speak with Eldora, and I arranged it when she came to have lunch with me. But it's not really something I would know anything about. That's probably between you and her. And Eldora. And Carson."

Pearl was out of the kitchen before Adelaide could stop her again.

"What is she going to *do* here, Pearl?" Adelaide said as they walked, her voice a rasping whisper.

"Take a reading on the house, of course," Pearl whispered back.

They arrived back in the drawing room. Only Caroline was still there.

"Where's Eldora?" Adelaide asked.

"Mother, what is that woman doing here?" Caroline's tone was gentle but urgent.

"Where is she?"

Caroline nodded toward the open doors Adelaide had just come through. "She went off to explore the house. Marielle followed her. What is she doing here? Is this…is this about Susannah?"

Adelaide looked over her shoulder. She could hear low voices now in the parlor. Pearl apparently heard them too.

"Oh my lands, Adelaide. Eldora and Marielle are in the parlor. I think I will just wait here." Pearl walked over to the sofa and sat down quickly.

"Mother, please tell me what's going on," Caroline said.

"I just… Something happened the day I fell, Caroline. I can't explain it. I—"

"But what is she doing here?"

"Eldora has special sight," Pearl said, leaning over to speak as softly as she could. "She can talk to the spirit world. Well, sometimes she can. Sometimes she can just see it. Sometimes she can hear it. Sometimes she can see ghosts. That's why Adelaide wanted her to come. Because of Susannah. Susannah pushed her down the stairs."

"Pearl!" Adelaide exclaimed.

"Well, that's what you told me!"

"That is not what I told you! I said it felt like I had been pushed. I didn't say I had been."

Caroline looked first to Pearl and then to Adelaide. Her countenance was calm but set. "Is that true, Mother? Did you ask Eldora to come here because you think there's a ghost in this house?"

"It's not as simple as that—"

"No, indeed. Ghosts are complex. Eldora told me that." Pearl sat back on the couch, satisfied.

Caroline ignored Pearl, her gaze still fixed on Adelaide. "Then tell me what you think it is."

"I don't know what it is! I thought I did, but now I'm not sure. Eldora had been here once before, ten years ago. She sensed a presence inside Holly Oak. She believes it was my great-grandmother, stuck here in some kind of self-imposed limbo because of what happened here at this house."

"And you believed her?" Caroline asked, sounding incredulous. Adelaide was struck dumb for just a second. Caroline sounded like the parent. And she, the child.

"No, I didn't believe her. I thought it was something else. Something else entirely."

Caroline blinked at her. "Thought *what* was something else? What?"

"But now she thinks it *is* Susannah, don't you, Adelaide?" Pearl interjected. "Because Susannah pushed her down the stairs because she let Marielle go poking about the studio."

Caroline stared at her, and Adelaide saw flashes of the young girl who had left Holly Oak at seventeen, hating it, hating her. "What have you told Marielle about this house, Mother?" Caroline said evenly.

"I said nothing about a ghost—"

"That's true, she didn't. Eldora told her about the ghost," Pearl interrupted. "Well, actually first it was me—"

Adelaide turned to her friend. "Pearl, please. I'd like to talk to my daughter alone."

Pearl frowned but rose from the couch and left reluctantly.

"What did you tell Marielle about this house?" Caroline repeated. "I'd like to know."

Adelaide's arm began to throb. "I never said there is a ghost at Holly Oak. Pearl told her that. You remember how Pearl is. I told her it's like the house doesn't know how to let go of its past. It wants to but it can't. I knew Marielle would hear the rumors around town that the house is cursed. Sooner or later she would hear it. I told her that the people who think there's a curse on this house are wrong."

Caroline breathed in and out. A breath of resignation. Or maybe indignation. "Are they wrong? Think about it, Mother? Are those people wrong?"

Her daughter strode past her.

"Where are you going?" Adelaide called after her, afraid that Caroline was headed up the stairs to grab her suitcase and leave.

"I'm not leaving Marielle alone with that woman," Caroline muttered.

Caroline was out the drawing room door, and Adelaide pivoted to follow her. "Caroline."

Caroline said nothing. She crossed the foyer and made her way to the far end of the entry and the half-open parlor doors. Adelaide hurried to catch up, her bruised body protesting.

Inside the parlor, Eldora stood, her arms lifting slightly from her sides, palms out, and her head to one side, looking somewhat like a waiting antenna. Her eyes were closed. Marielle stood wide eyed a few feet away from her.

Adelaide was mesmerized by the sight, but Caroline spoke into the strange silence as if to break the glass around a fire extinguisher. "What's going on in here?"

Eldora, apparently unfazed by Caroline's interruption, slowly moved her head in a circle, like a warmup exercise. She opened her eyes. "I feel the presence strong in here," she said. "So strong. Stronger than last time."

"Look, I don't mean any disrespect, but I don't think this is a good idea," Caroline said.

"You feel it too. Don't you?" Eldora said, turning to Caroline. Her voice was sweet, inclusive. "You are in touch with the spirit world."

"I think we need to go back to the family room and sew." Caroline turned to Marielle and nodded to her.

"Don't you want me to check the other rooms, Adelaide?" Eldora asked. "What about the garden? And the slaves' quarters? And your cellar? Do you remember how strong it was in your cellar? Do you not want me to see if she is in there?"

Adelaide saw Marielle flinch, and she opened her mouth but no answer came. She didn't know what she wanted Eldora to do. What would Eldora find if she kept at it? What would she hear? What would she see? Adelaide realized with a shudder that she wasn't prepared to hear she'd been wrong all these decades—that Susannah did indeed haunt the house. A tiny squeak escaped her throat.

"That's enough." Caroline stood at the parlor doors and held them open, like a nanny shooing little ones out of a room they had no business being in.

Eldora took a step toward Adelaide. "I will leave if you want me to. But only if *you* want me to."

Adelaide nodded. "I think you should go."

Caroline walked out of the room without a look back. Eldora took Adelaide's good hand in her own. "I wonder if you aren't in some kind of danger, Adelaide. Your daughter senses it too or she would not be so insistent that I leave. She is afraid I will provoke this presence by being here. Caroline touches the spirit world. I felt it in her when I shook her hand. She thinks you can ignore this and it will go away, but I ask you, how long have you known your house is not like other houses?"

The answer came easily, before she had a chance to rein it in. "All my life," Adelaide said.

Eldora squeezed her hand. "What would you like me to do?"

An image of her great-grandmother seated in her wingback chair, dead, rose up before her.

I did everything I could.

I did everything I could.

"What can you do?" Adelaide asked. "What is it that you can do? Can you fix what is broken here? Can you?"

Eldora's grip on her hand lessened. "No, I can't. I can only tell what I sense, what I feel. I cannot fix anything for you."

"Who can?" Adelaide whispered.

"The deceased who can't move on from this world needs to be empowered somehow. She needs something. If you want me to try and find out, I will."

The doorbell sounded.

From behind her, Adelaide felt Marielle place a hand on her shoulder. She had almost forgotten she was there. "I think the lunch is here, Mimi," Marielle said.

Adelaide turned to face her. Marielle's face was pale. "You must think I'm crazy. Don't you?"

Marielle shook her head. "No, I don't. Let's go have lunch."

Adelaide took a step toward the parlor doors with Eldora on one side and Marielle on the other. "I almost wish I was crazy. Then none of this would matter. It would all just be in my imagination."

"Do you want me to check the other rooms, Adelaide?" Eldora asked.

"Eldora, I think maybe we've had enough for one day," Marielle said before Adelaide could answer.

And she leaned into her new granddaughter-in-law and thanked Eldora Meeks for coming.

She did not ask her to stay for lunch.

arielle stood over the long table in the family room surveying the work she had done on the uniforms that lay before her, resplendent in the light from the chandelier above. Her rows of shining buttons, spread across the coat fronts like runway lights, glowed warm and straight. She'd had to remove and resew a few that hadn't been perfectly positioned. Adelaide had gently insisted. When officers go to war, they set the standard for everyone else, Adelaide had told her. Everyone looks to them for direction and inspiration. Especially the young soldiers because they're wondering what war will do to them. Will it turn them into barbarians? The perfect rows of buttons show them it will not.

There had been less conversation in the sewing room after lunch, after Eldora left. Pearl, pouting a bit, had decided they needed music to regain their party atmosphere and filled the room with Frank Sinatra tunes from the stereo. Marielle had caught Caroline looking at her more than once, and each time she tipped her head as if to silently encourage her. By the time Pearl left at six, Marielle's arms and shoulders ached from bending over fabric and needles all day long. But the uniforms were nearly finished. Just a few more swirls of braid to attach. Caroline had said she could finish them tomorrow—Pearl didn't have to give up another day—and Pearl had said she was fine with that because she had her jewelry party to get ready for.

Now, as Marielle waited for Carson to get home from work, the house was eerily quiet. Adelaide had gone to her room to lie down before dinner, and Caroline had gone for a walk. For the first time since they had left,

Marielle realized she missed the children. She smiled to herself. Surely that was a good sign. She wondered if she should call them and tell them she missed them. Carson talked to them every night, and sometimes he gave the phone to her to say hello and sometimes he didn't. She didn't think it was some kind of conscious decision on his part when he didn't. She supposed he was still getting used to the idea that his children had a new stepmother, just as she was getting used to the idea that she was it. She would definitely call them.

She heard the front door open and the sound of Carson walking into the house, hanging his car keys on the hook by the door, setting his briefcase down.

"Anybody here?" he called out.

"I'm in your study," she said, and a few seconds later he was at her side, his arms around her from behind. She rested her head on his chest.

"Wow. You gals were busy. Are they done?"

"Nearly. Just some trim left to do. Caroline said she'd finish them up."

He kissed her temple and she closed her eyes. "This was a wonderful thing you all did for Mimi. I know this would've bugged her, not getting them done in time."

She looked up at him. "See the nice rows of buttons? Those are mine."

He smiled. "Lined up like little golden soldiers. Well done." He kissed her again. "So you had a good day?"

She hesitated. "Mostly."

"Mostly?"

She turned around to face him. She wanted him to know who had been at the house. "Pearl invited Eldora Meeks over."

A rush of surprise fell across Carson's face. "Why?" He sounded almost angry.

"She thought she was doing Mimi a favor. Mimi said something to Pearl at the hospital about…" Marielle suddenly felt like she was saying too much. Betraying something.

"About what? What did Mimi say at the hospital?"

Marielle moved away from him to take a seat on the couch. He followed her. "She...well, you know how she feels about this house, and when she fell, she felt like...like she needed to talk to Eldora again. Pearl assumed it was okay to ask her over today."

"She felt like what?"

"Maybe Mimi should be the one to tell you."

"To tell me what? Why can't you tell me?" He sounded disappointed, like she was keeping something from him that he had every right to know.

"She felt like she didn't just fall."

"What's that supposed to mean?"

"She...she felt like someone or something pushed her."

Carson looked away for a moment. "What did Eldora say?"

"Caroline didn't like her being here. She didn't stay long. She only went into one room—the parlor. She left after that."

"And?"

Marielle shuddered slightly at the memory of Eldora standing as if in a trance, her head cocked in the pose of someone listening to something faint but present. "And it was creepy. She said she sensed a presence. Stronger than the last time she was here. Much stronger. Freaked me out, actually."

Carson exhaled and shook his head. "What else did she say?"

"She wanted to go into the other rooms, but Caroline wasn't going to let her and I certainly didn't want her to. She wanted to go back to the places where she had sensed this presence before. The studio, the cellar, the garden. But lunch arrived, and Adelaide didn't ask her to stay."

Carson stroked his chin with his hand, thoughtful and silent.

"Do you think... Do you think Eldora knows what she's talking about?" she said. "I mean, I've never believed anything like this could actually happen. Eldora said Holly Oak isn't like other houses. Is that even possible?"

He turned his head to look at her. "I think Adelaide hit her head too hard, and I think Pearl made a mistake by bringing Eldora here. Caroline was right to ask her to leave."

"But do you think it's possible?"

"Do you?" His tone suggested he didn't.

"I didn't think I did."

He took her hand in his and kissed it. "I'm sorry about this. I told you Adelaide had some quirky notions about the house, but I didn't think she'd take it this far. You shouldn't have to worry about any of this. I'll talk to her."

"To who?" The sense that she was betraying someone again pricked her. "Talk to who?"

He laughed gently. "To Mimi, of course. I'll tell her to please keep her odd superstitions to herself. They're upsetting you. I can see that they are."

"Don't do that. Don't tell her that."

"Why not? I really don't want Eldora coming back here. This is my house too, and I don't want her here."

"But that's just it, Carson. This isn't our house. It's Adelaide's house. Right now, it's just *her* house."

He still held her hand, and she felt it tense in her palm.

"What do you want me to do?" he said.

Marielle felt the weight of the house's history envelop her as she considered his question. Adelaide was not likely to change in the years left to her. She had lived a lifetime believing what she did about the house. It was up to them to lessen the weight if they could. She and Carson.

"Leave Adelaide be. I don't think you can say anything that will make her feel differently about the house. But I think cleaning out the studio is a good place for us to start feeling differently about it."

Carson closed his eyes and pressed his head to the back of the couch. "Yeah. About that."

"What?"

"I have to fly to Houston on Friday. I'll be gone until Sunday night late. I can't clean it out on Saturday. I'm sorry. We'll have to do it another day."

Disappointment settled over her. It surprised her how much.

"The following Saturday then?" she said.

"Sure."

"I can help her clean it out this Saturday." The voice from behind them was Caroline's. Marielle and Carson both whipped their heads around to see her standing in the doorway. Marielle had no idea how long she had been standing there.

"What was that?" Carson said quickly, but Marielle could see by the look on his face that he had heard her.

Caroline moved farther into the room. "I said I can help her on Saturday. Marielle and I can clean out the studio."

"Oh. No, that's...that's too much to ask of you, Caroline. It's a mess in there. And I don't mean just random art supplies." Carson sounded alarmed.

"I'm sure I've lived in places in worse condition than the studio," Caroline said. "You'd be surprised how many ways I know to kill a rat."

"Yes, but there's a lot of...stuff. You'll need some muscle, I think. I'm afraid it would be too much for both of you," Carson stood and faced Caroline, met her gaze eye to eye.

"I don't think a few old art tables and crumbling shelves are a match for Marielle and me. I've seen what's in there, Carson. We'll be fine."

Carson cocked his head in surprise. "You've seen the inside of the studio?"

"Yes, I have. Sara was my daughter. What's left in there is all that is left of her for me. So, yes, I've been inside. And I know Marielle and I will be just fine, won't we, Marielle? You've been inside it as well. You didn't see anything in there the two of us couldn't handle, did you?"

Marielle stood too. She took Carson's hand. "I think we'll be okay, Carson. Caroline and I can take care of it. And then it will be done."

His hand was limp in hers but gradually he took hold of her palm. "You're probably right." He turned to her. "Sorry I won't be there. It can't be helped."

"We'll be fine," Caroline said. "Now, I say we order Chinese. Who's hungry?"

She didn't wait for an answer.

Carson was quiet but congenial the next two days. He seemed genuinely happy when Marielle said she wanted to call the children after they'd finished plates of szechwan beef and vegetable lo mein. And Friday morning, as he packed his suitcase for Texas, he kept apologizing for the lousy timing of a business trip that had the audacity to fall on a weekend. He lingered over breakfast and pulled her into his arms three times before he left, assuring her he would call her when he landed in Houston.

After he left, Marielle was keenly aware that the house was empty except for the three of them. Adelaide. Caroline. And herself. And yet the house didn't seem empty. Quiet, yes. But definitely not empty. It was a queer sensation, as if the house was marveling at the turn of events that had ousted everyone but the women.

Saturday dawned misty and humid. Marielle dressed in old jeans and a faded T-shirt a decade old. She pulled her hair into a ponytail and took off her wedding ring. For a second she considered slipping it back on. But she turned from it, leaving it on her dresser where it would be safe from the dirt and debris in the studio. Then she went down the stairs, taking them quickly, her eyes on her sneakered feet.

It was early and the house was quiet. She wondered if Caroline would be up soon or if she would have to wait long for her. As she entered the kitchen, she saw that coffee had already been made and a cup sat in the sink. She touched it. Cold. Marielle moved to the door that led to the garden. Unlocked. She opened it, walked onto the patio, and looked toward the studio. Caroline was already there. Four large trash cans were placed at its entrance, one already full, and Caroline was tossing boxes out of the entrance as if she were in a great hurry. Or angry.

Marielle walked quickly across the patio stones. She reached the grassy knoll and began the gentle descent, the toes of her shoes quickly becoming moist from the dew on the grass. When she reached the studio steps, Caroline appeared at the entrance with an armful of curling magazines. She tossed them into one of the trash cans. Hurled them in. She nodded to Marielle and went back inside. Marielle followed her in. Clouds of dust swirled about Caroline's ankles.

"Why didn't you wait for me?" Marielle said.

Caroline, breathless and already sweating, pushed away a lock of hair that had worked itself loose from her hair clip. "Why in God's name were you waiting at all? How could you have lived here all these weeks with all of this in here?"

Caroline grabbed a wooden bolt of rotting twine. She heaved it outside. It landed on the stone steps and broke in two.

Marielle, stunned for a moment, found her voice. "I didn't think it was my place to make demands, Caroline. Especially about this room."

"Your place? You didn't think it was your place? For Pete's sake, you're his wife!" She grabbed an armful of tiny gift boxes, gray with age and misuse. She tossed them into the nearest trash can.

"So you think I should've told him he can marry me when this room is cleaned up."

"You got that right." Caroline stopped and put her hands on her hips. "Did you really think you were doing him a favor by letting him keep this room like this?"

"I..." Marielle didn't finish. She suddenly felt naive. Foolish.

"What is wrong with you people?" Caroline shook her head, her eyes narrowed in pitiable frustration. "It's like the minute you step inside that house, you fall under its miserable, godforsaken spell and you start letting the dead—the dead!—tell you how to live your lives."

Marielle shuddered. "What do you mean?"

"You've fallen for it, you have." Caroline pressed her lips together. Emotion roiled across her face, and her eyes grew misty. "Just like all the rest. God, help us."

Tears sprang to Marielle's eyes as well, surprising her. "I don't know what you mean."

Caroline leaned back against Sara's art table and raised a hand to her forehead. She rubbed the flesh there as if to rub something out. "And people wonder why I left." She laughed without mirth. "People wonder why I went crazy. Good Lord, it's this hell of a house. I thought it was me. But it's this house." She turned her head to look at Marielle. "And now you're getting sucked into it just like I was. Just like we all were."

Two tears slipped unchecked down Marielle's face. It occurred to her in a random thought that she'd never realized that fear could make you cry.

And she was definitely afraid.

"Is this house haunted?" she whispered. "Am...am I not safe here?"

Caroline stared at her and then looked away and sighed. "No one is safe here."

Marielle swallowed the lump of dread in her throat. "Is it...is it Susannah? Does she haunt this place? Is she going to try to hurt me?"

Caroline brought her gaze back to rest on Marielle. "Sweet Jesus," Caroline murmured, incredulous. "Is that what you're thinking? That this house is haunted by a ghost desperate to be absolved for her many sins? Is that it?"

"I...I don't know," Marielle stammered.

"You believe it all, don't you?"

"I don't know what I'm supposed to believe!"

Caroline said nothing for a long moment. Then she grabbed Marielle's arm. "Come with me."

Caroline trudged up the hill toward the house with Marielle in tow. At the patio stones she grabbed a heavy garden shovel leaning against a small shed, then kept walking.

"Where are we going?" Marielle tried to wrench her arm away from Caroline, but the woman held her fast.

Caroline continued past the patio table, the french doors, the kitchen door, and turned toward the little door that led to Marielle's office. But then she stopped. In front of them were the wooden cellar doors, locked and pitched at an angle that seemed to invite intrusion.

Caroline let go of her arm. "Stand back."

"There's a key in the garage—," Marielle began, but Caroline raised the shovel even as she said it. She brought its strong metal head down on the hinged lock, sending a resounding whack across the stillness and the pieces of the hinge scattering.

She tossed the shovel clanking to the patio and lifted the doors wide. A yawning darkness appeared.

"Go get a flashlight," Caroline commanded.

"I don't want to," Marielle whispered, childlike fear clutching at her voice. Eldora said she had sensed something in the cellar the time before. The Yankee soldiers buried there?

"Fine. If I break my neck trying to find the light switch, I don't want gladiolas at my funeral. I hate those." Caroline disappeared down the first couple of steps even as Marielle yelled a protest.

Seconds later, Marielle heard a click, and a sallow light emerged from the open cellar doors.

"Caroline?" Marielle bent down and peered into the gaping opening. She saw wooden stairs, an earthen floor, and shelves of dark boxes and dusty jars.

"Come down here, Marielle."

"Please, Caroline. I don't want to." Her voice sounded juvenile in her ears. "Not until you tell me why," she said with forced authority.

Caroline's face appeared at the opening. Her features had softened. In her hand she held a key on a ring. Webs hung off the metal and dangled from Caroline's fingers. "I need to show you something."

"I don't want to see where those soldiers are buried," Marielle said, closing her eyes to the thought of traipsing across the bones of dead men.

Caroline said her name gently, and Marielle opened her eyes. "There are no Yankees buried down here."

"But Adelaide said—"

"There were. A long time ago there were. But they were reburied ages ago, properly and in a cemetery, I promise you. There are no ghosts down here."

Marielle hesitated and then crouched to her knees and dropped a foot onto the first step.

Part Four

THE CELLAR

arielle eased her body down the wooden steps, her sodden sneakers turning brown with subterranean dirt and dust. Remnants of an ancient handrail offered no support, so she took Caroline's outstretched hand to make it safely down the last few steps.

A heavy dampness clung to the air, which smelled of age and darkness. The humid morning air that had followed her down whisked its way back out, unable to compete with the weighted chill inside the cellar. Utility shelves lined one wall, and two wooden benches lined another, blankets wrapped in plastic covering them. Carson had told her if there was a storm advisory when he was at work and she was instructed by the weather channels to take cover, she was to bring Adelaide and the children here. She shuddered now at the thought. Being inside the cellar was like being inside someone's grave.

"Over here."

Caroline had walked away from her and was now in another section of the cellar. Marielle followed the sound of her voice. Shelves of old Mason jars and garden decor sat along a wall of foundation stone. It was even cooler in this section. A large, metal trunk sat in the corner. It looked old. And its size seemed incongruous to the size of the room, as if the cellar had been built around it. Caroline was kneeling at it. She inserted the key into the lock and turned it.

"This trunk has been here since the house was built," she said. "Everyone thinks it's empty and that the key is missing. But it's not. I found it." She held it up. "A very long time ago."

Marielle took a step forward. "Why does everyone think it's empty?"

Caroline looked up at her. "It looks heavy. But it actually doesn't weigh that much. It doesn't make a sound when you rock it. It sounds empty."

She opened the chest. On the underside of the lid, welded to the metal, was a mesh pocket about the size of a casserole pan. Caroline reached inside and withdrew a package wrapped in plastic sheeting. She looked up at Marielle.

"Susannah Page isn't the person you think she is, Marielle. She wrote letters. A lot of letters." Caroline began to unwrap the bundle. Marielle knelt to the floor next to her.

"Adelaide told me about these letters. She told me she gave them to you when you were a teenager. She thinks you threw them away or sold them for—"

"For drug money; yes, I know. She wanted to think that, so I let her. And I didn't care. I brought them down here to hide them from her, actually, because I was mad at her and I wanted her to think they were gone for good. I had found the key in the old slaves' quarters—what you call the studio. But that's not what Susannah called it. I didn't know the key belonged to this chest. I just decided to give it a try. When it worked, I found that I wasn't the first person to decide to hide letters inside it. There were others already there."

Caroline let the plastic fall away, revealing a length of dark cloth which she also unwrapped. In her hands were letters, yellow with age. Some were loose, and some were bound with a blue ribbon that now fell in pieces to the dirt floor.

Caroline held up the loose letters. "Susannah was very close to her cousin Eleanor Towsley in Maine. Susannah wrote to her often after her father died and she and her mother moved back here. Holly Oak was her mother's childhood home. And the loss of Susannah's father was devastating to her mother. She never quite recovered from it." Caroline handed the loose letters to Marielle. "Those were all written between 1860 and the middle of 1862. After that Susannah couldn't mail any more letters north because of the war. Eleanor kept these letters, long into her adult years. She didn't keep any of Susannah's letters written after the war, even though I'm sure there were others. They both lived into their eighties. Before Eleanor died, she asked that these be sent back to Susannah, which they were. My great-grandmother had them in her escritoire. My mother found them there after Annabel died. And when my father died, she gave them to me."

Marielle fingered the delicate, aged paper and studied the flowing script and the ancient postmark. The letters felt warm to the touch despite where they had been slumbering. Marielle looked at the other stack in Caroline's hands, the one that had been bound by the ribbon.

"What are those, then?" she asked.

Caroline stroked the top letter. Marielle could see that the envelope was different. No postmark. No address. Just one word. *Eleanor.*

"These are the letters to Eleanor she never sent. She wrote them but she never sent them. No one ever saw these letters. They were here in this trunk in that little hiding place when I opened it. They had been there a hundred years, Marielle."

Caroline extended the second stack to her. "Take them. Take them up to your room and read them."

Marielle reached for them, her hands shaking a little. "Are you saying no one even knows about these letters except you?"

"And now you. I want you to go upstairs and read them."

Marielle sat staring at the letters in her hands, unable to move, overcome by what she held. "Why are you doing this?" She looked up at Caroline.

"You need to know the truth."

Marielle slowly rose to her feet. "What about the studio?"

Caroline closed the lid to the trunk and stood up. "I'll take care of cleaning out the studio. I'd like to do it alone, actually. It would mean a lot to me if I could."

"Adelaide will wonder why I'm not helping you when I said I would."

"I'll tell my mother I sent you away so that I could wrestle with my old ghosts in the studio alone. She'll understand that." Caroline handed Marielle the cloth that had been around the letters. "Do not show the letters to Adelaide just yet. I want to talk to you when you're finished reading them. And then I have something I need for you to do. After that, I will show them to her myself. I promise."

Marielle wrapped the cloth around the letters and said nothing. She thought of Sara's journals hidden in her room, more words unseen and hidden. Holly Oak was a veritable depository for buried truth. She looked at Caroline. It was on the tip of her tongue to tell her that she, like Caroline, had also found something a young author had hidden from view, when it suddenly occurred to her she hadn't considered that the studio would soon be empty and she hadn't made a decision about the journals. It was too late to put them back.

"Go on," Caroline said. "If my mother is awake, she will wonder where we are."

Marielle tucked the bundle under her arm and headed for the cellar stairs. As she climbed them she decided that when she was done reading Susannah's letters, she'd show the journals to Caroline. It seemed to be a good day for the unveiling of secrets.

She'd let Caroline decide what should be done with them.

Behind her she heard the click of a light switch and Caroline on the stairs behind her. Marielle emerged into the warm air of a July morning. Low-lying clouds were giving way to a sticky sun. Caroline clambered out after her, and she closed the cellar doors.

"Carson will wonder why you broke the lock," Marielle said, looking at the shattered hinges.

Caroline started to walk away. "Carson shouldn't worry about what doesn't belong to him. Come find me when you're done."

Marielle watched as Caroline strode purposefully across the patio and then to the old slaves' quarters. She pushed the bundle of letters farther under her arm, walked to the kitchen door, and opened it quietly. The house was still bathed in quiet. She stepped into the main part of the house, listening for sounds of movement on the stairs or in the parlor. She heard nothing. Hopefully Adelaide was still in her bedroom and Marielle could make it upstairs with her package, unseen.

Marielle walked across the entry and took the stairs quickly, pausing only a second to look at young Susannah as she turned at the landing. She made her way to her bedroom, Susannah's bedroom, and closed the door quietly.

She stood for a moment, her back against the closed door. She closed her eyes and felt the wood against her back, solid and true. Marielle's earlier curiosity about the letters should have made her feel eager now that she held them—and others—in her hands. But as she opened her eyes, she felt like she was about to sit down and have an intimate conversation with the very ghost everyone at Holly Oak seemed to fear, in one way or another. And yet she was not afraid.

Marielle walked slowly to the bed and spread out the letters that had been mailed, making sure they were in order by postmark. The other letters she hoped were dated inside. She kicked off her wet shoes, pulled the band from her ponytail, climbed onto her bed, and arranged the pillows to support her in a sitting position. Then she reached for the first letter, opened it carefully, and began to read.

The Letters

12 April 1860
Holly Oak, Fredericksburg, Virginia

Dear Eleanor,

    Thank you, dear cousin, for the lovely parasol you sent for my birthday. It is the loveliest shade of rose, and I am very grateful to you for sending it. Such a happy color. I have not thought of happy things in such a long time, but the moment I opened your parcel, I imagined myself walking down the streets of Paris like we've always dreamed about, and this thought made me smile. Thank you, thank you, dearest cousin.

    I do not feel any different today at sixteen than I did yesterday at fifteen even though my grandmother and grandfather made a fuss over me at breakfast. We ate outdoors in the garden, which Grandfather loves to do and Grandmother does not. A fly rested upon my juice glass for only a moment, but she insisted Tessie throw it out and bring me a fresh glass at once. I could see in Tessie's eyes that she'd gladly drink that juice—it was only a fly, only for a second—and I wanted to tell her she could have it, but Grandmother doesn't like it when I talk to Tessie, so I didn't. My grandparents gave me a lovely hat that came all the way from New Orleans. And an amethyst brooch.

    Mama came out onto the garden, but it was almost as if the April beauty was too much for her. She merely kissed me on my cheek. Then she went up to her room, and I did not see her again until nightfall, when she bade me good night after supper and disappeared upstairs. I wanted to ask her again when we shall be able to come to see you, as she promised we would, but I can never seem to gather up enough courage to ask her.

We have been here in Fredericksburg for three months. Sometimes it seems like we only just arrived and will soon be going back to Washington after a lovely visit and Papa will be waiting for us. Sometimes it seems like we've always been here and I have been missing him in silence for years and years. Grandmother doesn't want to talk about my papa because she says it is too hard for Mama to hear me mention him.

Holly Oak is a pretty house on a lovely street in town, and it has many rooms, six of which are bedrooms; I have probably told you that before. You can see a bit of the Rappahannock River from my bedroom window and the steeples of the churches from the third floor. I am sleeping in the corner bedroom, where there is a lovely curve in the wall like a bell. I feel a little like I am in a room for a princess with that round wall on one side. There is a lovely garden on the south side of the house with roses and tulip trees and hedges of forsythia. And many trees. Grandmother said when my mother was my age she would have garden parties and there would be dancing and all kinds of cakes and young men in suits. I have not made very many new friends yet. Grandmother says she wishes she could've had a birthday party for me but that would've been too much for Mama. Mama isn't ready for parties yet. Not even ones that aren't for her.

Aunt Eliza is coming home from Philadelphia next month. She has been going to a tailoring school there. Or something like that. I am not sure I understand why she is there. Grandmother knows how to sew. She taught my mother to sew, and she is teaching me. Why could she not also teach Eliza? I asked Mama this. She took a long *time answering, as if she had to remember she has a sister named Eliza. Mama said sometimes a person with a will like Eliza's needs to be taught by someone other than her mother. Eliza is only seven years older than me. And she is not yet married, which is very strange because she is very pretty. Last summer, when we were all here together, Papa said something about how pretty she was and how she must have her pick of beaus. She just frowned at him as though he had told her she was plain and lucky if any old goat would have her.*

Grandfather spends most of his time at the farm with the sheep or at the mill. My grandparents own a woolen mill; did you know that? And Grandmother has a little haberdashery here in town. It was her father's store. It smells like my Papa in there with all the men's hats and gloves and scarves. Mother worked there when she was my age. I want to work there too. Grandmother said perhaps in the fall, after the summer months. Perhaps after I have come back from visiting you in Maine!

I miss you, Eleanor. And Cousin John. And Aunt and Uncle. And Grandmother Towsley. And do you have any news of Will? Is he well? Do you ever get letters from John? I hear cadets at West Point do not have time to write letters home. I do hope that is not true.

Yours most lovingly,
Susannah Towsley

---

20 September 1860
Holly Oak, Fredericksburg, Virginia

Dearest Eleanor,

It is with great sadness that I tell you we shall not be coming to Maine after all. The summer has ended, and Mama will not speak of us coming to visit. She speaks of nothing. Grandmother told me it would be too hard for her to visit my Papa's family so soon after his death and to kindly leave her to her grief. You cannot rush a widow's grief. She said someday I will understand this. I said, what if I am never a widow? She asked me if I wished to marry someday, and I said yes, of course I wish to be married someday. And she said if a woman marries, she will be widow. She is destined to be a widow. The husband always dies first.

I do not believe her. But it would not have been polite to say so.

I would come on the train myself, but Grandmother and Grandfather both said it is too far for me to travel alone. There is too much happening between here and there. I asked if perhaps I could bring Tessie with me, and Grandfather said Tessie is an ignorant child and it was foolish to think a simple Negro could provide me protection on such a long trip. Tessie is not ignorant nor a child. She is three years older than I am and we've had many discussions in the garden when she is supposed to be merely seeing to my lemonade. Tessie's mother and father live in North Carolina. So do her brothers. She hasn't seen them since she was eleven, when Grandfather bought her and brought her here to Holly Oak. Yesterday I asked her why she hasn't been to visit them, and she said, "When you're a slave it's best to reckon you have no family to visit. It's best to reckon you have nothing." "Don't you miss them?" I asked. And she looked away from me, toward the river. "Every day," she said.

I told her that when I am older perhaps I could take her on the train to see her family. Surely when I am older my grandparents will let me travel with Tessie. I see Southern women traveling all the time with their Negro slaves. North Carolina isn't that far. Aunt Eliza came out onto the garden at that very moment and told me, right in front of Tessie, that Grandfather would never let me take Tessie to see her family. I asked her why not? "Ask him yourself," she said in that *way she has. I can't explain it. It is like she is being sweet and mean at the same time. But not mean to me, exactly. And not sweet to me either. You see? I cannot explain it.*

Tessie turned and left us without a word, and I watched her walk down to the slaves' quarters at the far end of the garden. She always says, "Will there be anything else, Miss Susannah?" when she leaves me, but she didn't that time. I thought perhaps I'd made her sad, asking about her family. So then of course I felt sad. I asked Eliza if I should go after Tessie and apologize. "Apologize for what?" Eliza said to me. "I made her sad," I answered. Then Eliza turned to go too. "You're not the one who has made her sad. And your mother wants you." She started to go back into house. I picked up my writing things to follow. "But if Grandfather hadn't bought her, wouldn't someone else have bought her?" I asked. And Eliza turned back to me, and her gaze on me was cool like a funeral mist falling on my skin. "Yes, Susannah, someone else would've." Her skirts swished as she walked back into the house ahead of me.

Eliza disapproves of Grandfather having slaves. I look at Tessie, and I do not think I like it either. I wonder why he has them. There is no one here I can ask except Eliza and Tessie, and I do not possess the courage to ask either one that question. Not yet. There are other slaves here at Holly Oak. But I cannot ask them either. We have never had more than a couple of words pass between us. Perhaps I will ask Eliza later. Tomorrow maybe.

There is much in the newspapers these days of Southern states that wish to keep slaves and Northern abolitionists who wish to see the practice ended forever. Papa once told me that God would not have a man own another man as though he were a horse or a carriage, but he also told me that when I am at Holly Oak visiting my mama's parents, I am to respect them and their way of life.

I am not visiting Holly Oak now. I live here. Is this now my way of life?

I so wish Mama and I could come to Maine for the Christmas holidays as we did last year. Grandfather won't consider it right now because he said there are too many things happening in the North that he doesn't like. Political things. Sometimes he will have gentleman friends over to Holly Oak, and they will sit in the garden and smoke pipes and talk about all the things they do not like about Washington. I know they do not mean the city itself. They mean the government and who decides what the states can do and can't. The women are never allowed to sit with them. Not that Mama nor I would want to. Mama certainly wouldn't. Eliza wants to and they won't let her. It makes her angry. She sits and listens at the open parlor window anyway.

I miss you all so very much. Shame on you for telling Will I asked about him! But I am glad he and John are well and have survived the first year at West Point. Perhaps at Christmastime, if Mama and I are there, they will come home on the train in their uniforms as they did last year, and this time we will recognize them!

Love to Aunt and Uncle and Grandmother Towsley,

Yours most sincerely,

Susannah Towsley

27 December 1860
Holly Oak, Fredericksburg, Virginia

Dearest Eleanor,

I trust you had a happy Christmas and that Cousin John made it safely home for the holidays. Thank you for the beautiful drawing.

You have such talent! And Mama loves the scarf you made. Did you see Will? Is he well?

Christmas here at Holly Oak was very strange. We had a nice goose and presents and carols, but everyone's thoughts were only on what South Carolina has done. And what it might mean for us.

I hardly know where to begin, dearest cousin. So much has happened since last I wrote you.

Grandfather is never home now, and when he is, he is always stomping about the house, angry. This morning he said what has happened with South Carolina is only the beginning. "The beginning of what?" I asked. He was talking to Grandmother, and he didn't realize I was even in the room. I had just begun this letter to you. Mother was in the room with us too. But everyone always forgets when she is in the room. Sometimes even I do. Grandfather looked at me—stared at me—and it was a strange look. It was like, for a moment, I was not his granddaughter; I was someone else. Someone he didn't like. Then he looked away and his face seemed sad.

"These are not good times," he finally said. "These are hard times. What South Carolina has done, more states will do. Mark my words. More states will leave the Union." And Grandmother told him to please hush. "No. I will not hush," he said. "This is my home. This is Susannah's home. We are Virginians." He turned back to me, and it was as if he were waiting for me to say something. I could only stare at him. I didn't know what it was he wanted me to say.

"Leave her out of it," my mother said, and every head turned to her. She had barely said anything in days. She wasn't looking at any of us. She was looking down at her hands, lying still in her lap. Then she stood and walked out of the room without another word. We all watched her go. As she neared the doorway to the parlor,

I saw that Eliza was leaning on the door frame and had certainly heard everything.

No one said anything as Mama left. Grandmother excused herself to follow after her. Grandfather watched her leave too. His gaze rested on Eliza for just a moment and then again on me. Then he told us he was going to the mill. And he left.

Eliza was quiet for just a moment. Then she nodded toward this letter you are holding, Eleanor. "Writing to your cousin in Maine?" she asked. And I said yes. Then she walked over to me, stood over me and the letter. "Your grandfather sometimes forgets that your papa and his family are from Maine and that you were born in Washington. And then on days like today he remembers." She paused, as if she wanted those words to settle in on me.

"What is this the beginning of?" I asked her. "Why is Grandfather so angry?" And she said, "Nothing good will come from South Carolina leaving the Union, Susannah. And if the rest of the South follows suit, God only knows what will happen." I asked her if all this was happening because the South wants to keep its slaves. And she said, "It's because the South doesn't want to be told by Northerners who don't live here what to do or how to think. The slaves are objects of ideologies and philosophies, but they labor and sweat and die like slaves. How long do you really think we can pretend we don't see that?" And then she left me too, and I now I am alone in the room.

I do not know what the New Year will bring, Eleanor. Say nothing to Grandmother or Cousin John of my concerns. And if you see Will before he and John return to West Point, tell him hello for me.

Yours always,
Susannah Towsley

12 April 1861
Holly Oak, Fredericksburg, Virginia

Dearest Eleanor,

Thank you for your letter and the lovely necklace you sent for my birthday. It was quiet this year. No one seemed to think it a remarkable occasion. Grandmother took me to Richmond to buy two new dresses, and we ate at a restaurant where the waitstaff brought me a little cake with tiny pink roses on top. But when we returned, it was like any other day. Mama sent for me after we arrived, and when I went into her room, she was still in her dressing gown. She kissed me on my cheek, whispered, "Happy Birthday," and then pressed her grandmother's diamond and pearl ear bobs into my hand. I've always loved them, but she just handed them to me like they had been mine all along and I'd been careless and left them in her room by mistake. I thanked her, and she nodded and turned away toward the window—the one that faces north.

I am sorry I have not written to you sooner, but I have been in a bit of a daze with the goings-on of late. I cannot think of Mr. Davis as my president and not Mr. Lincoln. Papa liked Mr. Lincoln. He would've wanted him as president had he lived. And I cannot quite grasp the notion that so many states have left the Union. Grandfather says Virginia is sure to follow. He says it like he cannot wait for it to happen.

I have been at the haberdashery more and more these last few weeks. Sometimes Grandmother is at the store too, but most days it is Eliza and me. Eliza is happiest when she is away from Holly Oak and at the haberdashery, and I do not think it is solely because men are forever coming to buy gloves and hats and ruffled shirts and trying to woo her. She and Grandfather argue about nearly every-thing, which makes for an unhappy house. Plus, Mama's inability to emerge from her grief makes Eliza angry. It makes me sad, but it irritates Eliza. My mother used to be like Eliza. She is her older sister, so this should not surprise me. But it is getting easier for me to forget that my mother was once a lively woman who wasn't afraid to say whatever she felt needed to be said.

I have met a few girls at various parties. Yet even there the only talk is that of secession and freedom from Yankee chains. The parties have not been enjoyable.

Pray for us, Eleanor. I am afraid. No one smiles in this house anymore. Inside the house all the anger feels heavy. The heaviness scares me some. How long can you hold up something heavy before your arms give out and it crashes down on you?

Love to you and Grandmother. Do you think Cousin John would like it if I wrote to him at West Point?

Yours always,

Susannah Towsley

---

27 April 1861
Holly Oak, Fredericksburg, Virginia

Dearest Eleanor,

It has happened, Eleanor. Virginia has seceded. Shots were fired at Fort Sumter. Grandfather says there is no turning back now. He says the Confederacy, if is it to endure, must now be prepared to defend itself. Eliza told me President Lincoln has called for seventy-five thousand militiamen. Dear Eleanor, will he call upon the cadets at West Point? Have you heard from John or Will?

I pray for their safety. And ours.

Yours,

Susannah Towsley

27 July 1861
Holly Oak, Fredericksburg, Virginia

Dearest Eleanor,

Terrible news. We have heard there has been a battle at Manassas. There was dreadful fighting.

Men and women came to watch the battle on the hillsides as though it were a spectacle and had to flee from the gunfire. Many Union soldiers were killed. There is shouting in the streets today because the Confederate Army was victorious. This was all Grandfather talked of at supper tonight. And all the while he was boasting, Tessie was serving us without so much as a crease of consternation on her brow. What does she think of what the South has done? Is doing?

Eliza said nothing the whole meal. She left the table before dessert and announced she was going to bed early. Her room was very quiet when I went upstairs later. The news of the battle must have tired her.

I do not know how I will get my letters to you. Our mail is no longer being carried across the Union lines. If you do not hear from me, you will know it is not because I am not thinking of you, dear cousin. John and Will are safe, I trust? And Uncle?

Grandfather has joined the cavalry. I didn't even know he liked horses.

I pray for you all,
Yours always,
Susannah Towsley

16 September 1861
Holly Oak, Fredericksburg, Virginia

Dearest Eleanor,

I do not know how this letter will reach you. But Eliza assures me it will. I was gathering my paper and pen to write to you today, supposing I would just save the letter until a time where I would be assured you would get it, and she whispered to me that she would see to it that this letter would be delivered to you and that all my letters would be delivered to you. I, of course, thought she was teasing me, and I told her it was not a very funny jest. She said she was not jesting. "What can you possibly mean, Eliza?" I whispered back. She told me she knows how dear you are to me and how much it would mean to me to keep writing to you and to know that you would actually receive my letters despite this war. "I know a way," she said. "What way?" I asked. But she told me I didn't need to know. She told me to give her the letter when I was done, and that you would soon have it. And to tell no one. How can she possibly move mail when no one else can? I am much afraid she is involved in something that could get her into trouble.

Tomorrow the four of us—Mama, Grandmother, Eliza, and I—are to be shown how to sew Confederate uniforms. An officer came to the house today and told us we were needed because of our sewing skills to make uniforms for the Cause. His name is Lieutenant Nathaniel Page, and he works for the quartermaster. He is very tall and has the reddest hair I have ever seen. He told us the cut pieces for the uniforms will be brought to us from Richmond and we are to sew them together using the patterns he brought us and to attach the braid and buttons. And that someone from the quartermaster's headquarters would come to Holly Oak once a week to inspect our progress, tally our quotas, and take our finished uniforms to the field.

After he left, Eliza pulled me aside. "You are never to mention you have family in Maine around him," she said. Her words nearly sent me into a faint. I had no idea what she meant. I thought the lieutenant had been most polite, and her words alarmed me. "You think he is dangerous?" I asked. "No," she said. "He is not someone to be worried about. He is someone who does not need to know you have relatives in Maine. Do you understand? He does not need to know that." I asked why she was so anxious about Lt. Page if he was someone we weren't to worry about. But she did not answer my question. She remarked instead that Lt. Page had been quite taken by me. I said she was quite mistaken. She said, "No. He has taken a fancy to you, Susannah. I am sure he will be the one to deliver the fabric and inspect our progress." And though I felt my face warm to crimson, I told her I had no desire for a beau right now.

And she said these days are not about me.

Eleanor, I do not know what to think. Please, please, say nothing to anyone. Especially not to Will. I know Will does not know I am fond of him, but even so, please do not tell him what Eliza said about the lieutenant.

I know you perhaps will not be able to get a letter back to me. Or maybe you will. I am not really sure what Eliza is capable of.

You are always in my prayers,

Susannah Towsley

──────※──────

20 November 1861
Holly Oak, Fredericksburg, Virginia

My dearest Eleanor,

I am writing to you now in secret. Only Eliza knows that I am still sending letters to you. Twice I've told myself I must simply stop *writing to you because surely my aunt is involved in something dangerous. But here I sit writing you anyway. You are my only friend, the only person I can trust. Eliza tells me she is certain my letters are being delivered to you. But she also tells me it is not possible for her to get any of your letters to me. I asked her why not. She told me—in that way of hers that is both gentle and scalding—to pull my head out of the clouds and remember that we are at war.*

Grandfather has gone off with the Virginia cavalry, so it is just us women in the house. Every day there is talk of a battle here or a battle there and of Union soldiers being taken prisoner and of the rebels putting the sorry Yankees in their place. Some here in Fred-ericksburg are loyalists; at least there were some who are loyalists. I think perhaps they've all been chastised into silence or have left. If you are a loyalist, Eleanor, you are treated with such contempt, like a criminal. Grandmother has told me not to mention to anyone where I was born or where Papa was from, because I am a Southern girl now. But there are people in this town who know me, who remember that my mother married a man from Maine and that we used to live in Washington. "What about them?" I asked my grandmother. And she said my only concern is to give no one any reason to recall any of that. She did not ask me if I was a loyalist. If she had, I would have told her I don't know what I am. It's as if she doesn't want to know what I think.

Sometimes I think Eliza slips out of her room at night and leaves the house while we are all sleeping. She is home every morning, and her shoes are never muddy nor her hems wet. But sometimes I smell the outside air on her and in her room. And it is too cold for the windows to be left open at night. I think perhaps she is involved with loyalists. I can't help but wonder who she is giving these letters to and what would happen if she were to be caught. And of course I wonder if she reads the letters before she hands them off to whoever is taking them across the lines. But she offers no evidence that she has read them.

Grandmother took me to Richmond last week to buy inventory for the haberdashery, and all the streets were atwitter about the sickly Yankee prisoners who are languishing there in the ship chandlery on Tobacco Row. Richmond is cold and gray. I was happy to come home.

Eliza was right about Lt. Page. He has been the one to make rounds at Holly Oak to inspect our progress with the uniforms. He comes every Friday; Grandmother always invites him to stay to supper, and he always accepts. I think Grandmother is hoping Lt. Page will find Eliza an attractive and suitable girl to woo and marry.

But I am afraid Eliza was right about Lt. Page in other ways too. I catch him looking at me over his wine glass and his spectacles, and when he inspects my stitching, he leans in close enough for me to catch the fragrance of the starch in his collar. It makes me very nervous. Eliza watches him all the time, and I think Grandmother thinks Eliza is jealous of the lieutenant's attentions toward me. But it is plain to me that Eliza is not jealous in the least. Eliza is thinking. Always thinking. She doesn't spend her days wondering how to win the war; she spends them wondering how to end it. Two different things.

I wish I knew where Cousin John and Will were. I know it is too much to suppose you might get a letter to me to let me know they are safe and well. I worry that they are here in the South somewhere, cold and far from the woodlands of Maine, or caged like animals in the Richmond ship chandler building. Or wounded or ill. I wish I knew they were safe. I dreamed of Will last night.

I dreamed he was the one leaning close to me. Instead of smelling
starch, I smelled pine.

> *I pray for you all,*
> *Yours always,*
> *Susannah Towsley*

---

25 January 1862
Holly Oak, Fredericksburg, Virginia

Dear Eleanor,

The streets are quiet today. The Confederacy has lost its first
major battle in a place called Fishing Creek. It is far away from
here, in Kentucky. But you'd think it was right next door. The young
men and all the fathers and uncles and brothers are gone, so it is
just old men pottering around in their wool coats and mittens,
wondering what this defeat means. And of course the women here
can only suppose that a defeat means Southern men are dead.

Eliza read the news of it in the newspaper and said not a word.
Grandmother read it and promptly asked Tessie for a hot cup of tea.
Mama, like Eliza, also said not a word. She is talking more these
days but only to herself. She whispers things but not to anyone in
particular. I told Grandmother it didn't seem right that she was
doing that, and she said of all the things to worry about right now,
a little whispering is not so terrible.

I told Eliza later when we were alone that I was writing another
letter to send to you and, I don't know why, but I suddenly asked
her if what she was doing with them could get her into trouble. She
hesitated for a second and then said, "We are already, all of us, in
trouble. If this"—and she pointed to the newspaper's front page,

which was covered from top to bottom with nothing but inky words about the war—"is not trouble, then I surely don't know what is." And then I asked her if she was a loyalist. And she just smiled, like I had said something sweet and comedic. "How much do you really want to know, Susannah?" This she practically whispered to me. "About what?" I said. "I think you know what," she replied. "Where do you go when you go out at night?" I whispered. And her eyes widened just a little. I don't think she knew I had discovered she was doing this. "If I don't tell you, you will never have to lie for me," she said softly, as if she knew I would lie to protect her. That I was just like her. That there were two sides and she and I were on a side together and if someone asked me about her, that someone would be on the other side. I was suddenly very afraid for her. "Why are you doing this?" I asked. Even as I was asking her, there was a caller at the door. We heard Tessie open it and welcome Lt. Page. "We all have our part to play, Susannah," she said. And she rose to greet our guest.

Lt. Page stayed for dinner. Then he asked me to walk with him out to his horse and might Eliza join us? It was not a bitterly cold night, but still, it is winter and it surprised me that he would ask. A winter's night is not the time for strolls. When we were properly wrapped and scarved, we stepped outside. The sky was shimmering with stars. Lt. Page told me his duties with the war will prevent him from coming to Fredericksburg as often as he'd like but that he would like to write to me. He told me he had already asked my grand-mother, since my grandfather was away at the war, if he might do that, and she had consented. I could feel Eliza's eyes on me as Lt. Page spoke to me, I could feel her urging me to accept whatever attentions Lt. Page wished to bestow on me. And that she wished it for reasons all her own. I could only guess what she might gain from my having a liaison with a Confederate officer. I wanted to shake that look of hunger out of her. I politely told him he could write to me. He kissed my hand and left with our weekly quota of uniforms tucked under his arm, smiling. What else could I say? It would have been rude to refuse him.

As soon as he was away, I turned to Eliza and told her I am not the kind of person to entertain someone with the intent to deceive. "I am not in love with Lt. Page," I said. "He is a kind man who deserves honesty. I don't care which side of this war he is on. I will not let you use him. I am not like you." As she turned to go back into the house, she told me everyone is like her. We all want what we want, and when it matters enough to us, we will do what we must to have it.

6 March 1862
Holly Oak, Fredericksburg, Virginia

My dear Eleanor,

I trust you are well and that you would have only good news of Cousin John and Will and Uncle if I were to hear from you. I shall make this letter short since I do not know if you will get it. Grandmother and Eliza had a terrible argument last night, and Eliza left the house. It is nearly noon and she has not returned. We had been sewing all day, and my fingers were sore, so I was in my room resting when I heard them shouting. I stepped out onto the landing. Their raised voices were coming from the parlor, but I couldn't make out the words. I thought I heard my grandmother say something about my grandfather, that he was in danger. Or maybe she said Eliza was in danger. I could not tell. My mother was standing just outside her bedroom door, listening. I started for the stairs, and Mama quietly said, "Let them be." Then she turned, went back inside her room, and closed the door. I went downstairs anyway.

Tessie was standing just outside the parlor doors, which were half open. She had a tea tray in her hands, and it was obvious to me she couldn't decide if she should bring the tray in and intrude on the argument or stand outside with it until the yelling ended.

I stood next to her, and we both heard my grandmother say, "This isn't a game, Eliza!" And Eliza said, "I am the only one in this house who realizes it has never been a game! From the beginning this has never been a game!" Then Grandmother said, "Where do you go at night, Eliza? Where can you possibly be going in the middle of the night alone and without a chaperon?" For a second there was silence, and then Eliza said, "To meet a lover. Will that satisfy you? I go to meet a lover." But there wasn't an ounce of shame in her voice. I think even Tessie could tell she was lying.

Grandmother didn't say anything for a moment. But when she found her voice, she didn't yell. She said what she said as if she were holding back a hurricane. "I will not let you put this family in danger. You will not set foot out of this house at night. You will not." And Eliza calmly said, "You think I am the one putting this family in danger? You think I am? Think again, Mother."

Again there was silence. And then the swishing of skirts. Tessie and I just stood there to see who would emerge from the room. It was Eliza. She looked at me, and her eyes were shining with resentment. "I didn't tell her," I whispered. And she said, "I know you didn't." She grabbed her wrap off the hall tree, and she was out the front door. A swirl of chilly air spun into the house as she slammed the door.

A second later, Grandmother called to Tessie, as if she knew she had been standing outside the door with the tray, and asked for her tea.

I don't know what to think, Eleanor. Sometimes I admire Eliza, sometimes she scares me senseless.

Lt. Page has written me three times. I have written him once.

He wants to come visit me when he comes back through Fredericksburg. He didn't mention anything about the uniforms. The officer who comes for the uniforms now is my mother's age and frowns all the time. Grandmother has never asked him to stay for supper.

Lt. Page has begun signing his letters, "Yours very sincerely" and "With much affection, Nathaniel."

Just writing those words to you makes me blush, Eleanor. I wish I was in Maine with you. I wish I was writing letters to Will from your house in Wiscasset instead of letters to Lt. Page from Holly Oak.

I wish my mother would stop whispering to ghosts. I wish my papa had not died. I wish there was no war.

Missing you dreadfully,
Susannah

P.S. Eliza returned last night before we all retired to our beds. She didn't say where she had been. She came to my room and asked me if I had any letters I wished to send to you. I told her I did. This one. But she said she will not be able to arrange any more deliveries after this one. Not for a while. I will write anyway, Eleanor, and keep the letters safe until a day comes when I can send them. I shall go mad if I cannot write you.

15 March 1862
Holly Oak, Fredericksburg, Virginia

Dearest Eleanor,

Lt. Page called on me today. He told me he has spoken to Grandmother about courting me and would I do him the honor of thinking of him as my beau? My face felt as if it were on fire when he said this, and I am certain he saw my cheeks turn crimson. I think he found it endearing. My blushing made him smile. He reached for my hand and kissed it and told me I was the sweetest of angels, and then he touched my burning cheek. I did not know how to tell him he mistakes my embarrassment. I did not know how to say there is a young man from Maine who I can't stop thinking about and that it is this young man who makes me blush. And that although I am fond of the lieutenant, Will alone has my heart. I could summon no words to tell him this. Lt. Page is a kind man. A good man. But he took my bashful silence as agreement. He said he could not wait to tell his parents about his lady. And I had no courage to tell him he was misguided.

Grandmother so wished to have Lt. Page to stay for supper though we had nothing to serve but ham and potato soup and cornbread. Our few remaining chickens we cannot eat or we will have no eggs or chicks to replace them. Most of the preserves are gone, and there will be no fresh fruit or vegetables to eat until after the summer months produce a harvest. There are jars of beets in the cellar. And molasses. There are only so many things one can put molasses on.

But Lt. Page did not stay. He told us there is much activity in the area and we are to be very careful. It seems the Yorktown Peninsula is soon to be attacked. He also gave us more fabric than usual and told us it may be several weeks before anyone from the quartermaster's office would be calling on us. The roads in and around Fredericksburg are not safe.

When he left he kissed my hand again, and this time his lips lingered.

Susannah

11 April 1862
Holly Oak, Fredericksburg, Virginia

My dear Eleanor,

I do not feel a year older; I feel a hundred years older. Once there was a time when I dreamed I would be married at eighteen and sewing infant smocks and living in a lovely house in Maine and Will would be coming home at night smelling sweet of wood and sap and we'd spend our summers at the seaside looking for shells and playing with our little ones. That dream seems so far away.

Eleanor, I can barely express to you what has happened since last I wrote. Lt. Page has asked me to marry him. He wrote to me from Richmond, wished me a happy birthday, told me he fears the war shall keep us parted, and he asked if I might agree to marry him at Christmastime and join him there in Richmond. I received his letter two days ago. He must have told Grandmother of his intentions, because she knew when the letter came by courier that it was from Lt. Page. When she informed me that the courier was waiting for me so that I could send back a letter of response, she told me I was a very lucky girl to have won the affections of a Virginian gentleman.

"He comes from a very prominent family," Grandmother said. We were alone in the parlor. I was sitting at the table where we sew.

"I cannot accept!" I said to her, and her face clouded with disappointment so fast that I quickly added that I hardly knew Lt. Page and that I could not leave my mother in her present state and that I did not wish to marry anyone during the uncertainty of the war.

"It would be very unwise of you to decline this proposal," she said. "What do you think will happen if the war continues and the food and money runs out? Have you thought about that? Have you wondered how I can be expected to provide for this family when that happens? You're not a child anymore, Susannah. I cannot be expected to care for all of you as if you were."

She delivered this effortlessly, but her eyes misted with tears she did not shed. I saw fear in her eyes, something I hadn't seen before. Ever. Fear for us, I think—the women at Holly Oak. I have not missed my papa as much as I missed him at that moment. I knew he would not want me to do what Grandmother wanted me to do. He would not. Even if it meant we would be hungry.

"I cannot accept," I whispered.

Grandmother walked over to her writing desk, drew out a page of stationery, ink, and her pen, and handed them to me. "You will kindly thank Lt. Page for his proposal, and you will tell him that you are hopeful of seeing him in person to discuss your future together. I will not allow you to make so important a decision without thinking on it. And we cannot expect the courier to wait until you come to your senses."

I felt very alone as I wrote those words, Eleanor. But I wrote them and the courier left. My grandmother went up to her room without saying another word to me. Not knowing what else to do, I went to my mother's room, but she lay asleep on her bed in the middle of the afternoon. I turned and sought Eliza, who I found in the library rifling though the drawers of my grandfather's desk. I didn't even care what it was she was looking for. I showed her the letter from Lt. Page.

"I don't love him," I said, needing someone to hear those words.

"Will that be your answer to him?" she asked. She did not seem surprised that Lt. Page had proposed. I told her about the note Grandmother had me write. She seemed to consider this, and then she told me perhaps that was wise, that much could happen *between now and the next time I see Lt. Page. "I won't change my mind," I said. "I am fond of him, but I am not in love with him." And Eliza just shrugged and then asked me if I had seen Grandfather's keys to the gun cabinet. I told her I hadn't, and I did not ask her why she needed Grandfather's guns. I went to my room, alone and so tempted to steal a horse and ride to some faraway place untouched by war.*

Eliza now makes no attempt to hide her excursions at night. She does not announce them and leaves the house after we have all gone to bed, but she doesn't hide the evidences of her comings and goings since the argument she had with Grandmother. I do not think she does it to be brazen. She merely sees there is no purpose in pretending she has this secret when she does not.

And since she does not seem to care that we know she slips away after dark, I followed her last night. She went to the river to where she had a little canoe hidden in the rushes. I watched her get in and paddle away in the moonlight to the other side. I waited as long I could, but I became afraid to stand out there alone in the dark. I made my way back to Holly Oak and watched for her from my window. I had to pinch myself to stay awake. When at last I saw her return, I could see that she was not alone. Two men were with her. They wore hats and long dark cloaks. I watched them move soundlessly across the garden and make their way to the slaves' quarters. They went to Tessie's door. It was too far away to see if she was the one who opened it. I saw the door open and the three of them disappear inside.

I grabbed my wrap and flew down the stairs as quietly as I could. I stepped out in the garden. The night had grown colder, and I shivered as I made my way to Tessie's. I only wanted to listen at the window. I was nearly there when the door opened, and I suddenly realized I had nowhere to hide. Whoever was coming out

would see me, and there was nothing I could do to conceal myself.
I froze and prayed.

It was Eliza. She didn't seem angry, just surprised. She closed
the door quietly behind her. "What are you doing here, Susannah?"
she said, calm and quiet. "Who are those men?" I asked. I tried to
sound brave and curious, but my voice cracked, and I sounded like
a scared child. "Come back up to the house," she said. And she just
walked past me as if I would obey her. "Are those men going to
hurt Tessie?" I asked, even though somehow I knew, I knew, those
men were Union men. They had no intention of hurting Tessie. Tessie
was hiding those men. Tessie was helping them. And so was Eliza.
She knew I had answered my own question. She just kept walking.

I caught up with her. "Are they going to help Tessie escape to
the North?" Eliza shook her head, and even in the shadowy moonlight I could see she was smiling at my naiveté. "No, Susannah. Come
with me." We went back into the parlor, and she led me to the
finished pile of Confederate uniforms. She took two officers' great-
coats and trousers and handed them to me. "I haven't asked for your
help before, Susannah, because I did not want to involve you. But
I need you to do something for me. I need you to hide these in your
room. Will you do that?"

At first I could not even breathe. Two men were hiding in our
slaves' quarters. Two Northern men. And she was asking me to hide
two Confederate uniforms. "What for?" I said, when I was able.

"For later," she said.

As I stood there holding those uniforms in my arms I knew Eliza
wasn't just a frustrated loyalist. She was more than a simple Union
sympathizer. She was more than someone who wanted to see the horrible practice of slavery ended. She was aiding the Federal troops.
She was out at night meeting with them, talking with them, hiding
them. Helping them. And now she was involving me.

"Who are they for? Are they for those men in Tessie's quarters?" I asked. But she went on with her instructions, ignoring my questions.

"Wrap them in a sheet, and put them deep inside your feather bed. Sew up the place where you cut to put them in. Then turn your feather bed over so no one can see the seam. Do you understand?"

"The man from the quartermaster's office will know two are missing," I said to her. "He's coming tomorrow."

"That's why you have to hide them tonight. I don't think he will be bringing us more fabric after tomorrow."

Her words sent a chill into my bones. I asked her how she could know this. She said it does not matter how she knows. All that matters is keeping the two uniforms safe and hidden until she needs them. I asked her when that will be, and she said hopefully never.

The next day the man from the quartermaster's office came and took our finished uniforms. He counted them. He counted them again. He asked for all the unfinished pieces too, and we told him they were all finished. And he counted them again. I dared not to even glance at Eliza. Then he said our count was off. Grandmother told him he was mistaken. The count couldn't possibly be off. He counted them again. "There are fifteen," he said. "There should be seventeen." Grandmother told him confidently that someone must have made a mistake. She opened the cabinets where we keep all our sewing supplies: the thread, the buttons, the braid. The space where the fabric sat was empty. "You have them all," she said. And he thanked her and left. But he did not look convinced, Eleanor.

My dearest cousin, I know you will probably never read this letter. How I wish you were here or I was there. I feel so alone.

Yours always,
Susannah

21 April 1862
Holly Oak, Fredericksburg, Virginia

Eleanor,

I am in a daze. Words escape me as I try to describe what has happened. I do not know how to begin. Fredericksburg is occupied. Union soldiers have taken the city. Eliza told us they were coming, and she instructed us to hide whatever food and valuables we could. When she said this, Grandmother glared at her. And Mama just sat in her chair like she didn't have the slightest care that the Yankees were coming to set up camp in Fredericksburg. Grandmother said to Eliza, "You brought this trouble upon us!" and Eliza looked angry enough to slap her. "I take responsibility for everything I've ever done, bad or good. But this is not my doing," Eliza said. "Now unless you want to let the Yankees have your silver, I suggest you hide it!"

We spent the night digging up the cellar floor and hiding our jewelry and our coins and the silver in the dirt. I felt like a pirate hiding booty from other pirates, and my dress was covered in earth when we were done. We climbed the stairs to our rooms and stripped to our chemises. Eliza took our filthy dresses. I was too tired to ask her what she planned to do with them. Before I fell into bed, she told me to go into the parlor and remove all the braid, the buttons, the thread from our uniform making. Everything. She told me to put it all in a sack with some rocks and toss it into the river. "It is the middle of the night!" I told her. And she said, "Indeed it is, Susannah. Thank God it is."

The next morning they arrived. Soldiers in blue. They poured into the streets. Eliza and I were at the haberdashery when they arrived, more and more and more of them. Some of them came into the store, said hello, then just started taking anything they wanted. Hats, gloves, watches, scarves, pipes.

Eliza was red faced with anger, but she merely said what they were doing was wrong. They laughed at her. Told her she was a lovely girl even when livid and asked if her husband was away at the war. She told them to get out. And they laughed harder. It was a very strange laugh, Eleanor. It was not a cruel laugh reserved for villains but the kind of laugh a superior might have for a childish fool engaged in something that is doomed to fail. Beyond our shop windows I could see more Yankees in other stores, walking out onto the streets with clothes, picture frames, garden tools, and tins of tobacco. Storekeepers were running after them, yelling at them that they couldn't just take what didn't belong to them. And the Yankee soldiers simply ignored them.

I stood there unable to comprehend what was happening. I didn't know war could also be like this. I know there is gunfire and cannons and killing in faraway fields, but I didn't know it was also this.

Eliza grabbed my arm and whispered to me. "Use the back door. Get to the house as quick as you can. And lock all the doors. I will follow as soon as I can."

"I can't leave you here!" I whispered back.

She turned to me, eyes bright with force. "GO!" she rasped. She pushed me to my knees, and I crawled to the back of the store. I heard Eliza yelling at the Yankees to get out, but I kept on my hands and knees. When I was no longer in the soldiers' line of sight, I rose to my feet and pushed open the back door. I could hear whoops and hollers in the street—more Yankee revelry. I picked up my skirts and ran. I heard voices calling, shouting. They might have been shouting at me. I didn't stop and I didn't turn around. I just kept running, tears of dread running down my face. I could hear shouts of anger and panic coming from other houses as my neighbors reacted to the presence of Yankees, walking boldly and uninvited into their homes. But I didn't stop. I just kept running until Holly Oak came into view. I stumbled up the front steps, crashed the front door open, and fell to a crumple, out of breath, onto the foyer floor. I slammed the door shut with my foot and gulped in air, eyes shut tight.

Then I sensed movement. I opened my eyes and saw boots approach me. Men's boots.

I looked up, and men in blue coats and hats stared down on me. Half a dozen or more of them. One of them stretched out his hand. I covered my head, ready for a blow, already feeling the sting of it. But then the man said my name.

My hands fell away from my face. Will was standing above me. And Cousin John.

Eleanor, they were standing in Holly Oak. Standing there in their Union uniforms. The incongruity of them being there, like that, swooped down on me like a crashing hammer. Will's hand was still outstretched to help me up, but I could not will my arm to lift itself. The world had gone mad. And since I was part of the world, I had surely gone mad too.

John dropped to his knees beside me. "Susannah, it's John and Will. Do you not recognize us?" The other men with them snickered, though not unkindly. "Are you all right? You have been crying."

Will was bent over now too, his arm now lightly reaching for my arm. He pulled me gently to my feet.

"You're here," I whispered, and all of them laughed.

John handed me a handkerchief. "Cousin, are you quite all right?"

I suddenly remembered why I had run home. "Where's my mother? Where's my grandmother?" I looked for a parting in the group of them, and there wasn't one. They were circled around me.

"We were wondering that too," John said. "We'd like to ask

*your grandmother if we can stay at Holly Oak while we're here.
Better us than strangers you do not know. And where might your
aunt Eliza be?"*

*The room seemed to be spinning. Where was my mother? Where
was my grandmother? Why were they asking about Eliza?*

*Will placed his hand under my elbow. Tender, as a father might.
"Susannah, what has happened? Where is Eliza?"*

*Behind me the door opened, and Eliza charged inside, the store
keys dangling from her hand. Her hair was loose and flying like I
realized now mine was.*

*"What the devil is going on?" she exclaimed angrily. She
glowered at the Yankees standing in our foyer, at my cousin, and
at the man I had loved since I was fourteen. Her eyes were blazing.*

*I opened my mouth to tell her one of the Union soldiers standing
in our entry was my cousin from Maine and the other was a good
friend, but they stepped forward and told her that what was happening at the shops and houses had never been ordered by the
general. And they didn't approve of it.*

*Eliza turned to Will. "They are sacking the town, Will! There
are just innocent women and children left here. And a few old men.
We're not one of your battlefields! This is a town of civilians!"*

She called him Will.

*John shook his head. "And I am telling you Gen. McDowell did
not order this."*

*Eliza whirled around to face my cousin. "Well, who's going to
order them to stop? Tell me that, John? Who is going to order them
to stop?"*

She knew them both. And they knew her.

*The room began to feel warm and sticky like a late July evening.
I felt Will's arms suddenly around my waist. As I fought to stay
conscious I was aware of how close Will was, how solid he felt*

against my body. Not some distant dream of a man, but here, in my house, guiding me and then picking me up off my feet and carrying me in his arms as I always dreamed he would do.

When I awoke minutes later on a couch in the drawing room, the other soldiers had gone off with Eliza to find my mother and grandmother, who apparently were hiding in Tessie's quarters. I found out later Tessie had run away. As had all the slaves. The gardeners, our houseboy, the cook, the groomsmen. They all left not long after the Yankees arrived because they knew there was no one who could make them stay. John had stayed behind with me and now held a cool cloth to my head as consciousness returned to me.

"You know Eliza," I said to him.

"Yes."

"Has she... Is she...," but I didn't know what question to ask.

"Will and I were part of the scouting party to take Fredericksburg. The general didn't want there to be any reason to use violence. The army is only here to position themselves to march into Richmond. That's all. Eliza was...helpful."

"The Yankees were in the streets, in the stores. They were taking things."

John pressed the cloth to my head. "That is unfortunate. We do need places to stay, however. And we need provisions."

"Doesn't your army supply you with provisions?" I said. "Besides, they were taking dress gloves and picture frames. And they didn't even ask. They just took!"

"They aren't supposed to be doing that."

"But they are!" I struggled to sit up. "Like common thieves."

"Dear cousin"—John shook his head—"I'm afraid war is ugly."

"People are ugly," I said.

John flicked a curl from my brow and smiled sadly. "Yes. Sometimes they are."

He suddenly seemed much older to me. And I seemed older to myself.

Eleanor, your brother and Will and the other men are sleeping in the parlor and drawing room. They don't know how long they will be here—not long, they say. Guards have been posted at all the houses and stores so that there will not be any more ransacking. Other soldiers are sleeping in our neighbors' houses. Many soldiers are sleeping in little white tents all along the river. But many more are in our houses. The haberdashery is closed and locked for now, much of the inventory is gone anyway. A curfew has been imposed, and none of us are allowed out after dark.

Grandmother found someone to take her out to the farm today. We still have our carriages but not our horse. When she came back she said the foreman and all but the oldest slave are gone. Abner is near to sixty and was reluctant to leave with the others on foot because he cannot walk without limping. The rails for the pasture fence are missing—taken for Yankee campfires, we have heard—and so most of the sheep are gone too. Grandmother made Abner the new foreman and told him to sleep in the farmhouse now. And to keep the few remaining sheep in the barn. I wonder if Abner knows he is a foreman of no one. There is no one there for him to manage.

Since the cook is gone, Eliza and I are making the meals now. The men eat in the dining room, and we ladies eat in the pantry.

At dinner tonight Grandmother lamented to Eliza that what had happened to the haberdashery was abhorrent. Then she proceeded to complain that the Yankees sleeping in Holly Oak are eating all our food and using up all our soap and oil and candles. I think Grandmother wanted to know why, with Eliza's surreptitious liaisons, our house and the business weren't spared, though she never said it. While we washed dishes I asked Eliza the question.

"Why do you think we were not spared, Susannah?" she said, in a very tired voice.

I thought about it for a moment. And then I knew. "No one in Fredericksburg knows that you have helped the Yankees," I said. "If our house had been spared, if the haberdashery had been spared then—"

"And no one but John and Will and a few others on the Union side knows either," she interrupted. "No one needs to know anything. It is not common knowledge that John is your cousin. And that's the way it needs to stay."

I realized then that Eliza had to be in the employ of someone. Someone has to be orchestrating her activities. A secret loyalist perhaps. Someone I would not expect, maybe. "Who...who are you with? Who are you doing this for?" I asked.

She dried the cup I had handed her and told me it doesn't matter who she is with. She is not doing this for a someone but because the South cannot win this war. The sooner it is over, the sooner the bloodshed will stop.

I suddenly thought of my letters to you, Eleanor, all the letters Eliza had been secretly getting to you. It occurred to me that she had used me, used the letters to somehow get an inroad with the Union army. I wondered if you had seen any of those letters at all.

"What about my letters to Eleanor?" I asked. And she said, "What about them?"

"Did you use my letters to communicate with Will and John?" I could sense my anger rising at the thought of my letters being opened by Union spies. Read by Union soldiers perhaps. Maybe even read by Will. Those letters were meant only for you, Eleanor. Only for you. I asked her if you had seen any of them or if she just used them to make contact with Will and John's scouting party. I was

very angry. Eliza calmly assured me you probably received every one. But yes, she did use them first.

I asked her how.

She told me messages were written in between my lines of writing with a special ink. It can't be read without a special solution.

My letters to you, Eleanor. Opened. Trifled with. I was livid. "You said no one read my letters! You said Eleanor most certainly received them. You lied to me!"

She frowned at me. "Lower your voice, Susannah. I have not lied to you. No one read your letters. I wrote the messages in between the lines. I did. And I assure you I did not read your letters!"

I didn't believe her. Eleanor, how could she not have read them?

She told me she had no desire to read them. No one did. It was only the messages in between the lines that mattered. When the messages were received the letters were sent on their way to Maine. She said it was as simple as that.

I asked her if Will had read them. I had to know.

"For heaven's sake, Susannah." Her skirt hissed as she turned to leave me. "Do you really think men at war have the inclination to read the trivial journalings of a naive girl?"

She left me there with my hands red and puffy from scrubbing dishes.

I stepped outside the house to let the night air cool my face. I was angry, sad, ashamed, and I wished for a soothing touch or a soft assurance that my secrets were safe with you, Eleanor. But the garden was silent, including the slaves' quarters. There wasn't a calming voice singing a child to sleep, or a laugh or a cough or even a wisp of music. Nothing. The buildings were dark.

I went back inside to climb the stairs to my room. The parlor doors were closed, and the Union soldiers were inside. I could smell *pipe tobacco and hear their deep voices as I walked past. Will was in that room. Closed away from me. Wearing blue. And your brother, Eleanor. My cousin. They were both in that room where I had sewn Confederate uniforms, and those men were the enemy of Virginia.*

My fingers are aching from writing, Eleanor. Everything is aching.

Susannah

10 May 1862
Holly Oak, Fredericksburg, Virginia

Dearest Eleanor,

And so I begin another letter you will likely never read. I do not need Eliza to get it to you. I could easily ask John to put it in his haversack for you. I am sure he would not mind slipping my letter in with his own to you and Auntie. But I don't want to ask him.

I spend my days pretending he and Will are insufferable Yankees outstaying their welcome in our house. John told me to show him and Will no extraordinary kindnesses since they will be leaving soon, and Eliza and I will remain in Fredericksburg among its angry people. The scouts will be on their way in a few days to Williams-burg or maybe Richmond. I don't know. I am not supposed to know. I don't want to know.

Sometimes I think the Will that I love is still in Maine and this other man who looks like him and sounds like him is some warped mirror image of him, a deviation. I've spent so many long weeks sewing abstract gray pieces together, day after day after day, that I cannot quite grasp the notion that I had been creating clothes a

Southern militia man would wear, perhaps as he sat inside a Northerner's house, drinking a Northern woman's whiskey and eating her food and taking her absent husband's books and tobacco. I had not pictured Southern soldiers inside those uniforms, doing what soldiers do. I should have.

Will caught me staring at him after supper tonight. I was clearing the last of the plates, and he was sitting alone at the table, preparing to light a pipe. The other men had stepped out into the garden. I must have lingered, motionless and staring, because he looked up at me. "What is it, Susannah?" he asked, thinking perhaps I was angry about something. But I was contemplating this bizarre paradox of his lovely nearness and yet strange distance, and because I was so entranced in this pondering, I was dazedly forthright. "It's like you are here but not here," I said, blushing at once. And he laughed. Light and sweet. The way I remembered it.

"That is a very interesting observation, Susannah. Are you telling me you think I am invisible?" His smile was wide and perfect.

I struggled to assemble words that would make sense, that would explain but would not embarrass me further. "The last time I saw you, you were wearing a brown-checked shirt and you had sawdust in your hair and no beard and you chased me with a lizard."

His eyes danced with merriment. "Ah, yes. You do not care much for reptiles, as I recall."

The memory made me smile too. Do you remember that day, Eleanor? Remember how I screamed? It had been exhilarating. "No. Not reptiles," I said.

"But now I am sitting here in your parlor, and a map says we are on opposite sides of a terrible war," he said. Gently. And I nodded. I told him I just wanted everything to go back to the way it was.

And he just said, "No, you don't."

Peaceful images of my papa and our pretty house in Washington and the summers we'd spent in Maine and Will chasing me filled my mind. And then I thought of my mother's mindless mutterings and the empty larder and the Union soldiers laughing at Eliza as she yelled at them in the haberdashery and Lt. Page's lips on my hand, and I said yes, I do.

"You want to go back to being a child?" Will laughed.

No, I told him. I wanted to go back to being happy. And he said happiness is not something we go back to get. We pursue it. It is ahead of us, not back in time. And that's what the North was doing. Pursuing a peaceful end to the dreary set of circumstances the Confederate Army had set into motion.

He struck a match and touched it to the bowl of his pipe, puffing on it as it took the flame. The room filled with the sweetest of scents, powerful and painful. I swayed for a moment. My father's tobacco.

"Where did you get that?" I whispered.

Will looked at me quizzically. "This was my grandfather's pipe."

"The tobacco," I said. "Where did you get that?"

"I found a whole tin of it in a crate of books and papers in your root cellar. It's a shame for it to go to waste down there," he said.

Tears began to slide instantly down my cheeks. It was if they had been hanging there ready to fall for all these many long months since Papa died. Just dangling there like a curtain poised to drop.

Will's brow crinkled and he cocked his head, ready, I am sure, to ask me why I was crying, but the doors to the garden opened and the soldiers began to file back into the house. I grabbed a plate from the table and dashed back into the pantry.

The soldiers had caught two rabbits for breakfast tomorrow. They are tired of ham, they said. And that is all we have. They have already eaten all our chickens. The soldiers brought the rabbits into the pantry while I was wiping the tears from my face. They wanted me to clean and skin them. I have never touched a dead animal. I bolted from the room. I heard one of them yell for me to come back and he'd teach me, and Will told him to leave me alone.

I ran to my room and opened the window. The orchards are in bloom.

---

18 May 1862
Holly Oak, Fredericksburg, Virginia

Dear Eleanor,

Will is recovering from a fever. Grandmother put him in my bed, and I have been made to sleep with Eliza. The Confederate uniforms are still buried inside my bed. But I suppose it will not be the end of all things if Will discovers them. Eliza had me hide them for Will and John anyway. They were the two men she hid in Tessie's cabin the night I followed her.

I miss Tessie. I wonder if she misses us. Probably not.

I will finish this letter later. Eliza found some stray hens and their chicks out along the river this morning. We need to find a way to hide them.

Seven o'clock.

The chickens are in the attic. Eliza made a hole in the roof to let sunlight in and covered it with a pane of glass she took from the carriage house. It is my job to make sure the hens stay quiet and happy. We made a dirt floor for them to peck at, and after supper I had the unfortunate task of catching crickets and grasshoppers for them. We can only spare so much corn. We hope and pray the hens will lay eggs for us.

Will's fever returned this afternoon, and he was most angry about it since he and the others are to leave soon. I brought him a basin of cool water and a cloth, and I confess I found much enjoyment sitting at his side, soothing his brow with my cloth.

He told me fever or no fever, he's getting up tomorrow, and I told him even soldiers can't tell a fever what to do. That made him smile. "When did you grow up, Susannah? You're not the girl I chased with a lizard."

I smiled back at him. "I would guess if you had a lizard to chase me with, I would still run."

"You must have a string of beaus writing you letters from battle," he said, still smiling.

And my heart seemed to take a stutter step. "No," I told him. I didn't tell him about Lt. Page. I didn't want to think about Lt. Page at that moment.

"Surely at least one," he continued. "Your grandmother tells me a certain lieutenant is sweet for you. Wants to marry you."

My face roared with anger and color. "She...she is... I am not..." But Eleanor, I couldn't finish! How could Grandmother have said such a thing? It was not her place to say it. And yet Grandmother does not know I love Will. And she thinks I will accept Lt. Page's proposal of marriage. She thinks it's just a matter of time before I will.

"So, the lieutenant's sweet for you, but you are not sweet for him," Will said, assessing my stuttering to silence. "You are sweet for someone else perhaps?"

I could do nothing but stroke his brow with my cloth. Words utterly failed me. The door opened, and I was at first glad for the interruption. Eliza came in bearing a tea tray. But then I saw Will's eyes brighten at her approach. His body, so close to mine, seemed to tense with veiled anticipation regarding her presence. Surprise walloped me.

And I seemed to sink into a gray place of denial, sitting there on my bed with Will lying inches from me, and him watching my aunt cross the room with a tray in her hands. I did not want to accept what I was seeing.

Eliza set the tray down and left with barely a word. And for that small miracle, I was grateful.

She is not in love with him, Eleanor. But I think he might be in love with her.

Susannah

---

29 May 1862
Holly Oak, Fredericksburg, Virginia

My dear Eleanor,

Will and John have left, along with the other soldiers who were staying here, and Holly Oak is ours alone once again. More soldiers came after the scouting party left, wanting to sleep in our bedrooms, but Grandmother told them no. I worried that they might insist, but they didn't. They went to the house next to ours, and I saw them go inside. I don't know why they were allowed in. Surely our neighbors put up the same resistance.

The curfew is still in effect, and Yankee soldiers still walk the streets, bored, but there aren't as many. Many of them are staying on the hill across the river, including the commanding officers, at the Lacy house. We hear the Lacys have left. Other Fredericksburg families have left too. Grandmother says we will never leave Holly Oak.

There are cooking fires at the slaves' quarters at the edge of the garden again. Negroes making their way north are spilling into occupied Fredericksburg to rest, organize, and disperse for destinations they have probably dreamed of their whole lives. At first Grandmother said she would not allow runaway Negroes to sleep in our slave quarters, but this was something she could only complain about while we women ate together in the pantry. There was nothing she could do about it. Eliza told Grandmother she could not stop what was happening by simply ordering it not to happen.

After supper yesterday, Eliza took me down to the slaves' quarters to see if those who were staying there for the night needed anything. There was a Negro woman with a new baby who was very ill. The baby was weak with hunger and listless. Eliza handed me the baby and asked me to go ask all those staying in our slaves' quarters if there was a nursing mother who could feed the child while she tried to help the woman eat something. She pushed me out the door before I could protest.

I did what she asked, but there was no one who could feed the child. I took the baby up to the house, and Grandmother tried to feed it some watered porridge, but the infant could not swallow it. Grandmother told me the child would likely not last the night and that I should take it back to its mother so that it would die in her arms, not mine.

I went back to Eliza and the sick mother. Eliza was mopping the woman's dark brow with cool water, and the woman kept whispering, "My child, my child." And Eliza told her I was right there in the room with her and I was holding her baby. Eliza started to sing to her. And to the baby. To me too, I think. And I fell asleep in Tessie's rocker with the baby in my arms.

When I awoke in the gray light of dawn, the baby was stiff in my arms. The mother had also died in the night. Eliza took the baby from me and placed the child in the dead mother's embrace. Two Negro men took two of our shovels and went to dig a grave for them at the slaves' cemetery at the edge of town. We asked them if they knew the dead mother's name, and they said they did not. No one else did either. Eliza told them to give the mother her name, Elizabeth. And to make sure someone put up a marker for her and the baby.

I went into the house with the weight of the dead child still in my arms. My hair had fallen from its pins and was tumbling about my shoulders, my dress was wrinkled, and I smelled of campfire.

I could not get the smell of smoke out of my hair and skin. I can still smell it. And I have bathed twice.

Now that the Yankees are gone, we are getting news from the outside again. A newspaper from Richmond reached us today, nearly a month old. I could not bear to read the front page. A Union spy posing as a secessionist was hung in Richmond. Eliza read it, but I think she had already heard of this man's execution before. She did not seem surprised. And she would not speak to me of it, not even in whispers.

Susannah

17 June 1862
Holly Oak, Fredericksburg, Virginia

Dearest Eleanor,

There are fewer Yankee troops in Fredericksburg, but those that are here are still looking to us for meals and soap and lamp oil. The chickens have soiled the attic beyond belief, but at least we have eggs. Several of the chicks are roosters. Perhaps, if we can keep their crowing from drawing attention, we will soon have more chicks and then something besides cured ham to eat.

The time I used to spend sewing uniforms I now spend tending Cook's vegetable garden. Half of what I planted has shriveled and died or been eaten by rabbits. I don't know how Cook managed to grow anything. Eliza says it doesn't matter how much I lose to my ineptness or the rabbits; it only matters how much I can save. At least the trees in the orchard are faring well. We shall have peaches, if not carrots and peas.

Negroes continue to move in and out of Holly Oak's slave quarters. I think word has traveled—albeit quietly—that if you are a contraband on your way north, there is a house in Fredericksburg where you can rest and gather your family members together. That house is our house. Eliza is down there every night making sure there are no quarrels or hurting children or hungry souls. I go with her sometimes.

The haberdashery is open again, but Yankee customers must pay for what they want. Business is actually good, but there isn't much to buy with the gold they pay us, nor will we be able to restock the inventory we have sold. At least not for a while. The Yankee soldiers are the only men in town, and when you own a men's haberdashery, that makes a difference. Eliza refuses to be genial with the Yankees who come to the store; she treats them with the same disdain as do all the other shopkeepers who were treated poorly during the first days of the occupation. I do not think it is an act for the other townspeople. She is highly aware of what would happen if her liaisons were found out. We do not speak of it, she and I. Mama doesn't seem to know or care. And Grandmother doesn't want to know and asks no questions.

We are being pressed by the Union soldiers who are still here to declare our loyalty to the Union. Some townspeople have been ordered to sign oaths of allegiance. As if you can obtain allegiance by brute force. I told Eliza this was a very strange concept—the idea of forcing someone to be loyal to you. And she just said, in that way of hers when I say something she finds silly, that it's been happening in the South since the first slave ship docked.

I have had no word at all from Lt. Page.

Susannah

20 July 1862
Holly Oak, Fredericksburg, Virginia

My dear cousin,

Will and John were here again. I think perhaps I was not meant to see them. They came in the early morning hours. I had awakened before the sun and was making tea when I heard low voices in the parlor. I found them there with Eliza. She was fully dressed and so were they, although they were unshaven and dirt covered. And there I was in my dressing gown. They looked surprised and Eliza looked annoyed. She told me I may as well make them tea too. When I came back with a tray, I think they had discussed what they needed to and had made a point to be finished when I reentered the room.

After only a sip of tea, John asked to be able to shave and bathe, and he and Eliza left to see about hot water. Will sipped his tea slowly as he watched them leave. It stung a little, watching him watch Eliza.

"There has been no more ill treatment from the Union soldiers, has there, Susannah?" he asked me. "You seem troubled."

I shrugged. "It doesn't seem the time to be tranquil."

"But you haven't... There hasn't been any... No soldiers have harmed you?"

I blushed as I realized what he meant. "I have not been harmed." And he nodded, clearly relieved. And I hung onto that relief like a warm embrace for several seconds.

"And Eliza?"

As the embrace seemed to slump away, I told him that I did not think Eliza had been harmed in any way either.

"Do you hear from your lieutenant?" he asked.

I bristled a bit. "He is not mine. And I have not heard from him." I stood, ready to clear away the tea things, to go back to the simple quiet of a nameless dawn. He reached out and touched my arm.

"I know your grandmother wants you to marry this man," Will said. "But do not marry him to make her happy. Or to escape this house. I would not want to think of you shackled to a man you did not love."

The tenderness in his voice moved me to wordless silence, Eleanor. Oh, that I would've had the audacity to tell him the name of the man I do love. But I didn't have it. I don't have it. How could I tell him, knowing the way he looks after Eliza whenever she is near?

"I am fond of you, Susannah. I don't want to see you hurt. Promise me you will only marry for love?" he continued.

I promised him. They were gone by noon.

---

15 August 1862
Holly Oak, Fredericksburg, Virginia

Dearest Eleanor,

There are no more Negroes staying in the slaves' quarters, and the Yankee troops are continuing to thin. Eliza and I moved the hens and roosters out of the attic and put them in Tessie's old quarters, which was no small feat. I have the wounds to prove it.

It took us two days to clean out the attic. And it still smells like chicken manure.

The vegetable garden is a sight to behold. You would be proud of me. Grandmother has been washing out the preserve jars. We shall have vegetables this winter. And peaches. And chickens.

1 September 1862
Holly Oak, Fredericksburg, Virginia

My dear Eleanor!

The Yankees are gone! The last of them marched away two days ago. We have survived. The Yankees have moved on to other campaigns, and we have our city back. Confederate troops have arrived on the outskirts of Fredericksburg and some are now patrolling our streets. Some folks wonder where they have been all this time. Others are cheering them.

Eliza told us not to remove the gold and jewelry we buried in the cellar, however. She said the war is not over.

And I have heard from Lt. Page. He was most anxious to know that we were all well and unharmed from our long, troublesome summer. I wrote to him and told him we had lost little compared to some and that we were glad to see the Union soldiers make their exit. I didn't mention who our houseguests had been nor that our slaves' quarters had been a meeting point for contrabands.

He is hoping to come see me in October. I did not encourage or discourage his desire to visit. I made a promise and I must keep

*it. You cannot break a promise you have made to someone you
love.*

4 October 1862
Holly Oak, Fredericksburg, Virginia

Dear Eleanor,

*The canning is at last done, and the chickens have all been
transported to the farm for Abner to care for. He is now a foreman
to chickens and a handful of sheep. We kept just a couple of laying
hens here at the house for eggs in the morning. I am quite happy to
see the chickens gone.*

*I think the trains are running again. And there is mail. We
have received letters from Grandfather. He has not been well. There is
no mail going to the North, however, hence my pile of unsent letters
to you continues to grow. Some who left Fredericksburg this summer
have returned. But not the Lacys. The big house on the other side of
the river is dark.*

20 November 1862
Holly Oak, Fredericksburg, Virginia

Dearest Eleanor,

*A brittle wind is blowing today, and with it comes news to
chill us. The Union armies are again amassing across the river
on the Lacy house hilltop, more of them this time. But there are
Confederate troops here in town daily watching them. We have*

heard that there are scores of Southern militia settling in behind us on nearby Marye's Heights. The only thing standing between the two growing armies are the Rappahannock—and us. Not a pleasant thought.

Eliza has been out and about at night again, doing who knows what. I have begged her to please cease her forays into activities not meant for a woman to engage in. Especially with Confederate snipers patrolling the streets. But she will not listen.

And Tessie is back, Eleanor. She told us she is with child. She came to us sick, numb with cold, and broken in spirit. Mama was the one who found her slumped against the door of her old quarters, which we keep locked because of the chickens.

Mama brought her in, took her to Cook's room, and put her to bed. My mother hasn't shown any interest in anyone's affairs since Papa's death, not even mine. Her exuberant compassion for Tessie has surprised and flummoxed me. While she was preparing dinner for Tessie today, I asked her why Tessie had decided to come back. Mama said Tessie had been hurt in the worst way and had nowhere to go. Something beautiful and precious had been taken from her— the last thing which had been truly hers.

And then I understood what drove my mother to Tessie's bedside. Loss.

Lt. Page was not able to come see me in October, but I did receive another letter from him. He said with the activity around Fredericksburg, the quartermaster's office is supplying Virginian troops via other routes. He thought perhaps after Christmas he would be able to come see me. He wrote that he missed me, that the thought of Yankees again nearby was driving him mad. He said we should leave Holly Oak and come to Richmond and that he and his family would take us in. And he closed by writing that I was the first thing he thought of when he woke and the last thing he thought of when he fell asleep.

I wrote back that I missed his company as well and that Grand-mother would never leave Holly Oak. Neither was a lie.

We've had our first dusting of snow. It fell like tiny pieces of ice. It seems we are in for a long, brutal winter.

Susannah

---

9 December 1862
Holly Oak, Fredericksburg, Virginia

My dear Eleanor,

There are no conversations about the coming Christmas holiday. The only talk is of the amassed Union army on the other side of the Rappahannock. The troops have been there for weeks and have only now begun to move about. It was as if they had moved to the Lacy House and Stafford Heights to stay until spring and had no plans to do anything until then but scrape the hillside bare for their camp-fires and play cards.

Eliza is very quiet these days. I am sure she knows there is more to the troops' recent inactivity than the desire to play cards.

Lt. Page has written me and again begged us to come to Richmond for our safety. He told me we could marry straightaway at his parents' church and that my mother and grandmother and aunt could come with me and we could all live at their spacious home in Richmond. He doesn't like our being in Fredericksburg with two massive armies on either side of us.

I told my Grandmother that Lt. Page had asked us to come to Richmond to live with his family. I did not tell her he wanted to marry me the moment we arrived.

She told me for the third time that she will never leave Holly

Oak but that I should certainly consider it. I told her I could not leave my mother. Nor her. Not now. Not while our world is at war. This seemed to please her somewhat. And she let the matter drop. I wrote to Lt. Page that my grandmother and mother are not willing to leave Holly Oak and that I could not leave them.

Tessie has begun taking care of the cooking and cleaning, but Eliza told her she will never again sleep in the slaves' quarters and that she would be paid a fair wage for her services from now on. She also told her that she and her unborn child would always have a home at Holly Oak if they wanted it, but that she was free to leave if she wanted that instead. Grandmother was strangely absent from that conversation. Tessie thanked her, saying that she was grateful, but I think she is sad to have had to come back to us. I doubt she ever made it to North Carolina to find her parents.

There is no garden for me to keep or uniforms for us all to sew or silver to polish, since it is all buried, or even cooking to do now that Tessie is here—she is a better cook than Grandmother, Eliza, and me put together—so I spend my days wondering and waiting to see what will become of us.

14 December 1862
Holly Oak, Fredericksburg, Virginia

My dear Eleanor,

I am glad you shall never see this letter. No one should have to read words as miserable as these will be. I would ask you to brace yourself, Eleanor, if I knew you would be reading this.

Fredericksburg is decimated. Houses and stores lie in ruins, smoldering still, even as I write this. And among the shards of devastation are the ruins of men. Blood, like the Rappahannock after too much rain, runs everywhere—in every frozen field, on every gray street, in every parlor of every house still standing in Fredericksburg. Our downstairs has been transformed into a hospital for dying Northern men. It is too much for the mind to make sense of. Hospitals are places to get well. But our odd hospital is a place to bleed and groan and die.

How can I begin to record for you what has transpired here? We awoke three days ago to the warnings of gunfire and the sight of Union soldiers on the other side of the river lacing pontoon bridges together—bridges wide enough for many men to march across. On the banks, wagons and Union soldiers—as far as my eye could see—stood ready to cross. And if that weren't appalling enough, in the ethereal morning mist, two giant orbs floated above the bridge builders—like strange, silent ghosts—balloons that carried armed Yankee surveyors. Every so often a Union cannon would boom and we would see the blink of its fiery charge. From my mother's bedroom window I could see various bridge builders fall into the water as Confederate sharpshooters, crouched in the windows of nearby houses, picked them off. But others quickly took their places.

When we first awoke, Eliza was nowhere in the house. But she soon returned and told us, with great intensity, that we must leave at once, that all the rest of Fredericksburg was also fleeing. Fleeing to where, I wondered? Where would we go? When Grandmother said she'd rather die than let a Yankee desecrate Holly Oak, Eliza grudgingly instructed us to take blankets and candles to the cellar and as much food from the pantry as we could carry. Tessie moved at once to obey. Her urgency compelled me to set about Eliza's directions. But Grandmother chased after Eliza, demanding to be told what the Union soldiers were doing. As I raced up the stairs to gather my blankets, I heard Eliza exclaim, "For heaven's sake, Mother. Isn't it obvious what the Union soldiers are doing? They are building a bridge!"

Mama was reluctant to leave her room. When I told her she could take all of Papa's pictures and books with her to the cellar, she began to slowly gather her things. By late morning we had the cellar floor lined with jugs of water and blankets and candles. We came back into the house for a quick meal and soon learned our timing had been providential. Not long after the clock struck noon, the sporadic booming of guns became instead a piercing hailstorm of wrath. There are no words to describe the sound of it, Eleanor. It was as if God Himself were splitting the sky in two and raining down destruction on us. Only this was not of God. These were Union soldiers and their barrage of shells.

Holly Oak shuddered against the assault, and we ran to the cellar. My mother, thinking it was the end for us, was actually smiling as we hurried her down the stairs. She believed she would be in heaven with Papa in a matter of minutes. And as I heard something wicked and demanding slam into the wall next to us, I nearly believed I would see him too.

All afternoon we cowered in the cellar, the five of us, listening to the hostile roar and wondering if Holly Oak broke apart above us, would she entomb us or protect us? Would we die in her loving embrace or in the collapse of her furious ruin?

We huddled and prayed and waited for the nightmare to end. When at last there was quiet, we emerged from the cellar. Holly Oak still stood. We stepped outside onto our porch, and Grandmother nearly fell into my arms with the shock of what we saw. Columns of smoke, banners of dying flame, and shattered homes and buildings. Night had fallen. It was too dark to see the ruin in its entirety. My grandmother began to cry, something I had never heard her do. Mama, moved by her mother's tears of grief, took her inside. Tessie followed them.

As Eliza and I stood on our steps and looked to the plumes of smoke coming from the direction of Princess Anne Street and the haberdashery, I asked her if we could sleep in our beds that night. Was it over?

And she said it was only beginning.

We did sleep in our beds. I lay awake for a long time, and it was nearly dawn when I finally fell asleep. I was awakened mid-morning by Eliza and other sounds. I heard a far-off yelling. And voices in our entry. She was sitting on my bed next to me. She had shaken me awake.

"What is it? What's going on?" I said.

She hushed me. "Susannah. You must do exactly what I tell you. You must stay in your bed and pretend to be ill. Do you understand? Under no circumstances are you to get out of your bed. You are ill."

The voices downstairs were male.

"What is happening?" I asked. I started to get up, but she pushed me back onto my pillow. She placed a hot compress on my forehead. It burned.

"The Yankees have crossed the bridges. They are in Fredericksburg. They are here. And they are downstairs."

I heard footsteps on the stairs. The Yankees were outside my door. Grandmother was yelling at them. One of them yelled back at her. And then my door was thrust open.

I gasped and Eliza pinched my arm. She held the compress to my head with her other hand.

"Get out of my house!" Grandmother was yelling. I had no idea where Tessie and my mother were.

One of the soldiers took a step inside. He looked young, and he was not an officer. "What have we here?" he said.

"My niece is very ill. You risk contagion if you come any closer. I do not advise it." Eliza said in that calm voice she has. The soldier stared at me. My chest was heaving—in fear, not illness—but to him it must have appeared that I was deathly sick. He took a step back out.

"Keep this door closed then!" he barked, as though he were a pharaoh or a god. He turned to my grandmother. "We'd like break-fast. And tobacco. And some decent coffee."

"You'll not get a—," she began, but Eliza stood and interrupted her. "Come sit with Susannah, Mother. I will make these scoundrels breakfast." The soldiers laughed heartily and proceeded to tell Eliza they would also like hot baths and a shave. Grandmother looked as if she would spit daggers. Eliza gently guided her into the room to take her place at my bedside. Then she left with the soldiers, closing the door behind her.

"What has happened?" I whispered to my grandmother. "Where is my mother?"

Grandmother sprang off the bed and began to pace the floor, surely to cool her anger. "Your mother is sitting in the parlor with a cup of tea as if it's Easter Sunday. As if those damned Yankees haven't plundered what is left of the city. They are looting every store they haven't smashed to bits with their cannons, and they are dumping the contents of bureau drawers into the streets and tossing furniture out of windows. It is hell outside your window, Susannah."

I rose from my bed and parted my curtains. In the sallow glow of a December sun, I saw the smoldering ruins of my street— timbers, stone, and glass—and the incongruous addition of beds and broken pianos and chairs and tea carts, all strewn about with plumed hats, hoops, and parasols, as if there had been a concert for sick people in the street and a devil had come and scattered the musicians and spectators with a giant hammer. A couple of soldiers were laughing as they pretended to waltz, drunk and wearing hoop skirts and summer hats. A stray horse galloped past them, dodging debris. The stretch of destruction in the street had no end.

Before, the Yankees had wanted what we had; now it appeared they wanted to destroy what we had. Eleanor, I do not understand what these Yankees hoped to gain by such senseless destruction. I think I might have whispered, "Why?" at the window.

I turned back to my grandmother. She had stopped pacing. "Why does Eliza want you to stay in bed and pretend you are ill?"

I was about to say I didn't know, but then I looked at the warm whiteness of my feather bed and remembered what lay hidden inside it. My grandmother didn't know about the uniforms. And apparently Eliza did not want these Yankees to know about them either.

"She didn't tell me why," I said as I climbed back into bed and replaced the compress.

By late afternoon, Holly Oak was bursting with Yankees who were tired of sleeping in tents and eating camp stew. They wanted the warmth of our house and full bellies and every tin of tobacco my grandfather had. I stayed in my bed as Eliza had asked me to. Mama joined me in my room later and then Grandmother, and then finally at nightfall Eliza and Tessie joined us. Grandmother gave Eliza a grating look for bringing Tessie into my bedroom, but Eliza just said it was not safe for a woman of any color downstairs.

The house was quiet when we awoke. Eliza went downstairs first. She came back within minutes and told us the Yankees who had slept in Holly Oak were gone but we were to prepare ourselves for how they had occupied themselves during the night. We dressed and then made our way downstairs. The rooms smelled of wood smoke and tobacco and men. Evidences of where they had eaten and slept were everywhere, and they had burned nearly every chair and table in the fireplaces, obviously intoxicated with warmth after many nights sleeping in a tent. The larger tables were too big to burn, and the sofas and rugs were too convenient a place to sleep to have wanted to burn them. They had drunk all of Grandfather's whiskey and port and the remains of glasses and decanters lay in sticky pieces across the parlor floor. The pantry was strewn about with the remnants of their meals. Every jar that we hadn't brought down into the cellar with us was empty and broken. Every tin had been opened and scraped clean. On our back doorstep I found the heads of our two remaining chickens along with their feet and feathers. I found out later the soldiers had roasted them in the drawing room fireplace. And had relieved themselves wherever they pleased.

We took it all in in stunned silence. Tessie was the first to find a broom and begin to clean up.

I asked Eliza where the soldiers had gone. And then I heard gunfire and the booming of cannons, and I knew. They had gone to fight.

We checked on our immediate neighbors, but they had fled during the night. After we had cleaned the worst of the filth, we again retreated back to the cellar. The battle was being waged where the Confederate army had dug their trenches on Marye's Heights, a mile or so away from us. It was not safe for us to leave, and it was not safe to stay.

By midafternoon the wounded started pouring back into the city. And the dead were carried in. Eleanor, I have never seen the human body treated this way. Were I to describe it to you, you would think I was a demon. These men, no doubt the same who had reveled in our streets the night before, were now half-men, crawling and being carried through our streets, some without arms, some without legs, some, if you could believe it, without faces.

No one asked if they could bring the bleeding men into Holly Oak or any of the other houses still standing. They just began to bring them in. And the Yankee doctors did not ask us to help them with their horrific task; they just handed us a basin or towel or—God preserve me—a saw and told us to hold this or pull that or take this outside. And as we obeyed, we heard the soldiers talking, crying, pleading, cursing, and praying.

As the cold day gave way to an even colder night and the ghastly work continued, we learned that the Confederate army had held the Yankees. The Union soldiers had not been able to gain the Heights. Most of the dead and wounded—hundreds of them—still lay in the field, where one soldier said you could not take a step without walking atop a dead or wounded man. He said he was able to be spirited away but many others could not even raise an arm to signal a stretcher bearer because Confederate riflemen on the Heights would shoot it clean off. This same man grabbed me with the one arm he had left and asked if I had a Bible. He was pale with blood loss and had a hole in his torso where something round and black had careened into him and then sped out the other side. I said we did, and as I left to go find it, I heard Eliza ask the man what unit he was from. He said the Twentieth Maine, and she straightaway asked if he knew John Towsley and Will Black. I hurried back to the man's side. The soldier asked if they were the West Point cadets that joined up with them in October. And Eliza said yes, they were. She asked if John and Will were also out there on that field where he had been. And I sensed a rare thing in her voice. Dread. It matched the fear that had immediately sprung into my heart as well.

The man coughed and we waited. It seemed a very long time before he finally said no, they were not. But our joy lasted only a moment. He told us John and Will had been on a scouting mission in November and had been captured. They were in Richmond. In the Libby Prison.

Eliza raised her eyes to mine and implored me with her eyes to say nothing. She held my gaze for several long seconds as we each adjusted to this news. I would've thought the soldier might ask how we knew two Union soldiers. Maybe on a better day he might have asked. But he didn't. He just asked again for the Bible. And Eliza nodded to me to go get one.

When I came back to his side, the man asked me, in as polite a voice as I have ever heard, if I might please read to him the 145th psalm. And I did. And then he asked for the 34th psalm and then the 90th. When I had finished the 90th, I looked up to see which psalm he wanted next. The man's eyes were open and unmoving, and I realized at some point during my reading he had begun to see in another place. I closed his eyes and left him. I left it all. I climbed the stairs to my room and fell upon my bed, my blood-soaked dress staining my coverlet, and I did not care.

I wished to see what that dead solider in my parlor was seeing. Heaven. Heaven without war.

I cannot write any more.

Susannah

17 December 1862
Holly Oak, Fredericksburg, Virginia

Dear Eleanor,

The defeated Union army has left. They have retreated back over the river, leaving us with their dead. The ground is too hard and cold to bury them very deep. Tessie says there are two Union soldiers buried now in our cellar where the ground is not so cold. I cannot take even one step down there to see if she is right. But why would she lie?

And all the gold, silver, and jewelry we had buried there this spring? Did the Union gravediggers find it as they dug? Did they take it? Were they too tired of war and loss to care? Did they find some poetic justice in burying their fallen comrades atop Southern trinkets?

Tessie has brought up from the cellar the few jars of preserves that are left. The jugs of water and our blankets are gone. Union medics used them. The blankets that they didn't take with them are bloodied beyond use. Eliza has taken them outside to be burned.

Mama, who went wordlessly from wounded man to wounded man, offering the comfort of a kind face and feminine touch, has taken to her room now that the soldiers are gone and has not uttered a word in three days. Not even one of her eerie whispers. It is as if she has taken a trip but left without her body.

Eliza went out this afternoon and has not come back. It is long past nightfall.

———◦———

20 December 1862
Holly Oak, Fredericksburg, Virginia

Dear Eleanor,

We have received word that Grandfather has died of dysentery in a field hospital. Grandmother is still holding the message in her hand as I write this, hours after receiving it. She is sitting by a fire Tessie made using splintered wood from the house that used to stand across the street from us. I am glad our neighbors are not here to see what is left of their home. The more of their sad ruin we burn away, the less they will have to face when they return.

I don't know how to feel regarding my grandfather's passing. I sense an odd relief that he died of illness on a hospital cot instead of in pieces in the muddy snow somewhere. It doesn't seem right that I didn't miss him after he left. I reminded him too much of the Northern man who married his daughter, I think. Grandmother wants his body to be sent to us by train. No one can promise that it will be.

A message also arrived today from Lt. Page. He wrote that he is desperate to know if we are well and safe. I do not know how to reply to him. Are we well? Are we safe? We are breathing. We are awaking each morning. We are watching the sun set each evening. We are here.

21 December 1862
Holly Oak, Fredericksburg, Virginia

O my dearest Eleanor! Eliza has been arrested! I hardly know what to think. She came to my room this morning wearing traveling clothes and carrying a traveling case, the kind of case a man might carry. Her face was flushed, and she appeared to be out of breath. She had been gone when I awoke at dawn, and when I asked her where she had been, she ignored me. She asked me instead to remove the two uniforms hidden inside my bed and to do it quickly. When I asked her what she was going to do with them, she told me she had a plan to help John and Will escape prison, but she needed to leave right then and she needed the uniforms. She told me to hurry. I was afraid for her, but I turned over my bed anyway and exposed the seam. Eliza opened the case and drew out two dresses. Again she told me to hurry. I took my sewing scissors from my mending basket and cut the seam in my bed. I reached into the feathers and drew out the wrapped bundle. A flurry of feathers spilled out. Eliza grabbed the package from me.

"Help me place them inside the folds of the dresses. Don't let any of the gray wool show!" Her voice was urgent. My fear for her doubled. She told me that if Grandmother asks where she has gone, I am to say I do not know. If anyone comes to Holly Oak asking for her, I do not know where she is.

"Do you understand, Susannah?" she asked me. "John's and Will's safety depends on it."

I could only nod my head. Terror silenced me.

"Are you bringing them back here?" I whispered, knowing, of course, she could not. Fredericksburg was again under Confederate control. She could not bring John and Will back here.

"Sew up the seam at once," she said. "Turn your bed back over as soon as I leave." She took the dresses with the uniforms now inside their skirts and placed them carefully back inside her traveling case. She latched it shut and reached for the handle.

Then we heard the front door open and voices. The voices of men. Eliza froze. We both heard someone ask for her. She whirled to face me. "Cover the opening!" she whispered. My heart clanged inside my chest as I grabbed the coverlet for my bed and flung it across the open seam. A few stray feathers fluttered into the air like white butterflies. Again we heard her name, this time louder.

She handed me the case. "Put it under your bed. Let no one see it."

I took the case, bent down, and shoved it under my bed.

"Now take the chair by your window. Pick up a book. You are reading."

I wordlessly obeyed, tears of dread forming as I sat down and opened a volume of poetry. One of my father's favorite books. Eliza listened at the door. Then she ran to me wide eyed and knelt before me.

"I think they are coming for me, Susannah. You must listen to me. Will has taken ill. We must get him and John out of Libby Prison. Will is sure to die there if we don't. Take the noon train to Richmond. Today is the only day it will be available for civilians until after Christmas. Take the case with you. Go to the Libby Prison on the corner of Twentieth and Cary Street. Make your way to the southeast entrance. The southeast entrance, do you understand?"

"The southeast entrance," I whispered, as tears slipped down my face.

"Ask for Cpl. Stiles. Say his name."

"Cpl. Stiles," I gasped.

"Tell him Dr. Prewitt has sent the medicine that has been requested. Repeat it to me!"

"Dr. Prewitt has sent the medicine that has been requested." The words tasted like shards, Eleanor. I could nearly feel the blood on my tongue.

Then Eliza handed me a small leather pouch from the pocket of her cloak. I could feel the heavy weight of gold inside it. "When you see Cpl. Stiles, he will take the case from you, and you are to give him this. Do you understand?"

The men were on the landing.

"Hide it!" Eliza whispered. And I shoved the leather pouch under the cloth-draped side table next to me. There was a knock at the door, and then Tessie was telling us there were some officers here to see Miss Eliza.

"What do I do if I get caught?" I whispered.

Eliza stood and smoothed the hair at her temples. "Do not get caught. And Susannah, when they open the door, you must pretend to be surprised."

"Miss Eliza?" Tessie said from behind the door.

"Don't leave me!" I mouthed. And Eliza reached out and stroked my cheek and chin.

"Be who I already know you are," she said.

And the door flew open.

I gasped as three men in gray wool uniforms stepped into my room as though it were a common parlor.

"You can't just walk in there!" Tessie yelled, and one of them told her to mind her own affairs.

One of the officers, blond and tall and heavily mustached, walked over to Eliza. His accent was sugary slow and lyrical. "Miss Pembroke. If you would be so kind as to accompany me and my men to our field headquarters, we have some matters to discuss."

It took every ounce of my being to stand and ask them what, pray tell, was the meaning of such an intrusion. What matters did they wish to discuss?

The blond officer turned to me. "I believe your aunt knows exactly what matters we need to discuss." He turned back to Eliza. "Don't you, Miss Pembroke?"

Again I fought for courage and asked what they could possibly want from my aunt.

But the blond officer ignored me and asked Eliza if she would prefer he arrest her in front of her family. He pointed to the door.

She turned and without a word began to walk to it. I played my part.

"Eliza! Where are you going? What is happening?" I called out.

She turned to me, and I saw such peace and relief there; she was proud of me. She was proud of me. "Tell your grandmother not to worry about me, Susannah."

And then she was out the door. The men followed her. I ran down the stairs after them to the front door and watched them take her outside to a waiting wagon. She climbed into it. A frosty morning mist had turned the bare and splintered trees into silvery spikes and arrows. They glistened as the wagon rumbled away.

Tessie said nothing beside me. Not at first. Then she said she would accompany me to the train station. Surprised, I turned to face her. She knew. She knew everything.

"Please tell me they will not hang her," I said.

"I seriously doubt they will hang a woman, Miss Susannah."

"If she doesn't come home, find out where they take her." I said, sounding like Eliza, and Tessie told me she would.

Eleanor, I am leaving Holly Oak in an hour for Richmond and taking with me the two Confederate uniforms hidden inside Eliza's traveling case.

My traveling case.

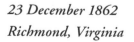

23 December 1862
Richmond, Virginia

Dear Eleanor,

I suppose I am a fool for writing down the events of the last two days, but unless I am also cursed, no one shall ever see this letter. I cannot express how glad I am that no one ever will. I may be a fool, but I am not without a sense of shame.

I write this from a beautiful room decorated in blue. A hot cup of tea is at my elbow, and the day promises to be warm—for

December. The maid who brought me breakfast told me it is a lovely day for a wedding.

Did you know, Eleanor, that one tiny broken thread in a seam can lead to the eventual ruin of the entire garment? One simple bubble of air can ruin a jar of peaches? One decision you make in the blink of an eye can alter your life forever?

I am not talking about the decision I made two days ago at Libby Prison. I am talking about the decision Mama made the summer I was sixteen. We were to come visit you in Maine. Remember? Papa had died only a few months before. And we were to come visit you. But Mama let her parents convince her not to come. And so we didn't. And I can't help thinking that if we had, Mama would have found a different way to spend her grief. I imagine that had we come, we would have stayed. Mama would have found comfort in being near all the things that Papa loved. The woods, the smell of fresh-cut lumber, the smell of the sea, the house where he grew up, the streams in which he had fished as a boy, the same starry skies where he had wondered what married love might be like. And if we had stayed, we would have been living in Maine when the war started and I would've seen Will on his visits home before duty called him South and I'd be writing letters to him instead of you and so he wouldn't have met Eliza and he wouldn't have been where he was when he got caught and sent to prison and I would never have had to get on that train to Richmond.

I know I cannot have changed the course of the war had we come to Maine, but I know that the course of my life within the war would have been different if we had.

What is done is done, and what will be will most surely be. I did take that train to Richmond. I didn't tell my mother, not that she would have heard me. And I didn't tell Grandmother. She would've heard me, but she would've ordered me not to go. From the station I took a hansom to Libby Prison, and I went to the southeast entrance, where I asked to see Cpl. Stiles. When asked what business I had with Cpl. Stiles, I said the medicine that Dr. Prewitt had requested had been sent.

But Cpl. Stiles did not come to the entrance as Eliza said he would. Instead, I was told to come inside to deliver the medicine to the infirmary. Perhaps I should've declined, Eleanor. Perhaps I should've left the case and made my exit. But I still had the gold. If Cpl. Stiles had been bribed to give those uniforms to Will and John, then I had to get that pouch to him or he would not do it. And who knew what would become of Will and John then? I had heard about the atrocities that took place inside Libby Prison. And I knew sick men at Libby soon died. I could easily guess what would become of them.

And so I went in. And I was taken down a long hallway with doors on either side and then told to wait on a bench while someone went to the infirmary's office to tell Cpl. Stiles I was there. The man who escorted me went inside the office, and as the door closed, I heard him tell someone else that I had a delivery from Dr. Prewitt. Then I heard the other person say, "Who the devil is Dr. Prewitt?" I sprang from that bench before I could even think what I was going to do next. I knew I had to find a way to get those uniforms to Will and John. I had to. I began to open doors as I made my way down the hall, fearful that the door by the bench would open and there would be a posse to take me away as Eliza had been. I didn't know at the time what was compelling me to open those doors. For all I knew, I was taking a greater risk than just sitting on the bench and waiting for the people behind the door to realize there was no Dr. Prewitt.

I saw tattered men in dirty beds, sick men. Broken men. Bandaged men. All chained to their beds. Union prisoners in Libby's attempt at an infirmary. I began to quietly call out Will's and John's names. I'd opened perhaps half a dozen doors when I heard a familiar voice.

Will.

I ran to the bed where the voice had come from. Will lay hot with fever, his face mottled with yellow bruising. He had been beaten, perhaps when he was caught. The bruises looked old. I sank to my knees at his bedside.

"Eliza," he whispered.

The pain was swift but I could not entertain it. "It's Susannah," I said, as soft as I could. I did not wish to awaken the other men sleeping in the cell. "I've brought you and John the uniforms. I am going to put them under your mattress, Will. Do you hear me? And the pouch of money. When Cpl. Stiles asks about it, give it to him. Do you understand?"

"Susannah?" His eyes now focused on me. He smiled. Then he grimaced. "Susannah! What are you doing here?"

"Did you hear what I said, Will?" I whispered. I opened the case and lifted out the dresses, then shook the uniforms out of them. "Roll over." I commanded. And Will obeyed me. I shoved the uniforms under him. "Now roll back."

Will groaned and rolled back to face me. "Run, Susannah. Before you get caught." His voice was weak, but his eyes were bright with fear for me. That wild concern made up for his confusing me with Eliza.

I showed him the leather pouch. "I am putting this inside your shirt. Cpl. Stiles will not help you and John escape without it. Do you understand?"

"Susannah..."

"Do you understand!"

He nodded. I slipped the pouch inside his shirt. His chest was hot to my touch.

"Where is John?" I asked. "Is he all right?" And again he nodded.

I knew I had to run then. But there was something I wanted to do first. I knew that Will might not remember that I had been the one to deliver the uniforms to him. Or perhaps he would remember but the memory would be foggy and indistinct because of his fever.

And that is why I kissed him, Eleanor. I didn't care that I might also become sick with whatever he had. I was afraid I might not ever have another chance. And, of course, I know now that I won't.

I leaned down and kissed him, on his lips. It was my first kiss. His mouth was soft and warm like bread from the oven. Sweet like bread too. I kissed him again. And I felt him kissing me, a slight turning of his head, his unchained arm now on my arm drawing me close. I knew I would remember that kiss always. Strangely, it was all that I had imagined it would be. It did not matter that he was a prisoner chained to a bed and burning with fever and that I was in danger of being caught and quite likely arrested. That one fragile moment when I kissed him seemed a moment outside itself. It would always be a tiny fleck of time outside the war, outside of me.

I heard voices outside the cell. I stood and stuffed the dresses back into the case and snapped it shut.

He reached out his hand to feebly push me away from him. "Run," he whispered.

As I approached the door, I turned to look at him one last time. "Go!" he gasped, and his eyes were bright with tears.

I opened the door and saw a pair of soldiers making their way to the door by the bench. Their backs were to me and they went inside.

I tiptoed out and began to walk away from the bench, the door, and the man I loved in the cell behind me. I was nearly to the end of the hall when a voice called out.

"Miss! You there with the case!"

I thought for a moment of running, but I knew I could not outrun a man, not in a dress, not in heeled shoes. And I knew that Eliza would not have run. Eliza would turn around calmly and think of something clever to say.

Eliza would not have run.

I prayed for strength and wisdom and slowly turned around. "Yes?" I said, sweetly as I could, my hands shaking.

"Are you the one looking for Cpl. Stiles?" He started walking toward me.

My mind raced for a response. "Corporal who?" I said.

"Were you asking for Cpl. Stiles? Did you tell the private at the south entrance that you had a delivery from a Dr. Prewitt?" He was now only feet from me. I could see the wariness that lay in his eyes.

And the way he said Dr. Prewitt's name, Eleanor, I knew I could not maintain that ruse any longer. There was no Dr. Prewitt. I had to think of a lie. Fast.

"I know of no Dr. Prewitt," I said, and then it came to me, the answer I could give which would keep Will and John safe and the uniforms I had just delivered from being discovered. "I think I am lost. I am looking for Lt. Page."

"For who?" The wariness receded only a notch.

"I am looking for Lt. Nathaniel Page. He works at the quarter-master's office." I said this as if I were a daft girl. Simple. Decidedly so.

"Miss, this is Libby Prison. Who told you this was the quarter-master's office?"

I bit my lip. "Well, I asked at the train station where all the important Confederate people were, and this is where they told me to come."

He still wasn't convinced. "What is your business with Lt. Page?"

I attempted an attitude of self-importance. "Why, I'm his fiancée!"

He blinked at me. "His fiancée."

"Yes, of course!"

"And your name is?"

I told him. Susannah Towsley.

The soldier stood there looking at me, looking at my case, waiting perhaps for my story to somehow collapse all around me. "Well, then. We must see to it that he knows you are here. I will send a messenger. Come, let's get you to a nicer place for you to wait for him. I am Lt. Carruthers." He took my arm, gently but firmly, and led me down the hall to a set of stairs.

He looked down at my case. "May I ask what you are carrying in that case?"

I swallowed hard, but he was ahead of me and did not see. "Why, my clothes, of course!" I said.

Now he looked at me. "You always carry your pretty clothes in a travel case like that?" He laughed but his tone was dubious.

I could almost feel Eliza feeding me an answer. "Those despicable Yankees ruined all our luggage. They ruined practically everything we own. I am from Fredericksburg, you know."

This seemed to satisfy him. At least at that moment. We came to another floor, and I was escorted into a waiting area. Lt. Carruthers offered me a chair and asked if I would like anything. To keep up my harmless reason for being in the wrong place, I told him a cup of tea would be lovely.

The cup was brought to me, and then Lt. Carruthers told me a message had been sent to the quartermaster's office to Lt. Page that a Miss Susannah Towsley had wandered into Libby Prison looking for him. He watched me for my reaction to the word wandered. It seemed that way to me. I told him I hadn't wandered; someone gave me bad directions.

"Of course. Let me know if you need anything," he said.

I had no plans to run, but he lingered as if I might. In less than fifteen minutes' time, the door to the waiting room opened and Lt. Page swept in, pink cheeked from the cold. He ran to me and took me into his embrace. I closed my eyes, but not before I saw Lt. Carruthers's eyes widen a bit in surprise.

"Susannah! I have been so worried for you. You are well? Everyone at Holly Oak is unharmed?"

I nodded. "Yes, I am so sorry we've not been able to get word to you."

He kissed my hand. "Did you come by train? If I had known you were coming, I would have met you at the station."

"I wanted to surprise you," I demurred.

Lt. Carruthers cleared his throat. "Apparently your fiancée was told at the train station that this was the quartermaster's office."

Lt. Page swiveled his head to look at the sergeant and then turned back to me. His eyes were glistening with surprised pleasure. "Fiancée?"

"Is she your fiancée?" the lieutenant asked.

His eyes implored me. And I nodded.

A smile broke wide across his face. "You have decided then? You will marry me?"

Eleanor, I have never seen such joy and happiness on a man's face as I saw at that moment. I think I began to love Nathaniel just a little then. I know I shall never love him as I should. But it is not like I do not love him at all.

"Yes," I said.

He kissed my hand again.

Lt. Carruthers took a step toward me. "I see congratulations are in order. And there should be no reason why then I could not have a look inside your case?"

Nathaniel frowned. "What for, Lieutenant?"

"Your fiancée came here saying she had medical supplies from a Dr. Prewitt. We know of no Dr. Prewitt."

Nathaniel turned to me, a crease of worry across his brow. "Susannah?"

I had been telling lies for nearly half an hour. It was not hard to come up with another one. I pouted. "I wanted to surprise you, Nathaniel. I didn't know I was in the wrong building. I made it up. I knew you worked with supplies. I thought I could surprise you at your office. Don't you work with supplies?"

Nathaniel smiled and kissed my hand again. "Aren't you a dear?"

"So if I were to have a look in your case...," Lt. Carruthers said.

"If I had known how much trouble this was going to be...," I said, and I set the case on the floor, unlatched it, and opened it fully. Eliza's two dresses lay in messy folds, their bows and lace and frills nearly cascading over the sides.

"Satisfied, Lieutenant?" Nathaniel asked, clearly perturbed. "If so, we shall be going. My bride-to-be and I have many plans to make."

The lieutenant nodded without a word, and Nathaniel bent down to close the case. "First thing we will do is get some better luggage for you, my dear." Nathan took the handle of the case in one hand and mine in the other.

"Good-bye, Lieutenant!" I said gaily, because I knew that's what I should do.

We left Libby Prison, where Will lay atop pilfered uniforms.

Nathaniel kissed me as soon as we were in his carriage. Light and sweet. But it was Will's kiss that still lingered on my lips, even after I met Nathaniel's kind parents and even as I sank into the guest bed at his parents' house.

Nathaniel wants to marry me at once, before he is called away to the field again. He asked if we might send a message to my mother and grandmother so that they could come on the next train and attend the ceremony. But I knew my mother couldn't travel and Grandmother was still mourning the loss of her own husband. And I really don't want anyone I know and love to witness what I am about to do. I told him I already have their blessing and that I didn't want to wait.

I will wear his mother's wedding gown today. We marry at five o'clock.

I kept my promise to Will. My decision to marry Nathaniel has kept my beloved Will alive and will secure his escape.

I will marry out of love.

Yours,

Susannah.

---

28 December 1862
Richmond, Virginia

Dearest Eleanor,

My wedding to Nathaniel took place in a lovely little church that was all decorated for Christmas. His parents were there, his married sister from Port Royal, his father's mother, some neighbors, and a few colleagues from the quartermaster's office. No one asked about my family other than to express condolences at the loss of my

brave grandfather and offer a remedy or two for my ailing mother,
whom they were told was too ill to travel. Nathaniel did ask if my
aunt Eliza might have come, and I told him she had gone away for
a few days before I left Fredericksburg and I didn't know where she
was. Not entirely a lie.

I will not embarrass you or myself by describing what it was
like to share a bed with a man whom you only love a little. I can tell
you that Nathaniel is a good man, a kind and gentle man, and that
he is the same refined soul in even his most intimate moments.

I do not deserve him.

There is something about the bond of the physical that I had
not known, could not have known. The oneness in flesh binds you
to the other person in almost the same way Tessie was bound to us.
But yet not the same. I don't know how to explain how I feel toward
Nathaniel after sharing his bed. It was not altogether unpleasant,
Eleanor. The intense and raw loyalty I now feel for Nathaniel has
surprised me. It is a strange, new devotion. But I know it is different,
less somehow than what I carry in my heart for Will. The love I have
for Will is purer than what I have now shared with Nathaniel. It is
above it. And always will be. And it shames me to admit it.

Nathaniel is attentive to my every desire, and I suppose I will
learn to love him the way he loves me. I will try very hard to return
that love.

Will's kiss returns to me at odd moments. When I am brushing
my hair, when I am putting on a stocking, when Nathaniel places
an arm over me in our bed in his sleep. Will's kiss will replay itself.
Part of me wants it to stop, and part of me wants to hold onto it
with every ounce of strength I have.

Nathaniel's parents are kind and thoughtful, but I can see they
are brimming with unasked questions about why I came to Rich-
mond the way I did. When I walk into a room, they assume a

different pose than they had before. Most of the time his parents are engaged in quiet conversation and they cease when they hear me approach. They trust Nathaniel's judgment, I can see that, and they are committed to accepting me because they love their son. But I do not think they trust my judgment. They surely think it is odd that I married Nathaniel with not a family member in attendance. They showered me with presents on Christmas nonetheless.

I wish I knew where Eliza spent her Christmas. I have written home to announce my news and inquire about Eliza, but it is too soon to expect a letter back from my grandmother. It has been less than week that I wrote to her.

I wonder if you have had a happy Christmas. I pretend that I did. In truth, it wasn't all pretend. The news on the street on Christmas Eve was that two Union soldiers escaped Libby Prison and no one knows how they accomplished it.

That is a gift to me.

Yours,

Susannah Towsley Page

7 January 1863
Richmond, Virginia

Dearest Eleanor,

The Richmond paper reports that a dozen people suspected of espionage and crimes against the Confederacy have arrived from Northern Virginia to be imprisoned. They have been sent to Castle Thunder to await their trials; two of them are female. I simply had to know if Eliza was among them. I showed the paper to Nathaniel and told him Eliza had been escorted from Holly Oak by Confederate officers the day I left for Richmond—for reasons unknown to me. I told him the officers threatened to arrest her if she didn't come with them willingly.

Nathaniel grew concerned at once, not just for me, but for all of us. He asked me if I had reason to believe Eliza might be aiding the enemy.

"The enemy," he called them.

I began to cry, and it was not an act to convince my husband of anything. The tears fell because my world is at war and there is an enemy and I do not even know really who it is. Nathaniel took my response as childlike fear for my aunt.

"If she has indeed made herself a traitor to the Confederacy, it is nothing you could have seen or prevented," he said, and this only made me cry the harder.

Nathaniel kissed my forehead and told me he would learn the names of the newly arrived prisoners to Castle Thunder.

Castle Thunder sounds like a place where knights and princesses might dance and dine, doesn't it, Eleanor?

It is a prison for traitors.

Susannah Towsley Page

---

10 January 1863
Richmond, Virginia

Eleanor,

Nathaniel secured the list of names. Eliza's name is there, as I had feared it would be. He went straight to his commandant's office and showed the colonel Eliza's name. He swore that his new wife—me—had no knowledge of her aunt's alleged activities.

Nathaniel said his commandant was pleased Nathaniel had been so forthright.

And when I asked Nathaniel if I might be permitted to visit my aunt, he told me not only was that terribly unsafe for me, his commandant would not allow it.

A letter from my grandmother arrived today. She congratulated me on my marriage. She wrote that my mother sends all her love.

Did you hear the news, Eleanor? President Lincoln has proclaimed all slaves are emancipated. You wouldn't know anything has changed here in Richmond. The Cause rumbles on as if he had merely welcomed the New Year with a toast to the weather.

Susannah Towsley Page

29 January 1863
Richmond, Virginia

Eleanor,

Nathaniel is to be sent afield to oversee the Confederate Army's supply wagons and sutlers across Northern Virginia. He came home with the news today at noon. He is distraught that we are to be parted, but he is hopeful that the war will end soon and that he will resign his commission, return to managing his deceased grandfather's bank with his father, and we shall build a house of our own.

He told me I will be warm and safe with his parents in Richmond while he is away, but Eleanor, I cannot live here while he is gone. Nathaniel's physical presence, his daily care for me, his intense admiration and loyalty and devotion, and yes, even his nearness in my bed—these are what sustain me in this new life I have chosen. When he leaves, I will have nothing.

I begged him to let me return to Fredericksburg to care for my grieving mother and grandmother. With Eliza gone, they have no one. It would be unkind and unchristian for me to ignore them when his absence would allow me to care for them in their grief. And he, of course, implored me to send for them, to have them come to Richmond. And again I reminded him that Holly Oak is their home and that my grandmother, especially now that she is in mourning, would never leave it. Then I told him that I couldn't bear to be there in Richmond without him, which indeed is quite true.

My pleading won him over, Eleanor. He is that disposed to grant me my every desire.

I leave tomorrow on the first morning train north. His parents do not seem overly sad that I am leaving.

Susannah Towsley Page

1 February 1863
Holly Oak, Fredericksburg, Virginia

I am home, Eleanor. Tessie, round with the growing bulge of her unborn child, met me at the station. I had forgotten how much Fredericksburg had suffered at the close of the year. The ruins of houses and buildings still line the streets. Fences are gone; trees are gone—fuel for Yankee fires. People are gone too, having fled before the battle and now having heard there is little reason to return.

Princess Anne Street is still littered with remnants of war and cruel revelry, and it saddened me only a little that I am only visiting this place. When the war is over, I will never call Fredericksburg home again. My home will be in Richmond with Nathaniel. It is a strangely acceptable notion.

On my arrival, Holly Oak looked plain and gray and lonely. I stepped inside and immediately noticed its sparseness. Tessie had cleaned away every hint of death and injury, but in its place was a melancholy emptiness. It was like the house was in a state of quiet bewilderment. My grandmother was waiting for me in the parlor, looking both forlorn and elegant in black taffeta.

"You didn't have to come," she said as she kissed me hello.

"I wanted to. Nathaniel will be gone for perhaps many months. I did not wish to be alone there in Richmond," I said.

And she said, "But you would not have been alone."

I told her Nathaniel's parents are very nice but I barely know them. I would've felt alone. For a second she said nothing, and then she asked Tessie if she might bring us some tea. Grandmother asked me to sit with her. When I had taken a chair, she asked me why I left for Richmond in such haste without saying good-bye, why I could not have told her I was taking the train to Richmond to marry Lt. Page.

I reminded her that in my letter I had said the horrors of the battle and what had happened inside our house had taken their toll on me. I had to escape.

"I know that is what you wrote, but that is not why you left. You left the same day Eliza was arrested. Did your leaving have something to do with that?" she said.

I don't know if it was this new knowledge that I belong to someone else or that I was only visiting Holly Oak now, but I suddenly had no great desire to keep up the pretense. "What does it really matter now, Grandmother?" I said. "You wished me to marry Lt. Page. I married him."

Tessie came in with the tea tray, but I stood. "I'd like to say hello to my mother before we have tea," I said.

And I left the parlor and climbed the stairs to my mother's

room. I found her seated at her writing table with a book open to the middle. As I approached her, she slowly raised her head. She looked afraid.

"Hello, Mama," I said gently.

"Susannah." She spoke my name not in greeting but more as if to remind herself that that name meant something to her. I kissed the top of her head and squeezed her shoulders. She stared at me.

"I am married now, Mama." I showed her my ring, and she stared at that.

"Remember Lt. Page, who first brought us the uniforms to sew?" I continued. "Remember he asked me to marry him?"

She nodded slowly.

"He's away at the war right now," I said. "So I've come to stay with you and grandmother for a while. I've missed you."

She looked back to her book, unable I suppose, to deal with having been missed. I looked at her book too and saw that the pages were upside down.

If I were going to send you this letter, Eleanor, I would tell you not to tell Grandmother Towsley or Aunt how poorly my mother is faring. She has all but disappeared. She has found a way to manage her losses—my father, her home, her father, her sense of peace and safety, the virtues of compassion and decency—missing now these many months. She has withdrawn from reality. I don't know exactly where she spends her days mentally. Her nights I would guess she spends dreaming of my papa and our house in Washington and maybe of me as a little girl who hasn't dashed off to be married.

I kissed her head again and told her I would bring up some tea. We drank it in silence.

I am suddenly very tired, Eleanor. I cannot hold the pen to write anymore.

Susannah Towsley Page

12 February 1863
Holly Oak, Fredericksburg, Virginia

I have been sick the last few days, Eleanor. Too ill to eat and lacking energy to write a word to you. Tessie came upstairs this morning with a warm drink to settle my stomach, and I told her I hoped I would be better soon so that she wouldn't have to run the house all by herself in her condition.

She smiled at me. Then she said, "You surely will get better, Miss Susannah. I'd say long about September."

It took me a full minute to realize what she was saying. She asked me when was the last time I had my monthly bleeding.

Eleanor, I am with child.

Susannah

15 March 1863
Holly Oak, Fredericksburg, Virginia

Dearest Eleanor,

I am finally feeling well enough to rise from my bed and not spend the morning retching into a basin. I asked Tessie if this is how her pregnancy began, and she said all pregnancies begin with the woman's body struggling to leave off meddling with the little one growing inside. But she wasn't nearly so sick as I.

And then I asked her what I have wondered since she returned to us in November. I asked her if the father of her baby will come to Holly Oak looking for her. She answered that the child she carries has no father. A heartless man did what he did, not a father. So, no, there would be no father coming to Holly Oak to look for her. Then she offered to take a few of my dresses down to the parlor to begin letting out the seams.

Grandmother seems pleased that I am to have a child but worried that we will not be able to properly outfit a nursery. Mama touched my stomach when I told her, a quiet recognition that she understood my words, but then she withdrew her hand and her mental presence and spent the rest of the day looking out her window.

A man from the quartermaster's office came a few days ago and asked us to again sew uniforms. He was short and portly and balding— nothing like Nathaniel at all. The cut pieces were delivered this afternoon. Tessie just stared at those sections of gray cloth, and I told her she didn't have to sew anything for the Confederate Army if she didn't want to, but she told me she will take my mother's place at the sewing table. Mama will perhaps be aware enough to sew on buttons, but I doubt she will have the understanding to do anything else.

Tessie knows President Lincoln says she's free. But Holly Oak is the only home she has right now, and every baby needs a home.

10 April 1863
Holly Oak, Fredericksburg, Virginia

My dear Eleanor,

A birthday parcel arrived from you today! Somehow it made it across the trenches of battle and found its way to me. Your note was so lovely, short as it was. I know you would have said more if we were not at war. I shall send you a note thanking you. It will not be this note. This I will add to the hatbox where I have stashed all the others since I learned what Eliza had been doing with them.

Thank you, dearest, for the lovely chemise. After the baby is born, I am sure it will fit me.

I am nineteen. More than three years have passed since my papa was taken from my mother and me, since I have seen you and Aunt and Uncle and Grandmother Towsley. My life is not what I had imagined it would be.

I wonder if you have heard from Will and John? Are they well? Are they safe? I wish you could have said more in your letter. You wrote that all is well. I am trusting you included Will and John in that declaration. Surely you did.

Nathaniel writes that he will be traveling near Fredericksburg in late April to supply the troops near Chancellorsville and will ask for three days' leave to come see me. He says he dreams of me every night. I have not written to him that we are to have a child. It seems something that should be told to someone face to face, not in a letter. He wrote that his father is sensing pressure to join the Cause and seek his commission. He will surely receive one. Alexander Page is a successful banker and respected in Richmond. No doubt he would be made an officer straightaway. He wrote that his mother will relocate to her parents' home in Savannah if his father is to be sent afield. Perhaps it was providential that I had been called away to Fredericksburg, he said.

Providential. Now there is a word that defies definition in these days of war. The Confederates pray for God's protection and blessing and favor. And the Yankees pray the same prayer.

Sometimes I sense within the walls of Holly Oak the bizarre state heaven must be in. Holly Oak is meant to be a refuge, as is heaven. A haven of rest and reward. A place where goodness dwells.

What does heaven do with these opposing prayers? It must drive the angelic hosts to their knees, if they have them. It drives me to mine in this house of woes.

We have heard nothing new regarding Eliza. She is still in Castle Thunder, awaiting her trial. At my urging, Grandmother attempted to visit her, but she was turned away. I don't think she will attempt another visit for a while. And I think she was relieved she was turned away. She is appalled by what Eliza has done.

Susannah Towsley Page

28 April 1863
Holly Oak, Fredericksburg, Virginia

Dearest Eleanor,

Tessie delivered a healthy baby boy on the twenty-sixth day of April. A midwife was summoned, and I assisted, despite my grand-mother's protestations. I wanted to see what childbirth will be like. It was both dreadful and wonderful to behold.

The baby is light skinned with fine, fuzzy hair the color of tea. Tessie had not mentioned the man who attacked her was white, but why would she? And in the end it does not matter if an embittered Southerner forced himself upon her or a vindictive Yankee or a Negro whose life of deprivation had robbed him of decency, does it? It does not matter. Any man can be kind like Nathaniel or endearing like Will or cruel like the man who hurt Tessie. Any man of any color can be any of those things.

She named him Samuel and asked me if she might give him the last name Holly. Tessie does not have a last name. I offered to give her mine if she would take it. But she would not, though she thanked me.

My mother was drawn from her bedroom by the baby's cries. She has scarce left his cradle. Tessie stayed abed only a day. The next morning she was up and about, seeing to the house and the garden, leaving Samuel in my mother's care. For the first time in many months, my mother is smiling again.

No word yet from Nathaniel. We hear there is much troop movement west of us.

---

5 May 1863
Holly Oak, Fredericksburg, Virginia

Dearest Eleanor,

There has been another battle on Marye's Heights. We woke to the echoes of gunfire two mornings ago. But this battle was not like the last one. Scores of wounded Union soldiers did not come crawling back to Holly Oak this time. Not from Marye's Heights. And not scores.

That same morning, before the sun had even begun to glisten off the Rappahannock, Tessie came to my bedside and awakened me.

"I need you to come downstairs to the cellar, Miss Susannah," she said. Her voice was strained. "We might need a sheet from your linens. And your shears from the parlor. And thread and a needle."

A thousand questions rushed to my tongue, but she dashed out of my room and was on the stairs as I rose from bed. I dressed quickly, grabbed a bed sheet from my cabinet, and headed downstairs to the parlor for my shears and sewing things. My heart was pounding in my chest, and the tiny child within me fluttered about.

Tessie stood by the cellar stairs just outside our back door with a jug in her hands, dusty and with web fragments clinging to it. A gray dawn rimmed the horizon.

I pointed to the jug in her hands. "What is that?"

"Spirits," she said, and she reached for the things I carried. "Hold the rail, Miss Susannah. You don't want to fall down them stairs. And it will be a good idea not to wake the neighbors with any yellin'."

I swallowed hard. "What is down there, Tessie?"

"Someone who needs our help."

Her tone didn't frighten me; instead, it compelled me. I grasped the railing and took the stairs as quickly as I could. Two lamps had been lit, and the dank cellar was awash in sallow light. I saw a man stretched out on the floor on a bed of hay and another man leaning over him. As I neared them and my eyes adjusted to the light, I could see the uniforms—blue. And then the kneeling man turned around.

Eleanor, it was Will. The man on the floor was John, bleeding from his side. I ran to them and dropped to my knees. I touched Will's face, gashed a bit and bloody, and then John's, wanting to embrace them, wanting to cry over them, wanting to erase their wounds and erase time too, I suppose.

"What has happened?" I said, my eyes again on John. I felt Tessie kneeling beside me with the things we had gathered.

"There was fighting in Chancellorsville." Will gently tore away John's shirt, revealing a gaping hole in John's side. "There's smallpox in our company from a bad vaccine we were fortunate to miss out on. We've been camping away and helping the First Division scout out weaknesses in the rebels' flanks. We were fired upon, and John was hit. They chased us and had us surrounded. We couldn't get back to the company, but we managed to lose them in the woods. I knew we were close to Fredericksburg, so we waited for nightfall and then rode here."

John moaned, and I reached for one of the lamps and pulled it closer to the wound. It looked big and dark and wicked. Eleanor, I've never seen anything that scared me as much. "He needs a doctor, Will!"

"No, I don't," John groaned. "I'll be fine."

"Get him sewed up, and I can get him to a Yankee doctor, I promise," Will said, and he motioned for Tessie to bring him the other lamp.

"I don't know how to sew up a person!" I exclaimed, my voice rising above a whisper for the first time. Tessie touched my shoulder.

"It's no different than sewing a uniform. Besides, you must have seen plenty doctoring last December when Holly Oak became a field hospital. You'll do fine." Will asked for the jug Tessie had in her hands. "Get me his cup out of his pack," he said.

Tessie reached into a pack by John's head and handed Will a tin cup. Will pulled the cork out of the jug and poured. A tangy and burning odor filled the room. "Help him drink this." Will handed the cup to Tessie, and I watched as she made John drink, though he coughed and sputtered.

I asked Tessie where she got the liquor, and she said there were four more jugs buried in the slaves' quarters.

Tessie made John drink another cup, and then Will told me to thread my needle. He poured a cup of spirits over the wound, on both sides, and John groaned. The musket ball had left John's body out his back. Tessie put her hand over his mouth.

I tried to thread the needle, but my hands shook. Will took it, threaded it, and handed it back to me.

I looked at the folds of flesh on John's side, the angry red spill of blood, the spirits dripping down his skin. "I can't do this!" I whispered.

Will touched my arm, the same way he'd touched it when he lay in the infirmary in Libby Prison. Gentle but insisting. "Yes, you can. I will hold the light. Tessie will hold the skin together. You can do this. We will help you."

His eyes in that pale light were tight on mine, and I knew, as I have always known, that there wasn't anything I would not do or attempt for Will.

I prayed to the God who has had to listen to all our selfish and desperate prayers, from both sides of this hellish war, and asked Him to help me. Tessie poured the spirits over our hands, over the needle and thread. And so I stitched your brother's skin as if it were gray wool.

When I was done, Tessie tore the sheet into bandages and wrapped John's torso. My hands were covered in blood. Will brought me a basin of water, and I washed them. I had been kneeling for too long. So when I stood, I faltered. Will sprang to his feet to assist me. And when he did, he saw two things that he hadn't seen when I first entered the cellar. I was keenly aware of him noticing both. First he saw the wedding band on my finger; then he saw the little round bump at my waist.

Eleanor, what I wouldn't give to have never seen the look on his face. I wouldn't call it betrayal, more like utter disbelief and disappointment.

I had disappointed him.

"You married him." He said it, he didn't ask it.

I just nodded as red heat blasted across my cheeks.

"When?" he asked, wondering, I am sure, if I was already married when I delivered the uniforms in Richmond. When I kissed him. Did he remember I had kissed him? Did he remember it was I who delivered them? I wasn't sure.

"Two days before Christmas," I said. I could not look at his face.

He was quiet for a moment. "Two days after you brought me the uniforms."

So he remembered. I nodded.

When he didn't say anything, I forced myself to look at him. The disbelief was gone. The disappointment had doubled and was now joined by something else. Shame, maybe?

"Did Eliza put you up to this?" he said, and the pain with which he said this stung me. He did not want to believe that Eliza, whom he clearly still had affection for, would ask such a heartless thing of me.

I could not bear to see that ache on his face, Eleanor. I could not bear it. I had to relieve him. "Eliza had already been arrested when I accepted Nathaniel's proposal," I said.

He stood inches from me as Tessie moved about—cleaning up and pretending she was hearing nothing of this—pondering my answer.

"But you promised—," he began.

"I broke no promise," I said quickly. "You asked me to marry only for love, and that's what I did."

"So you love him?" Will asked, daring me, it seemed, to prove it.

"I broke no promise." I found a bit of strength somewhere, Eleanor. I don't know where it came from. But when I said these four words a second time, I looked Will in the eye and my voice did not falter.

He took a step closer to me. "You kissed me," he said softly, brow furrowed as if he were still trying to make sense of my having pressed my lips to his while he lay in a sickbed at Libby Prison. "In the prison, you kissed me."

"Yes," I said.

He asked me why. And I told him because I wanted to.

Will looked at my hand and at my wedding band. He shook his head like he wished he could turn back time. Not for him, but for me. Not so he could undo something but so that I could. "What have you done, Susannah?" he finally said.

"What I had to do, same as you." And I turned from him,

pretending to be sure and brave, but I took the stairs as quickly as I could, knowing he wouldn't follow me. I could hear Samuel's morning cries as I dashed inside into the pantry and then onto the carpeted hallway and stairs, where my hurrying footfalls were graciously hushed.

My sleeping mother and grandmother did not hear me crawl back into bed in my bloodstained dress, nor did they hear my cries which I gave over, with all my heart, to the generosity of my pillow.

You are the only one who understands, Eleanor. The only one who knows.

I am glad Will brought John here, even though Tessie and I have taken a tremendous risk in hiding them. I think Tessie and I have helped John, perhaps saved his life. We will know more in the next few days as John regains his strength.

But I don't know if I am glad Will was the one to bring him to me. Will seems to regard me differently now, like I am not the same girl he chased with a lizard. And he misses that girl. But not like he misses Eliza. He has asked about her. His face grew most troubled when I told him she is imprisoned at Castle Thunder. He knows the place. Libby Prison was right down the street from it.

It is nearly midnight. Time to check on John.

Susannah

———

8 May 1863
Holly Oak, Fredericksburg, Virginia

Dearest Eleanor,

Will there never be an end to this upside-down world of war, dear cousin? Yesterday a woman came to the door, a neighbor who, *before she married, had been a good friend of Eliza's. She carried a few dresses in her arms, told me they were dresses she had worn three years ago when she was with child. She said she would be happy to loan them to me. As she put them into my arms, she leaned in close and whispered, "You must get those Yankees out of your cellar. There is someone in town who suspects you of hiding them."*

Then she gaily bade me good morning and was gone before I could assemble my thoughts. I could not imagine how anyone could know of Will and John's presence. Even Grandmother did not know. I tossed the dresses onto the couch in the drawing room and began to search the downstairs for Tessie.

But I could not find her. I searched Cook's room; I went to her old quarters; I searched the garden and the orchard, but she was nowhere. I went back inside the house and upstairs to search the bedrooms, calling her name. I found Mama in her bedroom with Samuel in her arms, rocking and singing him to sleep. She pressed a finger to her mouth to hush me.

"Where is Tessie?" I asked, feigning a casual tone.

"She had errands to run. Hush now, or you will wake the baby."

She went back to her lullaby, my presence for the most part forgotten. I left my mother and began to pace the landing, contemplating the wisdom of a daytime escape. It seemed ludicrous. But what could we do? How long could I wait? Should I wait for Tessie to return? Grandmother was at the haberdashery. With my mother rocking Samuel behind a closed door, I might possibly be able to get them to the river without being seen. But what then?

As I pondered these questions, the front door chime rang and I froze. Was it the neighbor again? Was it the person she said suspected us of hiding Yankees? I couldn't move. The door chimed again. I slowly descended the stairs. I steeled myself against my fear and fought to consider what Eliza would do. Eliza would be calm,

*Eliza would not shudder or shake. Eliza would display convincing
resentment at such a ridiculous notion as us harboring Yankees.*

*I crossed the foyer as the chime rang a third time and opened
the door slowly.*

*My fears melted in an instant. There on the other side of the
door was Nathaniel. I fell into his arms in sweet relief he clearly
misunderstood. He wrapped his arms around me and at once noticed
the hard bulge at my abdomen.*

*He pulled back and studied me as if needing to see with his own
eyes the mound that was his unborn child. He broke into a wide
smile, tears glistening at the corners of his eyes. He pulled me into
his arms again, this time off my feet. "Susannah! Why didn't you
tell me?"*

*"I didn't want to tell you in a letter. I wanted to tell you myself,"
I said, scanning the street behind him to see if there was anyone else
lining up to ring the door chime at Holly Oak. No one else was in
sight.*

*"Are you well? Are you getting rest? Do you need anything?" He
rushed his questions at me as I led him into the house. For the next
hour, while I waited for Tessie to return, I spoke to my husband as
if the day were an ordinary one, aside from his wonderful arrival.
Mama came downstairs to greet Nathaniel with Samuel asleep in
her arms. Grandmother arrived home for the noon hour, and I was
happy to see she had put on a dress of cobalt blue that morning, the
first dress she had put on in months that wasn't black. She was, of
course, distressed that Tessie was running errands when we had a
guest.*

*We sat in the drawing room while Nathaniel told us of the battles
he had weathered and how Virginia was faring and where his parents
were. As soon as I heard Tessie use the back door I jumped up and
announced that I would have Tessie bring the tea in.*

But I was gone too long, Eleanor. I should've known it would only take a moment to ask Tessie to bring in a tea tray. When I didn't return at once to the drawing room, my husband came looking for me. And I didn't hear him coming. Tessie didn't either. We were immersed in a hushed conversation about how to get Will and John safely out of the cellar when I suddenly heard Nathaniel's voice behind me.

"Who are you hiding in your cellar?" he asked, and it was plain by the distressed sound of his voice that he had heard quite a bit. He knew we were hiding two Yankee soldiers. He wanted to know who they were, because he couldn't for even a moment fathom that the woman he loved could possibly be a traitor. He had to know the reason.

It would've done no good to lie, Eleanor. He had already heard far too much. And I had wounded him as surely as if I had stabbed him in the chest. I could see that in his eyes. I had kept something from him. Something huge. Something dangerous.

I rushed to him. "Nathaniel, listen to me. It is true I am hiding two men in my cellar. But they are not Yankees to me. Not to me! One is my cousin. The son of my father's brother. He is family! My family is your family, dearest! And the other is the good friend who risked much to bring my cousin here after he was wounded at Chancellorsvillle."

Nathaniel stared at me, absorbing what I was telling him without a word. I went on.

"They became separated from their unit! And my cousin was shot. He needed help and they came here. I could not turn them away! I stitched my cousin's wound, and I have been caring for him. They will leave as soon as my cousin can travel. They will leave tonight, I promise you!"

Nathaniel still had not said anything. I pleaded again with

him. "Please, Nathaniel! Say nothing! They will leave tonight. I will make sure of it."

"I will make sure of it," he finally said, very quietly. And I felt my heart sink to my toes.

"Nathaniel, please..."

Then he took my hands and kissed them. "I will make sure of it. I will make sure they escape safely. I promise you they will make their getaway tonight, as soon as the sun sets. You are not to give it another thought."

His voice was so sincere, Eleanor. So kind. I almost could not believe it. He turned to Tessie.

"Better bring in a tea tray, Tessie. Susannah's grandmother and mother will be expecting it," he said.

Tessie nodded, wide eyed, and began to bustle about the pantry.

Nathaniel still held my shaking hands in his. "How long have you been hiding your cousin and his friend?"

"Only a few days," I whispered. "But Nathaniel! A neighbor came by just before you arrived today and said someone in town suspects they are here. And Tessie and I have told no one! Not even my mother and grandmother!"

He placed a finger gently on my lips. "Do not worry. I will take care of everything. They will be borne safely across to the Union lines tonight."

Eleanor, could you even bear to read a word from my wicked hand? I do not deserve a man like Nathaniel. I never will. I threw myself into his arms and thanked him, over and over. He stroked my hair and back and told me to think no more of it, to compose myself so that he and I could make our way back to the drawing room. He assured me that when I woke tomorrow my only concern would be what color to have the nursery painted.

He was as good as his word. When Will and John emerged from the cellar at nightfall, I hugged John good-bye, careful of his stitches. I could only give Will a polite peck on the cheek, as if he were nothing more than a compassionate soul who took pity on a wounded family member. I wanted to kiss him the way I had at the prison infirmary, wretch that I am. And God in his mercy—or perhaps in his punishment—saw to it that I could not, as Nathaniel stood right beside me.

As I stood watching Nathaniel shake Will's hand, gentleman to gentleman, it became clear as glass to me, Eleanor. Will is fond of me as I am fond of Nathaniel. But he loves Eliza as I love him. As I have always loved him.

As Nathaniel helped John mount his horse, Will smiled at me, an approving smile, a remorseful smile. He was wordlessly telling me he had been wrong to assume I had married for less than admirable reasons. What could I do but smile back? Will shall no doubt come to the conclusion that, aside from being a rebel Confederate, Nathaniel Page is a decent fellow. The girl Will is fond of shall be happy with this man. As he mounted his own horse, this smile still on his lips, tears sprang to my eyes for so many lost reasons. Nathaniel stepped back to my side and at once put his strong arm around me, kissed my cheek. Then he got onto his horse and told me not to wait up.

Tessie handed Will and John the provisions she had packed, and then they headed for the woods, the three of them—my cousin, my husband, and the man I must stop loving. When I could no longer see the backs of their horses in the mangled woods, I listened for the pat-a-pat sound among the trees of their quiet departure.

I fear I shall never see Will again, Eleanor.

Morning.

Nathaniel returned in the middle of the night. I tried to stay awake and could not. He told me he found me curled up on the couch in my room with a candle still burning, an open book on my lap, and a cold cup of tea on the table next to me. He carried me into my bed—our bed—and when I awoke this morning, the warming rays of the sun were stretched across us; I had forgotten to draw the curtains closed. The day outside my window seemed triumphal, even in its infancy, though my bedroom was still swathed in shadow. I laid my head upon Nathaniel's chest, and his arm was around me in an instant.

"I don't deserve you," I whispered, before even considering how that must've sounded.

But he just grinned and rubbed my shoulder. "You don't have any other cousins in the Union Army, do you?" he said.

"No." I looked up at his head on my pillow. "Are they safe?"

"As safe as a soldier can be when he is at war, my love. I am quite sure they are now across Union lines."

I reached out my hand and touched his cheek. "Thank you," I murmured. And a tear slipped out of my eye and landed on his nightshirt.

He kissed the top of my head. "They are good men. They didn't seem like Yankees to me either, my sweet. Not last night. But today, my darling, you must know, that is who they are."

And I nodded. I know who Will is. He is the man on the other side. Will is the man I must let go.

———≫————

15 May 1863
Holly Oak, Fredericksburg, Virginia

My dearest Eleanor,

Nathaniel did not stay here three days as he had hoped. The battle at Chancellorsville had been fierce and claimed the *life of Gen. Jackson. Nathaniel was called away after only one day.*

We had visitors to the house the hour before he left, however. Two officials from the mayor's office came to Holly Oak announcing they had received an anonymous message that we were hiding Yankee soldiers. Both of these men had been arrested and jailed during the occupation last year. They asked to see Grandmother, who of course showed all the necessary indignation at such an accusation.

Nathaniel and I heard her raised voice from upstairs, where Nathaniel was packing his things. We went at once into the parlor, where Tessie had shown the men. As we took the stairs, I quietly asked Nathaniel what we should do, and he said I was to entrust the matter to him. He patted my arm.

Nathaniel was resplendent in a clean uniform when we entered the room, and the men rose, uncertainly, it seemed, to meet him. He asked them what their business was at Holly Oak. They again said they had come on information of the most grievous nature. Someone had told them we were hiding Union soldiers in our house.

In a calm and authoritative tone, Nathaniel told them they had received faulty information. He assured them as an officer in the Confederate Army that there were no Yankees in the house.

One of them begged Nathaniel's pardon and said that perhaps Nathaniel did not know that Eliza Pembroke of Holly Oak had been arrested last fall for conspiring with Yankees and now sat behind a locked door at Castle Thunder.

"What has that to do with your unfounded accusations?" Nathaniel said politely.

The men both looked at me, and the same one said, "These Yankees were seen before you arrived, Lt. Page. And your wife, we know, is very fond of her aunt."

I felt the blood drain from my face. "What...are you suggesting?" I stammered. I sounded appalled, which, lucky for me, is very much like sounding terrified.

Nathaniel did not give them time to answer. "You will respect my wife in her home and in my presence," he said evenly.

"We mean no disrespect, sir, but—"

Again Nathaniel cut him off. "I find it highly disrespectful that you do not take my wife at her word—or mine. I swear to you before God there are no Yankees in this house."

They stood there a moment longer, running their fingers along the brims of their hats. Finally, the one who had been doing all the talking bowed to me. "I beg your pardon, Mrs. Page."

I said nothing. I tipped my chin in silence.

They bade my grandmother and Nathaniel good-bye. Grandmother rewarded them with stony silence. Nathaniel maintained his polite but firm tone and asked Tessie to kindly show them out.

When the front door closed behind them, Grandmother rose from the chair she'd been sitting in, smoothed her skirt, and then began to walk regally out of the room.

"I do not wish to know anything about this, Susannah," she said. But her back was to me, indicating she wanted no response from me, not even confirmation that I had heard her.

I looked to Nathaniel, and he just patted my arm and nodded once. It was over. This situation with Will and John was over.

Nathaniel left within the hour. I asked if he could tell me where he was headed, and he said all eyes are on Pennsylvania, including the regiment Will and John are hoping to reconnect with. Nathaniel told me his supply wagons were numerous. Gen. Lee was amassing a huge army to march north into Union territory.

He kissed me good-bye and then placed his hand over my abdomen. "If it is a boy, would you consider naming him Albert?"

he asked. "That was my grandfather's name. He was a great man. You would've liked him, Susannah."

I had not given any thought to the notion that I would deliver this child at Holly Oak alone, without Nathaniel pacing an adjoining room. "Of course," I whispered, though I could hardly imagine the moment of the child being real and outside of me and needing a name.

He took me in his arms for one last embrace. "I love you, Susannah," he said.

It took only a moment for me to say, "And I, you."

There are many shapes to love, Eleanor.

I watched him ride away, alone this time and into the streets of Fredericksburg, not the woods behind the house. It was a different sound this time.

As soon as he was gone, I stepped back into the house. Holly Oak seemed tomblike again as it had when I first returned. An air of foreboding seemed to seep through its walls. Like it knew something that we did not yet know.

---

15 June 1863
Holly Oak, Fredericksburg, Virginia

Dear Eleanor,

The summer heat is ovenlike, pressing in on us like a punishing hand. I spend as much time as I can out of doors among the remaining peach trees that the Union Army did not cut down for firewood last winter; it is unbearable inside the house. Mama and Samuel often sit with me under the shady boughs.

Tessie's garden enjoys the jungle warmth and is green with

happy, living things. We are all of us looking forward to eating
something besides fish from the river and cornmeal cakes. The only
good thing about the heat is it strips us of appetite most of the time.

There is no wind, Eleanor. The air is still and wet and heavy.
Like a hammer ready to fall.

Susannah

5 July 1863
Holly Oak, Fredericksburg, Virginia

Dearest Eleanor,

There has been a terrible battle in a place in Pennsylvania
called Gettysburg. We have been told there have been thousands of
Confederate casualties. Thousands. We've had no word from Nathaniel and certainly nothing from Will or John. All we can do is wait
for the list of names to be posted.

And still the unrelenting heat rails on.

I long for a blinding white blizzard to sweep us all under its icy
coat, to cover our horrors, bury our cannons and trenches and, yes,
even our dead. I want it to freeze us into statues that cannot pull
triggers or thrust bayonets or even walk to the post office to see who
has died and who has not.

I am almost out of paper and ink, Eleanor, none of which are
available anymore. That is why I am writing as small a script as
I can, pressing my letters together to the point of bare legibility.

Perhaps it is well that I shall soon be unable to pacify myself
with writing sentences you will never see and I, no doubt, should
not be writing.

Susannah

23 September 1863
Holly Oak, Fredericksburg, Virginia

Dearest Eleanor,

This shall be my last letter to you. I have no more paper beyond these last two pages, and there is no more ink in Fredericksburg.

It is fitting that when this letter is complete, I shall bind all these letters together and hide them away somewhere inside Holly Oak, perhaps forever. You will never know I wrote them, and perhaps one day I will forget that I did.

Nathaniel was one of the thousands of men catastrophically wounded at Gettysburg. The sharpshooter's bullet that sliced through his neck did not kill him, but he lost a terrible amount of blood. He was expected to die.

Perhaps it would have been a kindness if he had. But I do not deserve such kindness, and he is not aware that he does.

Nathaniel returned to me from a field hospital on the nineteenth of July, whole but broken. He can barely speak or walk, and he does not quite remember me. He doesn't remember that he loves me.

This, Eleanor, is my recompense for marrying a man I did not love and loving a man I did not marry. Nathaniel's devotion to me, his ardent affection, and even his physical presence was what I fed upon since I was denied what I truly desired. And now I am a stranger to him.

He sits in a chair all day long, unable to read a book or strike a match or even run his hands through my hair. When he first came home, it took Tessie and my mother both to get him out of bed in the morning. Tessie would not allow me to help. She was afraid the baby might come early.

Tessie told me it would be up to us to teach Nathaniel how to walk and talk again. How to live again. This thought terrified me to my core, that I was now burdened with restoring to Nathaniel all that the war had stolen from him. I told her it was too much, I could not do it. And she said, "You owe him at least that much."

Tessie has always known more than we gave her recognition for.

And she is right, of course. I owe Nathaniel that much. He would do as much for me and not have thought twice about it. This is how I will learn to love him, Eleanor. It shall do no good to ask who will teach me how to live again. My mother is proof enough that sometimes you either teach yourself to live again or you sentence yourself to slowly disappear.

Eliza came home on the tenth of August, released along with four hundred other wayward Southerners and Confederates. She only stayed a week, though I begged her not to leave. Even Grandmother cried when she told us she was leaving for Ohio; she had made friends with Southern abolitionists while in Castle Thunder, and that's where they were headed. She told us it would be unbearable for us if she stayed, far more so than if she left. There are probably only five hundred people left in Fredericksburg, but they all despise her. Eliza wasn't found guilty, but apparently eight months in prison as a suspected traitor and Union sympathizer is the same as a conviction.

Nathaniel mumbled good-bye to her, though I do not think he remembers her. She had procured a pass to travel; how she got it, I do not know. She asked Tessie to accompany her to the train station. The rest of us were to remain at home. She told us when the war is over she will write. She did not say when the war is over she will return.

And she did not say she had any plans to travel to Maine when the war is over. I wonder, Eleanor, if Eliza knows of my feelings for

Will, these feelings that I am slowly learning to pound out of myself. She said she didn't read my letters to you, but I know she had to have seen the words. She wrote her secret messages above my words. How could she not have seen them? And so I wonder if perhaps she does not entertain the thought of responding to Will's advances because of me. I think she knows what I sacrificed to secure Will and John's escape from Libby Prison. And if she allowed herself to fall in love with Will and to marry him—think of it, Eleanor! He would be my uncle! Always a part of my family, my world, my heart, and in the most awkward and torturous of ways. Out of her love for me, she will not do this.

You see? Love has many shapes.

And dearest cousin, the baby did come early after all, by three weeks. On September 6, I delivered a small but healthy baby girl. I named her Annabel Grace. And do you know what, Eleanor? Nathaniel, who struggles to say her name, loves to hold her. He loves it. I do not know if he understands she is his daughter, but I am optimistic that someday he will.

Nathaniel does not know his father was mortally wounded at Gettysburg. I have written to his mother in Savannah and offered my condolences. I told her Nathaniel's recovery will be long and that perhaps when the war is over, he and I and Annabel will take a train to visit her. But I can't envision that day yet. I can only see the day that I am living at the moment. And I do not see myself ever leaving Holly Oak for good.

This page is filling with the last of the ink, sweet cousin. You have been the dearest of companions these last three years. Someday I hope to share with you how you saw me through my darkest moments. And how writing to you has given me hope for the days ahead, which are still clouded in mist.

I am indeed living out the harvest of my choices here at Holly Oak. But I think it will be the very thing that will save me in the end. This is why God did not take Nathaniel on the battlefield when He so easily could have. He brought Nathaniel, an empty vessel, back to Holly Oak, where I, too, have become an empty vessel.

This place shall be my redemption. And what redeems us, saves us, does it not?

Yours always, my dear cousin,
Susannah Page

Part Five

HOLLY OAK

delaide awoke with a start and a scorching pain in her arm. The morning sun was brilliant through her half-closed curtains.

She had overslept.

She rose slowly out of bed, swung her legs to the side, and waited as the room settled. The pain medication that helped her sleep at night made her feel like a daft idiot in the morning. And thirsty as a refugee in the desert. She needed water, with ice.

Adelaide fumbled one-handed with a pair of elastic-waist pants and a pullover top and made her way barefooted down the stairs, holding carefully to the rail with her right hand. "Leave me alone, Susannah," she whispered, only half in jest as she rounded the landing and continued down. "I need a glass of water, for pity's sake."

There was no sound in the house. She stood in the entryway and listened, but she could not detect any signs of human life. She poked her head in the drawing room. The long table was still there. The boxes of uniforms sat ready to be mailed on Monday morning. But the room was empty. She shuffled to the kitchen and filled a glass of water, drinking it down in one long swallow. She set the cup in the sink and poked her head in Marielle's little office. Empty as well.

Marielle and Caroline must already be working on the studio, she thought, and she grabbed a sweater off a hook by the kitchen door, slipped on her garden clogs, and stepped outside. A blast of warm air met her, so she tossed the sweater back onto a kitchen chair. The day was already on its way to becoming blistering. As she walked across the patio, she wondered if Carson was truly ready for the studio to be emptied of the last of its treasures. He said he was, but she had watched him prepare to leave for his weekend trip to Houston. She had watched him linger over saying good-bye to Marielle, his head turned toward the garden and what lay at the edge of it. It was as if he were saying good-bye to other things than just Marielle. It was probably best. There was nothing beautiful left in the studio. All the pretty things were long gone.

The knoll down to the studio beckoned, but her aching body was protesting. She would probably need a cane to get down the hill. She had one in the hall closet, and she frowned at the thought of going back inside to get it.

Then Caroline appeared at the entrance to the studio. Her daughter looked up from the trash cans that were stationed at the studio entrance like bodyguards.

"Mother, what is it?" she called up to her.

"I just got a little lonely inside. Too quiet."

"Stay there. I'll come for you."

A moment later Caroline was helping her negotiate the slope of the grass. At the entrance to the studio, Adelaide peeked inside the trash cans.

"None of it is worth saving, Mother. You'll have to trust me," Caroline said.

Adelaide turned to look inside the studio. Already it looked foreign to her. The shelves and tables were empty. "Where's Marielle?"

"She graciously allowed me the opportunity to do this alone."

"I wish you could've seen the studio when Sara worked in it," Adelaide said thoughtfully. "It was so colorful inside. So full of...beauty. It's such a shame what time has done to it."

"I did see it once."

Adelaide turned to her. "Oh yes. I guess you did. Before Brette was born. You were on your way to... Where was it?"

Caroline wiped at a cobweb on her collar. "Doesn't matter now."

"Somewhere in Canada, wasn't it?"

Caroline shrugged. "I don't know. Maybe. I don't remember."

A torn canvas poked out of a trash can, and Adelaide stroked its rough edge. Half of a giraffe had been drawn on it. Sara hadn't added any spots yet. It looked like an alien creature. "I wish things had turned out differently. It doesn't seem right that you never got to know her. I wish..."

"'If wishes were horses, beggars—'"

"'—would ride,' yes. You remember me saying that?"

Caroline smiled. "You said it a lot."

"You had a lot of wishes."

"I suppose I did."

Adelaide turned again to the studio, to the last fragments of Sara's strange creativity. A pull at her heart made her grasp at her shirt. "I tried to do right by her, honestly, I did. When she was little, she would ask about you, you know. Often. She would ask about her father too. She wanted to know who he was and where he was. I had to make up stories. I didn't know how to tell her the truth."

"She figured it out, Mother. When I came to visit the summer she turned twelve. She had figured it out. She knew I didn't know who her father was, and she knew I wasn't well. The stories made you feel better, and that was important to her. So she let you keep telling them."

Adelaide turned back around and leaned against the exterior wall, closing her eyes to the image of Sara pretending she believed the excuses Adelaide made up and remembering how she wished she could also believe them. "We were always trying to make restitution for each other, weren't we?" she said a moment later.

Caroline picked up a broken piece of pottery and chucked it into the trash can. "Most of the time it's best to clean up your own messes. Who are you really helping when you try to fix something you didn't break?"

Adelaide looked at her daughter, unsure what Caroline was intimating. It sounded like an accusation of some kind. Against her. "What are you saying, Caroline?"

"I think you know."

An old wound slowly reopened, and Adelaide tasted anger on her tongue. How could Caroline even hint that she had butted into Caroline's messes, unwanted? "You brought your infant daughter to me and asked me to raise her and love her and care for her. To fix your mistake. And that's exactly what I did. It wasn't like you gave me much of a choice! And now you lecture me on cleaning up your own messes?"

"I wasn't lecturing. Just stating the obvious. I should've cleaned up my own messes. I missed out on everything. I missed out on loving my daughter, and I'm going to have to live with that. Me. Just me. You don't have to carry that weight. No one does but me."

Adelaide raised her good arm and pointed a finger at Caroline. "You're wrong. I have always had to shoulder your burdens. Always!"

"Yes, I know you did, but you chose to. You've chosen to bear the weight of everything and everyone who has ever lived here."

Anger rippled through Adelaide, so intense it made her cough. "That's what mothers do! But how would you know anything about that?" The words flew out her mouth like an arrow; they stung her lips and she clasped a hand to her mouth. For several moments there was silence between them. Adelaide waited for Caroline to spin on her heel and storm back into the house to gather her things and leave. She was already picturing the last of her years stretching into the mist with no word from Caroline ever again when her daughter spoke.

"You're right," Caroline said. "I don't know much about being someone's mother. But I'm not talking about holding on to your children's burdens; I'm talking about letting go of things that do not belong to you."

Her daughter's calm voice frightened her. Caroline stood with dusty hands and smudges on her face and webs clinging to the silvery brown braid down her back as if they were at a garden party making small talk.

"What is it you want to say, Caroline?"

Caroline looked up toward the house and then back again. "I want you to tell them to go."

"I beg your pardon? Tell who to go?"

"Carson and Marielle and the kids. You need to tell them to go."

She could not believe what she was hearing. "I could never do that. This is their home!"

"No. This house is not a home. It is a mausoleum. You've made it a crypt, Mother. You didn't mean to, but you did. I couldn't see it before. I wasn't well enough to see it before. But I see it now as clear as day. You're the one who can't let go of the past. You're the one with regrets. Not Susannah. Not this house. You."

Adelaide staggered back against the wall of the studio as if stricken. "How dare you say that to me?"

"Because it's true," Caroline said gently. "You needed a reason to explain all the bad things that have happened to you. The house became your reason. You found your great-grandmother dead in her chair after she told you things that didn't make any sense, and that became the image on which you pinned everything. The house and its terrible grudge. A grudge you couldn't understand because you were too young and then would never understand because you didn't know about the other letters. If I had known what you had become, I would have shown you long before this. I had no idea. I was too ill to see it. Susannah doesn't haunt this house, Mother. You do."

Adelaide felt lightheaded. Terribly old. Fragile. "Other letters..."

"Yes. Other letters. Susannah wrote other letters. Letters she never sent to her cousin. She never sent them to anyone. They've been here the whole time. Hidden in the cellar."

The cellar.

You walk upon it. We all do.

"I don't know what you are talking about," Adelaide breathed.

"I know you don't. But you will. Marielle is reading them right now. And when she is done I want you to read them. And then when Carson gets home tomorrow I want you to tell him to take his family and leave."

"I...I can't do that!"

"You have to. You have turned Carson into a shadow of what you are. Addicted to the echoes of his past, just like you. You let him choose to live in this funeral parlor of a house where his first wife died, and you let him keep her picture on the stairs with all the other ghosts, and for heaven's sake, you never insisted he clean up Sara's studio. Then he asks to bring Marielle here, and you just let him? Do you know you almost had Marielle believing Susannah was out to get her?"

"But Susannah..."

"Was innocent! She was innocent. Come up to the house, Mother. Read the letters. And then, by God, you will unbind Carson and Marielle and Sara's children from this house and let them go."

An instant image of every room at Holly Oak being empty and silent pushed itself to the forefront of her mind, and her body trembled at the thought. "You would have me live here alone?" Adelaide didn't recognize the childlike timbre of her voice.

Caroline hesitated before reaching out her hand and laying it on Adelaide's good arm. "Isn't it time you gave it a try? You've never let yourself enjoy this house with just you inside it. Just you and no one else. Never."

Adelaide turned her head to look at Holly Oak at the top of the sloping lawn, its windows glistening in the morning sun. A tiny fissure seemed to crack across the fear that gripped her, like a valve letting off pressure—a tiny stream of it.

She trembled slightly, and her broken wrist sent an aching reminder to her brain that she was presently unable to entertain such a heady thought as enjoying her house with just her inside it.

"I can't even tie a shoelace right now," she said as she turned back around.

"No, but soon you will," Caroline said. "And until you can, I will stay here with you."

arielle sat on the edge of her bed after she had read the last letter, in awe. Susannah Page was nothing like what Adelaide or Eldora had imagined her to be. She had simply been a young woman in love, a young woman who loved to the point of sacrifice. It was impossible that Susannah haunted the house in search of absolution. She already had that, and in Susannah's eyes it was the house that had given it to her, not kept it from her. Eldora Meeks was wrong.

And so was Adelaide.

Marielle gathered up the letters and rewrapped them in the cloth. Caroline had told her that when she was done there was something she wanted Marielle to do. She couldn't imagine what it was other than giving the letters to Adelaide.

Marielle slipped on a pair of sandals and opened her bedroom door. It was nearly noon and still the house was quiet. She wondered for a moment if Adelaide was sick or worse, and she hurried to Adelaide's bedroom to see if she was still in her bed. But Adelaide's bed was empty and made. Relieved, Marielle made her way down the stairs. When she reached the bottom, she heard movement in the dining room. Someone was pulling up a chair.

She walked to the dining room doors. Adelaide was seated at the table, looking a bit ashen. Caroline sat across from her. Both had teacups. Adelaide's, steaming, had been recently filled.

"Adelaide, are you all right?" Marielle said.

"She's waiting for the letters." Caroline stood and reached for the bundle in Marielle's hands. Marielle handed the letters to her. Caroline thumbed through them, setting the postmarked ones off to the side.

"Those you have read," she said to Adelaide. She set the unpostmarked ones in front of her mother. "These you haven't. Marielle, if you don't mind?"

Caroline motioned for Marielle to follow her. She led her to the kitchen and then out to the patio. Caroline pulled out a patio chair and sat down. Marielle did the same.

"So you told Adelaide what you told me—about the letters?" Marielle asked.

"Yes."

"They don't explain everything."

"What is unclear to you?" Caroline said.

"This whole thing about the house doesn't make any sense. I don't see how Adelaide could have thought all these years that the house had some sort of grudge against Susannah. Or why anyone in town would have thought it was haunted or cursed."

"No, you're absolutely right. It doesn't make any sense."

"And Eldora Meeks insists there is a presence in that house and that it's Susannah and her boatload of regrets. I'm not saying Eldora is a fraud, but that doesn't make any sense either. Susannah didn't do all those things people have accused her of."

Caroline nodded. "No, she didn't."

"So Eldora is a fraud."

"I know nothing about Eldora's capabilities. I would imagine she is indeed more insightful than most people. She knew I'd had an encounter with God at that convent when no one else could see it. So I believe it's possible that she has been able to pick up on something deep and binding here."

Marielle shivered despite the heat of the noonday sun. "Something... evil?"

"Something strong. However, I think it's my mother's incredible fear that Eldora picked up on. The gnawing sense of sadness my mother senses inside Holly Oak is hers. Not the house's. Just hers. A hard life is difficult enough on a healthy person. But when you throw loss upon loss upon a fragile person, well, it can be too much. I know that better than anyone. We're not strong people, us Holly Oak women. From way back, it is fairly obvious the illness that stole my life away from me began here with someone else."

Caroline's words were lost on Marielle. "Here?" she asked. "I'm not sure I understand. Susannah wasn't—"

"I'm not talking about Susannah."

"I don't...I don't follow you."

"Think about it, Marielle. Who was ill? Ill like I was."

And then Marielle understood. "Susannah's mother."

Conjured images of a grieving woman lost in mental illness filled her mind. The inability to deal with truth had started with Susannah's mother.

"We've all been susceptible to it," Caroline said. "That's how mental illness is, I'm afraid. It runs in my family." She leaned forward. "It runs through my family."

"But Adelaide's not... She's not..." Marielle couldn't finish. She didn't know if she believed what she had been about to say.

"No, she's not crazy. We're not crazy, Marielle. We're unskilled at dealing with reality. Some of us are less so than others. Susannah was more adept than her mother, more adept than I was. And more adept than Adelaide has been. We didn't all suffer from it in the same way."

Marielle thought of Sara's poems, her thoughts of suicide, her failed relationships, all the things about her that Carson probably didn't know. "Sara. She... I think maybe she struggled with this."

"I think she did, too."

"I have her journals," Marielle blurted, and warm blood rushed to her cheeks.

Caroline leaned back easily in her chair. "I know you do."

Stunned, Marielle whispered, "You do?"

"I saw them in your hands the night I arrived. I knew what they were. I had read them before. In the studio. Sara kept them there, and I saw them once during one of my epic and short-lived returns."

"You...you didn't say anything about my having them."

"I guess I wanted you to read them. The night I got here I didn't know how I felt about your having them. But then you and I talked, and I got to know you. And I realized you needed to read them."

"I *needed* to read them?" Marielle asked.

A slight breeze lifted a wisp of hair off Caroline's neck and toyed with it. "It just seemed very odd to me that you were a happy new bride living in the dead first wife's house. And yet I saw you trying to hide those journals that night I arrived. That's what you were doing. Right? You were trying to hide them. You were wondering, maybe without even fully realizing it, if Sara's fading presence was keeping your new husband bound to her old house, not just his concern for the children."

Silence fell across them as Marielle considered for a moment that perhaps Caroline was right.

"But I don't know what to do with them now," she finally said. "I don't think Carson knows about some of the things Sara thought. Or did. I think if he read these, he would... I think it would hurt him."

Caroline smiled. "You're a kindhearted soul, Marielle, to want to let Carson think only the best things of his deceased wife. I will take them. I will keep them, and I will show them to him when the time is right. Then you will have had no part in his learning what, at some point, he needs to know."

"Does he need to know?"

"For Brette's and Hudson's sakes, yes, he needs to know. We'll need to watch them as they grow, Marielle. I'll help you. I don't say that to alarm you but to keep us all from making the same mistakes if the situation presents itself. Perhaps it won't. We can wait."

"All right." Marielle felt herself begin to relax again. "So now what? What are we supposed to do with these letters?"

"Nothing."

Marielle echoed the word in surprise. "Nothing? How can we do nothing? People think Susannah was a traitor. They think it was her fault her husband was almost killed. They've got it all wrong. She had nothing to do with it. We have to do something with those letters."

"There is no 'we,' Marielle. My mother and I will take care of the letters."

Even as Caroline said it, Marielle knew the letters would remain hidden at Holly Oak. "You're not going to tell anyone about them, are you? You're going to keep them here without telling a soul."

"Susannah never wanted them seen. She lived another sixty-five years after she wrote those letters, Marielle, so she had plenty of chances to set the record straight. She didn't. It was her wish that no one ever know about the choices she had to make. I think we need to respect that."

"And so that's what you want me to do? Not call the newspapers and the TV stations? You said back in the cellar that there was something you wanted me to do."

"There is. But that's not it. "

"What? What do you want me to do?"

Caroline reached out her hand. Marielle hesitated before taking it. "I want you and the children to leave Fredericksburg," Caroline said. "Move closer to DC. It's ridiculous the amount of time Carson spends commuting every day. I want you to leave this house. You need to leave it."

Marielle had heard every word, but she couldn't keep herself from saying it. "What?"

"You need to make your own life, away from this house. Away from everything about it."

Caroline's urgent words flummoxed her. "But you said there's nothing abnormal about this house," Marielle said. "It's just a house, right?"

Caroline squeezed her hand. "Is a house just the wood and stone that comprise it? Think, Marielle! You know it's more than that. The perception of Holly Oak is that it is a house of ghosts. Do you think a stack of letters will erase that perception overnight? It's a house where ghosts are welcomed. Loved. Do you hear what I'm saying? Ghosts are expected here."

For several seconds, confusion alone spun in her head. Then clarity fell upon her. She shifted her gaze to the studio at the edge of the garden. "Sara," she whispered and Caroline nodded.

Sara lingered at Holly Oak. Not as a ghost but something like it.

"You need to make a home that is just yours and Carson's," Caroline continued. "The kids will be happy wherever you are happy. Trust me on this. You need to leave this house."

Tears that had welled as she looked at the studio spilled out, and Marielle wiped her cheeks. Inside, her heart stung. "Are you saying he is still in love with her?"

Caroline reached out her other hand and covered Marielle's trembling fingers. "No. He is not in love with her. But he loves her memory. A little too much. That's what this house is doing to him. To you both. That's what this house does, because the people living in it have empowered it. It's us who have made this house what it is. We've done this. You must leave."

"I don't think Carson will think this is necessary. He will think"—Marielle swallowed hard—"that I'm being irrational. I don't know how I'm going to convince him."

"You won't have to," Caroline said. "My mother is going to ask you to leave. Gently, of course. And when she does, you need to persuade Carson to honor her request."

"Adelaide wants this? Can she live alone here?"

Caroline took a deep breath. "She needs to live alone here. But not while she's recovering from her fall. I'm going live with her until her arm is better. I owe it to her."

"But…but you said you would never live here again."

Caroline squeezed her hands and let go. "I know. That was before I knew."

"Knew what?"

"That I could somehow make up for what I did. That I could clean up my terrible mess. I can. I must. God spoke to me at that convent, Marielle. He told me to come home and fix what is broken here. You and Carson and my grandchildren are my future. You're the reason I came back. You're my redemption. Susannah found hers here, and I'm going to find mine."

Marielle looked up at Holly Oak. "Did she find it? Do you know what happened to the people Susannah loved?"

"I know Eliza never left Ohio," Caroline answered. "She married a retired Union colonel. They never had any children. She is buried there beside him. Susannah's grandmother died here when Annabel was ten, Susannah's mother died a year after Annabel married. Tessie married in 1873 and moved to Maryland."

"And Will?"

"Well, I can't really say what happened to Will. He didn't marry Eliza, I can tell you that. He survived the war; he and John both did. They were both discharged at the war's end. John married a couple of years later and took over the family lumber mill. Will no doubt married too. I suppose you could find out if you wanted to."

"So Susannah never saw him again, never heard from him again?"

Caroline cocked her head. "I doubt she went out of her way to make that happen. What would've been the point?"

"But if she visited Eleanor and John in the years after the war, then surely—"

"She cared for an invalid husband for ten years before Nathaniel died of pneumonia. I doubt she ever left the house."

"But after he died?"

Caroline stared at her. "Did you not understand what saved her in the end, Marielle? Those ten years were the years she and Nathaniel learned to love each other. He for the second time, she for the first. That is what saved her."

"Saved her from what? What horrible thing had she done that she needed to atone for?" Marielle didn't hide the disgust in her voice. No one should have to pay the way Susannah had paid. It was senseless.

Caroline closed her eyes and then opened them slowly. She sighed, as if she were tired. "You don't get it, do you?" Caroline said. "Susannah was saved from herself. From a lifetime of regret over what might have been and wasn't. Adelaide had it backwards, all this time."

Marielle sensed color rising to her cheeks. She had missed the point. She was still missing it. "Backwards?" she asked.

Caroline locked eyes with her. "The house, if it indeed could speak, would tell Adelaide—and me—it doesn't want absolution. It wants to absolve. It doesn't want to be paid. It wants to give. To be a haven. To shelter and protect. That's all it has ever wanted."

Marielle's eyes were drawn again to Holly Oak's stone-and-timber expanse. A sighing in the trees beyond the patio seemed to whisper, "At last…"

Epilogue

Yards of gray wool lay across the polished surface of the long table in the parlor. Adelaide squinted as she lifted a corner and scrutinized the fabric's weave. Caroline stood across from her.

"If you don't like it, I think you should send it back," Caroline said.

"It's just new, that's all. I'm not used to this company. The fabric smells different."

"I think it smells like the inside of a car," Hudson said from underneath the table. "It smells like cars."

"Thanks for that insight, Hudson, dear. Can you please tell me why you are under my table?"

"I'm waiting to scare Brette. She's going to come in here to ask you if you've seen her seashell purse, and I'm going to jump out at her when she does."

"And how do you know she is going to do that?" Caroline asked, bending down to look at him.

"Because I have it, Grandma." He held up the purse.

"Wouldn't you rather go play with your rabbit or race some cars in the playroom or something?" Adelaide rubbed her arm where the stitches had been. It itched.

"No, I like this."

"You might want to take Mimi's advice and find something else to do," Caroline said as she stood back up. "Pearl is coming over. She likes you."

"Maxine and Deloris too," Adelaide added.

"Why?" Hudson whined.

"They need to talk business, Hudson," Caroline said.

"I'm outta here." Hudson crawled out from under the table. "When are Dad and Marielle getting back? They've been gone forever. How long does it take to buy a scarecrow anyway?"

"Scarecrow?" Adelaide said to Caroline.

"Escrow," Caroline said. "They're closing escrow on your new house, Hudson. It's a big deal. They're probably going to drive up to the Capitol and celebrate with the president afterward."

Hudson stared at her and then puckered his mouth. "They will not. You're teasing me."

Caroline nodded toward the stairs. "Go give your sister her purse back."

The boy left them but headed for the drawing room, not for the stairs and Brette's bedroom.

"This house won't be the same without them," Adelaide said.

"Yes, I know."

"The children don't even seem to be bothered by the idea of moving."

Caroline began to roll the fabric back on its bolt. "Anything new will require adjustment. They'll find that out when they're actually living in Fairfax and attending a new school and making new friends. Right now they feel only the thrill of the unknown. Not the danger."

"Oh, to be young," Adelaide said. She stared at the fabric as her thoughts now took her to imagining an empty house. "So it's a smart idea to invite the Blue-Haired Old Ladies into my business, right?" she asked.

Caroline laughed. "Is that what you call them?"

"They have blue hair and they are old."

"Some of them are younger than you, Mother. Pearl is—"

"Yes, I know. Pearl is seventy-nine. They all have blue hair but one. It's ridiculous. The color of your hair is the color of your hair."

"Well, yes, I do think inviting them into the business is a good idea. That is, if you're sure you want to keep doing this. You can retire, you know."

Adelaide exhaled heavily. Yes, she could retire. She had thought long and hard about it. But then, what would she do? Especially now that Carson and Marielle and the children were leaving. She needed something to fill her days. Besides, there was no one to appease by making the uniforms. There never had been. So why should it matter if she kept at it?

"I'll go crazy if I don't have something to do," Adelaide said.

"You could sew quilts instead."

Adelaide let her eyes travel over the spread of gray wool—stiff, smooth, and clean. In a few days it would be a Confederate States Army major's greatcoat for a grand game of pretend. No blood would be spilled on this coat. "There are some things that are worth remembering, Caroline," she said. "Be a shame to forget what the past has taught us. Especially when it about near killed us." Adelaide reached for the chair behind her and sat down. "Although Pearl will make a fuss about sewing in the parlor."

"But you told her about the letters, right?"

"I did. She says Eldora's never been wrong about anything."

Caroline waited until Adelaide raised her head to look at her. "Nobody is ever right all the time," Caroline said. "Nobody."

Adelaide smiled wanly. "I suppose you're right."

And Caroline laughed.

When she stopped, Adelaide spoke. "I already miss her a little."

"Who? Marielle?"

"No. Not Marielle. The ghost I never had. I miss her a little."

Caroline walked over to Adelaide and knelt down. The little golden cross at her neck glittered in the sunlight spilling into the room from the windows. "It's not a crime to long for spiritual things, Mother. It's what you're meant for. We all are. And in time I'm going to prove it to you."

Spiritual things. The notion made Adelaide tremble a bit. "Not sure I've the courage for all that," she said. "Not after all that's happened."

Caroline smiled. "You've lived your whole life wanting to reverse what most thought was a terrible curse. You could've left this house long ago. But you bravely believed you could end its suffering, and you stayed. You've the courage to discover what you're meant for, Mother. Trust me."

Adelaide felt her cheeks grow warm, and she sniffed to dispel the warm rush. "I suppose I shall have to hang around then."

Caroline patted her knee and rose. "I think you should."

The front door opened, and Adelaide and Caroline both turned toward the sound. Carson and Marielle had returned. A few seconds later they appeared at the parlor door, the smell of late summer clinging to their clothes. He held up a set of house keys.

"It's done," he said, a smile easing across his face and Marielle in the crook of his free arm.

"Congratulations," Caroline said.

"Yes, congratulations," Adelaide echoed.

Hudson was at their side in seconds, followed by Brette, both asking multiple questions about the new house, and Carson and Marielle moved away from the parlor doors to answer them. Brette slid her hand into Marielle's as they walked away, and the child leaned against her hip. Carson had his hand on Hudson's shoulders and his other hand on the small of Marielle's back. Adelaide was struck by how they were all connected to each other by touch. Joined. Bound.

Watching them walk away like that, Adelaide became aware of a sudden urge to touch that which she had never had the desire to touch before, though others had. Many others. Many times. She would have to make her way outside, though. "I think I might want to poke about in the backyard for a few minutes before the Ladies get here," she said. And she rose slowly from her chair.

"Want someone to come with you?" Caroline asked.

"No. I'll be fine." Adelaide made her way out of the parlor and into the foyer. "And you probably want to spend some time with the children before you head back to Bethesda."

"Actually, there's something else I'd like to take care of before I head back," Caroline said, following her out.

"Fine, fine," Adelaide said, intent now, but wanting a few minutes of quiet before heading to the north side of the house to do the thing she had never done before. She made her way into the dining room and through the french doors as Caroline followed after Carson and Marielle in the opposite direction. Adelaide opened the door to the patio and stepped out, inhaling the scent of warm flagstones. The late afternoon sun had slipped behind the house, and the patio was now under the house's ample shadow.

A breeze from the summer's heat was kicking up spent leaves that had collected under the patio furniture. They danced around her feet like tiny adoring fans. She pulled out a patio chair to sit for just a few moments and enjoy the applause before heading to Holly Oak's north side. The air smelled preautumn—sweet and playful—and she could hear the tinkling of her next-door neighbor's wind chimes. Someone nearby was operating a leaf blower, and a dog began to bark. Despite the various noises, the garden was serene and golden hued. Adelaide had only been there for a few minutes when she heard the patio door open. She turned to tell Caroline that she was truly fine sitting out on the patio alone, but the person who had emerged from the house was Marielle. She had car keys in her hand.

"Off somewhere?" Adelaide asked.

"The kids and I are going out for ice cream." She looked as if she was going to say more. But she didn't.

"Just you and the children?"

Marielle nodded. She paused for a second. "Caroline is… Caroline has decided to show the journals to Carson while she's here today and before we start packing things up for the move. We both thought a little uninterrupted time would be nice for him while he looks at them. The kids are so excited about the house; they're kind of bouncing off the walls here."

So that's what Caroline had said a moment ago that she wanted to do before she left.

It had been eight weeks since Caroline told Adelaide about the journals Marielle had come across in the studio and that she planned to show them to Carson when the time was right. Adelaide had hoped Caroline would offer to show them to her, but she hadn't.

"Let's let Carson be the one to share them with you. If he chooses to. I think in time he will," Caroline had said.

Adelaide now looked up at Marielle, knowing Marielle had read them before handing them over to Caroline. And she thought of Susannah's unsent letters, safe now in her bedroom and for the moment known to only a few. "You've read them. Will they change anything? Those journals?" Adelaide asked.

Marielle ran her finger absently across the circle of her key ring. The diamond in her engagement ring caught a snatch of sunlight and sparkled. "I don't know, Mimi. I guess I hope they do."

Adelaide cocked her head, surprised. "You do?"

"Well, sure. If Carson reads them and has no reaction at all to anything that Sara wrote, I think I'd be a little worried. They were her journals, the one place where most people aren't afraid to tell the truth."

Marielle was right. Truth always changes things.

"And I know you're wondering if he really needs to read them at all," Marielle went on. "He does for the children's sake, Mimi. And for the memories of Sara he will keep. Those are what he gets to hang on to. Right? We get to keep the memories of what was, not what might have been or—"

"Or wasn't," Adelaide finished for her.

"Yes."

The two of them were quiet for a moment. The wind chimes from next door clanged a fairylike tune in the silence between them.

"Want me to bring you back some pecan praline?" Marielle asked a second later. "I know it's your favorite."

Adelaide thought for a moment. "I'd like to try your favorite, Marielle. Bring me back that."

Marielle smiled. She turned to go back into the house, and Adelaide called her name. She turned back around. "Yes?"

"I'm really very happy you and Carson bought the house in Fairfax. Really, I am."

"Thank you, Mimi. I am too."

"And I am sorry I didn't insist on it from the beginning. I didn't... There was a lot I didn't..." But she couldn't piece the words together.

"It's okay," Marielle said softly.

Adelaide shook her head. "Anyway, I am actually looking forward to rediscovering my house. I don't think we know each other very well."

The minute the words left her mouth, Adelaide knew she only had it half right. It was she who didn't know the house. The house had always known who she was.

The patio door burst open, and Hudson poked his head out. "I thought we were going!" he said.

"Coming," Marielle said. She waved to Adelaide and went back inside the house, closing the door gently behind her.

A few minutes later Adelaide heard the sound of a car starting and then driving away. All was quiet. The leaf blower had stopped, the dog had ceased its barking, and the breeze had abated, leaving the wind chimes voiceless. Inside the quiet house, Carson was reading Sara's journals. The past was again making itself clear within the walls of Holly Oak.

Adelaide was reminded then of why she had stepped outside in the first place, and she stood and pushed in her chair. She walked to the edge of the house and paused for a moment at the beginning of the long row of hydrangeas at the west end. Below her the grassy knoll stretched to the steps of what had been Holly Oak's slaves' quarters, now a modest home for a lop-eared rabbit and a playroom where a ball could be flung in any direction and nothing would break.

She walked the length of the back of the house and then turned to face Holly Oak's north side. She hadn't been back there in years. She couldn't remember the last time she had stood there. Adelaide's gaze traveled up the massive wall to the cannonball half buried in the stone. For decades she hated the thought of even looking up at the black half-orb, that terrible reminder of what the house had endured. Her house. The only house she had ever known. She thought of her great-grandmother, fleeing to the cellar, running down the same stairs she had fallen down, as cannons rained destruction on Fredericksburg. Susannah had not deserved what happened to her. Few survivors of war ever do.

She stood on tiptoe and stretched as far as she could with her good arm, but her fingers couldn't quite brush the cannonball's flinty surface. It was beyond her reach. Instead her hand brushed the stone around it, warm and smooth, and her fingers tingled where she touched it.

She had feared that sensation for as long as she could remember; the cannonball was a ghastly memento of what the house had been subjected to, and the stone and wood around it were the wound it had created. But now, as she pulled her hand away, she marveled at the lingering sensation on her fingertips. She was aware of something invigorating on her skin, something sharp and vivid. Different. Alive. The cannonball was more than just a reminder of what the house had suffered; it was a reminder of what the house had survived. She closed her eyes against the ache of suddenly realizing that it had always been this way, from the very moment the ball slammed into the house and did not crush it.

And she had only ever seen the half of it.

"I'm sorry," she murmured to the hulking back of Holly Oak. "I am so sorry." She reached up again to rub her fingers on the ancient stone surrounding the cannonball—a caress that begged for forgiveness.

Then she brought her fingers to her mouth and nose and breathed deep the heady fragrance of resilience.

AUTHOR'S NOTES

The Battle of Fredericksburg as my fictional Susannah describes is a historical event, and much of what she pens in her letters to Eleanor is based on fact. Holly Oak is not a real house, but I saw many beautiful and stately homes in current-day Fredericksburg with a view of downtown and the Rappahannock the way Susannah describes Holly Oak. As for the military details, I endeavored to stick to the facts as much as possible. It was not unheard of for West Point cadets to join up with a volunteer infantry from their home state, as I have suggested here, though it was likely not the norm. And I have placed the infirmary at Libby Prison in such a way as to make it convenient for my story. Other liberties with historicity were taken with care, and every attempt was made to make the story ring true whenever possible. I recommend the following resources for further reading and study:

Chesnut, Mary Boykin. *A Diary from Dixie.* New York: Barnes and Noble, 2006.

The Civil War: A Film by Ken Burns. DVD. Arlington, VA: Public Broadcasting Service, 2004.

Foote, Shelby. *The Civil War, a Narrative.* 3 vols. New York: Vintage, 1986.

Gallagher, Gary W., ed. *The Fredericksburg Campaign: Decision on the Rappahannock.* Chapel Hill, NC: University of North Carolina Press, 1995.

McPherson, James M. *The Illustrated Battle Cry of Freedom: The Civil War Era.* New York: Oxford University Press, 2003.

READERS GUIDE

1. Describe Adelaide. What is her greatest strength? her greatest weakness? What is her relationship with Holly Oak, and how has it colored her entire life?

2. Holly Oak withstood the Civil War but not unscathed. Along with the cannonball embedded in its walls, it acquired a reputation. What do people like Pearl think of the house? How does Adelaide think of the house? What about Susannah? Which is true? Do you think a home can take on any of the characteristics assigned to Holly Oak, or is it simply a building?

3. Why does Marielle agree to live in the same house her new husband shared with his previous wife? Do you think she was right? What would you have done in her situation, coming into a family as a stepmother far from the only home you'd ever known?

4. Susannah is referred to as a spy, a traitor, and a ghost. Who was she really? How does knowing the truth about Susannah's life free Adelaide? How does it free Marielle? Caroline?

5. Why does Caroline come back to Holly Oak? What do you think would have happened to Adelaide and Marielle if she had not?

6. Eldora claims to be in contact with the spirit world. Do you believe her? What did she feel in Holly Oak? What happens when she meets Caroline?

7. When she is interviewed by the journalist, Adelaide says, "People will think what they want. They will always think what they want." How is this statement a key theme of the story? In what ways does it

apply to Holly Oak, Susannah, the Blue-Haired Old Ladies, and even Adelaide and Marielle?

8. In a way, *A Sound Among the Trees* is a ghost story without a ghost. Who is Adelaide's ghost? Carson's? Does Marielle have a ghost?

9. Adelaide tells Marielle that Holly Oak is stuck, like a needle on a record. What does she mean? At the end of the book, Caroline explains that it is actually Adelaide who is stuck. In what way do the characteristics Adelaide gives to Holly Oak refer instead to herself? Why do you think she projects her unhappiness upon her home in this way?

10. With which character do you most closely identify? Adelaide? Marielle? Susannah? Caroline? Someone else? Why do you relate to this character? What similarities does her story have to your own?

ACKNOWLEDGMENTS

Every book I write bears the influence of so many wonderful people in my life. I am deeply grateful:

- To Jeff and Sarah Sumpolec and their sweet family for sharing Fredericksburg with me, for opening up their lovely home and driving me from museum to battleground to historic street to cemetery as I researched for this book.
- For the keen editorial minds of Shannon Marchese and Jessica Barnes at WaterBrook Multnomah, and Jennifer Peterson and Lissa Halls Jackson. Thank you for the trips to the crucible. The book, if it shines, shines because you saw where it needed the Refiner's fire and sent me there.
- To my agent and friend, Chip MacGregor, for words of affirmation at every juncture.
- To dear friends Kathy Sanders, Mary DeMuth, Barb Anderson, Tanya Siebert, Susie Larson, and Jeanne Damoff, for cheering me on in the tense days of the homestretch.
- For the love and support of my husband, Bob, and our four amazing young adults, and my mother, Judy Horning, for expert proofreading and encouragement.
- To God for His whispers in the trees and elsewhere, reminding me in that quiet way of His that the past is not just a collection of happenings He orchestrated; it is also a collection of my responses, both good and bad.

SOMETIMES WE FIND *The* TRUTH ABOUT OURSELVES IN THE LIVES *of* OTHERS.

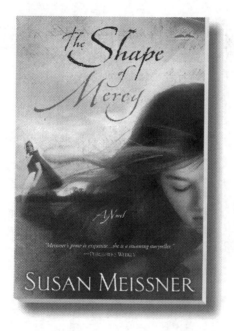

Expected to gracefully embrace a life of privilege, a young woman cuts the purse strings that bind her to plot a new life course. But startling self-realization challenges everything she knows as she begins to study the tragic life of a seventeenth-century victim of the Salem witch trials.

An ancient *ring,*
                two women separated
        by nearly five hundred years,
    and the *freedom* to *choose* one's life.

Manhattan antique shop owner Jane Lindsay is jolted into a new reality when she
suddenly has to face the fact that her marriage is crumbling. While she grapples
with her husband's abandonment, she comes across an ancient ring that may have
belonged to Lady Jane Grey. As she traces the origins of the ring and Lady Grey's
story, Jane has to decide whether she will default to habits of powerlessness or
whether she will take the first steps toward real truth and happiness.

Read an excerpt from this book and more at
WaterBrookMultnomah.com!

Printed in the United States
by Baker & Taylor Publisher Services